CINEMA LUMIERE

CINEMA
Lumière

HATTIE HOLDEN EDMONDS

RedDoor

Published by
RedDoor
www.reddoorpublishing.co.uk

© 2014 Hattie Holden Edmonds

ISBN 978-0-9928520-8-5

A CIP catalogue record for this book is available from
the British Library

Cover design: Scarlett Rugers Book Design

Typesetting: typesetter.org.uk

 printed on FSC-certified paper

Printed in the UK by TJ International, Padstow, Cornwall

To my Dad, with love and hindsight

Chapter 1

'Nellie, that's disgusting.' I jerk my head off the pillow as a guff of foul air hits my nostrils. 'What on earth have you eaten?'

Nellie, whose face is about four inches from mine, opens one eye. She glares at me then lets out a cross little fart. The eye closes, there's another guff and a bubble of drool slithers from the side of her mouth.

I sigh. It's pointless trying to reason with Nellie so instead I haul myself out of bed and stumble across the room towards the kitchen. My feet and fingers are freezing and my toes have turned that mortuary blue you see on television corpses. In fact they're so bad this morning that for a sleepy split-second I wonder if maybe I died during the night. Maybe I'm just a ghostly shadow drifting back and forth from bedroom to kitchen, trapped for eternity between a gaseous bedmate and last night's pile of dirty plates.

The kitchen floor isn't helping – it's gravestone cold. I shuffle towards the fridge and feel something sticky underfoot. The bin, which is usually under the sink, is lying on its side with a selection of half-gnawed pizza boxes and shredded crisp packets spilling from its open mouth.

Nellie, I think.

I pick up the rubbish and lay out Nellie's breakfast in her bowl on the sideboard. Then I flick open the child's safety catch on the fridge and reach inside for the milk. My eyes blink to adjust to the light that shines from behind the out-of-date sausages, and it's only now that I remember my dream. Although it wasn't really a dream, it was more of a mini film, whose images were brighter and more vivid than anything I've seen before:

In it, I was sitting alone in a cinema on a red velvet seat. It was dark but I could make out the thick crimson curtains drawn across the screen in front of me. From the projectionist's booth behind my chair came the whirring and clicking of film reels being changed.

'Hannah!'

I jumped at the sound of the voice and twisted round to see a familiar figure standing behind the shaft of light streaming from the booth.

'Victor!' I said, both elated and astonished to see him.

Victor smiled from his elevated position and pointed towards the screen. Seconds later I heard the soft muffle of the curtains drawing apart. When I turned back, I saw that the screen was blank, except for one bright red feather in the top right-hand corner. There was something mesmerising about the feather and I watched it float downwards, gently swirling back and forth as though blown by an unseen breeze.

The moment it touched the bottom of the screen I awoke.

I close the fridge door and try to shake from my head the image of Victor high in the projectionist's booth. Why is he still hanging around the edges of my mind, sliding unbidden into my dreams at night? It's been over two years now, why can't he just leave me alone?

Nellie is still asleep when I carry in her breakfast so I waft the bowl past her nose to coax her from her morning coma. She opens both eyes and rearranges her mouth into something resembling a grin.

'Nellie, have you been in the bin?' I say.

Nellie looks at me as if I've suggested she's eaten the television.

'Yes, you,' I say. 'No breakfast till you come clean.'

Torn between greed and an admission of guilt, a variety of expressions flit across Nellie's face before her cheeks puff outwards with what I assume is a begrudging sigh.

Although a lot of people say that British bulldogs look like Winston Churchill, or vice versa, that's not the case with Nellie. With her soft pendulous cheeks, wide brow and crooked mouth, through which several teeth protrude at odd angles, she looks more like Les Dawson – only with a furry face and in dire need of a trip to the dentist. And like Les, she has quite a repertoire of expressions, which after a little practice, aren't too difficult to decipher.

'You'll make yourself sick again,' I say.

Nellie pointedly ignores me and eyeballs her bowl of breakfast.

It's not worth pursuing the argument because Nellie and I have been over the same ground since she arrived, and I always lose. So while I plunder the wash basket for a clean-ish skirt to wear for work, I listen to the sound of her eating, gums slapping together like wet nappies. By the time she's finished, it's already eight thirty and we're late for the morning walk.

Having heaved myself and 60lbs worth of sulking bulldog up the steps from my basement flat (Nellie's not a big fan of stairs… or walking for that matter), we set off for

3

the local cemetery, the nearest open stretch of grass to the cul-de-sac where I live. On the way we pass the Caribbean takeaway with its rows of freshly baked patties, then the Spanish delicatessen whose windows glisten with piles of chorizo sausages. Next comes the launderette, ruled by Mrs O'Connor and her permanently crooked wig. At the end of this little stretch is the Paradise pub, named after the last line in a GK Chesterton poem *To Paradise by way of Kensal Green*.

Once on Harrow Road, Nellie and I cross over to the white pillared gates of the cemetery. 'London's Foremost Necropolis', as it bills itself in the brochure, stretches over seventy acres and packs in more than 60,000 graves. Over the two years that we've been coming here, Nellie and I have got to know the more eccentric inhabitants. Our favourites include Thomas Hood, the poet who once mortgaged his brain with his publishers in return for a cash advance, and the Duke of Sussex, renowned for his house full of singing birds and chiming clocks and his diet of turtle soup and orange ices.

The cemetery is modelled on Père Lachaise in Paris and boasts residents from China, Chile, Italy, Egypt, Eritrea, Jamaica, Ethiopia, Hungary, Morocco and Iceland – all lying side by side, having come to rest in this little corner of the capital. Each grave, from lichen-frosted mausoleum and crumbling Corinthian column to moss-coated angel and simple wooden cross, is wreathed in ivy. Silence hangs like a fine mist, the sound of 60,000 souls between breaths.

The frozen ground crunches beneath our feet as Nellie and I traipse through the gates and the icy January fog is so thick that I can barely make out the gasworks on the far side of the Grand Union canal. After a lengthy dawdle by Trollope's grave – anything to delay my arrival at the office

4

– we head for the abandoned taxi which stands, inexplicably, on the edge of the Anglican side of the cemetery. I climb inside while Nellie does her usual two-minute dither before deciding where she fancies a crap.

While I wait, I gaze out of the window at the blanket of grey and try to remember the last time I saw a dazzling blue sky. According to an article I recently read, the average human eye can detect over five hundred different shades of blue. Five hundred? Me, I can't even see one.

A triumphant bark drags me from my thoughts and I look up to see Nellie squatting in the middle of the path.

'Not there,' I call. 'Go by the bush.' I am keen to avoid a rerun of the previous week's scene when Mrs O'Connor caught Nellie taking a shit on the grass and told me off for letting my dog do 'its durrrty business in a place of rest.'

This was bad enough in itself without the fact that it triggered an attack of what I've come to call 'the Mentals'.

You know what, Mrs O'Connor, I said, grabbing the collar of her little woolly coat and shaking her so hard that her wig slithered down the side of her head and onto her shoulder. Nellie can crap where she wants. In fact, you're lucky she didn't shit all over your shoes.

I've suffered from the Mentals since I was a little girl, and it basically involves a very overzealous imagination picturing in great detail the worst possible thing I can do or say in any particular situation. From the outside, no one would know that it's happening, but inside my head it's all kicking off. It can get pretty bad – enough to make me change dentists once, because whenever Mr Halford bent over me to poke around in my mouth, I imagined myself shouting, 'Fuck me, fuck me,' and I was petrified that one day I might actually say it aloud.

5

So I didn't really say or do any of those things to Mrs O'Connor. Instead I told her I was sorry, that it wouldn't happen again, and then I picked up the warm turd in the only thing I had on me at the time – a flattened-out Hula Hoops wrapper.

'Nellie, are you listening to me?' I call out again, but Nellie pretends that she hasn't heard by staring in the opposite direction. I start to get out of the taxi so I can scoop up the shit in my handy Boots plastic bag, but something catches my eye. At first I think it's my imagination, some fragment of the dream returning, but up close there is no mistaking it. Shining out against the black vinyl of the taxi seat, its tiny filaments waving like underwater coral, is a little red feather.

Chapter 2

'Welcome to the World of *Health and Wellbeing*,' I say to Ian, who's already by the office door when I arrive for work an hour later. 'I hope I didn't keep you waiting long.'

Ian shakes his head, stammers a hello and follows me inside. It's his first day in the job and I can tell that he's surprised by the size of the office. In fact it's not really an office at all but more of a customised storage cupboard on the third floor of a crumbling building on Denmark Street. We used to have the larger workspace next door, but since the magazine has been scaled down to just three issues a year, available only in health food shops, it's all we can afford.

'Dump your stuff wherever you like,' I say to Ian. 'We're not too fussy about tidiness round here.'

Ian nods and removes his blue rucksack and multi-zipped anorak, both of which are better suited to scaling the north face of the Eiger rather than sitting in a dolly-sized office in Soho. Beneath the anorak he's wearing grey flannel trousers and a blue V-necked jumper over a white schoolboy shirt, all of which make him look about nineteen even though I know from his CV that he's almost thirty.

'Ready for the grand tour?'

'OK.' Ian, who still hasn't looked me in the eye, fiddles with the fringe of his short reddish hair, which is gelled into a row of tiny shark's teeth.

Roz, my editor for the past six years, who interviewed him for the job, told me that he was shy, but I didn't realise quite *how* shy.

I point to the two desks squashed against the far wall by the window. 'Yours is on the right. If you twist your neck enough you can get a good view of Luigi's café and the guitar shop below.' I take the six steps over to the kettle and toaster in the opposite corner. 'And this is the kitchen,' I say. 'Feel free to knock yourself up a five-course meal.'

Ian smiles faintly, but still manages to look alarmed.

I reach over to the metal filing cabinet next to my desk. 'And this,' I say, 'is what I call "the shop".' I drag open the middle drawer and sweep my fingers over its contents as if I'm presenting a deluxe range of sparkly jewellery on the shopping channel. Ian stares down at the array of hemp snack bars, chlorella powder, 'natural' coffee, krill probiotic supplements, detox foot patches and two exfoliation gloves – all sent to us by health companies in the hope that we will feature them in the magazine.

'Help yourself to anything you fancy,' I say. 'I can recommend the hemp bars, but don't go near the natural coffee. It's made from acorns and it tastes foul.'

'OK,' says Ian. His eyes dart around the office. 'Where does Roz sit?'

'She works from home since we've downsized,' I say, 'so it's just you and me.' I'm tempted to add the word 'kid' but it will probably embarrass him even more, so I just smile.

'Right,' Ian gulps.

We both sit down and switch on our computers. Ian has been left a detailed list of instructions by our website consultant, and I've got a heap of articles to wade through. Now that *Health and Wellbeing* is only quarterly, the idea is to build up its online presence. It's Ian's job to do this and it's my job to supply the bulk of the copy.

I turn to the pile of packages that the postman has delivered. Today's promotional freebies include two packets of low-glycemic soya crisps, an 'Energy Pot' of quinoa and buckwheat, a mini tube of fennel toothpaste and a relaxation CD entitled *Stillness and Flow*. I arrange the new additions in the shop; soya crisps and energy pot on the left side of the drawer, fennel toothpaste and *Stillness and Flow* on the right.

My first article of the day is entitled 'Are you a Catastrophic Thinker?' and was inspired by this morning's 'Maybe I'm dead' train of thought, together with a recent visit to my GP, Dr Ling, who diagnosed me with having chronic catastrophic thinking. The 500-word piece will be part of the ongoing 'Mind Matters' series which Roz has recently commissioned. The basic idea of this piece is to help readers gauge their level of optimism and trust in the world by getting them to complete a short questionnaire. But I kick things off with a quote from Einstein – 'The single most important decision any of us will ever make is whether or not to believe that the universe is friendly'. There's nothing like a few *bon mots* from the world's best-known scientist to add an air of authenticity to what will otherwise be a distinctly flakey, fact-deficient article.

Then I get cracking:

'You feel a slight tingling sensation in your right hand. Do you think:

    a) You must have slept awkwardly. It'll pass in a couple of hours.

    b) It's probably from too much time on the computer and

may signal early stage repetitive strain injury. Better take it a bit easy.

c) It's definitely the start of locked-in syndrome and by tomorrow morning your entire body will be paralysed and you'll be strapped into a hospital bed like the man in *The Diving Bell and the Butterfly*, reduced to communicating with the outside world by blinking your left eyelid...'

I pause and read through what I've just written before pressing on:

'Your bank manager calls you in for a meeting. Do you immediately suppose:

a) He just wants a quick catch-up. He's keen on the personal customer service approach.

b) He's going to tell you off for falling behind on your monthly interest repayments, but together you'll be able to work out a viable new debt repayment plan.

c) He's just cancelled your loan, leaving you £27,000 in debt with the outstanding interest rocketing every second. After being evicted from your flat for rent arrears, you'll lose your job because you can't work after sleeping all night on the street. You're forced into sheltered accommodation but due to the capital's chronic housing shortage you'll be decanted to West Riding, where you will die from loneliness and a diet of low-quality hamburgers made from mashed-up cow's uteruses because that's all you can afford...'

Hmmm, I think, as I scan this second option C. That's pretty extreme. It's probably a level 5 in Dr Ling's opinion. Or even a level 6. Can you be a level 6? Isn't that veering into the 'crackers' department? Maybe I am crackers and Dr Ling is planning to section me next time I visit. Restraining straps, straitjackets, injections filled with enough tranquilizers to fell a mammoth... a vision of Jack Nicholson, comatose and dribbling in a hospital bed *One Flew Over the Cuckoo's Nest* style, fills my head.

I realise that although Roz is quite a liberal editor and most of the time leaves me to my own devices, the option C's are probably a little far-fetched for her. So I tone them both down, before knocking out a couple more slightly less extreme catastrophic scenarios. When I'm finished, I send them over to Ian.

'That's from me, by the way,' I say after the ping of his e-mail reverberates around the silent office. 'It's a questionnaire on catastrophic thinking.' Good to get Ian involved in the whole process, not just the on-line side.

'OK,' says Ian, eyes still averted.

I glance at the office clock. It's still only ten thirty and I'm already tired. I wonder if Ian would think me weird if I take a nap – something I've been doing so much recently that I may well be suffering from narcolepsy. In an effort to keep myself awake I click on my current favourite YouTube clip – 'Christian the lion' – and watch the eponymous Christian being reunited after a three-year gap with his former owners who rescued him as a cub from Harrods' pet department. I play it four times back to back but the final time an advert box pops up – '15,000 Chinese women are looking for dates' – which spoils it a bit.

My phone rings, making us both jump. I check the caller's number and see that it's my mother, so I let it continue until the answering machine clicks in. If it's urgent, she'll leave a message and I'll call her later. If not, then it can wait until my midweekly phone call. We certainly don't have the sort of relationship where I need to speak to her every day.

Seconds later, Ian's phone rings and after glancing over at me, he picks it up.

'Yes,' he mumbles into the receiver. 'No, of course I remembered. No, I won't be late.' There follows a brief conversation, during which he tugs on the shark's teeth fringe.

'Sorry,' he says after he's hung up. 'That was my mum.'

'Mothers, eh?' I roll my eyes in what I hope will be a bonding moment, but Ian's already looking back at his screen and there's a light humming from his lips. Roz has warned me about the humming.

I still have to complete this week's 'Healthy Eats' menu for the website, which basically means pinching vegetarian recipes from the internet and passing them off as my own. To avoid detection, I tinker a bit with the ingredients, so for example last week's Yugo bean soup contained borlotti beans instead of the dried haricot beans. Whether this actually works as a dish I have no idea, but it sounds like it would. This week's Healthy Eats – marinated mini tofu steaks – will have an extra tahini dip to go with it.

I send it over to Ian and glance at the clock again. I'd kill for a snooze, but then kipping on Ian's first day would be pretty antisocial, so instead I decide to engage him in some light-hearted office chat.

'Sorry there's not more of a buzzy atmosphere,' I say. 'It used to be quite lively here.' I explain that the building was once fully occupied and even had a French lift operator, but now it's just us hanging in here until the place can be sold and no doubt turned into a block of fancy flats.

'That's fine,' Ian stammers, 'I'm not really a buzzy kind of guy.' The corners of his mouth twitch, but I'm not sure if he's trying to smile or if it's just a nervous tic.

'Fancy a spelt bar?' I nod to the open the shop drawer. 'Or maybe a spirulina juice?'

Ian shakes his head and does that smile/nervous twitch thing again so I decide it's probably best to leave him in peace.

At lunchtime I direct Ian to Luigi's café but I'm still feeling tired and decide to have an in-house lunch so I can kip afterwards. I rummage around in the shop and select the quinoa and buckwheat energy pot. Removing the recyclable plastic lid I scoop up a fingerful of the claggy grey gloop. It's utterly tasteless, but I'm not sure whether it's the product or my taste buds, which recently seemed to have gone on an extended holiday. So I fish out a flaxseed bar from the drawer and take a bite to see if that's got any flavour. Nope – I might as well be chewing on bits of glued-together gravel.

It's one thirty so hopefully I can squeeze in a medium-length nap before Ian returns. Using one of the exfoliation gloves as a makeshift pillow, I rest my head on my desk. I'm just drifting off when a wisp of the previous night's dream spirals up from the depths, like smoke curling through a crack in the wall.

It's fitting that it was set in a cinema, given how many hours Victor and I spent sitting side by side in one. For it was he who introduced me to those landmark French directors whose films helped to forge our unlikely friendship, which began in the foyer of the building where I now work and ended four years later on a freezing December night, the memory of which I am still trying to erase.

Ian returns from lunch, and after a brief discussion on what sort of sandwich he had (ham and salad), we both settle down to the afternoon's work.

The big article today is entitled 'The Miracle of Manifesting'. It's Roz's idea, of course, she loves this sort of stuff: *The Secret, The Cosmic Ordering Service, Change Your Life by Lunchtime...* she's read 'em all.

I cut and paste an article from the internet written by one of America's newest 'manifesting gurus', then I sit back and wonder how I manifested my own existence: thirty-six years old, writing about fennel toothpaste from a customised storage cupboard and living in a basement flat with a fat, flatulent bulldog.

Like everyone, I had dreams when I was younger, but they didn't tend to be very realistic, like the one of becoming a gymnast (inspired by Nadia Comaneci) flick-flacking around on a big blue mat. Although I remember thinking at the time that the parallel bar part looked quite painful and how Nadia must be doing herself some damage when she came crashing down against it. I just hoped that I could give that bit a miss – make up for it with something a little easier on the groin, like some extra floor work with ribbons or hoops.

When I was growing up, I just assumed there'd be something that I would love doing and for which I would get paid. Admittedly I never had a big game plan, unlike, say, Suzy Beale at primary school who knew at the age of five that she wanted to be a nurse and would march round the playground with her mini medical kit, checking children's pulses and applying plasters to non-existent grazes.

Watford Grammar School went by and still there were no clues pointing to the kind of career which would make me happy, but I wasn't panicking. Something would turn up, surely. I only started to worry when I sat opposite my career's officer two weeks before leaving school. Frowning as she scanned my poor A-level results, she let out one of the longest sighs I've ever heard.

'Hmmm,' she said, massaging her temples rigorously.

'Any advice?' Perhaps a little foolishly, I'd pinned all my hopes on a complete stranger telling me what to do with my life.

'Have you thought about teaching?' she asked.

'No,' I said. 'I'm not very good with children.'

'Oh,' she said. 'That's a shame.'

I'm still contemplating the 'how did I manifest my life?' question when my mate Megan rings. Megan's a painter but works part-time in the framing shop in Golborne Road. She often looks after Nellie on the afternoons when she's at her studio.

'We're on the Scrubs and Nellie's just eaten an old hamburger bun that she found in the bushes,' says Megan.

'Don't let her eat anything else,' I say, 'or she'll explode.'

'You hear that, Nellie?' says Megan, away from the phone. 'Hannah says you're going to explode.' There's a pause. 'Nellie says she doesn't give two shits,' says Megan into the phone again.

'What are you writing about today?' Megan's always eager to take the piss out of my job. If I believed in half the stuff that I write about, maybe I'd be offended. But I don't, so I'm not.

'The Miracle of Manifesting.'

'Run me through that one again.' I can detect the lip curl in Megan's voice.

15

'Well, first you have to imagine how it would feel to be living your perfect life,' I adopt my standard Californian accent, used for such conversations with Megan. 'Then you do a bit of role play. So in your case, if you want to be a successful painter you have to act like one.'

'Genius,' says Megan.

'So which super-successful painter are you going to be?'

'Rothko.'

'Excellent,' I say. 'With a little bit of play-acting your pictures will be selling for fifty million quid a pop and you'll be considered one of the world's greatest artists. Of course you'll end up being a chronic alcoholic and slicing your arms to shreds, then bleeding to death on your studio floor, but it's a small price to pay.'

'Rothko it is then,' says Megan. 'I can start right away. The offie's just round the corner.'

After we've discussed several other people we could try modelling ourselves on to manifest interesting and action-filled lives (Joan of Arc, Jesus, Rihanna…), Megan says that she will drop Nellie off on her way home from Wormwood Scrubs and we wind up the conversation.

Next to me Ian is switching off his computer. It's written into his contract that he can leave at 5 p.m. every day. He stands up and unhooks his coat and rucksack from the peg by the door.

'Fancy a hemp bar for the road?'

'Why not?' He blushes, but his mouth twitches into what I now realise must be a tentative smile.

'Oh, and here's an office key so you don't have to wait outside again,' I say.

He takes the hemp bar and key and slips them into his rucksack. Then he zips up his padded North Face jacket in preparation for the treacherous mountain peaks for which Soho is famous.

'See you tomorrow,' I say.

'See you tomorrow,' he echoes faintly and, still blushing, he heads for the door.

Chapter 3

I step out of the tube at Notting Hill Gate and board the No. 52 bus which will take me home. There's a spare window seat on the top deck and I sit down. Leaning my head against the glass, I shut my eyes and doze off. I'm not sure how long I have slept for – a minute? An hour? Three weeks? – who knows with narcolepsy – but when I wake, I see that apart from a West Indian woman in the seat in front of me, I am the only passenger left.

'No idea!' I hear the woman saying into her mobile. "im go out, an' come back a couple of hours later, actin' all peculiar. When I open the door, 'im hug me like 'im been gone a lifetime.' She shakes her head and laughs.

But it isn't so much the woman's conversation that interests me – it's her hat, or more precisely the sprig of red and blue feathers sprouting from the side of it. As she chats away, I watch the feathers dance in the air, until after another particularly energetic shake, one of them, a red one, breaks free and floats gently down to rest on the wooden slats by my feet. At the same moment the bus jerks to a halt and the conductor's voice shouts up from the floor below. 'End of the line.'

Down on the pavement I am standing by a salvage yard filled with wrought iron gates and rusting claw-footed baths. Next to it is a Brazilian café and a hairdressers, and further down the road is an old library, whose doors are boarded up.

Directly in front of me is a short street lined with Victorian semi-detached houses, and at the end of it, I notice something glowing.

The conductor and the West Indian woman have already headed off and all the shops are shut. There's no one else about and the darkness is beginning to feel oppressive. That light is still shimmering at the end of the street, and beneath it I can make out what looks to be a video shop. Hoping that whoever works there will be able to tell me the quickest way back to Kensal Green, I walk towards it.

Several steps lead up to the video shop and in the window there's a poster of a black guy pushing a man in a wheelchair, advertising a film called *Untouchable*. Through the half-open door, I can hear the sound of a single oboe. I recognise the melody immediately from what was once my favourite soundtrack. I shiver and hurry up the stairs.

Inside, it's not a large video shop, just two small rooms with banks of plastic-cased DVDs lining the walls, interspersed with posters from the newest releases. The foreign section dominates the far left-hand corner, and from where I'm standing I can see at least four Truffaut films, including *La peau douce*, whose soundtrack is now playing.

'Can I help you?' The voice is soft and I don't need to turn round to see who's speaking.

'Victor,' I say, astounded. 'What on earth are you doing here?'

Victor is in the second room, halfway up a ladder with a light bulb in his hand. In marked contrast to the neat uniform he wore to operate the lifts, he is dressed in a frayed blue cotton shirt and creased brown corduroys. His hair is longer, whiter and uncombed and stands up at the ends, making him look like he's just been electrocuted.

'This is where I work now.' He quickly screws in the bulb and climbs down the ladder. His pale blue eyes hold mine as he walks over.

'I am glad that you have come, Hannah.'

I stare at him, still unable to believe that it's Victor standing in front of me. For a moment I wonder if last night's dream is somehow seeping through into the present.

'You've changed a bit,' I say to fill the silence, and I wonder what could have happened to him after he left his job so abruptly. All I know is that following his retirement he'd hoped to return to Paris and that in the two years since he's been gone, he's never once tried to contact me.

'And you?' Victor asks, his expression suddenly serious. 'How are you?'

'Oh, I'm fine,' I say quickly. Well, what else am I going to say? Actually, Victor, things aren't too brilliant. For starters I appear to be losing my senses – I can barely taste or smell anything and grey seems to be the only colour I can see. The panic attacks are getting worse, and on top of that, there's the tiredness. I mean, is it normal to feel tired all the time? In fact, I spend so much time sleeping that I've even found myself contemplating a catheter and how complicated it might be to fit, so that I can stay in bed all weekend. That's not right, is it?

Victor is still looking at me, obviously waiting for more of an answer than 'I'm fine'. I'm tempted to add a jokey aside, but I decide against it. I may be able to fool other people by attempting a bit of humour even when I'm feeling like shit, but Victor knows me better than that.

'Come.' Victor clasps my hand. 'I will show you where my real work is done.' He leads me to the back of the room and draws aside the curtain behind the counter. Beyond is a long thin corridor, whose walls are hung with black and white photos of famous French directors from the sixties and seventies. At the far end is a door with the words 'Cinema Lumière' painted on in gold letters. As we pass through it, I remember Victor telling me about the Lumière brothers, who were the world's first filmmakers and how, at the end of the nineteenth century, Louis, a physicist, and his photographer brother Auguste designed and built the original combined camera and projector, the cinematograph.

'What do you think?' The door shuts behind us and Victor is watching closely for my reaction.

I look around at the miniature cinema with the gold flocked-paper walls, the screen hidden by a swathe of thick crimson velvet, and the arched ceiling from which hang chandeliers with lights shaped like little flaming torches. Beneath my feet the carpet feels as springy as moss and the smell of mothballs hangs in the air. In the middle of the room just to my right, about five metres from the screen, is one red velvet seat.

'Do people have to stand to watch the films?' I ask.

Victor shakes his head and pats the arm of the solitary chair. 'One seat is enough.'

'I see,' I say, not seeing at all. 'But it is a cinema, isn't it?'

'Not exactly,' Victor replies. 'It is more of a private viewing place – a pre-view theatre, if you wish.' He gestures towards the raised room at the back of the auditorium. 'I have something else that I want you to see.'

The small space where we are now standing is exactly how I would have imagined a projectionist's booth to look. The ceiling is low, and into the wall nearest the auditorium is cut a square, through which I can make out the curtain-covered screen at the far end. On the opposite wall are several shelves stacked with round silver film cans. Aside from two chairs and a small cabinet, there is little in the way of furniture. Instead, the room is dominated by what stands in the middle, and although I've only seen one in pictures before, I know exactly what it is.

About eighteen inches in height and the same in depth, the large wooden box is mounted onto an old-fashioned tripod, bringing the whole construction to around the same height as Victor. On one side is a brass hand crank and on top an electric arc lamp, while set into the front panel is the projector lens. The shiny walnut wood from which the box is made has been polished to such a degree that I can see my face reflected in it.

'A cinematograph!' I say, amazed that Victor could own such a piece of machinery. 'Does it actually work?'

Victor nods, his eyes shining.

'Where did you get it?'

'It was donated to me by two of the backers for this cinema.' Victor smiles, running a finger along the side panel nearest me. Then he flicks the catch and the panel swings open to reveal a jumble of cogs, sprockets and brass hubs. Just behind the lens is a small bellow-like device, which he tells me is responsible for regulating the shutter speed.

I watch him as he talks excitedly about his cinematograph, and once again I am struck by the contrast between this new Victor and the Victor I knew from those early days when I had just joined the magazine.

We met on my first morning at the job. As I entered the building I saw a white-haired man of around seventy sitting, or so I thought, in the booth by the lifts. He was dressed in a stiff navy blue suit and matching peaked hat and had the palest blue eyes. His posture was buckled, and when he stood up I realised that he wasn't sitting at all – he barely reached my shoulder. The badge pinned to his lapel told me that his surname was Lever, which I knew from my faltering grasp of French meant to raise up or elevate, and which I thought quite apt given his job.

Over the next few weeks I would try to get Victor to talk as he was taking me up or down in the old-fashioned lift. I didn't learn a lot – just that he was born and brought up in Paris but moved to London in the sixties; he lived in West Kilburn and he spoke English as if he'd learnt it from pre-war text books. There was something very guarded about him which only made me more curious – and there was certainly nothing to indicate how close we would become over the following years.

'We should celebrate.' Victor's voice cuts through my thoughts. He's standing by the cabinet which contains three crystal glass bottles filled with liquids of varying colours – blood red, absinthe green and crème de cassis purple.

Victor pulls out the first bottle. '*Eau de vie,*' he says and pours a large measure of the gleaming red liquid into a glass, which he thrusts into my hand. I take a sip – it has a strong taste of port, but beneath that is something else, something with quite a kick.

'That's powerful stuff,' I say. It's the first thing I've been able to taste properly in months.

I watch Victor knock back the contents of his own glass in one and the dribble of red *eau de vie* that trickles down his chin.

'I thought you didn't like alcohol,' I say.

'There are a great many things I thought I did not like.' He turns, pulls open the drawer beneath the cabinet and whips out a family-sized packet of Doritos. 'Have you ever tasted these?'

'Errr, yes.'

He rips open the packet of cheese-flavoured Doritos and shoves a fistful of the triangle shapes into his mouth. A flurry of crumbs land on his shirt and trousers and the carpet below, where I notice there's quite a selection of other foodstuffs scattered.

'I see you're as big a fan of housework as I am,' I say.

Victor waves dismissively at the carpet. 'Pffff. There are more important things in life than housework.'

'I agree,' I say, 'all housework should come with a government health warning – it makes you soft in the head.'

Victor chuckles and sucks noisily at his fingers, presumably to remove the orange stains left by the Doritos.

'Would you like to hear a joke?'

'OK, then.' I'm still unsure how to take this new Victor.

'What do you call a woman with egg and bacon on her head?'

'I don't know.'

'Caff!' He bursts out laughing.

'Victor, are you on drugs?'

'Yes!' Victor shouts. 'LIFE. It is marvellous, is it not?'

As I watch him, still chuckling to himself, I am reminded of Scrooge when he wakes on Christmas morning after dreaming that he has died, to find that he is still very much alive.

'So why didn't you go back to Paris?' I ask Victor a little later after he has poured himself a second drink.

'Life had other plans for me,' he says. 'I was given an

24

opportunity which I could not refuse,' he nods towards the auditorium. 'My own cinema.'

I follow his gaze and peer through the hole in the wall through which I can still see the single red seat.

'What sort of films do you show here then?'

Victor thinks for a moment. 'Each one is different.'

'And who makes them?'

Victor grins. 'I do.'

'Really? That's brilliant,' I say. 'It's what you always wanted.'

Victor raises his glass in a toast. 'To fate.' He takes a mouthful then walks over to the shelves of silver cans. 'Actually I have a film which I would like you to see.'

He reaches up on tiptoes and pulls down one of the cans from the middle shelf.

'It is not yet finished,' he says, removing the film reel from inside. 'But I think you will find it interesting.' He opens up the side panel of the cinematograph and slots the reel onto the brass hub. 'Do you have the time?'

Although I'm not really in the mood to watch a film, I don't want to be rude. I also don't have the energy to argue, and since Megan isn't dropping Nellie back until later, there's no hurry to get home.

'Alright then,' I say.

'Excellent.' Victor clicks the door of the side panel shut and switches on the arc lamp. A shaft of light immediately pierces through the hole in the wall, spotlighting the single chair. Victor swivels round from the cinematograph and smiles. 'Your seat awaits you.'

I walk down to the front of the cinema and sink into the chair's soft velvet clutches, where I lean my head back and close my eyes. While I wait for the film to begin, I remember that very first film that Victor and I watched together.

It was in February, about three months after I started the job, and we happened to be leaving work at the same time. We walked down Charing Cross Road together, passing the queues for *Les Misérables* outside the Palace Theatre, where Victor told me that his mother named him after Victor Hugo, on whose book the musical was based.

A few minutes later he turned into a small side street, stopping halfway down in front of an old building squashed between a second-hand bookshop and a shop selling artists' supplies.

'What is this place?' I asked. I'd never even noticed the building before.

'It is one of London's first cinemas,' said Victor. 'I come here every Monday.' He pushed open the door and I peeped inside at the small circular foyer whose faded pink walls were papered with French film posters.

'It mainly screens French films.' He motioned to one of the posters showing a man leaping off a train with the words *L'amour en fuite* below. 'There is a François Truffaut film showing tonight in the original, but with subtitles. Perhaps you would like to watch?'

I hesitated. The only French films I'd ever seen seemed to revolve around complicated threesomes and long sullen silences. But it was a rainy Monday night and I'd nothing else planned.

'Why not?' I replied. And that was how it started.

From that first Truffaut film I was hooked, and within two months I was going to the cinema with Victor almost every Monday after work. Most of the films we saw belonged to the *Nouvelle Vague* or 'New Wave' era, whose directors Victor considered to be the world's finest filmmakers. Instead of the glossy, stylised studio productions of the fifties with linear plots and predictable scripts, the *Nouvelle Vague* directors, or *auteurs* as they were called, showed life as it really was. They insisted that the characters were the most important part of their films and that the audience should relate to these characters through their feelings and emotions.

After each film, Victor and I would retire to a French café in Greek Street and talk about what we had just seen. Aside from Truffaut, Victor adored Godard, Resnais and Chabrol and when he spoke of them his posture would straighten and his eyes would sparkle. Sitting opposite him at the wobbly wooden table with its worn green paint, I was intrigued that he should love films that focused so much on feelings and emotions, when he showed so little of his own.

'Are you ready?' Victor calls from the projectionist's booth behind me. Before I can reply, the lights dim and the crimson curtains slide apart. The screen in front of me is blank except for the words 'Lumière Productions' in gold script. The *accent grave* of Lumière is formed by a red feather which slowly detaches itself and drifts down across the white expanse until it reaches the bottom of the screen.

The opening shot of the film shows a young woman lying motionless on a sitting room floor. Her eyes stare sightlessly at the ceiling and one side of her head is covered in blood. In the background a curtain billows and the carpet around her is strewn with shards of glass. On the mantelpiece above the woman is a photograph of a young couple standing on a shingle beach. The man's arms are wrapped around the woman and they are laughing.

Seconds later, the screen fades to black.

The next scene shows the same young woman in a café, reading. A man sits down at a nearby table, and although he has a newspaper his eyes keep drifting towards her. Eventually he says something – I don't know what because the film has no sound – and she gives him a hesitant smile. He stands up and walks over to her table. Watching him, my heart begins to hammer. I take a deep breath and force myself to focus on the screen in front of me.

The scene has changed into a series of fast-moving images, like photographs being flicked through in an album; the young woman and man are speeding across a bridge in an open-top car; they're walking together through a street market, eating peaches; then lying on a rooftop gazing at the glitter of stars above them. Fleeting as these images are, the feelings that they trigger are so intense that it seems as though I am experiencing the exact same emotions as the female character. I can sense a giddy rush of euphoria when the car speeds across the bridge; little ripples of happiness wash through me as if I am also wandering through the market, eating peaches with the man I love; and I too experience a bloom of wonder while I gaze up at the stars.

I feel the sharp sting of tears so I shut my eyes. My hands are shaking and my throat is sandpaper dry. How is it that Victor has managed to steal scenes from my own life and recreate them on film? When I open my eyes again, the images have turned to black and white. A mother is holding a newborn baby, tracing a finger gently down its cheek; a father clasps the hand of his young daughter, pulling her along the pavement in her shiny roller skates; a woman (the same woman who held the baby) is sitting by her daughter's bed, reading her a story. Again, it seems as though I am part of each scene; when I watch the woman running a finger down her newborn child's cheek, I feel a fierce explosion of love. While the man is pulling his daughter along the pavement on her roller skates, my own body tingles with giddy delight, and when the little girl snuggles up against her mother, I am enveloped by a blanket of warmth and contentment.

Another jump cut and the film is now in colour again. The young woman from the café scene is standing in a kitchen, crying. The man is gripping her shoulders, shaking her hard and shouting into her face...

My palms are slicked with sweat and I feel dizzy. Memories that I've pushed to the far corners of my mind shoot to the surface and a rush of hot bile surges up from my stomach. I thrust myself out of the chair and race for the door, tears streaking down my cheeks.

Chapter 4

I am still thinking about the film seven days later – in fact I've thought about little else – when Nellie and I set out for our Monday morning walk. We're half an hour late due to Nellie's reluctance to leave the house, and by the time we enter the cemetery, icy sleet is falling around us. Nellie's face is set in a hard grimace.

'I know it's not fun, Nell,' I say. 'But you have to have a walk. Otherwise you'll lose the use of those legs.' I reach down and give her back a quick rub. 'If it gets any worse, we can take cover in the taxi.'

Nellie is in such a grump that she refuses to look at me. We round the corner to the first avenue of mausoleums and as we pass beneath the canopy of oak trees, frames from Victor's film spool through my mind once more. Although it's a week since I sat in that cinema seat, the images haven't faded at all. In fact they're as sharp and bright as the evening on which I watched them, stitched like a length of ribbon onto the inside of my skull.

It's not only the images which won't fade, it's also the feelings that each scene seemed to trigger. However much I try to ignore them, they remain stubbornly close to the surface – a huge and complex bundle of happiness, joy and euphoria, mixed with a deep dragging sadness that I can't begin to unravel even if I wanted to. I haven't felt emotions like this in over two years and their intensity is terrifying.

And finally there are the film's obvious similarities to my own life. I cannot believe it is just a coincidence and if it's not, why would Victor do such a thing, given our shared history?

The bewildering tangle of emotions, together with the unnerving parallels to my life, is too much for me to process right now. Instead, I find it easier to take a detached view and analyse the style and filming techniques just as Victor and I used to do. For in many ways it felt like one of the more experimental *Nouvelle Vague* films that we watched together. Littered with jump cuts and with a starkly realistic, almost documentary style, it could almost pass for one of Truffaut's earlier works.

My thoughts are still caught up with Victor's film, when Nellie lets out a little bark. I squint through the sleet and see a tall man in a red woolly hat loading dogs of varying shapes and sizes into the back of the taxi. When the last one is safely aboard, he climbs inside. But he must have seen us approaching because he leans out again and waves.

'You two look frozen,' he says, 'come inside and warm up.'

'Don't worry, we're fine,' I say.

'No, you're not. Your face is blue.' A smile creases the dark skin of the man's cheeks. He's wearing a thick workman's jacket, jeans and muddy boots, and I reckon he's in his mid-thirties.

'See. She wants to come inside.' He grins and points to Nellie, who's deploying her special pleading look which usually gets the sympathy vote from strangers.

I'm about to reply, saying that I'm already late for work, when Nellie lumbers up to the taxi, clambers in through the open door and flops down on the floor next to a terrified-looking whippet.

'One down, one to go.' The man pats the empty seat beside him just as a gust of sleet hits me full in the face.

I climb inside reluctantly

'I'm Joe and these are the girls,' says the man. 'I haven't kidnapped them by the way. I'm a dog walker.' He runs me through the names of the three dogs at his feet – one limpid Afghan, one fat black Labrador and a mongrel with bushy eyebrows.

'And that's Stan. He's sort of a girl.' He points to the quivering whippet who's trying to merge with the taxi door in an effort to get away from Nellie. 'He's new today. His owners live in Kensal Rise, which is why we're here.' He twists round in the seat to look at me, and I notice that his dark eyes are flecked with green. 'That's us. So who are you?'

'I'm Hannah.'

'Hello, Hannah.' Joe shakes my hand. 'And this is?'

'This is Nellie.'

Nellie gives Joe a cursory glance before resuming her stare-out with Stan.

'Do you come here often?' Joe grins.

I tell him I'm a regular.

'I bet you know some good stories about the place. Come on, what's the best one you've heard?'

In fact I do know quite a few stories about Kensal Green Cemetery after going on a guided tour with Victor one afternoon. Down in those echoing catacombs we learnt a lot about the burial business. I now know, for example, that coffins have to be lined with a special substance to protect them from 'coffin liquor' (the stuff that dead bodies excrete); that the bars across the front of each 'loculus' were to stop

32

the body snatchers from stealing the corpses and selling them to the hospitals for research; and that for a few extra quid you could buy a round metal container in which to keep your innards, thus preserving your body for a little longer.

But I don't want Joe to think me too morbid so I end up telling him about another famous resident, the tightrope walker Blondin, who crossed the Niagara Falls in 1859 and whose party trick was to wheel a small stove into the middle of the Falls before frying and eating an omelette in front of the crowds.

'Great story,' says Joe, clapping his hands when I finish, which makes all the dogs bark except for Stan, who's now squashed into the corner of the taxi, eyes popping and legs clacking with fright.

'Nellie, what are you doing to Stan?' I say.

Nellie glances briefly at me then her eyes swivel back to the whippet.

'Nellie's a bit of a bully,' I say to Joe. 'She needs round-the-clock surveillance.'

Joe smiles and pulls an envelope-sized foil package from his jacket pocket. 'This might distract her.'

Nellie's eyes dart from Stan to the package. *Mine.*

'You want some of my pattie then?' says Joe.

A noisy gulp escapes from Nellie's throat.

Joe unwraps the package, breaks off a small piece for Nellie and then offers me some.

'My cousin makes them for the Caribbean takeaway on Chamberlayne Road so they're obviously going to be delicious.'

'In which case,' I say, 'I can't really refuse.' I take it and bite into the pastry.

'Tasty,' I say, hardly tasting a thing.

'Not too hot? Esme's pretty liberal with the chili.'

I shake my head.

'What? You must have a mouth made of steel. Either that or someone has run off with your taste buds.' Joe's laugh is so infectious that I can't help joining in.

'That explains it,' I say. 'Do you know where I can get some more?'

A frown of concentration ridges between Joe's eyes. 'Taste buds, you mean? Well, there is one place in Soho, but it's very hidden away, just word of mouth so to speak. And of course, you have to know what you're after, the quality varies massively.'

'Taste buds come in different ranges?'

'Oh yes,' says Joe. 'There are the ones with a liking for tinned mince and frozen pizzas at the bottom end of the market, the middle end caters for people who buy fun-sized vegetables and Tesco's Finest, and the top of the range, that's for posh folks who want caviar, truffles, and...' he fumbles for a third example.

'Whippet's tongues?' I venture, nodding at Stan.

'Exactly,' Joe chuckles.

I feel my cheeks redden. I'm not sure if it's the way he's looking at me or the way his thigh is brushing against mine, but my mind is already off, having a field day.

Placing my hand on his leg, I turn to Joe. How do you feel about fucking in graveyards, or is that a bit Goth? If not, I'm sure we can find a grassy knoll somewhere...

Without waiting for a reply, I lunge at him and bury my head in his crotch, moaning urgently.

That's the trouble with the Mentals – you can never tell when, and with what intensity they're going to strike. This attack is pretty full-on, and I feel the flush of embarrassment spread from my cheeks to my neck and chest. My attempt to crush the image of my head in Joe's groin by staring at Stan's gluey eyes doesn't seem to have much effect.

'I should go,' I say quickly.

'You can't leave yet.'

I mumble something about being late for an interview with an American life coach and lever myself out of the seat.

'A life coach, huh?' says Joe. 'In that case, you're excused. But come and see us again,' he adds, with his head cocked to one side as if he's asking a question. 'We'll be here for the rest of this week.'

'Thank you,' I say, although I'm not quite sure what I'm thanking him for. 'Goodbye,' I add, but it sounds so stilted and formal that I tack on a ludicrous sounding 'Ta ra,' along with a little quiz-panel wave, before Nellie and I clamber out of the taxi and set off back to the flat.

Chapter 5

I am sitting opposite Anthony Brooks on a tan leather sofa in a massive hotel suite just off Park Lane. Anthony (the PR lady has instructed me to pronounce the *th* as though I have a lisp) is the American life coach whose most recent book, *Discover your Life Purpose,* is shooting up the Self-Help charts. Roz has insisted that I interview him.

Anthony is built of standard male life coach stuff – well over six foot tall, thick dark hair, firm chin, square jaw, capable hands and big feet encased in no-nonsense black leather lace-ups. He's wearing a smart black suit with a casual grey T-shirt beneath. His hands are clasped and he's leaning towards me in a rather overfamiliar way, awaiting my first question. The proximity of his face to mine makes me want to reach over and lick his chin just to see his reaction.

'So, Anthony,' I say and flip open my notebook with my ten questions, 'when did *you* discover your own life purpose?'

Anthony smiles, showcasing a set of bleached white teeth. 'Well, Hannah, I knew from a very early age that I would help others in some way.'

'How early?'

'I was probably about seven.'

'Seven?'

Anthony nods. 'I was blessed.' He puts his hands together

as though he's praying and does a little bow. Then he tells me that as a child he loved playing detective games and uncovering hidden clues. He now employs that very same skill to help others find their own vocations.

'So how *can* other, less blessed people go about finding their life purpose?' There's a spike of resentment in my voice. Seven is far too young to know your life purpose. Where's the struggle in that?

'Often clues to our purpose in life will be found in our childhood. Was there something you loved to do as a little girl, Hannah?'

I shrug, pretty sure that my clumsy cartwheeling attempts to copy Nadia Comaneci won't count. I also used to write rather macabre stories about my vicious pet guinea pig, Gilmore, most of which ended with him getting wedged down the waste disposal unit. But those won't count either.

'Not really,' I say.

'Hannah,' says Anthony, 'I'd like to let you into a little secret.' He leans even closer and I get a waft of minty breath. 'You already know what your purpose is.'

'I'm not sure I do actually.'

'Oh yes, you do,' says Anthony.

'I'd have to disagree there.'

Anthony shakes his head with a flash of that expensive white dentistry. I'm tempted to argue this one out till the end of the interview, but then I wouldn't have anything to write about so I let it go.

'You just aren't aware of it yet because you're not listening properly,' says Anthony.

'Listening to who?'

'To you. That's you with a capital Y.'

'Sorry, you've lost me there.'

37

Anthony starts to explain that there is a part of me which knows everything already and that if I can learn to tap into this part, then my life will be just peachy. I've heard this so many times before – Roz is a particularly staunch advocate of this idea – but I'm not convinced.

Anthony is now blathering on about my 'Higher Self', but I've zoned out. Instead I focus on his feet, which really are quite big. Size 16 at least. My uncle, Malcolm, took a size 16 and when I was a child, and he used to lift me up so that my little red patent T-bars rested on the toes of his ludicrously large boots, then we would shuffle round the room together to Randy Newman's 'Short People.'

'Our life purpose is usually linked to things that bring us joy,' says Anthony, 'so I want you to write down a list of five activities that bring *you* joy, Hannah.'

'What? Now?'

Anthony nods.

I flip over to the next sheet on my pad and stare down at the blank page. Then I write 'Five activities which bring me joy' and stare down at that for a bit.

I realise I'll have to write something, so I jot down the things that *used* to bring me joy before all the joy seemed to have been sucked out of my life by some giant, invisible Hoover.

1. Eating and sex (joint first)
2. Reading and watching films
3. Going to gigs and walking Nellie
4. Rummaging around in other people's tat at flea markets
5. Long train journeys, preferably through the Scottish Highlands.

When I've finished, Anthony asks me to read my list out to him, so I do, fully aware that trying to divine a life purpose from this lot is like trying to cobble together a gourmet meal from chicken breasts, custard creams, Gorgonzola and Castrol GTX.

'And what do you think is holding you back from achieving your life purpose?' says Anthony when I'm silent again.

'Err, life?'

Anthony laughs. 'Now if I had a dime for every person who's said that.' Then his expression turns serious. 'Hannah, do you *believe* that you have a purpose on this earth?'

'I'd like to,' I say. 'But no, basically I don't.'

Anthony taps the side of his head. 'It all starts with the belief.' He holds my gaze. 'The power of our minds is extraordinary, and if we use them correctly we can move many, many mountains.'

'If you say so,' I deadpan.

The sleet has turned to drizzle by the time I reach the office. My coat and skirt are sodden and my hair is slicked to my head like a little brown skullcap. I sink down into my chair and toss Anthony's book onto my desk.

'Sorry, I'm late,' I say to Ian. 'I've been discovering my life purpose.' I tap the front cover of the book, which features a huge headshot of Anthony, all teeth, hair and jutty jaw.

'He looks scary,' says Ian. After a week of working together he is now able to hold my gaze for longer than a second.

'He was.'

'So… did he tell you what your life purpose is?' Ian's voice still has a slight stammer but it's getting better.

'Apparently I'm going to breed miniature cockatoos and open my own nail salon.'

There's a short pause.

'That's a joke by the way.'

I watch the sides of Ian's mouth lift in a little smile. 'Yes, I got that.'

I open the three promo packages that the postman's brought and lay out the contents on the desk. There's a tin of braised tofu, a packet of spelt crackers and a sachet of Menop-Ease powder whose mixture of sage, nettle and ginkgo biloba will apparently help to 'ease' my way through this major life change. There's also a free Menop-Ease mug with a picture of a grey-haired woman leaping up in the air on a trampoline and grinning like a goon.

I decide to postpone my article on An*th*ony – there's only so much life coach talk I can take for one morning. Instead, I start a piece on panic attacks. According to recent research, over 10 per cent of the UK's adult population have experienced them at some time and that figure is rising. I have no trouble listing the main symptoms, given how many I've experienced myself (shortness of breath, heart palpitations, trembling, sweating, nausea and dizziness). The possible cures are a little more complicated, so I do a mix of advice that my GP has given me and internet-gleaned tips, which include deep breathing, physical exercise, meditation, magnesium and cognitive behavioural therapy.

When I'm done, I e-mail the copy over to Ian, then I click on another YouTube favourite to take my mind off the subject of panic attacks. For the next three minutes I immerse myself in footage of a humpback whale doing its 'dance of joy' after being cut free from tangled nets off the coast of Mexico by the aptly named Michael Fishbach. Halfway through the third viewing my phone rings.

It's my mother again. We only spoke four days ago, so I'm tempted to switch over manually to the answering machine. But before I can reach for the button, a black and white image from Victor's film bolts into my mind. It's the one of the young woman holding her newborn baby. She's smiling and her eyes are shining with a look of intense joy as she traces her forefinger very slowly down the baby's cheek. There's so much tenderness in that one gesture that, just as in the cinema, I feel an overwhelming rush of love.

I pick up the phone. 'Hi there, Mum.'

'Is that you, Hannah?' Mum sounds so happy to hear my voice that I wince.

No, actually it's Darth Vader.

'Yes, it's me. How are you?'

Mum tells me that she's fine then embarks on a story about yesterday's visit to the Harlequin Centre in Watford with Pam, who lives next door. She breaks off just as she and Pam are queuing in the food court for a mid-morning Danish.

'I'm not boring you, am I?'

I check my watch. 'Not at all,' I say, then I ask her how she's been getting on at the hospice charity shop this week, since the volunteer left. She tells me that it's been so busy she hasn't even been able to take a lunch break. After that there's a pause.

'I thought I might come and see you this Sunday,' I say, trying to inject as much enthusiasm into my voice as possible. Although it's been three months since I last saw Mum, I can't say that the prospect of a visit fills me with joy.

'Oh darling, that would be wonderful,' says Mum. 'What would you like for lunch? I could do a roast chicken, or what about that chicken and olive dish I did last time?'

41

Mum has a repertoire of about five dishes, all of which involve chicken.

'Roast chicken is lovely.'

'Are you sure? I could make a chicken casserole.'

'Roast chicken is perfect,' I say, frustration pricking my voice.

'Or maybe I should buy some chicken Kievs?'

'Roast chicken's fine, Mum.' I repeat. How many more chicken dishes do we have to wade through? Chicken à la King, chicken Maryland, chicken vindaloo, chicken in a basket...

'So, I'll see you on Sunday, will I?' Mum sounds as if she doesn't quite believe I will come.

'See you then,' I say. Chicken nuggets.

For lunch, the idea of the braised tofu and spelt crackers just isn't cutting it, so I decide to go with Ian to Luigi's. We join the queue and contemplate the sandwich fillings beneath the glass counter: egg mayonnaise, tuna and sweetcorn, an old-school Coronation chicken with added slithers of red pepper and some fat slices of ham.

'What are you having?' I say to Ian. 'I need inspiration.'

'Tuna and sweetcorn,' says Ian, 'with some salad.'

'Edgy,' I say with a smile.

Ian smiles back. 'I may even have a flapjack for pudding.'

'Steady on.'

Out on the street again, Ian says he wants to go to the comic shop on Charing Cross Road, so I head back to my desk to eat my cheese sandwich. With my chair positioned for optimum viewing of Luigi's, I stare down at the café's lunchtime crowd. Sitting at a corner table and set apart from the usual office worker clientele is a white-haired old man.

His shoulders are hunched as he nurses a solitary cup of coffee and gazes out of the window.

*

May 2006

'Are you still with me?' I ask Victor, who's sitting opposite me at our favourite spot in the French café.

Victor drags his eyes away from the window and looks over at me. 'Sorry,' he says, 'where was I?'

It's six months into our friendship and we've just watched Truffaut's *Les quatre cents coups*, a film about a young boy growing up in Paris during the early 1950s. I've been asking Victor about his own childhood, and so far he's told me that he was raised by his mother, a seamstress, in a top-floor flat near the Montmartre vineyards. He never knew his father, who was English and had met his mother as a student one summer when she was waitressing at a nearby café.

'You were telling me about the Occupation,' I say.

Victor nods, then takes a sip of his coffee before he starts speaking again.

'It lasted until I was seven,' he says, 'so I spent a great deal of time at home by our kitchen window, watching whatever was happening on the street below: Monsieur Olivier sitting on the bench outside the tobacconist; Madame Valjean singing to her budgerigar on her balcony; and later in the evening, Evelyne with the shiny black stilettos, who waited for customers beneath the Fleur de Madeline soap poster.'

Victor pauses for a mouthful of his apricot tart. 'We lived one street away from Paris's oldest cinema, and once a month after the Occupation ended, my mother would leave me with Madame Valjean and walk to Studio 28. There she would watch the films of Jean Renoir, Marcel Carné and the comedies of René Clair, and the next day, over breakfast, she would act out her favourite scenes. Each time I would beg her to take me with her until finally on my ninth birthday she agreed.

'Abel Gance's *Paradis Perdu* was showing that night, and nothing on earth had prepared me for the experience of watching my first film. Afterwards I told my mother that one day I would own a cinema exactly like Studio 28, with the same flocked wallpaper, the same red seats, even the same torch lights designed by Jean Cocteau. The only difference would be that I would not show the films of other directors, I would show films that I had made myself.'

Back in the café, Bernard, the small, neat French owner, hurries past to deliver a Dijon slice to the table next to us. He studiously ignores the woman sat at the table behind, because she is talking on her mobile. If you use a mobile or a laptop in Bernard's café, you don't get served.

'The next day, a Saturday, I started my new career,' Victor continues, 'I chose Monsieur Olivier for my subject and followed him when he left his apartment, pretending that he was the lead character in my first production. Using my eyes as the camera lens, I recorded all the details – the missing button on his coat, the sagging pockets of his trousers, the loose sole of his left shoe that flapped on the pavement like a brown tongue. I waited outside the tobacconist's while he bought a packet of cigarettes, then I followed him to the library to return a book, a romance. I do not know if he noticed me, but I spent the entire afternoon making my imaginary film, which in my head I entitled "Monsieur Olivier's Life".'

Victor takes another forkful of tart and chews slowly. 'From that day on, I made imaginary films of almost everyone in our neighbourhood: Madame Valjean, whose husband had been killed at the start of the Occupation, walking to the Montmartre cemetery each Sunday; Evelyne reapplying her red lipstick as dusk fell; and Edouard, the thin man in a tattered three-piece suit tap dancing for centimes on the corner...'

Victor glances out of the window again at a pigeon which is pecking at some peeling paint on the ledge. 'I was so convinced that this was to be my future career that I could not imagine any other life for myself.' He looks back at me with a shrug of his uniformed shoulders. 'It is strange how the lives we lead can be so different from the lives of which we dream.'

*

Sitting at my desk, a sadness swells inside me. I can remember that afternoon in the café so clearly: Victor's animated face when he talked of his childhood, his description of his neighbours' lives and the effect of that first film on him. The fact that I have seen him again won't change things, and it's unlikely that I will return to the video shop. If I do, it will undoubtedly mean having to talk about what happened between us and that's not something I can face.

But that doesn't stop me from thinking about Victor's film. Given his childhood preoccupation for documenting his neighbours' lives, perhaps it's not so strange that he chose to document mine. What is strange is the intensity of the feelings that the film produced, and the fact that despite all my efforts to push them away, they're not going anywhere.

Tentatively, like a skater circling a black hole in the ice, I skirt around the feeling that resonated most – that profound sadness which I know is connected to my mother. Of course, I've been aware for a long time that our relationship isn't exactly normal, and for the last few years it hasn't particularly bothered me. But now it seems that something has changed.

I finish my sandwich and wash it down with some freebie coconut water. Then, to distract myself from thinking about my mother, I decide to review some of the relaxation CDs we've recently been sent. I pick out three: *Navajo Chants*, *Rainforest Symphony* and *Orca's Song* – and stick the first one in the CD player.

Naturally, *Navajo Chants* opens with the sound of panpipes, without which any self-respecting relaxation CD would be stuffed. Whatever the location, be it a calming ocean, cool forest glade or serene summer meadow, they always manage to shoehorn some sort of wind instrument in there. I listen for about thirty seconds, then I press stop and consult my handy stash of stock health and wellbeing words (tranquil, harmonious, soft, flowing, inspirational, soulful, soothing, mystical…) before scribbling down my review.

I've just moved onto *Rainforest Symphony* when Ian appears through the office door carrying a plastic bag from the comic shop. He glances at the CD player.

'*Rainforest Symphony*,' I say. 'It's a blast.'

Ian's mouth twitches into what I now know is definitely a smile.

'In fact, I'm going to play it 24/7 in the nail bar that Anthony said I'd be opening.'

Ian chuckles, then takes out two comics from his plastic bag and places them neatly on his desk next to the hole punch. The top one has a picture of a tall, bald, silver man with massive biceps standing astride a big rock.

'Who's the dude?' I ask.

'Silver Surfer.'

'You really read those things?'

'I do.'

'But aren't they for kids and… well, sad men who live in bedsits?'

'Please don't be rude about my comics,' says Ian, 'or I may have to leave the room.'

'Oh, right, sorry,' I say, 'I didn't mean to…'

Ian breaks into a grin. 'That was a joke by the way.'

The rest of the afternoon is filled by a piece on how meditation can reduce your biological age by up to fifteen years and how even mainstream medical practitioners are prescribing it to reduce blood pressure, combat fatigue and boost the immune system. At 5 p.m. Ian and I leave the office and walk down Denmark Street together. We stop in front of the guitar shop, where Phil the owner is perched on a stool behind the till, cleaning one of the ukuleles.

'They're funny instruments,' says Ian, staring through the window. 'I wonder what they're like to play.'

'I'm sure Phil would be happy to let you have a go.'

Ian shakes his head. 'I'd feel like a prat.'

'So what? I won't tell anyone.'

We walk on, past the second-hand video shop whose windows feature a cardboard cut-out of Robert Pattinson and Kristen Stewart kissing.

'Ian,' I say, giving voice to something that's been preying on my mind for the last few days. 'If someone made a film of your life, would you want to watch it?'

Ian laughs. 'Not unless I'm in the mood to watch paint dry. What about you?'

I shake my head. In the distance the sound of an ambulance siren slices through the air.

Ian checks his watch. 'I'd better run, but see you tomorrow.' He gives me a little wave. 'I enjoyed today.'

'Me too,' I say and give him a little wave back.

I'm picking Nellie up from Megan's studio, so I hop on the bus to Wormwood Scrubs, where she shares a big, dusty storage unit with Kevin, a ceramicist, who never seems to be there. When I arrive she is priming a canvas, and as usual she's wearing her paint-splattered green boiler suit and a dark blue woolly hat over her frizzy red hair. Led Zeppelin is playing and Nellie is asleep, curled up on an old brown cardigan by the heater.

'I made her walk halfway round the Scrubs. You'll probably have to carry her home,' says Megan as she tosses two Yorkshire Gold into a chipped teapot.

'Cheers,' I bend down to stroke Nellie's back. There are little specks of red around her mouth.

'Jam,' says Megan. 'She found an old donut by the bus stop bin.' She splashes hot water into the pot. 'I tried to pull her away but she nearly took my hand off.'

'Nellie!' I tut, but Nellie just groans in her sleep.

'Good day at the office?'

'Same old.' I say. 'Although the new guy Ian is turning out to be quite a laugh.' I glance over at the canvas that Megan's been working on. 'Are you going to be ready in time?'

Megan has an exhibition coming up. It's her first in eighteen months and even though she pretends to be blasé about it, I can tell she's bluffing. I've known her for over ten years, from when we had a market stall together at Portobello, and although she may come across as a tough nut, she's not.

'Let's just hope I sell something.' Megan tips some milk into each of the mugs. 'My finances are nuked at the moment.'

'Worse than usual?'

Megan nods. 'Billy's not had any work in eight weeks.' Billy, Megan's boyfriend of five years, is a freelance sound engineer. She hands me a mug. 'So what's going on with you?'

I tell her about my interview with Anthony Brooks. Then I briefly mention meeting Joe in the cemetery, but I don't dwell on it because I don't expect to see him again.

'I saw Victor last week,' I add as casually as possible. 'He works in a video shop up in Willesden.'

Megan, who was about to take a mouthful of tea, sets her cup down on the window ledge. 'I thought he'd gone back to Paris.'

'So did I,' I say, 'but obviously not. He makes films now, which he shows in a little cinema at the back of the shop.'

'What sort of films?'

'Weird ones, very experimental,' I say. 'Actually, he showed me one of them. It was extraordinary...' I stop, unable to find the right words which will convey even a fraction of its effect on me.

'Let's just say it probably won't get distribution,' I add.

'How was it to see him again?' asks Megan.

'It was OK, I suppose,' I say. 'Not as bad as it could have been.'

Megan picks up her mug again, clasping it between her palms so the steam curls up towards her face. 'Did you talk about what happened?'

49

'No,' I say quickly.

'Will you go back?'

'I doubt it.'

'How did you leave it?'

'Very rapidly,' I say. 'I had a panic attack and ran out.'

'A bad one?'

'About 2½.' Doctor Ling, who clearly likes a 1–5 grading system when it comes to symptoms, has encouraged me to grade the panic attacks according to intensity, 1 being pretty mild and 5 being a full-on meltdown. She's also encouraged me to have counselling, but I said no.

'You poor luv,' says Megan.

I shrug. After two years of panic attacks, I'm getting more used to them.

'So you didn't even say goodbye to him?'

'Nope,' I say. A couple of times I've thought about sending Victor a note explaining my rapid exit, but then logic tells me he'll know exactly why I left like that. You don't make a film that close to the bone and expect the viewer, i.e. me, to watch without a whimper. Besides, I don't have the video shop's address.

Megan is still looking at me.

'What?' I say.

'Maybe this would be a good chance. If you won't see anyone professional then talking to Victor might help. After all, he was there with you when it happened.'

'Yes, I'm aware of that,' I say, much sharper than I'd intended. I've often wished that I hadn't told Megan about that night, but then it's not the kind of thing you can keep from your best friend. I glance over at Nellie, who is still snoring in the folds of the cardigan.

'We'd better go.'

Megan is leaning against the window ledge, staring at me. 'Hannah, how much longer are you going to ignore it?'

A fist of anger bunches in my stomach. 'It's none of your business.'

'Yes, it fucking is.'

I glare at her, heat searing my cheeks.

'It's because I care about you.' Megan's voice is a little softer.

I bend down and grab my bag. My hands are trembling. 'Well, don't,' I shout.

Chapter 6

Two weeks later, Nellie and I are sitting in the foyer of Mr Tierly's surgery waiting for the monthly nail cutting session. Perched on the bucket chair next to me is an old man with his wheezing Staffordshire bull terrier. Next to him a little girl clutches a small cardboard box from which a hamster periodically pokes its nose. Magda, Mr Tierly's Polish receptionist, is seated behind the reception desk with her face about two inches from the screen and her long black hair trailing across the keyboard as she concentrates hard on her computer game. From the new iPod dock on the shelf behind her comes the sound of Arcade Fire, Magda's favourite band. I imagine the iPod dock was her idea. Mr Tierly is in love with Magda, and whatever Magda wants, she usually gets.

The waiting room has undergone a bit of a makeover since Nellie's and my last visit. Instead of the usual adverts for worming powder and pet sitting agencies, the walls are now plastered with pictures of misshapen kittens, stick-legged dogs and crazed-looking guinea pigs. Above the drawings are the words 'My Best Friend', and below is a small sign inviting children to add pictures of their own pets.

While Nellie dozes, I flick through the stash of old magazines, finally selecting an ancient copy of *Bliss*. I turn straight to the problem page, which I used to do as a teenager. This one features a letter from Susan, aged fourteen, who's worried that one side of her labia is longer than the other. Immediately I picture poor Susan standing in her knickers with one 'labium' (as the Agony Aunt puts it), escaping under the elastic like an errant mollusc. I've just moved onto Tessa (fifteen), who wants advice on contraception, when Magda shouts over from reception that Mr Tierly is ready to see us.

Nellie's eyes narrow as soon as she catches sight of Mr Tierly through the door. They've never been close, which is probably why he's clutching the plastic head guard.

'We'll just slip this on.' He advances on Nellie, rictus smile fixed to his face. First he secures the head guard with a strap around her neck, then he attempts to circumnavigate her stomach so he can winch her up onto the table. 'Did you stick to the diet I prescribed last time?' he frowns.

'We tried,' I say. In fact Nellie lasted just one day on the shrunken lumps of protein before she did a dirty protest all over the kitchen floor.

'Well, then I suggest you try again,' Mr Tierly says tersely before reaching for the nail clippers.

Nellie does her best to ignore Mr Tierly while he clips away at her claws, and I stare at the shrivelled spider plant by the door, wishing I'd brought *Bliss* in with me so I could finish the problem page. I try to think what I would have written to the Agony Aunt about if I was fourteen – lack of breasts, that's for sure, and the fact that my hair seemed to be thinning already, even though I was barely in my teens. Maybe I could have asked her about the Mentals?

Dear Dr Anne,

I have this freaky condition where, whenever I feel nervous or out of my depth, I can't help imagining the rudest and

weirdest thing I could do. Like yesterday in geography, for
example, when I pictured myself lying starkers on scary Mr
Martin's desk and asking him to think of my body as a world
map and point out Namibia...

My phone beeps. It's a text from Megan asking me for Sunday lunch with her and Billy. We've spoken twice since I was at her studio, but both times we glossed over what happened. Even though Megan is not one for keeping her mouth shut, she knows where she stands on this one. After all, if I could cut Victor – the only other person who knows – out of my life so brutally, I'm more than capable of doing the same to her.

I text back that I'll be at Mum's this Sunday, but that we should meet for a drink the following week.

'All done.' Mr Tierly replaces the clippers in their plastic case and hoists Nellie down from the table. 'And,' he says while he unfastens the lampshade head guard, 'if you ask nicely, young Magda will give you some more of that diet food.'

'Hannah!' I hear someone call my name as Nellie and I step back into the waiting room. I look round and see a tall man balanced awkwardly on one of the bucket chairs with the copy of *Bliss* in his lap.

'Joe,' I say. 'What are you doing here?' My mouth is so dry it feels like I've swallowed half a packet of Philadelphia.

'Reading girls' magazines,' he grins, 'and picking up some gel for Stan's eye infection.' When he stands up, I see that he's well over six foot tall. Without his hat, his hair is cropped so closely that only the tips of the black curls are visible. Even though skulls aren't usually high on my 'What-turns-me-on' list, I notice that he has one of the most perfectly shaped heads I've ever seen.

'What about you?' says Joe.

I point to Nellie's freshly cut claws. 'Manicure.'

Joe laughs and bends forward to stroke Nellie's head.

'I wouldn't do that,' I say quickly, explaining that Nellie hates her head being touched.

'So where are you off to now?' Joe asks, scratching her back instead.

I try to think of somewhere more scintillating than my sofa.

'Have you got time for a mint tea at Hassan's café? It's only round the corner.'

I'm still fumbling for an excuse when a frame from Victor's film darts into my head. It's of the young woman lying on her bed staring dully up at the ceiling. With it comes that familiar feeling of numbed emptiness.

'OK,' I say quickly, before I can change my mind. 'But not Hassan's because Nellie's been barred. Last time we were in there, she peed all over the floor because I wouldn't buy her a cake.'

'In that case what about a look round the car boot sale up the road?'

I hesitate.

'Come on, just twenty minutes,' Joe coaxes. 'Besides, you never came back to see me at the cemetery, so you owe me one.'

Once Joe has managed to persuade Magda to take time out from her computer game and find him the gel, we set off up Ladbroke Grove. Along the way, he chats about the joys of car boot sales and how even second-hand turntables and chipped Toby jugs can seem exciting.

Nellie lags behind, dragging her paws listlessly along the pavement like a sulky teenager.

'Looks like she wants a lift.' Joe stops and reaches down to pick her up.

'She's a big girl,' I warn.

'I can take it.'

Joe obviously hasn't reckoned with Nellie's potato-sack weight, but he says nothing. Wedged under his arm, Nellie shoots me what I interpret as a grin of triumph. *See, this is how we do it.*

By the time we reach the car boot sale, which is in the playing fields of an old Victorian school, it's midday, and hundreds of figures are bent over trestle tables, sifting through other people's junk. Behind the tables the owners sit in their open car boots, clasping steaming polystyrene cups in woolly gloved hands.

'Wait here.' Joe sets Nellie down on the ground. He strides over to a stall selling children's toys and points to a pink plastic pram. After he's handed over the money, he wheels it back over to us and folds down the hood. Then he picks up Nellie and places her inside on her stomach.

We trundle round for the next half hour, inspecting and commenting on the bizarre assortment of stuff that humans collect, while Nellie lies snoozing in the pram like a spoilt, fat, furry child.

'Why didn't you come back to see me at the cemetery?' asks Joe.

'I meant to,' I say lamely, 'but things got in the way.'

Well, I'm not exactly going to tell him the truth – that I'd thought about it every morning, but each time I did I could hear that little voice at the back of my head. *You'll only get hurt again, Hannah. Look what happened last time.*

56

'I'll forgive you this once,' Joe grins, and picks up a book entitled *You've been snookered!!* On the front is a picture of Hurricane Higgins leaning over a billiards table about to take a shot. Someone has used a biro to turn the pool cue into a giant joint.

'You play pool, Hannah?'

'A little,' I reply. I should really say that I'm hopeless at it, but I've always fantasised about being a pool shark, so I don't.

'Any good?'

'Not bad.' I say. Sod it. It's not as if he'll ever find out.

Joe smiles. 'Well, I'll have to see some proof.'

Joe's just bought us both a slice of coffee and walnut cake. While we are eating it, we try to come up with theories for the stall opposite whose display includes an old SodaStream, four home waxing kits (that look suspiciously second-hand) and some Neil Sedaka records. I watch Joe out of the corner of my eye: his mouth, curved at the sides in a permanent grin, his dark eyes, the smooth brown skin at the nape of his neck...

'Joe!' I hear a voice shout from a couple of stalls away. I look over at a girl with a round freckly face, short blonde hair and an army jacket, who's standing behind a table piled with clothes and second-hand books.

Joe touches my arm gently. 'Come and meet my friend.'

'And this is Nellie,' says Joe after he's introduced Caitlin and I. He nods towards the pram where Nellie is still snoring.

'Nice wheels, Nellie,' says Caitlin.

A bubble of drool froths around Nellie's gums in response.

'So how's the writing?' says Joe.

'Good,' says Caitlin. 'The book's due out in May.' She explains to me that it took five years to get a publishing deal for her first novel.

'Congratulations,' I smile.

'Thanks,' says Caitlin, 'now for the next hurdle – getting people to buy it.' She laughs and begins to rummage under the pile of clothes, pulling out a tiny T-shirt. On the front are the words 'Pop Kid' in shiny press-on letters. 'It's about Maya's size, isn't it?'

'It looks perfect,' Joe replies. 'She'll love it.' He gives Caitlin a hug. 'Thank you.'

There's a short pause and I notice Caitlin glance over at me.

'I'm just going to check out that stall,' I say, pointing to a nearby trestle table.

Joe brushes my forearm. 'I'll catch you up.'

I wheel Nellie over to the stall and pick up a DVD of *Man on Wire*. But I barely glance at the cover because my head's too full of questions. *Who's Maya? Who's her mother? Are she and Joe still together?*

I look back to where he and Caitlin are standing.

'How have you been?' I hear Caitlin say.

'OK,' says Joe slowly.

'And Nadia?'

I hold my breath and wait for the reply.

'It's getting better. Thank God.'

'Good,' says Caitlin. 'It's about time you two sorted things out.'

See, I say to myself. You were right not to meet him at the cemetery. He's with someone else. And they have a child together. He was only being friendly when he asked you to look round the car boot sale.

I call over to Joe, saying that I need to go. Then I start to push Nellie towards the exit.

'Hey, what's the rush?' Joe runs up to me and places a hand on my shoulder.

'I have to get home,' I say. 'Otherwise I may be tempted by those home waxing kits.' I try to make my voice sound light and jokey, but it just sounds strange and stilted.

'Oh. OK.' Joe looks genuinely disappointed.

'What about the pram?' I say, thinking that Joe must have bought it so he could give it to his little girl afterwards.

'You and Nellie keep it,' says Joe. 'For now.' He looks at me, smiles, then takes out a chewed pencil and a small notebook from his pocket. Tearing out a piece of paper, he scribbles down his number and hands it to me.

'That's if you fancy a game of pool,' he says and kisses me lightly on the cheek.

As I push Nellie back down the road, I repeat the warnings to myself like a mantra. *Don't even go there, Hannah. He's got a child – and a girlfriend. Besides even if he was free, do you really want to get involved with someone again?*

When we get back to the flat, I take out the bit of paper and toss it into the bin.

Chapter 7

Nellie is flat on her back on the sitting room floor. Her four stumpy legs are waving in the air while her round pink tummy quivers with pleasure. A long string of saliva slides down onto the carpet by her right ear.

'Want some more?' I ask.

Nellie's gums galvanise into a wonky grin.

I flick the switch again and put the nozzle up to her neck, far enough away from her gums so they don't get sucked in too. Nellie lets out another little moan and wriggles her bottom against the carpet as her head rolls from side to side in delight.

After eating, sleeping and bullying, being hoovered comes fourth on Nellie's list of pleasurable ways to spend time. I discovered this a few weeks after she arrived, when I was doing some hoovering, and everywhere I went, Nellie seemed to be just in front of me, lying on her back like an overweight, overturned beetle. I'm not sure her many expressions cover 'Will you hoover me?' but I eventually got the message and since then, hoovering Nellie has been a regular Sunday fixture.

'Right, that's you done.' I unplug the Goblin while Nellie lies motionless on the carpet, eyes rolled back in a post-coital glaze.

I check my watch. 'Come on. Mum will worry if we're late.'

Nellie's eyes swivel towards the pram, which is parked in the hallway.

'No, Nellie, we're not taking it.' It was fine wheeling Nellie round the car boot sale with Joe, but on my own is a different matter. 'People will stare.'

Nellie glares at me. *Fuck 'em.*

Fifteen minutes later, after Nellie's refusal to budge from the hallway unless the pram came too, I am pushing her up the road to the tube station, trying to ignore people's stares. Nellie doesn't help things by insisting on sitting upright in the pram and twisting her head from side to side so everyone can see her.

The first leg of the tube journey is even worse due to a group of teenage boys, who spend the whole journey from Warwick Avenue to Baker Street, calling out comments like 'Who's the dad?' and 'Did you do it doggy-style?' while I stare out of the window and pretend to be deaf.

Having changed at Baker Street onto the Metropolitan line tube, Nellie immediately falls asleep, air whistling through her pink nostrils. She must be dreaming because every so often she shudders and lets out a little whine. I lean forward to stroke the fur on her neck and can't help thinking what a clever move it was on Victor's part to buy her for me before he left London.

*

December 2009

I only see Victor once again after that December night. It's four days later and I am still in bed at two o'clock in the afternoon when the doorbell rings. I ignore it, but whoever is outside keeps pressing the bell until I am eventually forced to open the door.

'We have an appointment,' says Victor. He looks tired and pale, but his voice is unusually brusque.

'I'm not sure I'm up for appointments,' I say. I have no idea what he means by an 'appointment', but I try to keep the tone light.

'It is important, Hannah. I am not leaving until you come with me.'

I stand there in the doorway, hair unwashed and still caked in blood. It's quite clear what's expected of me – Victor has agreed not to tell anyone what happened and in return I will have to agree to whatever he has planned.

We don't speak as we sit on the bus heading south towards the river, but it isn't our usual comfortable silence – this time the air bristles with tension. Victor's hands are shaking in his lap and there are still cuts on his wrists and arms. I twist away to stare out of the window, catching sight of my reflection and the deep red gash just above my left eye, which I've tried unsuccessfully to cover with my fringe.

'I think we should talk about the other night,' says Victor quietly.

'No,' I say, still staring out of the window. 'I can't.'

If I speak about it, then it will become real again but if I keep quiet, then with time I might be able to forget it, pretend that it happened to someone else.

The bus passes the empty shell of Battersea Power Station and pulls up at the next stop, where we get off. We don't talk again until we're inside the flat white building.

You forget how many types of dogs there are until you visit somewhere like Battersea Dogs Home. Kennel after kennel of Staffordshire bull terriers, mongrels, boxers, beagles, Alsatians, Jack Russells and collies, and that's just on the ground floor. Victor, who seems to know his way around, leads me to the third level, and once there, he walks a few steps in front of me, as if he's looking for something in particular. But I can't help staring into each kennel at the dogs inside, who bounce to the front bars, pushing their noses towards me. Others, presumably those who've been there longer, lie quietly on their blankets, following my movements with unblinking eyes, although their expressions all say the same thing – 'Please take me home with you.'

It's the greyhounds that I find most distressing. According to the cards pinned outside each kennel with details of the dog's character and history, many of them were once racing dogs. You wonder how they made sense of it: one day they're haring round the track, wind in their ears and grass underfoot, the next, they're pacing round a concrete kennel, waiting for someone to take them home, someone who won't care that their eyes are a bit cloudy and that they can't break the three-minute record any more.

'Here she is,' says Victor when we reach the kennel at the end of the corridor. He points to a barrel-shaped lump of fur with its back to us.

'Hello again,' he says.

The lump of fur continues to stare at the wall. A card is taped to the door. 'British bulldog. Age and original name unknown. Kennel name: Nellie. Would suit a more sedentary owner. Likes her food!'

'Talk to her while I find someone who can help us.' Victor's voice is quiet but insistent as he turns and heads towards the swing door.

I swivel back to Nellie. Something about the way she's

sitting, with her ears flat against her head and her nose almost touching the wall, makes me call out to her.

'Can I see your face, Nellie?'

The faintest twitch of an ear.

'Please?'

A slight shudder of fur.

'I won't hurt you.'

Only then does she twist round and look straight at me.

'So you want this one, do you?' says the kennel worker, who's just returned with Victor.

'I do,' I reply, without even thinking about it. And although I've never even contemplated owning a dog before, I know that I can't leave the kennel without taking her with me.

*

The train pulls into Chorleywood station and I unload Nellie and the pram and then set off for Broom Hill, where Mum lives. She and Dad moved here soon after they were married although Dad was always suggesting that they live somewhere else, maybe even abroad.

Midway up the paved path to Mum's redbrick semi, I notice some new additions to her garden accessory collection: a stone birdbath with a carved robin perched on the rim, a hollow log with two little squirrels peeking playfully from inside and a wooden wheelbarrow in which a pair of rabbits are curled up together. I've never understood what I secretly call Mum's 'Woodland fetish' – but then there are a great many things that I don't understand about my mother.

I can see Mum through the kitchen window by the oven, basting what I assume is the roast chicken. She's wearing her favourite light blue cashmere jumper, which she bought about twenty years ago from The Scotch House on one of her rare trips to London, although at the time she said that the jumper was far too extravagant. Her hair, once dark like mine, is now completely grey and caught up in a tortoiseshell clip.

We kiss awkwardly in the hallway and Mum leads us through to the kitchen. Nellie immediately takes up her post beneath the oven and I hover by the sideboard while Mum stands at the sink to drain the carrots.

'Chicken smells good,' I say.

'I hope it's alright,' says Mum.

'I'm sure it is.' I glance around for something other than poultry to chat about. 'New napkins?' I point to the daisy-patterned linen squares next to the two place settings.

'I bought them in the Harlequin Centre,' says Mum. 'They're pretty, aren't they?'

I nod, wondering when our conversations started to shrink like this.

'Can I do anything?'

Mum turns from the sink. 'No, it's fine. You and Nellie relax next door and I'll call you when lunch is ready.'

Relieved, I walk through to the sitting room with a disappointed Nellie trailing behind me. I know that if I stay in the kitchen with Mum, by the time lunch is ready we'll have exhausted what limited conversation we have and we'll be back on the chicken run.

I sit down on the pink sofa, surrounded by shiny satin cushions with Nellie slumped at my feet. From there, I study the figurines on the mantelpiece – mostly wistful-looking girls in bonnets draped around trees. But in the middle is a faded picture of Mum and Dad taken on the day the investment firm for which he worked promoted him to look after the Canadian clients. He's sitting behind the wheel of his beloved Alfa Romeo, the roof is down and the sun is glinting on his dark hair. In the passenger's seat, wearing a rose-patterned headscarf, Mum is gazing over at him. Her right hand is on his free arm, clutching at his shirtsleeve and causing the material to ruche.

I had just turned twelve and the summer holidays were about to begin, when Dad told us. We were having Sunday lunch and Mum had just cleared away the plates before pudding.

'Are we going to Cornwall again this year?' I said, handing Dad a slice of treacle tart.

'You'll have to ask your mother that,' Dad replied. He stared down at the bowl in front of him.

'Mum,' I said. 'Are we?'

'Maybe, darling,' Mum called over from the sideboard. 'But we'll need to book it soon,' I noticed her glance over at my father. 'Or we might go somewhere else, somewhere in Spain even.' She walked back over and sat down, placing her hand over Dad's and squeezing it gently. 'Wouldn't that be fun?'

Underneath, Dad's hand didn't move.

'I could go into the travel agent this week,' said Mum, removing her hand and laying it in her lap.

'Diane,' said Dad slowly. 'I won't be coming on holiday.'

'Why not?' said Mum.

'I'll be in Vancouver.'

'But you've only just come back from the last business trip,' said Mum.

Dad began to thread his napkin slowly through its wooden ring, which was weird because he hadn't even started his treacle tart. 'I won't be there for business.'

'Then why else would you be there, you dark old horse?' Mum's voice sounded much higher than usual.

Dad cleared his throat. 'I've met someone.'

'Well, what about Italy then?' Mum's voice was shaking now. 'Rome? You're always saying you want to visit Rome.'

'Diane, I'm leaving.'

Mum stared at him for what seemed like hours. Then she made a funny strangled cry and grabbed her napkin, stuffing it up against her mouth. Dad watched her for a few seconds, then he pushed back his chair and walked stiffly towards the kitchen door.

I sat there motionless, with Mum opposite, still making those weird sounds. Above us, we could hear Dad's feet as he moved around their bedroom, opening and closing cupboards. A few minutes later he was standing in the doorway, holding a small case. He walked round to where I was sitting, put one hand on my shoulder and started to say something, but then he stopped. His eyes were red and his hands were trembling. Then he turned to Mum, who was staring up at him with one hand over her mouth.

'I'm sorry, Diane.'

Mum went to grab his sleeve with her other hand, but Dad had already turned away.

I didn't move as he walked down the corridor towards the front door and let himself out. Neither did Mum. Instead we both sat there, staring at his chair, where he'd been just a few minutes before, about to eat his treacle tart. We could both hear the engine of his Alfa Romeo, but still we didn't move. It was as if the scene had been frozen, like the dining room scene in a doll's house where miniature figures are glued forever in front of plastic chicken drumsticks and brightly painted jelly trifles.

That night I heard Mum crying in her bedroom. Short, sharp gulps followed by muffled sobs. I didn't go in, though. Instead I lay in bed with a pillow over my head, trying to block out the noise. It's your fault, I thought. You made him go.

After that, Dad visited three times a year, once in early spring, then in August and at the beginning of the Christmas holidays. He'd sleep in the B&B next to the post office, and almost every day of his week-long stay he and I would take off in his hired MG. More often than not, we'd visit some attraction – Whipsnade Zoo, Madame Tussauds, the Tower of London. I don't know why we went to those places, but perhaps he felt that it gave us something safe to talk about. Afterwards, we'd go to a nearby pizza restaurant and Dad would ask me how school was, if I was in the swimming team yet or if I still wanted to be Nadia Comaneci. Sometimes, he'd let slip little details about his new life in Vancouver; how the snow had completely covered his car that year, how he was beginning to enjoy watching ice hockey, how he'd been fishing with one of his neighbours. Whenever this happened, I'd stare down at my Four Seasons pizza, trying desperately not to cry.

Although Dad invited me to stay with him in his new life with the snow that covered his car and the ice hockey games he was beginning to enjoy, I never went. That would prove that his other life was real and that he had deliberately chosen it over his old life. I preferred to pretend that when he left at the end of each visit, he'd just gone on an extended business trip.

At the end of one pre-Christmas visit, the year I turned fourteen, he handed me an envelope. The letter inside was written with his familiar Mont Blanc fountain pen and said that he needed to explain why he had left. He didn't expect me to forgive him, just perhaps to understand a little. He and my mother hadn't been happy for a long time because they were simply not suited. The depressions, from which he'd always suffered, had been getting worse, and although he'd been prescribed medication, he knew this wasn't the answer. Shortly after he tried to take his own life, he realised that things could not continue any longer.

Of course, he hadn't intended to leave like that, in the middle of Sunday lunch, but he knew that if he'd stopped to say a proper goodbye, to tell me how much he loved me and how much he knew this would hurt, he would never be able to go.

I will never fully understand my father choosing to live four and a half thousand miles away, but the letter helped a little. Gradually our conversations became less awkward. Dad would tell me how as a boy he had dreamed of living abroad, of climbing the world's highest mountains and swimming in as many oceans as possible. But when he had met Mum and she had become pregnant, obviously that had changed everything. He said that while he and my mother's marriage could never have worked because they wanted completely different things from life, she was the kindest woman he had ever known. In giving birth to me she had given him the greatest present any human could give another.

While I was at least beginning to grasp the reasons for my father's departure, my mother remained in complete denial. She'd talk about him in the present tense as though he had just nipped out to buy a newspaper and would be back at any moment. The fact that he was living on the other side of the world with another woman seemed to have passed her by.

When I was twenty-two, Dad's car slid on black ice on the Vancouver Highway, slamming into a concrete support pillar on one of the bridges and killing him on impact. One week later, Mum and I were standing in Vancouver's Mountain View Cemetery, where amidst the snow-packed fir trees, surrounded by strangers, I said my final goodbye.

'So how's the job?' asks Mum, opposite me at the kitchen table. The roast chicken has been carved and loaded onto the plates, along with piles of potatoes and carrots. Nellie has her own bowl of chicken and potatoes, in which she's now face down, chewing vigorously.

'The job's fine,' I say. 'How's the charity shop?'

'Good. I'm really enjoying it at the moment,' says Mum.

'That's great,' I say.

There's another pause, filled by the sound of Nellie's gulping.

'I see you've slipped in another visit to the garden centre.' I nod through the kitchen window at the rabbits in the wheelbarrow.

Mum smiles and glances down at Nellie, who is now using her nose to bump her empty bowl up against my chair leg.

'Would she like some more chicken?'

Nellie looks up at her expectantly. *Does a bear shit in the woods?*

'Just a little bit,' I say. 'But don't worry, I'll do it.'

'It's no trouble.' Mum jumps up from her chair and reaches for the roasting pan on the sideboard. 'There'll still be some left. Would you like to take it back to London? You could make a fricassée with it.'

I look at Mum, hunched over the chicken carcass, and wonder how we've got to this point. How can two people who are supposed to be related have so little in common that all they can talk about is chicken? I remember a man I once saw on a game show, who became so terrified with stage fright that all he could answer to any of the questions was 'turkey'. Perhaps that was how it would end between Mum and me, when all conversation had dried up – just endlessly repeating the word 'chicken' to each other.

After the washing up is done, we go through to the sitting room, where I read the Sunday papers, Nellie dozes and Mum flicks through a garden catalogue. As I watch her ticking seeds to order for spring, another black and white scene from Victor's film loops through my mind. In it, the young woman, the same woman who had been holding the baby in hospital, is standing in a kitchen, chopping vegetables. Her daughter, now aged about five, is on a chair next to her, laying out the chopped vegetables in a dish. Both of them are giggling at something and the little girl is hanging onto her mother's arm, her shoulders shaking with delight.

I glance over at Mum again and it's then that I feel that same deep dragging sadness that I felt in the cinema. It's so profound, visceral even, as if someone is reaching through my ribcage and squeezing my heart like a ripe fruit. Quite unexpectedly, I feel the prick of tears behind my eyes, and watching Mum opposite me, I wonder for the first time in years if it will be possible to rebuild our relationship.

Chapter 8

'What time do you call this?' I smile up at Ian, who's just entered the office.

'Sorry,' he says. 'I had to... brother... doctor.' He unzips his anorak and hangs it carefully on the peg by the door.

'You had to take your brother to the doctor?' Ian still has a tendency to mutter so I ask him to repeat himself to make sure I've understood. 'Nothing serious, I hope.'

Ian shakes his head. 'Just a check-up.'

It's the first time that he's mentioned his brother, although I know he has one from his regular phone conversations with his mother.

'And never apologise about being late,' I say, 'or I'll shop you.'

'To who?' Ian asks with that hesitant smile.

I tap my nose. 'Never you mind.' I point to the stack of products that came with the morning's post. 'More importantly, look what we got.'

Ian inspects the packet of multiseed rye crackers, the miniature bottle of flaxseed oil and the bright blue Eco eye shadow. There's also a silicone menstrual mooncup, which I have set slightly to one side and intend to use as a container for stray paper clips.

'What's that?' he picks up the ping-pong-ball-sized mooncup and turns it over in his fingers.

'You really want to know?'

Ian nods.

'It's like a tampon but it's better for the environment.'

'Oh right.' Ian flushes a deep crimson, coughs, then sets the mooncup quickly back down on the desk.

After I've tidied up the shop and installed the new products, I write five hundred words on 'The Natural Wisdom of your Body' for the next quarterly print copy of *Health and Wellbeing*. I pilfer the opening paragraph directly from the internet: 'The intelligence of the human body is far superior to that of the brain. It is capable of digesting a ham sandwich, regulating blood sugar, playing a Bach piano concerto, growing a baby and repairing a small cut made while slicing the bread for the ham sandwich all at the same time. This innate holistic wisdom should never be underestimated, and it can act as an essential guide to help us in our daily lives. By tuning into your body when you need to make a particular decision, you will receive a far clearer message than if you rely solely on your brain. If it *feels* right in the body, then it *is* right...'

When I'm done I take a little break and pick up Ian's copy of the *Guardian*, flicking straight to the jobs section. I used to scan this section every week when I initially joined *Health and Wellbeing*, hoping that something would leap out at me and announce in a very loud voice what I was meant to be doing with my life. At that point I was still convinced that, like Suzy Beale and her stethoscope, it was only a matter of time and a little legwork before I stumbled on my vocation. But as the months turned into years and still nothing materialised, each time I would close the paper a little more disheartened and a little less convinced. Until, one day, it seemed easier not to look at all any more.

Perhaps if I wanted children, a career wouldn't be so important to me, but I knew from fairly early on that I wasn't mother material. I remember exactly the moment this feeling crystallised into certainty – some girlfriends in the Lower Sixth were in the common room having one of those discussions about what they'd name their future children.

'What about calling them after man-made fibres?' I suggested. 'Dacron, Rayon, Draylon, that sort of thing.'

The girls stared at me, bemused.

'Or perhaps you could name them after STDs? Chlamydia, Gonorrhoea, Syphilis – Phylis for short, obviously...' I paused, trying to remember whether Candida was a sexually transmitted disease or simply a wheaty type of infection, but the girls had already moved onto the next round of Justins, Belindas and Susannahs.

That afternoon, during double biology, it occurred to me that if I wasn't destined to bring a clutch of Chlamydias into the world, I was going to have to find something pretty inspiring to fill the next forty-odd years of my working life.

My career to date, if you could call it that, doesn't really hold any clues. When I left school, I went for the obvious – a typing course at Watford's Cassiobury College, followed by a journalism course, which led to a job as junior reporter on the *Watford Observer*. But when it came to what should have been my big break, an interview with the local footballer John Barnes, I managed to leave my notepad with all my questions at home. Once I was sitting opposite him in the interview room, I had a complete blank-out, and knowing sweet FA about football, most of my questions revolved around what he ate for breakfast and whether he hated the gym as much as I did.

Having proved what I, and apparently the editor of the *Watford Observer*, already knew – that newspaper journalism wasn't for me – it was mutually agreed that I should seek employment elsewhere. So I moved to London and took a temping job with an advertising company. One month turned into six, which turned into a promotion as PA to Mr Forshaw, one of the partners, a job which meant spending a lot of time at the Old Compton Street off-licence buying quarter-litre bottles of vodka to smuggle back into his office. When Mr Forshaw's drinking habit got the better of him and he was offered 'early retirement', I went back to the Job Centre.

A short stint selling advertising space in the back pages of the specialist magazines *How to Knit* and *Making Your Own Soft Toys* (with free ring pull binder and monthly inserts!) confirmed that selling advertising space probably wasn't going to be my calling either. In the course of the first week I managed to sell precisely £104 worth of advertising, but due to my misspelling the advertiser's name, the money had to be reimbursed.

My next career move was on to the production side of *How to Knit* and *Making Your Own Soft Toys*, where I wrote copy. When the subeditor fell pregnant, I stepped into her sensible low-heeled shoes – which basically meant editing (and inserting captions into) reams of text about wool. But there are only so many captions you can come up with for knitting and soft toys and I exhausted them all – 'Get knitted! You've got Knits! Knit Wit! Bearly there! Grin and Bear it! (You'd think the readership had the IQ of a stuffed rabbit.) So before I went mad due to an overdose of exclamation marks and wool, I handed in my resignation (I Quit!) and applied for a job as subeditor of the other publishing house magazine, *Health and Wellbeing*.

At first I quite enjoyed the work. My editor, Roz, promised me that I could write about pretty much what I wanted as long as it fell within the remit of 'health and wellbeing'. So since I've always been interested in pop psychology, that became my department. But with the advertisers now wielding the chequebook, my 'department' has been scaled down to just four pages per issue. So now I spend the majority of my working hours banging out copy about multiseed rye crackers and silicone mooncups, and weirdly, it's just not doing it for me any more.

I can't spot anything in Ian's *Guardian*, although I do briefly consider 'Assistant Producer for Exciting New Home Makeover Show'. This leads to a lengthy fantasy about how I could take out my job frustration on the cheery homeowners by using them as a punchbag and instead of 'Bright, Sunny, Mediterranean Look', decorate according to the 'First Flat Away From Home' Guide Book. The off-white walls of the couple's sitting room would be painted purple and black, the logo from some speed metal band sprayed on the ceiling, the Shaker-style sofa replaced with a stained, lumpy mattress, and the original Victorian fireplace, the only feature they wanted to hang on to, ripped out and fitted with a cack-brown Calor Gas heater with dodgy wiring.

In my head I start on my application letter:

Dear Exciting New Home Makeover Show Producers,
    Although I know absolutely nothing about making telly

programmes, I did however once make a temporary kennel for my dog by covering a Walkers Crisps box (prawn cocktail flavour) with wrapping paper and carpeting it in an old winceyette nightie…

I hand Ian back his paper and try to fathom once again how some people know exactly what they will do with their lives, while others are left to flounder around, hoping they might stumble across something even vaguely fulfilling, before resigning themselves to getting their creative kicks from watching home makeover shows.

So how do those people like Suzy Beale, and say, Mozart, know what their calling is? OK, if you're Mozart then composing operas and performing them for royalty at the age of five might be a bit of a clue, and in Suzy's case, the home medical kit was a definite giveaway. But for the rest of us, whose talent and passions (assuming we have any) are buried a little deeper, how do we find them?

It's a subject that Victor and I used to talk about a lot and I can still remember our first conversation about the early days of his own film career.

*

November 2006

We've just been to see Godard's *À bout de soufflé* and are sitting in the café sharing the last apple tart. A customer has given Bernard an old cherrywood gramophone, which now stands next to the till and from whose shiny brass trumpet drifts the sound of violins playing a Ravel sonata. Victor has been telling me how Godard was so broke that he had to work on construction sites to raise the finance for his first few films.

'I wonder if I'd be able to hack working on a construction site if that's what it took to fund my passion,' I say.

Victor smiles. 'If you feel like Godard did about films, you would do anything.'

I pour myself a cup of tea and sip it slowly.

Victor watches me. 'Hannah, you will find your vocation, if you want it enough.'

'But what if I don't? What if I die and the only thing written on my headstone is: "She came, she wrote some stuff about 'Me-time' and then she left"?' I set my cup back down in the saucer.

'It's not that I want stacks of money or fame, I just want to find something with a bit of meaning which will pay the rent and which I hopefully enjoy. And yes, I know that's what everyone wants and I should have got over it by now, but I haven't.' I stop, sensing the irony of the violins in the background.

'I'm bored of banging on about myself,' I say. 'Tell me about your jobs in Paris before you moved over here.'

Victor wipes a stray crumb from his mouth and takes a quick sip of coffee. He's used to my questions by now and is much less reluctant to reveal details about his life before London.

'I started to work at Cinema 28 when I was fifteen.' Victor motions to Bernard for a second cup of coffee. 'At first I was sweeping out the auditorium, but later I was allowed to help the projectionist, Albert. It was from him that I learnt about the Lumière brothers and their experiments at their father's photographic laboratory which led to the creation of the cinematograph. The more he talked about them and their miraculous machine, the more convinced I became that together he and I could make something similar. So we began our own experiments using parts from the cinema's old projectors and any second-hand cameras that we could find at the flea markets. The biggest challenge was how to improvise the mechanism that made the film pass smoothly through the camera to take moving images instead of stills. Then one day, when I was watching my mother at her sewing machine, I had the idea.'

Victor looks over at the gramophone and smiles. The violins from the first movement of Ravel's sonata have now been joined by a cello and their strings fuse into one glorious heart-tugging harmony.

'What idea?' I tap Victor on the sleeve, impatient to hear the rest of the story.

Victor takes a quick forkful of the apple tart before he picks up the thread.

'We would use a device similar to that tiny silver claw on my mother's machine which pulled the material forward, and we would hook it onto the little perforations at the edge of the film. Using lengths of 16 mm film stock to practise on, after about six weeks of false starts, Albert and I finally succeeded. We had built our own cinematograph.'

Victor chuckles. 'The first film we made was a catastrophe. It was seven seconds long and completely overexposed, but it was a moving picture.' He glances through the open window at the slither of blue sky above the Soho rooftops.

'When Albert retired from his job, his parting gift to me was our makeshift cinematograph and as much empty film stock as he had been able to collect. From then on, whenever I was not in school or working at the cinema, I spent my time making miniature films from the window of the apartment of whatever was happening in my neighbourhood –

Monsieur Olivier on his weekly trip to the library to take out his romances, Madame Valjean buying lilies for her husband's grave every Sunday morning, Edouard counting out his centimes at the end of the day. Nothing grand or glamorous, just everyday moments of their lives. Then, each Saturday evening, I would draw the curtains in the sitting room at home, turn around the sofa to face the large back wall, and show my mother what I had made that week.'

Victor smiles at the memory. 'And each week my mother would ask me why I always filmed the same things. Paris was such a beautiful city, why did I not film the Art Deco winter gardens of the Jardin des Plantes or the Saint Eustache and its majestic 8,000-pipe organ? But I always replied with the same answer – that I wanted to film the lost souls of this life.'

As Victor delivers this final sentence, he looks me straight in the eye and I feel the skitter of goosebumps across my skin.

*

Nellie is waiting for me when I get back to the flat that evening, prostrate in the hallway like a skewered bullfrog. I know exactly why she's there – if Nellie's waiting in the hallway after work, it means one thing – rubbish night.

I potter round the flat emptying the bins, and Nellie follows until I reach the kitchen, where I haul the black bin liner from under the sideboard. I'm just tying it when Nellie head-butts the bag.

'No, Nellie, it's rubbish.'

Nellie head-butts the bag a second time and lets out a growl of frustration.

I'm in a hurry to get to Megan's exhibition, so as a diversionary tactic I give her one of her favourite snacks – a rusk. While she's eating, I quickly bag up the rest of the rubbish and put it outside. It's not until I'm changing out of my work clothes that I notice something stuck to my sleeve. I peel it off and see that it's the same piece of paper with Joe's number on that I'd thrown away after the visit to the car boot sale. I deliberate for a couple of seconds then drop it into the bin once again before heading off to the shower.

An hour later, I'm standing in a pop-up gallery under the Westway clutching a glass of Gallo Shiraz and staring at one of Megan's sculptures. Megan's boyfriend, Billy, is next to me, wearing the traditional West London uniform of jeans, Converse trainers and a mop of unbrushed blond hair.

'I don't get it,' I whisper.

Billy takes a swig from his glass of red wine and surveys the heap of broken plastic dolls with a big man's brogue balanced on top. 'I do.'

'Enlighten me then. You know I'm a philistine.'

'Come on, you must be able to—' But Billy never gets to finish his sentence because Megan is already walking towards us.

'I hope you two aren't slagging off my work.' Megan looks pointedly at me and laughs. We both know that I don't really understand her art, and she has the good grace not to be offended.

'There's some really great stuff here,' I say, 'and if I had an ounce of understanding about art, I'd be making insightful and complimentary comments about it.'

'Thanks,' says Megan. 'I appreciate that.' She loops her arm through Billy's and nods at his glass. 'Leave some red for me.'

'It's only my second,' Billy protests good-naturedly.

'Course it is.' Megan laughs, then points to a woman with

dyed black hair and bright purple glasses. 'She's a local gallery owner. I'd better go and arse-lick.'

Billy heads over to some friends at the bar while I try again to decipher the sculpture. I peek inside the brogue for inspiration and note that it's only a size 14. Disappointing.

My fascination with the larger foot has followed me around since my days of dancing on Uncle Malcolm's size 16s. I once went into High & Mighty, the outsize clothing shop on Edgware Road, to ask if the enormous pair of shiny black dress shoes in the window were real or a plant to lure people inside. The assistant, Christopher, assured me they were real, size 20 in fact, and we then had quite a chat, during which he told me that the biggest feet in the world belonged to Matthew McGrory of Pennsylvania (size 28½). He even let me try on the window display dress shoes and walk around the shop to get the full effect.

'Excuse me.' A tiny woman pushes past me and I stumble forward. There's a loud thud, and several plastic dollies clatter to the floor, taking the brogue down with them.

I squat down to shove the dolls back where they came from, but they're having none of it.

'Hi.' I hear a voice above me.

'Hi.' I clamber to an upright position, brogue in hand.

'That's a big shoe you've got there,' says Joe.

'I've seen bigger.'

Joe grins. It makes me want to kiss him.

'I didn't know that you knew Megan,' I say.

Joe shakes his head. 'I don't. I came with a mate who used to work at the frame shop.'

There's a short pause during which I try to think of

something amusing and informative to say about modern art. It's then that I see a childlike arm snaking itself around Joe's waist. It's attached to the tiny woman who's fluttering her ludicrously long eyelashes at him. 'Aren't you going to introduce me then?' she says.

I am standing at the opposite end of the gallery, looking at a painting of Wormwood Scrubs prison. I've been here for about ten minutes now but I don't want to turn around and be confronted by the sight of Joe and the woman I'm assuming is his girlfriend.

I dither a bit more in front of the prison picture then decide the best exit strategy is to stride purposefully through the crowd and bid a hasty goodbye to Joe while claiming to have another very important engagement.

'You're not running out on me again, are you?' says Joe as I stride by a couple of minutes later. He's at the bar with his mate now and the little woman is no longer at his side but chatting to a guy in a suit by the door.

I nod and say something about a supper that I have to go to.

'But we still haven't fixed our date,' he says.

'For what?'

'For that game of pool.'

My eyes swivel to the woman. 'Will your girlfriend be OK with that?'

Joe chuckles. 'That's not my girlfriend. She just latched onto me when I walked in.' He nods to the man in a suit. 'Thank goodness she got bored and moved on. So when's our pool date?'

I look up at Joe's wide mouth and green-flecked eyes and forget all about my previous resolve not to get involved.

'I think I'm free next Sunday,' I say, 'but only if you let me win.'

Chapter 9

I haven't been to All Saints Road in a while and it's certainly changed a bit. The jerk chicken takeaway, the picture restorers and the record shop are still here, as is the bathroom shop and Mercury taxi rank. But the little Jamaican restaurant that served saltfish and ackee off rickety tables for over thirty years is now a bar with expensive light fittings, the second-hand furniture stall is now an overpriced jewellery shop, while the old newsagent has been turned into a boutique selling cowhide poufs with matching slippers.

I'm early to meet Joe so I wander up and down, gazing into the new shops and trying to picture what sort of person would buy four hundred quids' worth of cowhide pouf. Catching my reflection in the window of what looks like yet another boutique, I notice that beneath my jacket a button on my shirt is missing and consequently I'm exposing a little more flesh than is seemly for a casual Sunday afternoon in the pub. I then wonder how much more will be on show when I bend over a pool table. I'm just leaning over to check when I hear a voice.

'Having fun?' Joe is standing right behind me, smiling.

'I was just… window shopping.' I'm hardly going to say that I was checking to see how my tits would look if I bent over a pool table.

It's not until I've said it and clocked Joe's raised eyebrows that I notice we're standing in front of a wedding dress shop.

The Pelican is full for a Sunday afternoon. A crowd of old Jamaican men are clustered around two tables adjudicating over a noisy game of dominoes. Next to them, a group of traders clutch pints and discuss their day's takings on Portobello Market. In the far corner, three public school boys in matching leather jackets glance nervously around them, presumably to see who they can score some dope off. On a high wooden stool at the bar sits a woman of about sixty, wearing black leggings and trainers several sizes too large. She's talking to a guy in a sharp blue suit with one fat grey matted dreadlock that hangs down his back like an armadillo's tail. Above them, a television shouts that day's racing results to no one in particular.

I sit at the only other available table while Joe stands at the bar, buying the drinks. He's taken off his jacket and is wearing a blue sweatshirt beneath. Through the dark cotton material I can make out the long ridge of his backbone and the curve of his shoulder blades.

'You 'ere wid him?' One of the Jamaican men, face wrinkled as a walnut, is standing by my table and pointing a long finger latticed with gold rings at Joe.

'I am,' I say.

The man rolls his eyes and clutches his chest. 'You wanna watch dat bwoy, 'e breaks all de pritty girls 'earts.' And with that, he bursts into laughter before his Cuban-heeled boots do a sideways shuffle across the sticky wooden floor towards the woman with the oversized trainers. 'Ain't dat right, Sally?' he says, giving her a wet kiss on the cheek.

'Don't listen to a word Benjamin says. He talks shit.' Sally, whose low voice has a curious home-counties twang, waves Benjamin away with a bony hand, which is missing two fingers. 'Oi, Arthur, get Benjamin a drink and shut him up.' She shouts in the direction of the barman.

I'm just wondering if I should say something to Joe about the wedding shop or if it will only make things worse when he returns from the bar with two pints of Guinness. He hands me one of them. 'Shall we go upstairs then?'

The pool table is on the first floor above the main bar and is set in the middle of a bare panelled room with no chairs, no tables, not even any other people for distraction. Anything would have been better than pool, I think. Golf. Paintballing. *Wicked*, the musical… there are so many other options we could have picked for a first date. I take another gulp of Guinness and try to think of possible excuses to get me out of the game at such a late stage: I've forgotten my glasses – which I have, but I'd never planned to wear them anyway; lifting my pint of Guinness has triggered my latent repetitive strain injury; I need to have a little chat with Sally about those missing fingers.

'Do you want to open?' Joe chalks his cue and blows a puff of blue dust from the tip. For the first time I notice the little groove between his nose and top lip. It makes me want to lean forward and kiss him, exactly there.

'No, you start,' I say.

Joe takes his first shot, scattering the balls across the table and potting two striped ones in the process.

'Show off,' I say.

Figuring that conversation might break his concentration, I start to tell Joe how Nellie and I went into Hassan's that afternoon, hoping to convince him that she had mended her ways. But while I was reading the paper, she snuck round the back of the counter, nudged open the sliding window of the glass counter and necked half a bowl of baba ganoush.

Joe laughs but doesn't seem at all distracted. He moves round the table to pot his fourth ball, so I decide on another approach – question time. How long has he been walking dogs? Eighteen months. Can he survive on just that? No way – he also does six shifts a week in the Paradise pub and the odd bit of painting and decorating. What was he doing before? He trained and worked as a lawyer, but he gave that up to focus on his passion for writing and directing plays. I ask him what his plays are about.

'Nothing fancy,' says Joe, cuing up for another shot. 'Just about people and life,' he pauses, 'and love, of course.' He hits the red ball in the far corner and sends it spinning into the far pocket.

Finally, with only two more balls to pot, Joe misses a shot and it's my turn.

I peer down the length of the pool cue and try not to be distracted by the fact that Joe's standing so close to me. When I take the shot, I miss and pot the white instead.

'Stage fright,' I say.

That and the fact that your crotch is two feet from my face.

'I didn't see that,' Joe nods to the white ball that I've just placed back on the table. 'Take it again.'

I lean down to cue up, but seconds later I can feel the familiar signs. Focus on the cue, Hannah, just focus on the cue. But it's too late.

I twist round from the pool table and look Joe straight in the eye while I slowly undo the buttons on my shirt and let it slip to the floor. Still holding his gaze, I pick up one of the balls from the table and run my tongue over its smooth surface. Then I reach down to unzip my jeans...

'Hannah?' I hear Joe's voice in the background. 'Stage fright again?'

'Sorry.' I force myself to focus on the spotted ball that I was meant to be aiming at. I miss again and pot a striped one instead.

'I may have been under-exaggerating when I said I wasn't bad at pool,' I say, retreating to the ledge by the window. 'In fact, I'm rubbish.'

'So you lied,' Joe grins.

'Basically, yes.'

I sit by the window and watch Joe clean up, wondering how many other people in the world suffer from the Mentals. I can remember exactly when it started. I was seven and we were having Christmas lunch at home. We'd just ploughed our way through Mum's throat-chokingly dry Christmas pudding and I was standing on a chair at the end of the table with Dad behind me. Mum, Granny and Granddad Morgan and Dad's dad, Grandpa Bailey (Dad's mum had died when he was young) were all looking at me, waiting for me to start the speech that Dad and I had written together the night before. Every year the speech was roughly the same, something about how Mum had managed to pull off a splendid Christmas lunch despite the odds being stacked against her and how it would take her months to recover during which we would be forced to subsist on cereal and protein drinks. But this time, when I opened my mouth to begin, the speech suddenly evaporated. I couldn't think of one word as I stared at the expectant upturned faces in front of me.

'There's no hurry, darling,' said Mum, before turning to Grandpa Bailey. 'She spent two hours learning it last night.'

And that was when it started.

Instead of trying to remember the speech, my mind careered off in another direction and I imagined all the other things I could say and do at that moment.

You know what? I shouted, jumping up onto the table and stamping my way down the middle until I reached the Santa and reindeer decoration with its snowy grotto made from cotton wool and twigs. I don't want to do this silly speech any more. I hate it. Aiming a foot at the grotto, I kicked the sleigh and a couple of reindeer into the air, before pulling up my blue dress to show my knickers and shouting Fuck off, fuck off, fuck off into the faces of my astonished family.

Of course, that was only in my head. Reality saw me still standing on my chair, silent and scared, until Dad came to my rescue and did the speech for me. Afterwards, Mum said that it didn't matter at all, that no one had noticed anyway (quite how she figured this, I don't know). Either way, it was too late – the seeds had been sown.

'So, Hannah, what do you do when you're not earning your living as a pool shark?' says Joe.

We're sitting with our drinks at the small table next to the bar downstairs, having decided that one game of pool was probably enough.

'I work for a health and wellbeing magazine,' I say and make the familiar joke about it keeping me in mink coats – only by now the line has worn more than a little thin.

Joe sips his Guinness thoughtfully. 'If you could do anything, what would it be?'

I shrug. 'That's the problem. I'm not sure what else I can do.'

'What are you passionate about?'

Aha, the dreaded question. Invent something. Anything. The rights of the Kalahari Bush people. The Amazon tree frog. My duck-down duvet.

'I'm still trying to work that one out.' I rise from the table even though we've barely finished our drinks. 'Another pint?'

I'm at the bar waiting to be served. Next to me, Sally's discussing with Arthur the future of the Pelican, which is about to be taken over. Joe is still at the table, talking to one of the Jamaican guys. I wonder if we'll see each other again or if a couple of hours in a pub will be it, then we'll say goodbye and walk in different directions. It's so difficult to know this early on and I'm so out of practice. After all, it's well over three years since that first date with Luke.

Luke, I say his name a few times in my head and the more I say it the stranger it sounds, as though it's part of some far-off world. But it's a world that's never going to go away.

I'm back sitting next to Joe at the table, having fetched our pints of Guinness and a couple of packets of crisps. Joe's been teasing me about my promising pool career, suggesting that he could get me a gig playing against Ronnie Sullivan at the Crucible next week.

'Excellent,' I say. 'I'll whip his arse.'

Joe laughs. 'I reckon you can whip anyone's arse.' He smiles and holds my gaze. Then he digs into his pocket and pulls out his wallet. 'Can I show you something?'

'Of course.'

He takes a small photograph from the wallet and hands it to me. 'This is my daughter, Maya.'

I study the little girl with brown dreadlocks and huge dark eyes looking very intensely into the camera. 'She's beautiful.'

There's a brief silence during which all kinds of questions jam into my head, but before I can ask any of them the bells of a nearby church peel six o'clock.

'Shit. I'm late for my shift,' says Joe. 'That went far too quickly.'

'Blame it on the pool. Nasty game.'

'Do you fancy meeting up again?' says Joe. 'Maybe I could take you out for dinner?'

'I'd like that.'

'Good, so would I,' he says and bends down to kiss me on the cheek, just to the right of my mouth.

Chapter 10

'Stay with the breath and try not to let your thoughts wander...' says Graham, the meditation guide with the thick-knit Arran jumper and sensible walking shoes.

'Whenever you feel your mind straying, come back to the present moment.'

The present moment – 9.42 a.m. on Monday morning – sees me sitting cross-legged with a dozen or so other journalists on a midnight blue carpet in a hotel conference suite near Marble Arch. Roz was meant to cover this 'Mindfulness' workshop but she's laid up with the flu, so it's down to me.

'Just follow the breath. Do not let it out of your sight,' says Graham from the podium.

Immediately I have a mental image of myself, dressed in a black cloak and balaclava, creeping down a long dark corridor, stalking my own breath. This thought segues seamlessly into a random fact that Megan told me about the walls of London sewers being coated in saturated fat, and naturally that thought spirals into wondering what's the best way to dispose of leftover fat.

'When thoughts arise, just let them be,' says Graham in his Scottish lilt.

Thoughts of Joe shoot into my mind, but of course I can't just let it be so the next few minutes are devoted to lavish fantasies about the dinner we'll have together, the possibility of after-dinner entertainment, the next morning in bed, the lovely few days we'll spend at the beginning of summer somewhere in southern Europe, maybe Naples, where we'll stumble upon a tiny trattoria overlooking the bay, which serves linguine with clams and a fruity but not too sweet white wine from the nearby vineyard…

'Stay in the present,' says Graham. 'Don't let your thoughts tempt you away.'

I hear the squeak of wheels and squint through my right eye at the trolley being pushed by Graham's assistant. There's tea and coffee as well as a selection of croissants, pastries and some boring-looking brown biscuits.

'However much your mind wanders, always come back to the breath,' says Graham. 'Inhale. Exhale. That's all you need to do.'

This last instruction reminds me of something I recently read about how atoms in the air that I inhale today will have once been in the lungs of a Kenyan goat herder, or a North Korean housewife – or a Mexican drugs baron. So it's only logical that I draw up a list of all the people whose lung contents I'm not so keen to inhale. After that I move onto Graham's home life. He's wearing a wedding ring, so I picture a strawberry blonde woman with freckles not unlike Virginia McKenna in *Ring of Bright Water*, only she'll be called Finella. Graham and Finella have two red-haired ruddy-faced children, perennially clad in chunky knits like their dad. They all live in a remote Highland croft, nice and quiet so Graham can practise his meditation. Of course, Finella is very house-proud and does a lot of home baking at the flour-dusted wooden table (hewn by Graham from the timbers of an old fishing boat), making Eccles cakes… Are Eccles cakes even Scottish? Maybe Dundee cake might be a better choice, that's definitely Scottish. Or shortbread – in a cheery tartan tin…

The sound of a gong reverberates through the conference suite.

'How was that for everyone?' says Graham.

Ian is making himself a cup of tea when I arrive at the office just after eleven thirty.

'Thought I'd try out the acai berry,' he says. 'Would you like one?'

'Why not? Although I really need a double brandy after what I've just been through.' I tell him about Scottish Graham's workshop.

'Everybody else except me seemed to love it,' I say. 'Weirdos.'

Ian drops an acai tea bag into the Menop-Ease promo mug and fills it with hot water before handing it to me. We both take the three steps over to the window and stare down at the guitar shop below, where Phil is tacking up a new poster by the till. It's from the film *Blue Hawaii*, and in it Elvis is standing ankle deep in the sea, strumming a bright yellow ukulele.

'What did you get up to at the weekend?' I ask Ian.

'Not much,' he replies, 'except for taking my brother Matthew to the swimming pool.'

'How is he?'

'He's good,' says Ian, 'thanks for asking.'

'That's kind of you to take him swimming,' I say. 'How old is he?'

'Almost twenty-eight,' says Ian. 'It's his birthday next month.'

'Oh right,' I say, 'I thought he might be a bit younger.' In fact I'd imagined he was around ten and that he must be a half-brother.

Ian shakes his head and is about to say something else, when his phone rings. He picks up the receiver with a look of relief.

A few seconds later my own phone rings. Thinking it might be Joe, I answer in my most relaxed, yet efficient, office voice.

'Are you alright, Hannah? You sound a bit strained.'

'Oh, Mum. Hi. I'm fine.' I ask her what she's been up to and she tells me that she's just finished a lengthy hoovering session.

'Nellie loves a Hoover,' I say and explain about the Sunday treats.

'That dog's strange,' says Mum.

'I know.'

Mum then tells me she's been promoted to manageress of the charity shop.

'That's brilliant. Now you can nab all the good stuff for yourself and sell it on eBay.'

Mum laughs. 'I hope you're joking, darling.'

'I am,' I smile from my end of the phone, then ask if she's been to the nursery recently.

Mum says that she went on Saturday and bought a new trellis for the clematis.

'Are you sure you didn't sneak a little sundial in there or maybe some more squirrels on a log?'

'Are you taking the mickey again, Hannah?'

'Just a little,' I say. 'But you might want to think about some counselling for your addiction. It's always good to talk about these things.'

Mum laughs at the other end of the phone, a girlish happy laugh which I can't help joining in with.

Moments later, I hear the sound of her doorbell in the background. Apparently it's Pam coming round for lunch.

'I'd better let you go then, Mum,' I say, and after I've promised to give her a ring at the weekend, we both hang up.

Afterwards, I try to pinpoint when I last heard Mum laugh like that. Various scenes from my childhood bubble to the surface, and I remember the time when she left a big Yorkshire pudding in the oven too long and it was so charred that it shattered when she dropped it on the kitchen floor. Or when Gilmore, my guinea pig, escaped from his cage and got trapped down the side of the sofa and she had to prise him out, wearing Marigolds so he wouldn't scratch her. Or the afternoon of my sixth birthday, which we both spent skidding in our socks along the recently retiled corridor by the front door, giggling hysterically.

At first, when I replay these memories across the screen of my mind, they're blurred and faded through years of neglect, but slowly the details become sharper and the colours brighter, like a Polaroid developing.

But another memory skates amongst them and I can feel it, circling in the background, waiting to be acknowledged. I must have been about seven and my parents and I were in the car driving back from St Mawes in Cornwall. We'd stopped at a service station so Dad could have a coffee, and I was sitting in front on my mother's lap with that week's copy of *Bunty*. My head rested against Mum's jade green jumper and its soft fuzz tickled my cheek. She had just given me a barley sugar and its outer coat was melting on my tongue. Above my head I could hear her and Dad talking about his next business trip, but 'Bella of the Bar', for me the best bit of *Bunty*, was far more enticing. It was a particularly exciting day for Bella because she was entering the county gymnastics finals, and although she was sure she'd win on the parallel bars, her mat work still needed some attention.

'It's only a week. Why do you always have to make such a fuss?' I heard Dad say.

'I'm not making a fuss,' said Mum.

I was still in Bella's world, right there at the county finals as she began her mat routine. It was touch and go for a while but she managed to pull it off, finishing with a double flick flack, by a fraction of a point in the lead, which meant she got to take home the shiny gold cup as well as earn her parents (who were very poor) £50, enough to keep her in gym lessons for two whole years.

I'd just turned over to 'Wendy's Wonder Horse' next, a story involving Wendy Barnes and Miracle, her 'electronic' horse, which her scientist father made for her, when I heard my father's voice once more.

'Do you have to be so emotional about everything? It's just a business trip.' His tone made me look up, and I noticed the muscle of his left cheek twitching.

Mum's hand reached around me to open the glove compartment and pull out the box of tissues. 'Why are you always like this, Michael?' she said with a slight tremor to her voice.

'Let's not start this again,' said Dad in a tired voice. Then he took his left hand off the wheel and patted my arm. 'Hannah doesn't cry when I leave, do you, Hannah?'

I looked back at him and I wanted to say that yes, I missed him like mad when he was away and I just wanted him to stay at home with Mum and me. But I didn't. Somehow, even at seven, I knew that this wasn't the answer he wanted to hear.

I pushed what was left of my sweet into the hollow in my right cheek, so I could reply. 'No,' I said quickly. Then I wriggled out from under Mum's arms. 'I'm too hot,' I muttered and scrambled into the back seat to sit behind Dad's chair.

I kept the sweet in my right cheek until it had completely dissolved, in case Dad asked me any more questions. I must have needed a filling because the nearest tooth began to ache.

As I sit at my desk, remembering that journey back from Cornwall, I feel a surge of shame at the hurt I must have caused Mum. The scene in the car certainly wasn't an isolated incident, but it's only now that I find myself imagining how my behaviour must have made her feel.

For lunch, Ian and I buy our sandwiches at Luigi's and take them to the little patch of green behind the office, where Victor and I would sometimes come when our lunch breaks coincided. The early March sun has just broken through the clouds and we sit down on the bench. Pale yellow and purple crocuses dot the ground in front of us and the air smells of freshly mown grass.

'Anything in the paper this morning?' says Ian. He now brings the *Guardian* in every Monday so I can scan the classifieds. Although I haven't said as much, he's obviously picked up on the fact that writing about detox foot patches isn't my dream vocation.

I shake my head.

Ian takes a bite of his sausage sandwich and chews thoughtfully. 'What did you want to be when you were younger?'

'Funny you should ask that,' I say. 'That's what "Discovering your Life Purpose" Anthony asked me.'

'Well?'

'A gymnast was top of the list. Then a writer.'

'Did you actually write anything?'

I nod. 'Lots of very short stories about my guinea pig, Gilmore, and when I was in my late teens, a much longer story about Mr Simpson, the old man who lived next to the bakery and who never came out of his house.' I laugh, remembering the ridiculous adventures I dreamed up for Mr Simpson to compensate for what I assumed must be an extremely boring life.

'Nothing else?'

'I tried to write two novels in my twenties, but they were autobiographical rubbish.' I tell him that I even misguidedly sent off the second one, the story of a young woman searching for a father figure in all the wrong places, to three agents. Only one of them replied, declining my manuscript and saying that if I was determined to write what was clearly very personal material, I would need to find a suitably engaging story to contain it.

'What about you?' I ask.

'A photographer and a chef.'

'Would you still like to be either of those?'

Ian thinks for a moment. 'Definitely not a chef, but I'd love to do something with photography.' He glances up between the buildings where little wisps of white cloud are scudding across the sky. 'We can all dream, can't we?'

I nod and take a bite of my own tuna and sweetcorn baguette. I don't know if it's the al fresco lunch location or the sunshine, but it tastes pretty good.

'Nellie would have your sarnie off you in seconds,' I say

when I've finished chewing. 'She's a nutter for sausages.' Over the past few weeks I've told Ian a bit about Nellie and I elaborate now with that morning's stand-off on the way back from the cemetery when she refused to move from outside Ramón's deli until I took her inside and bought some chorizo.

'My brother would love her,' says Ian. 'He's always badgering Mum to get a dog, but I keep telling him that it would just be too much work for her on top of everything else.'

'If you don't mind me asking, what's wrong with your brother?' It's something I've been wanting to ask for a while, but I'm never quite sure how to phrase it.

'There's nothing wrong with him.' The sudden harshness of Ian's tone makes me jump. 'Sorry, I didn't mean to snap,' he says quickly. 'It's just that sometimes...' he hesitates, 'Matthew was born with cerebral palsy and has learning difficulties.'

'I'm sorry,' I say clumsily.

'Don't be,' says Ian.

'And your Mum cares for him full time?'

Ian nods. 'I've offered to pay for some help, but she refuses.'

'What's Matthew like?' I ask.

Ian smiles. 'He's funny, he's loud and he's incredibly self-confident.' He breaks off a piece of his sandwich and throws it to one of the sparrows hopping expectantly at our feet.

'So Matthew's a bit like you then?' I say.

Ian does a quick double take then breaks into a grin. 'Ha ha.'

We finish our sandwiches in silence, enjoying the space and

light away from the office. It's warm enough to take off my winter jacket and I tilt my face towards the sun. A feeling of contentment washes through me. It's a similar feeling to the one I experienced in Victor's cinema when watching the mother read to her young daughter, although much less intense.

Sitting here in the sunshine with the purple and yellow crocuses at my feet, I find myself finally returning to those emotions triggered by the film. Was their intensity caused solely by the film's disturbing similarities to my own life or was there more to it?

Perhaps the answer also lies in Victor's apprenticeship. After all, he did train with one of France's greatest filmmakers, a man with a gift for conveying even the most complex and powerful of human emotions.

*

March 2007

'I love crocuses,' I say as I take my seat on the bench next to Victor for our lunch break. 'They're such plucky little flowers.' It's a warm March day and these are the first crocuses I have seen this year.

Victor smiles. 'My personal favourites are margaritas. I used to give my mother and Madame Valjean a bunch every Saturday from the flower shop by the grocers where I worked.'

'I thought you worked for the cinema.'

'I did. The grocery was my second job at weekends.' Victor unwraps his baguette with a sideways glance at me. 'Although once I began to work for Truffaut I had to give it up.'

'You worked for Truffaut! How come you never mentioned that before?'

Victor shrugs. 'It was so long ago.'

I put my sandwich down on my lap and swivel to face him. 'Come on, tell me everything.' By now he knows me well enough to know that I am genuinely interested in his stories.

'I met him the week before my twenty-first birthday,' says Victor, setting his own baguette down on the bench next to him. 'I had taken the day off work, but just before the afternoon screening, the manager of the cinema called to ask if I could fill in for another usher. I really did not want to, but something told me that I should say yes. When the audience filed in, I noticed a young man sneak in through the emergency exit and sit down in the seat nearest the old piano, which used to be played during Charlie Chaplin's films.'

Victor pauses to take a sip of Luigi's Lavazza coffee.

'When the screening ended, the manager asked if I would help to sweep out the auditorium because the cleaner had called in sick. Again, I did not want to but again my intuition told me that I should. When I came to that seat nearest the piano, I found a small notebook filled with scribbled lines of dialogue, telephone numbers and scene locations. I took it home with me, and I still had it in my pocket the next day when I was driving the grocery van. After my final delivery, I ended up in a small side street in Pigalle, where I saw a crowd of people standing around a film camera. Behind the camera was the same man who had crept into the cinema without paying. I stepped out of the van to watch. But a few minutes later, Truffaut, as I now knew his name to be, announced that filming would have to stop for the day. Apparently the van, from which the moving shots were to be filmed, had broken down and Truffaut had lost his notebook with the number of a back-up vehicle. That is when I stepped forward to return his notebook and offer him the use of the grocery van.'

Victor's eyes are trained on the sparrow by his foot, which is hopping from one spindly leg to another, waiting for crumbs.

'At the end of filming, Truffaut invited me for a beer and a steak with the rest of the crew,' says Victor. 'That night was a revelation. About twenty people, including Jean-Luc Godard and Eric Rohmer, crammed round a table in La Fourmi bar, all of them debating and shouting about everything and anything to do with film.

'I was entranced. For the first time I had met people as passionate about cinema as I was. But as usual I said very little. Finally, at around 2 a.m. the party began to disperse until it was just Truffaut and I left. The beer had made me a little less shy and I found myself telling Truffaut about the sort of films I longed to make.

"You and I are very similar," Truffaut said when I had finished. "I have no interest in the rich or the glamorous. What fascinates me are the people in our streets and apartments, the fragile and the timid, those unable to speak for themselves."'

Victor tears off a small piece of his baguette and throws it to the sparrow. Immediately a pigeon swoops down and snatches it from the ground, flying off before the sparrow can even react.

'Over the next few weeks Truffaut came regularly to Studio 28,' says Victor, 'and when he began making a short film several months later, he asked me to help out as the driver. For his next three films, which included *Jules et Jim*,

I was again the driver, but I also assisted the cinematographer, Raoul Coutard. On his fourth film, *La peau douce*, in 1964, I was appointed Coutard's assistant. By then I had started writing my own film…' Victor stares down at the baguette in his lap. 'But it did not come to anything. It was a foolish little film and I was a foolish man to make it.'

Victor stuffs the remaining baguette back into the paper bag and stands up abruptly. Although he still has fifteen minutes left of his lunchbreak, he marches towards the exit, muttering something to himself although I cannot hear what.

*

After lunch, Ian and I wander back to the office, where I start on the day's main article. It's called 'Stop Thinking. Start Feeling' and there's quite a lot of research to do. Trawling through various mental health websites I learn some interesting facts. For example, the average person will have around 55,000 thoughts a day, most of which will be focused either on the past or the future, but rarely on the present. This obsessive overthinking is apparently making us ill, both mentally and physically. To limit it we should aim to develop 'present moment awareness' by paying more attention to our feelings and the sensations in our body.

I always feel a fraud when I tackle articles like this. My own mind isn't exactly the finely honed, disciplined instrument to which we should all aspire – the sleek, well-trained dressage horse which obeys every order and never puts a hoof wrong. Instead, I've got a grubby, stubborn Shetland pony with attention deficit disorder and a tendency to gallop off in every direction but the one I've asked it to go in.

I glance out of the window down onto Denmark Street. Some late-lunchers are queuing in Luigi's, and I picture all those obsessively repetitive thoughts whizzing around their heads. In fact there are so many of them that their skulls start to split open with the added pressure of the sandwich filling decision. Thousands upon thousands of thoughts scamper out like miniature Gollums, taking refuge behind the Gaggia coffee machine.

My phone rings, interrupting my little Gollum montage. It's Megan. She's with Nellie in Oporto's, a café on Golborne Road.

'Those yoga women are behind me and they're talking about energy again,' she says. Although I can't see her, I know she'll be doing ironic speech marks with her index fingers at the word 'energy'.

'Shall I give them a slap?'

'Yes, please,' I say. I may work for a health and wellbeing magazine, but that doesn't stop me finding yoga fanatics intensely irritating.

'You know who else needs a slap?' says Megan crossly. 'That woman with the stupid purple glasses. She spent hours at my exhibition gushing about how she wanted to put my work in her next group show. Now she won't even return my calls. Rude bitch.' Megan pauses and from the sounds of the groaning in the background she must be rubbing Nellie's back.

'Oh fuck, how was the date with the cemetery guy?'

'His name's Joe and actually it was OK,' I say. 'Considering I'd lied and told him I could play pool, which as you know, I can't.'

'And you like him?'

'I do,' I say. 'In fact we're going out for supper next week.'

There's a short pause. 'You'll be careful, won't you?'

'Yes, Megan, I will,' I sigh. I raise my hand to touch the puckered line of flesh above my left eye, which is normally covered by my fringe.

'What time shall I pick up Nellie?' I ask, deliberately changing the subject.

'Seven o'clock suits me,' says Megan. 'She's in a filthy mood so watch out.'

We finish the conversation and hang up. Next to me, Ian is turning off his computer.

'You up to anything tonight?' I ask.

'Just supper and some telly.' Ian zips up his rucksack. 'Since Mum looks after Matthew all day, it's only fair I stick around in the evening.'

'Do you ever get to go out?'

Ian shrugs. 'Not really.'

'And girls?' I say. 'Are you courting at the moment?'

Ian laughs and shakes his head. 'Unless I meet someone on the way to work or at the swimming pool, the chances are fairly slim.'

'But you'd like to meet someone?'

Ian nods and then blushes a deep red.

'Have you thought about internet dating?'

Ian shakes his head. 'No, thanks.'

'Why not?'

Ian holds up his hand. 'Honestly, Hannah, it's not for me.' Then he puts on his coat, his cheeks still a vibrant red. 'Can I go now, or do you want to carry on embarrassing me?'

Chapter 11

Joe is already sitting at one of the small wooden tables in the restaurant when I walk in on Friday evening. He's reading a book and his head is slightly bowed, so the sweep of his lashes looks even longer than I remember, and his cheekbones are even more pronounced. The curls on his head have grown; they are black and springy now, which makes me want to run my hands through them.

When he rang last night to say which restaurant he'd booked, I tried to conjure up the details of his face as we spoke. I could remember his almond-shaped eyes with their green flecks, his wide mouth, the dimples in his dark cheeks, and the small thumbprint groove between his nose and top lip. But now there are more details to be added, like layers to an oil painting.

The restaurant, which is further up from the cemetery on Harrow Road, has just eight tables packed inside one room. The walls are covered with pictures of the Grand Palace in Bangkok, sunrise over the Mekong River and orange-robed monks kneeling in front of a golden Buddha. Waitresses weave like cats through the jumble of chairs, tables and elbows, carrying steaming bowls of noodles, soups and coconut curries, while from the kitchen behind comes the clatter of plates and the hiss of frying woks.

'Sorry I'm late.' I shake out my umbrella and slide into

the seat opposite Joe with my back to the window. I don't offer up the reason for my lateness – that it took four changes of outfit before I settled on the jeans, cream shirt and black jumper. Nor do I tell him how I had to rewash and redry my hair because the first time I added too much mousse, which failed spectacularly in its promise to deliver 'full volume and the appearance of thickness to fine, flyaway hair', and instead left me with limp strands crusted with sticky white flakes.

'You're forgiven,' Joe smiles. 'Anyway, punctuality is very overrated. In fact, I've only been on time twice recently – tonight and for pool the other Sunday. Funny that.'

'What? Funny that you were on time or funny because I was so rubbish at pool?'

'Both,' Joe grins. 'So how's your week been?'

'Fascinating,' I say. 'I know a lot about pork now.'

I explain that twice during the week, Nellie dragged me into the Spanish deli, where Ramón insisted on giving me a lengthy lecture on how he makes his chorizo and the exact ingredients for *cachelada* (pork, eggs, tomatoes and onions).

Joe laughs. 'Good old Ramón.'

'You know him?'

Joe nods. 'He's Nadia's… my ex's, uncle.'

'Oh,' I say, unable to think of anything else to reply, because I'm too busy revising my original picture of Nadia. Perhaps swayed by Caitlin at the car boot sale, I had imagined Joe's ex to be Irish, with long, thick red hair, a pale cream complexion and dark green eyes. Now that picture has to be erased and replaced by an admittedly pretty stereotypical image of a Spanish woman with lustrous black tresses, olive-coloured skin and voluptuous hips.

'Is beer OK for you?' asks Joe. 'It's BYO so I've got a couple more stashed in the fridge by the till.' I nod and he picks up the bottle of Cobra on the table and pours me a glass. Watching his long fingers curve around its neck, I wonder what they'd feel like on my skin.

'I brought you a present,' he says when he's finished pouring, and holds out the book he's been reading. It's a collection of Pablo Neruda's poems.

'I thought you needed some more poetry in your life,' he says with a smile.

'Too right,' I say.

We talk a little about Neruda and Joe tells me that the film *Il Postino* was based on the Chilean poet's life. We've just moved onto Italian films in general – Joe loves Fellini's *La Dolce Vita*, while *Cinema Paradiso* is my favourite – when the waitress arrives to take our orders.

'How's Nellie?' he asks when she's gone.

'She needs therapy,' I say, and I tell him about her making a lunge for a Pekinese on our walk that morning.

'I've got an idea,' he says. 'How about I take her out with the other dogs? That way, she'll be forced to be more sociable.'

'I'm not sure that'll work,' I say. 'Besides, it's not fair on the other dogs, particularly Stan.'

'I'd keep her on a lead.'

'That's an idea. How much do you charge?'

'Thirty quid an hour.'

'What?' I say, choking on my beer. 'I love Nellie dearly, but...'

'I'm kidding,' Joe chuckles. 'You don't have to give me anything,' he pauses, 'well, maybe the odd game of pool to boost my ego.'

'But I'd want to pay you something.'

Joe thinks for a moment, then grins. 'I'm sure we'll find a way for you to pay me back.'

This time it's his expression that triggers it. Head tilted to one side, eyes looking straight into mine, with that smile playing around his lips.

Tell you what, I say, I could pay you in blow jobs. That sound fair? We could get cracking right now, while we're waiting for the food.

I slip under the table and crawl over to his side, so that my head bobs up by his lap, in line with his crotch. I start to undo his belt…

A plate appears to my right and is set down on the table in front of me. 'Thai chili squid and coconut sticky rice?' says the waitress.

Every table in the restaurant is now full, each one pushed so close to the next that diners are knocking body parts and jostling those sitting behind. The noise of laughter and chinking cutlery joins the cacophony of clattering pans from the kitchen.

'Shall I ask for a bib? You seem to be dribbling a bit,' I say, as another spoonful of Joe's curry lands on his sweatshirt.

'What?' Joe cups his hand over his ear.

'Bibs,' I shout. 'Shall we ask for some?' I point again to the blob of curry on Joe's chest. He glances down, and then he scoops off the gloopy liquid. 'I usually have more social skills than this, I promise,' he shouts back to me.

'It's OK,' I shout. 'You're making me feel at home.' I point to a noodle nestling on the sleeve of my shirt.

Joe leans towards me and wipes it off with his napkin. Then he stands up and walks over to my side of the table, dragging his chair with him. 'Unless we want to shout or mime for the rest of the night,' he says, slotting in beside me. 'Oh, and there's another,' he laughs, lifting a stray bit of squid from my cuff.

'At least I have an excuse,' he says. 'I had two fillings at the dentist this afternoon and the anaesthetic's only just wearing off.'

'Ouch.'

'It's OK,' says Joe. 'Mr Halford's a good dentist. I just wish he wouldn't play Radio 3.'

'You go to Mr Halford?'

'Why, do you?'

'Not any more.'

'Why not?'

'Radio 3 and…' I hesitate.

'And what?'

'Nothing.'

'Come on, tell me.' Joe grabs my wrist. 'I won't let go until you do.'

'I can't,' I say, laughing. 'You'll think I'm strange.'

'No, I won't.'

'Well,' I say slowly. 'Like a lot of people I have a pretty active imagination and sometimes it gets a bit out of control.' By the time I've finished telling him, Joe is laughing so much that he's managed to spill beer all over the table, smack his head against the glass behind him and choke on a mouthful of Pad Thai.

'Does it happen often, this condition?' he chuckles, rubbing the back of his head.

'Quite a lot.'

'Had any today? Tonight even?'

Oh yes. In fact I've had one just now where I go down on all fours and suck your cock in front of the entire restaurant.

111

'Nope,' I say.

Keen to change the subject, I point to another little trickle of curry that's just landed on his left sleeve. 'Maybe they'll have some plastic macs we could borrow?'

We've been talking about Jamaica, where Joe hopes to take his daughter, Maya, when she's old enough, but I'm having trouble staying focused. Instead, my mind is scampering ahead to what might happen after dinner. Then it fast forwards a few months to fantasise about that long weekend in Naples with the little trattoria and the not-too-sweet white wine... Stop it, I say sternly to myself. Focus on your body and the physical sensations, like you keep telling the *Health and Wellbeing* readers.

I can feel my skin prickling with heat and my jumper is hot and scratchy against my neck. There's a piece of squid lodged between two upper-right molars. I try to coax it down with my tongue, but it's not budging. I remember how my Gran used to hold up her left hand and discreetly conduct removal operations from behind her palm. But a similar gesture coming from me would look a bit nineteenth-century prim. Like Glenn Close in *Dangerous Liaisons*, only with a hand coyly fluttering in front of my face instead of a lacy fan.

'You look worried,' says Joe.

'No, no,' I say. 'Just very relaxed and happy, here with you and my Thai chili squid.'

The heat is becoming unbearable and I wonder at what point the Little Thai restaurant will turn into a sauna and I can get them on the Trade Descriptions Act. Beads of perspiration are dripping down my neck between my breasts, leaving small wet patches on my shirt, which I try to cover with my napkin. Joe's forehead glistens with sweat, while behind us long thin silvery trails of condensation slither down the glass of the window. Even the bottles of beer seem to be perspiring as miniature droplets of moisture glide down the sides and collect in tiny pools on the table.

Joe reaches down to take off his jumper. He pulls it over his head and it catches on his T-shirt below, lifting it and for a moment exposing the smooth dark skin of his stomach and the faint line of black fuzz that starts at his belly button then creeps down to disappear into the waistband of his jeans.

'That's better,' he says, turning back to face me. He cocks his head a little then leans forward to touch my cheek with a forefinger. It feels cool against my hot skin and I have an urge to take it in my mouth and suck. I smile at him in what I hope is a seductive way, but he's still staring at my cheek with a frown of concentration. It takes another few seconds before I realise what he's doing.

'Got it,' he says and holds out his index finger on which is balanced one tiny eyelash. 'Make a wish.'

Behind the counter, a small Thai woman of about ninety is snatching up the slips of paper from the waitresses, before shouting the orders into the kitchen fug. To her left is the fridge, where customers can put their BYO booze, and in front of which Joe is now waiting to get two more beers. I watch him joking with the man in front and I think how different he looks from Luke. Naïve as it sounds, I hope, I really hope, that this physical difference is somehow proof of other differences.

'Let me take those away.' A passing waitress stops by the table and reaches over to pick up the empty bowls of rice. I smile up at her, but my thoughts are still on Luke, reeling back in time to the day that he and I first met.

*

'I'll just clear away those empty cups,' says the waitress, standing beside the table where I've already sat down with my coffee. I'm in Oporto's café and it's a sunny morning in late September. I've brought along a book on Truffaut – having seen so many of his films, I am now almost as big a fan as Victor.

I'm aware of the background chatter and of the man at the table next to me, but I'm engrossed in a chapter about the making of *La Nuit Américaine*, one of Truffaut's later films.

'Isn't French cinema a bit passé?' I look up to see the man smiling at me as he empties a sachet of sugar into his espresso.

'No,' I say. 'Not at all.'

'And you don't find New Wave films pretentious?' he asks after he's introduced himself as Luke. His eyes are a blue-ish grey and he's wearing a battered flying jacket.

'Some of them are,' I say, 'but have you ever seen *The 400 Blows* or *Day for Night*?' I deliberately use the English translations of the film titles so I don't sound pretentious.

Luke shakes his head. 'Three-hour films with no plot aren't my style.'

'What is your style then?'

'You really want to know?' He points through the café window at the black Norton motorbike which stands next to the Moroccan fish stall. 'Then come with me to the Coronet cinema this afternoon.'

I shake my head. 'Call me old-fashioned but I'm not in the habit of hopping on strangers' bikes.'

'Where's your sense of adventure?'

'Neatly filed next to my sense of self-preservation.'

Luke sighs loudly. 'Shame. I would have bought you popcorn and everything.' He picks up the napkin by my plate, takes a pen from his top pocket and hands them both to me. 'Can I at least take your number?' he says. 'Surely that's allowed.'

I still can't remember why I gave him my number. Although I found him attractive, he was obviously a player and therefore exactly the kind of man I usually avoid. Just a quick drink, I thought to myself as I handed him back the napkin. That can't hurt.

'Hop on.' Luke pats the low-slung leather seat of his motorbike which is parked on the pavement outside my flat at eight o'clock on the following Tuesday evening.

'I thought we were just going to the Paradise for a swift pint,' I say.

Luke shakes his head. 'Change of plan.' He takes a second helmet from the pannier behind him and holds it out to me. 'I'm taking you to the movies.'

We arrive at the Coronet just in time for the opening credits. Luke insists that we sit in the front row with the massive bucket of sweet popcorn that he's just bought, balanced on his lap.

'This is what a real film looks like,' he grins, tossing a couple of popcorn up into the air and catching them in his mouth. He nods towards the screen on which the film's title – *Bonnie and Clyde* – has just appeared. 'Brace yourself.'

It's past three in the morning when he finally drops me back at my flat. In the seven hours since he picked me up, we've watched Warren and Faye shoot their way across America, we've been to Charlie Wright's pub in Old Street, the twenty-four hour bagel shop in Brick Lane and a basement bar in Soho. Along the way I've learnt that Luke works for a production company making TV adverts and pop promos, his passion is a documentary he's putting together on the making of *Easy Rider* and he's lived in LA for five years. He also makes me laugh till my stomach cramps.

Now we're standing at the top of my steps.

'When can I see you again?' he says.

'Is that a good idea?' I say. 'After all, you like American films, I like French ones, you like sweet popcorn, I like salty – it's doomed from the start.'

'You're right. What was I thinking?' says Luke, grabbing me by the waist and kissing me hard on the lips.

Before I have a chance to take a breath or to steady my hammering heart, he pulls back. 'That's sealed,' he says with a grin. 'You're mine now.'

*

I force my mind away from the memory and back to the restaurant. Those feelings that I experienced when I first met Luke are still there, but it's only since watching Victor's film that I am even able to acknowledge their existence, buried as they are beneath everything that came later.

My heart is thudding and my hands are shaking. Joe is still chatting with the man by the fridge and I hope he'll stay there for a bit longer. I try to focus on my plate in front of me, breathing deeply, but the telltale light-headedness is making me nauseous.

Not here, I say to myself. Please not here.

I take several more deep breaths and another wave of dizziness sweeps over me. I can taste the bile surging up from my stomach. I shove back my chair and race for the loo.

I am standing outside the restaurant on the wet pavement. I'm still doing the breathing exercises that Dr Ling taught me, and I can feel Joe's hand on my back between my shoulder blades.

'It's alright,' he says gently. 'We can stay here as long as you need.'

I'm feeling a little better – at least the dizziness has gone and I reckon I can make it home. Another lash of rain slicks the road in front of me. Joe opens my umbrella and holds it over both of our heads.

'You don't have to walk me home,' I say. 'I'm through it now.'

'Don't be ridiculous,' says Joe and takes my hand in his.

We walk up the short stretch of Kilburn Lane, past the Paradise pub which is just shutting for the evening, and past the launderette, where the machines are finally still after a day washing the neighbourhood's clothes. Outside the Caribbean takeaway the queue stretches down the street – mostly drinkers from the Paradise buying post-pub patties. A couple lean against the outside of the window, kissing.

'How long have you suffered from panic attacks?' asks Joe.

'Two years,' I say.

'Do you take anything for them?'

I shake my head. 'I don't want to go on medication and...'

I hesitate, 'my GP says I should have cognitive therapy, but it's just not for me. All that talking, my head's busy enough as it is…'

We've reached my basement steps so I fish my keys from my bag, relieved.

'This is my penthouse palace,' I say.

'Are you going to be alright?' says Joe.

I nod.

'Sure?'

'I'm sort of used to them now.'

Joe bends forward to kiss me lightly on the lips. 'Sweet dreams, Hannah. I'll call you tomorrow.'

There's a pause, a pivotal moment when it can go either way. I take a deep breath. 'Would you like to come in?'

Nellie is splayed out on the sofa when we walk into the sitting room. Her eyes swivel straight over to Joe.

My house. What's he doing here?

'You remember Joe, don't you?'

'I brought you the pram, so you have to be nice to me,' says Joe and bends down to rub Nellie's neck.

'I'll make some coffee,' I say. 'You two can chat amongst yourselves.'

When I come back, Joe is squatting by my record collection. 'Nellie and I want to hear this.' He holds up my copy of Nick Drake's *Pink Moon*.

We sit in a line on the sofa, me, then Joe, then Nellie at the far end. Joe and I are each holding a cup of coffee, which neither of us has even sipped. Nellie keeps on peering round like a maiden aunt, as if to check that we're not doing anything.

'Nellie, would you go into your kennel, please.'

Nellie glares at me.

I don't want to start up a one-sided squabble with Nellie in front of Joe – that wouldn't exactly give a good impression of sound mental health, especially after the panic attack, so I lug her off the sofa and over to the kennel. She flops down, head inside and bottom sticking out of the doorway.

'We still love you, Nellie,' says Joe. Then he pulls me to him, cupping my face in his hands. 'Are you sure you're alright, Hannah?'

I smile. 'Much better.'

Joe hooks a stray bit of hair behind my ear. 'You really have no idea, do you?'

'About what?'

'How beautiful you are.'

As the title track of *Pink Moon* fades into 'Place to be', Joe softly kisses the side of my neck. I put my hands under his shirt, feeling the warmth of his skin and the smooth knots of his spine. He draws back and gazes at me, before kissing me on the lips, at first gently, then again, this time harder.

By the time the song has finished, our clothes are all over the floor and we're pulling each other into the bedroom.

Chapter 12

'How was your date?' says Ian, when I arrive at work three days later on Monday morning.

'Rollercoaster,' I say. 'I was half an hour late, I was nearly boiled alive, I slopped food all down me, then I had a panic attack,' I stop and smile, 'but after that things improved.'

'And you like him?' asks Ian, with a trace of his old stammer.

'Just a bit,' I grin. Joe and I had stayed in bed till noon on the Saturday, then he cooked me scrambled eggs and hash browns. After arranging to see each other on Tuesday night, he left for his shift at the Paradise.

But I don't want to jinx things by talking about Joe too much so I tap the neat pile of that morning's free samples which Ian has already unwrapped.

'I hope you don't mind,' says Ian. 'I didn't have breakfast and I needed a snack.' He points to an opened packet of chia seeds and wrinkles his nose. 'They're all yours.'

'What are those?' I pick up a pair of black plastic glasses with lots of tiny holes poked through the lenses.

'Trayner pinhole glasses,' says Ian, reading from the accompanying leaflet. 'Apparently they exercise the eye muscles to counteract eye strain, near-sightedness and computer stress.'

'Pop them on then.'

Ian takes them from me and sets them lightly on the bridge of his nose. They make him look like a skinnier, geekier version of someone from *The Matrix*.

The first article of the day is devoted to the downsides of spending too much time in front of a computer and how it can cause both drowsiness and insomnia, and a compromised immune system. I've done several pieces like this before so I already know a few tricks which will offset the negative effects: regular breaks and fresh air, along with plants, flowers, bowls of salty water and rock salt crystals next to the computer. There's also an exercise that I sometimes use myself which entails tapping your scalp with your fingers from the forehead to the back of the neck several times, then throwing your head upside down and shaking it around. It's surprisingly effective.

Next on the list is a short piece about how just twenty minutes of meditation is the equivalent to four hours of deep sleep. After that it's time for this week's Healthy Eats – a crafty combo of quinoa, lentil and feta salad and quesadilla wedges. I also include a simple pudding – Yofu soya yoghurt with agave syrup. When I've finished, I read it out to Ian. He pulls a face.

'You try coming up with Healthy Eats week after week, when you can't cook a pulse to save your life.'

'OK,' says Ian. 'I'll give it a go.'

'You can cook?'

'I wanted to be a chef, didn't I?'

'What sort of stuff can you make then?'

'Well, for Sunday lunch yesterday I cooked vegetarian lasagne followed by apple turnover.

'Wow,' I say, 'you're so wasted. Any girl would be lucky to have you.'

'I wouldn't go that far,' says Ian.

'I would,' I say and tap my computer screen. 'Won't you even *consider* internet dating?'

Ian shakes his head. 'I'm not interested, Hannah. So can we just drop it?'

It's raining hard by lunchtime so Ian and I pick up some sandwiches and return to the office. I've been a bit adventurous in my selection today and Luigi has made me one of his specials – a mozzarella and roasted pepper panini. For pudding, Ian and I are splitting one of Luigi's giant flapjacks with hazelnuts and honey.

While we eat, we trawl through the classifieds.

'What about this one?' says Ian, 'Head of IT for a new sports marketing company.'

'Sounds perfect,' I say. After three months of working with Ian, I am wising up to his quiet irony. 'You know how I adore sports, and IT… well, there's nothing I don't know about IT.'

'Or what about manager for a new womenswear brand in York?' he says, still reading from the page. 'The successful applicant will have a keen eye for fashion and the ability to spot future trends…'

'Are you having a pop at my clothes, Ian Collins? Because if you are…' I gesture to his blue V-neck jumper and schoolboy slacks, 'you're on very shaky ground.'

I lean over and scan the lower part of the page. 'Here's one for you then, smart ass. Senior lecturer in Slavic studies at Leeds University. You'd like that, wouldn't you? Standing in a huge echoey auditorium, talking to hundreds of noisy students.'

'When do I start?' Ian chuckles.

'Beginning of May. Just time to work yourself into a right old panic.'

After lunch, I finally tackle a write-up of Scottish Graham's Mindfulness workshop. But it's impossible to concentrate because my thoughts keep veering off-piste, heading straight for Joe. I spend a good half hour replaying Friday night and Saturday morning in minute detail. Next, I leapfrog forward and spend at least twenty minutes developing the fantasy of the Naples long weekend, during which Joe and I spend hours in the outsized bed of some bougainvillea-covered *pensione*. When we finally venture outside, we take a picnic to a little beach nestled beneath pine trees, where we swim in the sparkling water. It's here that the fantasy grinds to a halt and I start to fret about fitting into my old frayed bikini. I should definitely get a new one. Maybe I could find a nice fifties retro number from Portobello Market, but then buying second-hand swimwear is a bit rank. I mentally trawl through all the other possible places I could get one until I realise that I've already wasted an hour and I still need to knock out three articles before the end of the day.

But first I call Mum. Although we only spoke four days ago, I've got into the habit of ringing her a couple of times a week. She doesn't pick up, so I leave a message sending her my love and saying I'll try again tomorrow.

I leave the office at six, and since Megan's bringing Nellie round at eight I don't need to hurry home. The rain has finally stopped so I decide to take a walk. Loathing gyms as much as I do, I have to get the exercise where I can (especially if the Naples fantasy is going to become reality).

I wander down Charing Cross Road and without even thinking find myself turning into the side street just after Cambridge Circus. I've not been here since the cinema closed in May 2010, five months after Victor left his job. One day when I happened to pass, I saw two men loading a row of cinema seats into the back of a lorry, while a third was carrying the curtain that had once covered the screen. There was no sign of the owner, the walrus-moustached Monsieur Henri, but pinned to the door was a notice, written in a similar script to the closing credits of so many of the films Victor and I had watched:

Fin – The End.

Midway down the street, I see what looks like a pop-up bar where the cinema once was. The door is painted green and a sign outside says 'Kino' with a cocktail glass beneath it. It's not open yet, although standing in front of it is a short man wearing a big blue overcoat and a blue felt hat. I don't recognise him at first because he seems so out of context here. When I do, I stop abruptly, wondering if there's time for me to turn around. But it's too late, he's already seen me.

I walk towards him.

'Hello, Victor,' I say as though it's not at all weird that I should bump into him on the one day I happen to be revisiting the old site of the cinema.

'Hello,' he replies, turning his head away from the bar's locked door and looking at me.

I gesture towards the bar. 'You knew that the cinema had closed?'

Victor nods. 'But I still come here sometimes. Nostalgia is a hard habit to break.'

'I was here on the day it shut,' I say. 'Monsieur Henri's note made me cry.'

There's a short silence while I cast around for something else to say, something which has nothing to do with the last time I saw Victor and the film that he showed me. But he beats me to it.

'I was worried about you,' he says. 'You left so quickly.'

'I'm sorry,' I say. 'I wasn't feeling very well.'

'Are you better now?'

'A little.' I sense that he knows I'm not talking about a passing cold or a bout of flu here.

'I had hoped that you might come back,' says Victor.

'I meant to. It's just that things have been...' I trail off. It's pointless lying to Victor, given what's gone before.

'How is it going?' I say, steering the conversation to safer ground.

'Good.' Victor smiles. 'I have made another film.'

'Wow,' I say. 'You don't hang around.' I try to inject a lightness into my voice, but it just sounds odd.

The silence that follows is soundtracked by the rumble of traffic on Tottenham Court Road. Victor is still looking at me. I can't avoid the subject any longer.

'That film you showed me,' I say tentatively, 'why did you make it?' Sweat prickles my neck. Even the mention of it is enough to trigger those feelings again.

'Because I felt that you needed to see it,' says Victor.

A flare of anger scalds my cheeks. 'How dare you!' I say, 'I never asked you to...' I stop, knowing that I have no right to be angry with Victor after what I did.

'So now I am just another subject, like that old guy you used to follow in Paris?' I say quietly.

Victor shakes his head. 'No, Hannah, you are much more to me than that.'

It's the way he says it rather than the words that halts me in my tracks. I swallow hard, forcing back the tears, and for a few moments both of us stare at the building in front of us, which was once the symbol of our friendship. I have no idea what's going through Victor's head, but my own feelings are an intensely painful mixture of shame, guilt and a profound sadness.

'I'm so sorry for what I did to you,' I say.

'Ssssh,' says Victor. 'I forgave you a long time ago, Hannah.'

A tear trickles down my cheek. 'I loved watching all those films with you, I really did.'

To our right a motorbike enters the small street and roars towards us. Victor and I both step towards the bar's door, to make sure the rider has enough space to pass. But even so I can feel the wind snap at my legs as it hurtles by.

Victor is watching me quietly when I look back at him. 'Will you come to my cinema again?'

'Maybe,' I say. But I'm not sure that I will. The feelings that his presence provokes are just too distressing, knowing what he does about me.

Behind us, the bells of St Giles's church are ringing. Victor counts them with a nod for each one. Then he pulls a diary from his pocket and flicks over to today's date.

'I have a private screening at seven o'clock.' He reaches forward and pulls me into a brief hug. 'Please come to see me again,' he says, and after a quick salute he hurries down the street towards Tottenham Court Road.

I watch until he rounds the corner, and I remember a time when we would have exited the cinema together and walked arm in arm down this street. Usually, we would be chatting about the film we'd just seen – Truffaut's haunting images, Godard's deftly improvised dialogue or Chabrol's love of detective stories – but not always.

*

March 2007

'That was a bit heavy-going,' I say, as Victor and I set off down the street towards the café. It's a warm March evening and we've just watched Truffaut's *La peau douce*.

Victor doesn't reply and I wonder if he's still thinking about the rather depressing story of an old man and his infatuation with a younger woman.

By the time we reach the café he has still not said anything. We order and take our seats. In the background, the voice of Maurice Chevalier croons from the gramophone's brass trumpet. Although Bernard often plays this particular track, today *'Notre Espoir'* sounds especially sad.

'What is it?' I ask Victor.

Victor stirs his coffee. 'I thought that I would be able to watch that film by now, but it seems I am wrong.'

In the eighteen months that I have known him Victor has never once mentioned a love life, but instinctively I know that his present mood is somehow linked to a woman.

It's at least a minute before he starts to tell his story. He won't look me in the eye while he speaks, instead he watches the young art-student couple opposite us.

'I met Claudette on the set of the film we have just watched. She was in charge of costumes and make-up,' he begins. 'She had dark brown melancholy eyes and long auburn hair.' Victor drags his gaze from the couple to pour some milk into his coffee.

'One night at the end of filming she offered me a lift because she had heard that I also lived in Montmartre. On that first journey we talked only about Truffaut's skill as a director and her day job as a sales assistant in a local pharmacy. In fact, for all those journeys over the next four weeks when she kindly drove me home, we never talked about anything personal. But I came to know her through her love of Paris, for she rarely took the same route home. Instead, she made sure that we drove past at least one of her favourite spots. One evening it might be the Marché des Enfants Rouges in the Marais with its fragrant flower displays and wine stalls, the next it would be the misted glasshouses in the Les Serres d'Auteuil botanical gardens or the Pont Neuf, otherwise known as the Bridge of Memories.'

Victor stares down at the table's chipped green paint as Bernard sets on another record, Jacques Brel's '*Ne me quitte pas*', his sign to customers that the café is about to close.

'On Claudette's last day of filming she seemed very upset,' says Victor, 'and when we drove back that evening, we did not pass any of her special places. At the corner of my street, she stopped the car abruptly and burst into tears.

'"I'm sorry. Today has not been a good day," she said. Then she turned to me in the passenger's seat. "Let's go for dinner," she announced with forced gaiety. "What about Bofinger?"

'I knew the brasserie – everyone in Paris does – although I had never been there, mainly because I could not afford it. But of course I said yes.'

Victor glances up at me for the first time since he began talking.

'I have no idea what I ate that night. It might as well have been wood shavings for all I noticed, although the final bill would indicate that it was rather expensive wood shavings. I could focus only on Claudette. At first she talked about how her job in the pharmacy would now seem even duller than before. Only later, as the sommelier brought the second bottle of wine that she had ordered, did she mention her boyfriend, Philippe, who had recently cheated on her again.

"'Why do men always do this to me?" she asked, motioning to the sommelier to fill her glass to the top. "What's wrong with me?"

"'There is nothing wrong with you, Claudette," I said. "Philippe does not deserve you if he is unfaithful."

"'You're so right," she exclaimed with a sudden forcefulness. "I should be with someone like you, Victor! You would never cheat on me, would you?'"

Back in the café, Bernard taps his watch and glares at us. We are the only customers left and all the tables have been cleaned without our noticing. Victor tells Bernard that we will be leaving in a few minutes, then resumes talking.

'Claudette could scarcely walk by the time we left the restaurant. She had to leave her car there, and during the taxi ride home, she laid her head in my lap and told me over and over again how kind and special I was. When we arrived at her apartment, I escorted her up to the fifth floor where she lived.

"'Stay with me, Victor," she said. "I need you."

'I shook my head. "You need a good night's sleep," I said and kissed her on the cheek. Once I had made sure she was safely inside, I left.

'I knew that I would not be able to sleep that night, so instead I decided to visit those places that Claudette and I had driven by during the past month. At sunrise I ended up at the Pont Neuf bridge, where the river was slowly turning to a luminous gold. I was so overcome with happiness that I thought my heart would explode.'

Bernard is back again, impatiently jangling the door keys. Victor stands up and sets his hat back on his head. Outside in Greek Street, I ask him to finish the story.

'Not here, Hannah,' he says. 'Half of Paris already knows what happened and I would rather it stopped there. I will tell you next week.'

*

I often wish that Victor had kept the end of that story to himself. If I hadn't known about it, then I would not have been able to use it as further evidence against him and in doing so, wreck our friendship.

Chapter 13

Joe, Nellie and I are sitting in the park next to Portobello Market on a Sunday afternoon. The grass is warm from the April sun, and above us the branches of the cherry trees are speckled with small brown buds just beginning to unclench their tight green fists. All around, clusters of daffodils bob in the breeze, frilly yellow heads nodding earnestly as though deep in conversation. Their subtle marzipan-like fragrance fuses with the scent of turmeric and cumin from the nearby Indian takeaway stall. Splayed at our feet, Nellie chews on an onion bhaji.

'This is why I wanted to set it here,' says Joe. 'I love this place, and it's not going to be around forever.' Joe's been telling me about his play, a two-hander about the disintegration of a marriage. He's just finished the final draft and is due to send it out to several theatres and stage directors next week. Listening to him talk so passionately about his work, I feel my stomach tighten and a sweet almost painful ache in my chest. We've been together for just over six weeks now and each time I see him the ache gets a little deeper.

It's the small things that set me off, like the way he eats a piece of toast in three bites, how he stands at the fridge and drinks milk straight from the carton, or how he can't seem to remove his tops without the T-shirt or vest below getting caught midway, leaving him tugging and cursing from inside a jumper.

And then there are the other things: the press of his lips as he kisses the crooks of my elbows, the smell of his skin at the nape of his neck, the trail of his fingers across my belly... Even thinking about them now makes my insides contract.

'What's on your mind?' Joe grins.

'Nothing.'

'Liar,' he says, and kisses the top of my head. Then he draws back and looks intently at my face. 'Did I already tell you how gorgeous you look today?'

Under the canopied market, Joe seems to know all the stall holders, which means stopping every few steps to introduce me: first to a woman with bright orange hair in an electric wheelchair, then to the man with green varnished fingernails who owns the book stall, and finally to a guy selling old vinyl records who's plucking at a guitar in time to the sound of Etta James's 'I've got dreams to remember'.

Nellie follows us, tongue glued to the ground, suctioning up anything in her path – a couple of falafels, a half-chewed pitta bread and a flap of old naan. I'm just pulling her off the naan when a loud voice hurtles through the stalls from the other side of the market and a large woman in a dark green wool suit comes striding over.

'What are you doing here?' says Joe.

The woman waves the wad of leaflets she's holding. 'Canvassing for the local elections.' She glances over at me.

'Mum, this is Hannah,' says Joe. 'Hannah, this is my mum, Rosemary.'

I smile and shake Rosemary's hand, even though something about her makes me want to curtsy.

Rosemary returns my smile and my handshake, although I sense her eyes assessing me.

And then, of course, it starts.

Meeting people's parents, especially a boyfriend's parents, is probably the most fertile ground for my overactive mind. There are just too many embarrassing scenarios to imagine. Usually they revolve around bursts of filthy language or at least some weird face pulling, but there are variations. Like with Steven, who I'd gone out with in my early twenties. As soon as we sat down for that first Sunday lunch with his parents, I knew there was going to be trouble. His mother, Mrs Nicholls, was in her early fifties with a neat grey bob, lilac cardigan and eager-to-please eyes, while his dad, who was roughly the same age, had a blue cardigan and looked suspiciously like his own wife's brother.

'Do start before it gets cold,' said Mrs Nicholls and handed me a plate of two thick slabs of lamb, some cauliflower cheese and a pile of roast potatoes.

Both she and Mr Nicholls watched me, smiling expectantly.

I took a mouthful.

'Is it alright?' They both asked in unison.

I looked up at their kind faces and keen eyes and I was off.

Alright? You are joking, aren't you? It's fucking disgusting! Which one of you in this weird brother-sister set-up cooked this shit? I said, spitting a lump of lamb onto the table.

Umm, I did, said Mrs Nicholls nervously, raising her hand like a schoolgirl.

Well, it stinks! I shouted. Stretching over the table, I grabbed the remainder of the joint and hurled it against the wall.

Reality, of course, was a little different.

'It's delicious, Mrs Nicholls,' I said, sounding like I was eight years old and had just come over for tea.

With Joe's mum, my mind zooms in on her sizeable chest. *Just look at those breasts. They're MASSIVE. Do they even make bras that big?*

'What do you think, Hannah?' Rosemary's green eyes are boring into mine.

'Sorry, what was that?'

'Conservative or Labour?'

Since Joe has already told me what her job is, I assume she's asking me about my voting habits. 'Ummm, Labour, I suppose, although given their despicable performance over Iraq...' I stop there. However strongly I feel about the illegal invasion of Iraq, it's probably best not to get into a big argument about it on our first meeting.

Instead, I ask Rosemary how the campaign is going.

'We're doing OK.' She smiles at me before turning to Joe. 'Weren't you meant to be seeing Maya today?'

I notice Joe stiffen. 'No, Mum. Nadia's taken her to see her parents.'

'Oh,' says his mother. 'But I thought you were both going to take her to...'

Joe places a hand on her arm. 'Not now, Mum. I'll give you a ring later.' He turns to me. 'We should get going.'

After we've said a hasty goodbye, Joe, Nellie and I walk back down Portobello Road. On the way we pass a stall selling children's clothes, and the sight of those mini T-shirts printed with pictures of The Ramones and The Clash makes me realise once again how little I know about Joe's other life. Although he often talks about his daughter, Maya, he rarely mentions Nadia and why they split up. Whenever I ask, he manages to change the subject. Over the past few months I have however gleaned a few facts: I know that they were together for four years before Maya was born, but after that the arguing began. Shortly after Maya's second birthday Joe moved out of the flat, believing it would be the best for the three of them. A month later, he said he'd like to try and work things out, but Nadia wanted them to split permanently – Maya didn't need a father who kept walking in and out of her life. By then the situation was so bad that whenever Joe was allowed to see Maya, she had to be dropped off at his mother's so that Nadia and he didn't have to come face to face. Only recently had things started to improve.

But that's about all I know. Nine years of Joe's former life compressed into a few scanty facts.

I sense from Joe's purposeful stride that he doesn't want to discuss whatever had been planned for that Sunday with Nadia, so he and I walk on in silence with Nellie just behind until we reach Lancaster Road.

'That's Chris Blackwell's recording studio, the guy who started Island Records.' Joe points to the building on the corner, which looks like a church. Then he gestures towards the dark blue house a few doors down, 'And that place once belonged to one of my heroes, Joe Strummer.'

Just then, a woman emerges from the blue house, followed closely by a baby pug whose face is so squashed that it looks like it's run into a wall very fast and its eyes are still bulging from the shock of it. A little tartan coat is strapped onto its back, beneath which trot a set of spindle-legs.

Nellie is transfixed. *What the fuck is THAT?*

'Leave it, Nellie,' I warn. The pug's head is temptingly

bite-size and I have visions of the woman returning home with just a tartan coat on four legs.

Nellie sighs.

Turning into All Saints Road, we hear the sound of Aswad pulsing from the reggae shop, outside which sits a man in a knitted hat big enough to fit a football beneath.

'That's Duke,' says Joe, 'owner of the best collection of reggae records this side of Kingston.'

Duke looks over and raises a hand in greeting. Nellie grins up at him, and for a moment it seems like her head's nodding in time to the music.

Joe's flat, which is above the old bakery, consists of just one large room, a minuscule kitchen in one corner, a high bed in the other and a small separate bathroom. The walls are painted bright blue, and the white floorboards are covered with a huge red and yellow striped rug. The shelves by the window are heaped with books, records and photographs.

From the sofa where she has immediately made herself comfortable, Nellie surveys the room and then lets out a noisy fart.

'Nellie!' I say. 'Manners.'

Joe laughs. 'Looks like someone feels at home already.' Then he turns and points to a painting by the shelves of a man with an oversized head. Above the head hovers a bird which looks more like a potato with wings. 'What do you think of that?'

'Did Maya do it?' I ask.

'HANNAH!' says Joe. 'I'm shocked. That just happens to be one of my favourite paintings in the world. It's called *The Ascension* by George Milton. Ever heard of him?'

I shake my head. 'I've heard of John Milton, *Paradise Lost*. Any points for that?'

'Lots,' says Joe, kissing me on the nose.

While Joe puts on the Sister Rosetta Tharpe record he bought at the market, I glance through his books. There are several writers and playwrights whose names I've never heard of – Barry Reckord, Jacqueline Rudet, Bernardine Evaristo… There's also a copy of *The Bhagavad Gita* and *The Road Less Travelled*, which I try to ignore.

It's not that I don't like these kind of books *per se*, it's just that in my experience the sort of people who read them can sometimes be… well, a little tiresome. Steven (he of the lamb lunch) couldn't get enough of *The Bhagavad Gita*. He was studying philosophy at UCL and when he wasn't enthusing about 'the genius of the 700-verse Hindu scripture', he'd talk me through his thesis on Plato's theory that all humans were trapped in a dark cave, watching shadowy projections on the walls, thinking that they were real, while in fact the 'real world' lay outside the cave. Maybe if I met Steven now, I wouldn't be quite so dismissive, but for a twenty-two-year-old more interested in going to gigs and getting pissed, he was just irritating.

'So where's this "real world" and why can't I see it?' I once asked him.

'You can't *see* it,' Steven replied in his irritatingly patient voice. 'You can only sense it. It's a matter of perception.'

'Right. Oh, is that the time? Chuck us the remote, *EastEnders* is on.'

Seven weeks of Steven and the shadowy caves was quite enough, so we parted ways in the middle of a Pulp gig.

I let my eyes drift back to a book of Derek Walcott's plays, praying that Joe isn't going to turn out to be a second Steven. But even if he is, it's probably too late. I'm in too deep.

'Did you always know you wanted to be a playwright?' I ask him.

Joe shakes his head. 'It took a while to find out, but looking back, I suppose there were a few pointers. At school I loved drama lessons and was always writing plays for my sister and me to put on. My best birthday present was being taken to see Mark Rylance perform *Hamlet* for the Royal Shakespeare Company when I was fourteen.'

'So how come you ended up studying law?'

'I thought that it would be the sensible thing to do,' he replies. 'It was only after Maya was born that I realised how unhappy I was and that I wanted to go back to college and study drama. But Nadia didn't want me to quit my job. She said that I had a daughter to support and that I couldn't be selfish any more. And of course she was right.'

'But if you were passionate about the theatre...?'

Joe looks at me. 'It's not that simple, Hannah.'

While Joe unloads the shopping bags in the kitchen, I study the photographs on his shelves. I pick up one of a man in sandals standing in front of a small restaurant with a corrugated iron roof. His red T-shirt has the same logo as the wooden plaque above the door – 'Linton's Soul Food'.

Joe has told me a bit about his dad; how he moved from Jamaica to London in the late sixties, where he met Joe's mother at one of the few mixed race dance halls in Ladbroke Grove. The two fell in love, and when Rosemary became pregnant with Joe, they married. But by the time Joe's sister, Linda, followed two years later, his dad was homesick and wanted to go back to Jamaica. He hated the weather and his job working nightshifts as a hospital porter, and he longed to open a restaurant back in Ocho Rios, where he would raise his family. But Rosemary had just started a new job as assistant to a local Labour counsellor and had imagined a very different life. When Joe was nine, the marriage finally ended and his father returned to Jamaica.

'But you still speak to your dad, don't you?' I say.

Joe walks over from the kitchen to stand next to me. 'Every week – providing he's remembered to pay his phone bill.' He stares down at the picture in my hands. 'It hasn't always been like this, though. After he left I was so angry that I refused to speak to him for almost three years. But then I realised that I had a choice – either I forgave him or I never spoke to him again. It was that easy.' He shrugs. 'Actually, it wasn't that easy, but we got there in the end.' He sets the picture back on the shelf.

'You hardly ever speak about your father. What was he like?'

Joe's right. I rarely talk about Dad because even though he died over fifteen years ago, I still find it difficult.

I think for a few moments, wanting to select from my store of memories those things which best describe the man I idolised.

'He was daring and funny and had a very dark sense of humour,' I say. 'He loved swimming and fast cars.' I smile as I remember sitting in the passenger seat of his Alpha Romeo and speeding round the Chorleywood lanes. 'His big dream was to live abroad, maybe in Spain, or Canada… which of course he did when he and Mum split up.'

Sister Rosetta Tharpe is still playing in the background, a growly gospel drawl, accompanied by a frenzied electric guitar. 'Oh, and he could dance like a demon. Unlike me.'

Joe slides an arm around my waist. 'Bet you can.'

'Trust me, I can't. I dance like a broom.'

'Do brooms dance?'

'No,' I say. 'For obvious reasons.'

'Come on,' says Joe, 'just follow me.' He does a weird sort of hip jerky movement and kicks up his legs while his arms flail above his head. Nellie looks on from the sofa, baffled.

'Is that you dancing?' I say, trying to keep a straight face.

'Sure is,' says Joe.

'Did anyone ever tell you that you dance like a spirogyra?'

'What's a spirogyra?'

'It's like an amoeba, but it has long dangly arm things. I'll draw you one, if you like.'

Joe laughs and kicks up his legs again. 'I look forward to it.'

When the record finally comes to an end, Joe pulls me down onto the sofa with him.

'You make me very happy, Hannah. I hope you realise that.' He brushes my hair from my face then pulls back a little to study my forehead.

'I still don't know how you got this scar,' he says. 'Are you going to tell me?'

'This old thing,' I say. 'I've had it for years.' I laugh but not very convincingly. 'I ran into a door, if you must know,' I say, which actually isn't so far from the truth.

Joe lets my fringe fall back down onto my forehead. His hands drop from my shoulders and he pushes himself up from the sofa. 'I'd better start lunch then. I hope you like chili con carne.'

I watch him as he heads towards the kitchen and I want to tell him – tell him that I'm falling in love with him and how much it scares me, but the words spike in my throat.

I sit there, mute, trying to stop the past from bleeding into the present, to take this moment just as it is, but there's something dragging me back with the strength of steel cables.

*

'I hope you like Mexican food,' says Luke. 'If you don't, you can always chuck it out the window.'

I am standing in Luke's sitting room, surveying the blanket laid out with plates of fajitas, bowls of shredded chicken and guacamole, along with some bright red salsa, all of which Luke has ordered from El Camino's, the new Mexican takeaway under the flyover.

'I'm impressed.' I take the bottle of ice-cold Dos Equis from Luke's fingers. 'Even though you didn't make it yourself.'

Luke laughs and kisses me on the mouth. 'This is about as domestic as it gets with me.'

He's wearing his faded Levi's and a sweatshirt advertising the Stinkers Truck Stop, a bar in LA that he used to go to. As usual, he's not wearing any shoes around the flat, just a pair of woolly blue socks.

'I missed you today,' he says, folding his arms tightly around me.

'But we only saw each other this morning,' I smile.

'Twelve hours is way too long. You need to quit work.'

'You're full of smart ideas. You should patent them sometime.'

Luke laughs then skids over in his socks to his iPod dock on top of the television. He scrolls up and down the small screen, frowning with concentration.

I sip my beer and watch him trying to pick a song. A

fantasy starts to unroll in my mind, of us living together some ten, fifteen years down the line, me making dinner and Luke providing the tunes, still making each other laugh, still finding each other sexy and still believing that what we have together is never going to end.

I've been indulging in fantasies a lot recently and it's a bit of a new thing for me. I haven't tended to do it with previous boyfriends, mostly because I could never see it lasting beyond a few months. But with Luke it's different. I'm completely smitten and I want it to last a lifetime.

Of course, I haven't told Luke this yet. It's been barely two months and I don't want to scare him off. At the same time it's becoming increasingly difficult to keep it to myself.

'Found it,' says Luke triumphantly, pressing the volume button on the iPod dock. Music blasts from the speakers and I can't help grinning when I hear what he's selected – it's from the soundtrack to *Taxi Driver* – 'The days do not end.'

We've finished the Mexican picnic and are lying back on the sofa. The sounds of Portobello Road filter up through the window: some girls calling out to a friend to meet at the Castle for a pint; a snatch of Otis Reading from the bar opposite; the hum of traffic from the Westway.

I glance over at Luke.

'Are you happy?' I ask.

'Very,' says Luke.

'Me too,' I say. I take a deep breath, trying to slow my thumping heart. 'And I know we've only been seeing each other for a few weeks, but I need to say something…' The beer is making it a little easier, but the words still snag in my throat.

'I'm falling in love with you, Luke,' I say, 'and I need to know if—'

Luke doesn't even give me the chance to finish my sentence. He grabs me by both arms, his fingers digging through my jumper into the flesh.

'Isn't it obvious? I'm crazy about you.' He pulls back and stares me straight in the eye. 'This is for keeps, Hannah. Now I've found you, I'm not letting you out of my sight – so you'd better get used to it.'

*

I shake my head as if I can somehow dislodge the memory, forcing it back beneath the surface. But that memory, along with all the others, can no longer be contained. It's as if the last two years of suppression has only made them more powerful.

I stand up and walk into the kitchen.

'Joe?' I say. I'm not sure how I'm going to continue, but I'm determined to try and explain why it's so hard to tell him how I'm feeling.

'Yes?' says Joe.

I take a step towards him, just as a ringing sound comes from his pocket.

'Sorry.' He takes out his mobile, checks the number then answers it. 'Hi Nadia,' he says and turns away slightly.

Chapter 14

'Your mind is a magnet, so use it!' says Judy the facilitator in the camel-coloured slacks and matching silk shirt. 'Whatever you focus on, you will attract.'

I stare up at the large crack in the ceiling above me. It's just gone ten o'clock on Tuesday morning and I'm sitting on a grey chair in a hotel conference suite, listening to Judy, whose recent book *Abundance Mentality* is the new hot ticket in the world of 'Mind, Body and Spirit'.

'Any scientist will tell you that similar energy is drawn to similar energy,' says Judy to the fifteen journalists in attendance. 'You attract into your life what you think about and this applies to both positive and negative. So if you focus on the lack of something in your life – money, love, health, etc. – you will only experience more of that lack. If you focus on what you *do* have, however small you may think it is, more of that will flow to you.'

Since Sunday lunchtime I've been thinking almost exclusively about Joe and his telephone conversation with Nadia and how they are probably going to get back together again.

'Abundance is your birthright,' says Judy, who has certainly deployed abundance mentality when it comes to her jewellery. She's heaving with the stuff – a gigantic tortoiseshell necklace, several matching tortoiseshell bracelets, brown and orange disc-shaped earrings and assorted onyx rings.

'The trick,' says Judy, smoothing down a non-existent crease in the left leg of her slacks, 'is to remember a time when you felt healthy, happy, successful... or whatever it is you are desiring, and then to recreate that feeling in your body. This will align your energy to attract even more of that.'

I'm distracted by the clatter of wheels. It's the catering trolley – arriving a little prematurely, to judge from Judy's frown. I've not eaten since yesterday lunchtime and I twist my head to scan the contents. Clearly Judy is using the same catering company that Scottish Graham used for his Mindfulness workshop, which was held in the adjoining conference suite. I already know the score: the croissants, the sickly custard pastries and the dreary brown biscuits.

I count the croissants. Eight between sixteen people! That's just rubbish. No one's going to want those horrid pastries filled with curdled custard. And the cheap-seat biscuits might as well be binned immediately. Either Judy is penny-pinching (thus negating this entire workshop) or the catering company has cocked up. Either way, come breaktime I'm going to have to peg it to the refreshments table.

'A final tip for this first session,' says Judy, 'is to give away what you want. You desire more money? Be generous! Want people to appreciate you? Appreciate them first! Long for love? Give love away!' She checks her watch and nods towards the refreshments table, telling us we have fifteen minutes.

I launch myself up from the chair and march – as casually as possible – towards the refreshments. I'm almost there when the woman from *Holistic Health*, our main in-store rival, intercepts me.

'Wasn't that amazing?' she says.

'Not now,' I say.

I've finally elbowed my way to the croissant plate. There's only one left. I reach towards it, but another hand clanking with tortoiseshell bracelets shoots forward. I remember Judy's last tip for the session. Covet that last croissant? Then give it away!

Nice try, dearie, I think, then I snatch up the croissant, pop it onto one of the paper plates and give Judy a big fat abundant smile.

I board the No. 7 bus back to the office, and despite my efforts to follow Judy's advice, the entire journey is taken up with thinking about Joe and Nadia.

Standing a few feet away from him in his small flat, I'd heard almost every word of their conversation. The first part focused on Maya and practical stuff: Would Joe be able to give Nadia that month's money on time? Did he know that Maya had developed an allergy to nuts? Was he aware that on Fridays she finished school an hour later now? After that, they talked about an exhibition that Nadia was having, and that was when Joe's voice softened.

'We should try again for that coffee,' he suggested. From the other end of the phone I heard Nadia agree.

'OK then, Lisboa's café it is. What time?' There was a pause. 'No, I won't be late. Promise,' said Joe.

After he'd hung up, Joe didn't elaborate on their conversation, and we sat down at the small table by the window overlooking All Saints Road to eat the chili con carne.

'Everything alright?' I asked.

'Aha,' said Joe, then he pointed down at his plate. 'Hot enough for you?'

I nodded. 'So when will you see Maya next?'

'This Friday.'

'That's brilliant.' Joe didn't usually get to see Maya every week but this was the second Friday in a row. 'Maybe Nadia's relaxing a bit.'

'Maybe,' said Joe. Then he put down his fork and placed his hand over mine. 'So,' he said with a smile, which looked distinctly forced to me. 'What shall we do this afternoon?'

It's normal that Joe and Nadia are going to see one another, I keep repeating to myself as the bus crawls past Regent Street. That's what people do when they have a child together. Besides, it's only a coffee, what can happen over a coffee?

My mind, of course, has plenty of ideas about what could happen over a coffee. At first, it would all be polite, almost formal, with Joe and Nadia sitting opposite each other in Lisboa's, to discuss their daughter. But then Nadia would do something like brush a stray hair from her eyes or suck her teaspoon, and suddenly Joe would remember the first time he saw her do that and how it made him feel. After that, it'd be as easy as dot to dot; Joe would take her hands in his and tell her how much he missed her, Nadia would reach over to stroke his face – and before they've even finished their coffees, they'd be kissing and saying how stupid they were for throwing it all away.

I'm so caught up imagining Joe and Nadia getting back together that I miss my stop and have to double back on myself. When I finally walk into the office, Ian is frowning at his computer screen.

'We've got a problem with the print edition.' He swivels his chair to face me. 'The layout guys say there are still two empty pages and they need to be filled by midday.'

'Shit.' I thought I'd already wrapped up this issue. Now my mind is so full of Joe and Nadia that I can't think of one health and wellbeing topic.

'You could always do some more product reviews,' says Ian.

'Good idea.' I drag open the shop drawer and stare down at the jumble of promo stuff we've recently received. But I'm so exhausted from a shoddy night's sleep that everything just blurs into one big spelt bar.

'Need some help?' says Ian.

'Please.'

Ian surveys the shop contents for a few seconds then pulls out one of the relaxation CDs and sticks it into the player. An American woman's voice with a West Coast accent whispers from the speakers.

'Relax and dive into a lake called you...' I let it play for a few seconds, then I press eject, toss the CD back into the drawer and jot down a few words from the CD review stash (soothing, calming, inspiring, etc., etc.).

Next, Ian pulls out what looks like a giant silver metal spider on a silver stick. 'What's this?'

'It's an Indian head massager.' I set it on top of my head and press so that the metal legs scrape down the sides of my scalp. I assume some people like having their heads scraped up and down by a giant metal spider. But I don't. It makes me feel weird.

'You try,' I say and hand it to Ian.

Ian places it on top of his own head, pushes it down then pulls it up again. He does this a couple of times until his hair goes static and sticks to the spider legs.

'That feels quite nice.'

'Freak.' I say. 'Well, it's yours if you write the review.'

Ian takes his pad and scribbles down a few words, then reads them back to me. It's not bad at all. I take a picture of the Indian head massager with the office digital camera and e-mail it over to Ian, who's now sifting through the shop again. He pulls out a pack of three white candles.

'Hopi Indian candles,' I say. 'You stick them in your ear, light them and they draw out the toxins – allegedly.' I pat the desktop.

'You want me to play guinea pig?'

'Yep.' I set my napping pillow, aka the exfoliation glove, on the desk. 'If you liked the head massager, you're going to love this.'

We don't have much success with the Hopi Indian candles, probably because we're not doing it right, but I still manage to knock off a pretty convincing review. After that, Ian and I do a little tasting – starting with some raw cacao snack bars (a bit stale from lying around for six months but still quite edible) and ending with some savoury roasted soya beans (very strange). This time Ian photographs the products while I whizz off the reviews.

An hour later, we're done (although Ian drew the line at reviewing the menstrual mooncup). We're just having a cup of coffee when his phone rings.

'What?' When?' he says into the receiver. 'How bad was it?' He continues talking for a few minutes, tugging on his fringe.

'What's happened?' I say after he's hung up. I wheel my chair across the carpet so I can sit next to him.

'That was Mum. My brother just had another fit,' says Ian. 'Matthew suffers from epilepsy on top of everything else.'

'Do you want to go home?'

Ian shakes his head. 'Mum said he's sleeping now. I'll take over when I get back if it's OK to leave a bit earlier.'

'Of course.'

'Fuck it!' There's a loud thump as Ian's fist slams down onto the desk and both his stapler and hole punch clatter to the floor. He takes several deep breaths and stares out of the window.

'Sorry,' he says a few moments later. He bends down to retrieve the stapler and hole punch. 'I love Matthew to bits, but I really resent it that he causes Mum so much worry.' He shakes his head. 'I know it's not his fault, but some days I even hate him, then I hate myself even more.'

I put my hand on his shoulder. 'You're only human. You're doing the best that you can.' I stay sitting there for a few moments with my hand resting on his shoulder. Then I stand up and take his coat from the peg.

'Come on, I'm taking you for lunch.'

After we've been to Luigi's, Ian says he'd like to go to St Martin-in-the-Fields for the lunchtime concert. There's a bench just outside the main door, so we sit down to the sound of violins tuning up in the church behind us.

'Are you OK?' I ask.

Ian nods and unwraps his cheese and pickle sandwich. 'Let's not discuss Matthew any more. Let's talk about you for a change.'

'What's to talk about?'

'Why you were looking so upset when you arrived this morning.'

I glance over at Ian's open face and kind eyes. I hadn't intended to tell him about Joe and his conversation with Nadia, because it sounds so trivial compared to what he has to deal with, but I do.

'What makes you assume that they'll get back together?' Ian asks when I've finished.

'The way he barely mentions her name, his tone at the end of their conversation, the fact they have a child together…'

'Yes, but surely they broke up for a good reason, otherwise they would have already got back together.'

'So you think I'm being paranoid?'

'Maybe a little,' says Ian. 'I'm hardly one to give advice but isn't trust quite an important part of a relationship?'

'That's the problem,' I say. 'I don't do trust very easily.' I unwrap my own sandwich.

'So you've never talked to Joe about any of this?'

I shake my head.

'What's the worst that can happen if you do?'

'He'll think I'm needy.'

'Needy? To tell someone how you feel?' Ian takes a mouthful of his sandwich and chews slowly. 'I think it's just the opposite.'

Behind us, the sound of violins and a cello drift through the open church doors. I recognise the melody immediately – it's the Ravel piece that Bernard used to play in the café.

*

March 2007

'I love this music,' I say. 'What is it again?'

Bernard, who's behind the counter assembling our order, smiles. 'Ravel's streeeng quartet in F major,' he says in his heavy French accent.

'*Le premier mouvement*,' says Victor from across the table. His eyes are shut and his fingers are moving lightly over the table's surface, tracing invisible notes. It's a week since he told me about Claudette and I'm itching to hear how the story ended. But I wait patiently until the record has finished and Bernard has delivered our drinks and cakes.

'What happened with you and Claudette?' I say when I have poured my tea from the china teapot printed with little yellow roses.

Victor looks over at me with a shake of his head, then stirs his coffee. After sampling a small forkful of his lemon tart, he starts talking:

'Following that night by the Pont Neuf bridge, I did not see Claudette for almost two weeks,' he says, 'and of course I could never tell her how I felt. So I decided to make her a film of all those places in Paris that she loved. It was a difficult film and took a great many hours to complete because I wanted the light in each shot to be perfect; the orchids in the glasshouses of the Botanical Gardens that exact shade of purple; the leaves on the trees around the Marché des Enfants Rouges the perfect orange; the waters below the Pont Neuf bridge at sunrise that shimmering gold.'

Victor stops talking and his eyes take on that slightly unfocused look as if he has slipped back in time and is wandering amongst his memories. It's a couple of seconds before he continues.

'The following Sunday afternoon I walked round to Claudette's apartment with the film and my cinematograph. When she opened the door, gone was the distraught woman from Bofinger restaurant.

'"Victor. How wonderful to see you!" Her face was flushed and she was wearing a silk dressing gown.

'"I have made you a film," I stammered. "But perhaps it is not the right time?"

'"It's a perfect time," she said, waving me inside. "How marvellous!"

'"You seem to be much better," I said.

'"I am," she smiled. "And I have you to thank." She ushered me into the sitting room.

'"Me?" I said, hardly daring to hope.

'"Yes! That night in Bofinger you told me how I didn't deserve to be betrayed. And do you know what? For the first time in my life, I believed it." Claudette picked up one of the two empty wine glasses on the glass table in front of her with a little laugh. "What sort of film have you brought?"

'"It is an homage to Paris," I said, "and an homage to…" I didn't have the courage to finish the sentence, so I pretended to be busy setting up the cinematograph.

'We were just pulling the couch over to face the wall when the doorbell rang. I prayed that Claudette would ignore it, or at least tell whoever it was to go away. But her expression indicated that she was expecting the caller.'

Behind the till Bernard is complaining loudly about a man tapping away on his laptop. To our right, a woman with bouffant peroxide hair is feeding her poodle with morsels of her chocolate éclair.

'Who was the caller?' I say. I've grown used to Victor's way of drifting off mid-story.

153

'His name was Philippe,' says Victor. 'And from the way he was standing next to Claudette with one hand around her waist and a bottle of wine in the other, it was evident that he was more than a friend.'

'What did you do?'

'I tried to make an excuse, to say that I would come back another time, but neither of them would allow me to leave. Instead, Philippe opened the bottle of wine and filled three glasses before joining Claudette on the sofa.

'There was nothing I could do but start the film and try not to look at Claudette, whose legs were now entwined with Philippe's.

'Standing behind them, rooted to the floor next to the cinematograph, I watched the images of Paris, the ones I had chosen so carefully, slide by until the closing shot of the Pont Neuf bridge at sunrise. Across that final frame I had written the words: "'Thank you for the best summer of my life'".'

Victor shakes his head and glances over at the white poodle, which is now licking its owner's plate.

'When the film finished both Philippe and Claudette applauded, then Claudette said what a dear man I was, and had she known I was coming round, she would have cooked enough dinner for three. It was how she said it that hurt most – as though I was a small child who had just played an amusing piece on the piano, but now it was finished, the grown-ups wanted some time to themselves.

'Suddenly I was able to move again. Without even looking back at Claudette or at my cinematograph, I raced to the front door and down the stairs. Out on the street, I ran all the way through the alleys of Montmartre to Pigalle, then on to the Marais until finally I reached the Pont Neuf bridge…' Victor takes another deep breath and I see that his hands are trembling.

'I do not know if I would have found the courage to jump because I never had the chance. A couple, who were walking past, saw me on the ledge of the bridge and dragged me back down onto the pavement. I cannot remember what I said to them, but two days later, it was all over the newspapers. It turned out that the woman was a journalist and thought it would make a good story.' Victor smiles wryly. 'You know how the French thrive on unhappy love stories. Through Truffaut's film company she had tracked down Claudette, who was happy to give her an interview. In it, Claudette said she hardly knew me, that I was just someone on the film set who she felt sorry for.'

There's a scraping of chair legs and the woman with peroxide hair stands up, tucks the poodle under her arm and teeters towards the till in high black shoes. Victor watches her for a second then looks back at me.

'Other papers picked up on the story and soon it seemed that everyone in Paris, from the ushers at the cinema to the waitress at my local café, knew about me. Someone even wanted to turn it into a film – a sort of modern-day *Hunchback of Notre Dame*.' Victor laughs but the laugh gets caught in his throat and he ends up coughing.

'I could not bear to stay in Paris any longer. So I came to London, imagining that because my father had been English, it would be the easiest place for me to go.' Victor contemplates his barely touched slice of lemon tart. 'But I think I was mistaken.'

We're both silent for a few minutes after he has finished speaking. When I stretch out my hand to place it on his arm, he brushes it away, almost roughly.

'Please, Hannah, never ever feel pity for me.'

*

I feel a nudge on my arm and hear Ian's voice at my side. 'You're miles away, Hannah.'

I pull my thoughts back from Bernard's café and look over at him.

'Are you diving into a lake called you?'

I smile. 'I am, actually. It's pretty shallow, though.'

Ian chuckles, but then falls silent and plucks at the material of his grey schoolboy trousers.

'You know, I'm not normally like this with girls.'

'Like what?'

'So relaxed.'

'That'll be those relaxation CDs.'

'I mean it.'

'You know what the next step is, of course – if you're so relaxed?' I say.

'What?'

'We get you to go on a date.'

'Who with?'

'I'm still trying to figure that one out. But you're such a great guy and you'd make a brilliant boyfriend.'

'Really?'

I grin. 'Really.'

I can see Ian is blushing again so I leave it there. We both lean our heads back against the warm stones of the church wall and listen to the soft fluid notes of the three violins and the cello float in the air around us. For the next five minutes or so, everything else falls away except for the music and the feel of the sun on my face. I can't help smiling. I glance over at Ian and see that he's smiling too.

Chapter 15

'Do I look presentable?' I ask Joe. We're standing on the steps outside his mum's flat, which is on the third floor of a tall white stucco-fronted house on Powis Square. 'No stains anywhere?'

Joe checks my outfit – a cream cardigan and a red skirt that I bought at the Saturday market yesterday. 'Nope, you're stain-free – and you look gorgeous,' he says, giving me a quick kiss.

I smile back up at him. Over the past four days I've been trying to take Ian's advice and not let my mind torment me with paranoid scenarios of Joe getting back with his ex. It's not been entirely successful but at least I'm trying.

'Hello, you two!' Joe's sister flings open the door, hugging first her brother then me. Linda is a lot smaller and rounder than Joe but has exactly the same eyes and the same wide grin. Her clothes – a silver glittery jersey and a pink skirt – are matched with an armful of sparkling bangles that clatter whenever she moves.

'At last I get to meet you.' She takes my hand and marches me down the corridor while she fires off a volley of questions. Where did I buy my skirt? Have I ever had callaloo before? Did I know that they filmed *Performance* with Mick Jagger in the basement of this house?

We enter the kitchen, which is small, yellow and smells of

sweet potato. Joe's mother is stirring a pan over by the cooker.

'Hello again, Hannah,' she says.

'Hello, Mrs Fuller,' I say, sounding like I'm in nursery school.

Joe and I lean against the sideboard while Linda sits up next to the sink and continues with the interrogation: why haven't I brought Nellie? Where do I get my hair cut? Have I been into H&M recently? There doesn't seem to be much logic to her questions, and my answers, when she pauses long enough for me to give them, have no bearing on the next question. It makes me want to fire off a few myself: how many grams of sugar does it take to make a Victoria sponge? How long is the gestation period of a hamster? Who won the FA cup in 1976?

But I like Linda. There's something contagious about her warmth and the way she laughs, throwing back her head so that her hoop earrings jangle in sympathy with the bangles. Rosemary, however, is a whole different ballgame. She has this way of peering at me over her gold-rimmed spectacles that makes me think a massive weeping boil is slowly forming on my forehead. This, of course, adds to my nervousness, and soon the Mentals have really kicked in. First I imagine myself hoisting my skirt above my hips and performing a lively rendition of 'Strip the Willow' around the kitchen, then I'm scooping up a fistful of sweet potato from the pan and flinging it at Rosemary's face, and finally I'm sinking to the floor, gabbling high-pitched filth in an *Exorcist* devil-voice.

'You look flushed,' says Joe, holding a palm to my cheek. 'I hope you're not coming down with the flu.'

'No, no,' I say, 'just a bit hot in my woolly cardy.'

Lunch takes place next door in the sitting room on a round table by the window. Almost every surface apart from the dining table is covered with photographs: Joe on stage as a child bowing in biblical robes; Linda, who's a nursery school teacher, with a group of little children all jumping in the air; Joe receiving his lawyer's degree. At the end of the main mantelpiece, half-hidden by the picture in front, is a photograph of Joe holding a baby, and on his left, wearing his blue sweatshirt, is a woman with short dark hair.

I stare at Nadia's delicate face, at Joe's left arm looped protectively around her shoulders and at their heads bent low while they gaze at their daughter with joyous expressions. Nadia is smaller than I'd imagined and is wearing boyish jeans and trainers, which means my stereotypical picture of her as a curvy, long-haired Spanish beauty has to be revised once again.

Maybe it would be better if I knew nothing about her. Then at least I wouldn't spend so much time stitching together and embroidering every little piece of information that I've gleaned from Joe. When, for example, he mentioned that he and Nadia had been to Havana together, there she is with her lustrous black hair, drinking mojitos at Hemingway's favourite haunt; his casual comment about her recent art exhibition results in a whole montage in which Nadia is surrounded by admirers salivating over both her talent and her luscious Mediterranean looks; even their fights, which Joe said were pretty messy, become full-scale cinematic extravaganzas in my mind, filled with tempestuous head tossing, plate throwing and passionate post-argument love-making.

No, Hannah, I think as I study the photograph, don't let your mind torture you. Of course they are going to look happy. They've just had a baby together. But that was five years ago and things have changed since then.

'Have some more.' Linda is passing me the plate of fried dumplings stuffed with callaloo. 'This is Dad's recipe. Mum doesn't usually do traditional food but I begged her to make it today,' she grins, 'it reminds me of being a kid again.'

I take a second dumpling to be polite. I've just popped it in my mouth when Rosemary asks me what I do for a living.

I push the doughy lump into the far corner of my cheek, so I can reply.

Me? I say. Mostly drugs. Crack's my biggest seller at the moment, but of course there's always the soft stuff, E and weed, for the kids...

...Oh, didn't Joe tell you? I'm a high-class hooker. It's a hoot and the money's fantastic...

...Well, I used to be a female cage fighter, but I've just been taken on by one of the world's largest vice rings, so that's exciting, isn't it?

The imaginary answers to Rosemary's question are limitless, but eventually I manage to get something half-sensible out.

'Do you enjoy working for the magazine?' asks Rosemary.

'It's OK,' I say, 'for now.'

'At least it's a proper job.' Rosemary twists in her chair towards Joe. 'So how are your jobs going?'

'Good, thanks for asking.'

'Still dog-walking?' Rosemary has stopped eating and her arms are crossed over her chest – not an easy move, considering.

'Let's not talk about that now,' says Joe.

Linda is watching him carefully.

'Why not?' says Rosemary.

'Because it always ends in an argument.'

'Are you surprised? When you don't even have enough money to pay the maintenance.'

'Mum, it's none of your business,' says Joe evenly.

Rosemary's hand thumps down onto the table. 'Of course it's my business. She's my first granddaughter, Joseph.'

Joe pushes back his chair, grabs the water jug and marches into the kitchen.

Through the gap in the sliding doors I can see him standing at the sink, head bowed and hands gripping the edge. A few moments later Linda follows him, and after she's pulled the sliding door shut behind her, I can hear the two of them talking in raised voices. From their conversation it sounds like Linda lent him the money to pay Nadia that month's maintenance, but by mistake she'd let it slip to their mother.

'So where do you live, Hannah?' asks Rosemary as if nothing has happened.

'In Brent.'

'North or Central?'

'Errr, Central, I think?' I say, unaware that Brent was divided into two.

'Who's your MP?'

'Sarah Teather?'

'She's Central. What do you think of her?'

'I haven't made my mind up quite yet.' I'm hardly going to admit that I know almost nothing about Sarah Teather, except that she's Lib Dem.

'So you agree with all of her policies?'

'Like I said, I'm still undecided.'

Rosemary wipes her mouth carefully with her napkin. 'Do you know how many MPs there currently are in Parliament?'

I gulp.

'Have a guess.'

'Umm… three hundred?'

'Three hundred?'

'Give or take.'

'Six hundred and fifty, Hannah. And do you know how many of those candidates are women?'

I play it safe and shake my head.

'One hundred and forty-five,' says Rosemary. 'That's twenty-two per cent to represent fifty-two per cent of this country's population.'

'Crikey,' I say.

'And of those what percentage of those do you think are black or from an ethnic minority?'

'I wouldn't like to say.'

'Go on, have a try.'

'Fifteen per cent,' I say tentatively.

'Fifteen per cent?' Rosemary bursts out laughing.

'Ten?' I'm really panicking now.

Rosemary wipes the tears from her eyes. 'Now that's funny.' Her expression suddenly turns serious. 'four per cent.'

Suddenly I feel my legs propel me from my seat and up onto the table, from where I begin shouting hysterically. Back off, bitch. Can't you see I haven't got a fucking clue about politics? I know all of this stuff is really important, but the sad fact is, I only know that Sarah Teather is my local MP because I remember the campaign posters in people's windows. So if it wasn't for those, who knows what my answer would be? Zeinab Badawi? Judy Finnigan? Fearne Cotton?

Only that's not quite what happens. What happens is that I grab my glass of water, take a drink, slop half of it down my skirt and end up with a soaking crotch – just as Joe and Linda emerge through the sliding doors.

Lunch has finished and we're all back in the kitchen where Linda is washing up while Joe and I dry and Rosemary puts the clean plates away. The argument seems to have blown over and Joe is asking his mother if she's ever tried Chinese water torture as a way of getting people to vote Labour.

'I only tease you because I love you, Mum,' he says, kissing her on the cheek.

Rosemary snatches Joe's cloth from his hands and flicks it at him. 'You don't get round me that easily.'

I watch them laughing together and smile. I love the fact that they are so open and demonstrative with each other – and the fact that their relationship is clearly the polar opposite of the relationship Luke had with his own mother.

*

'It's my mother.' Luke is peering out of his window onto Portobello Road. 'What the hell is she doing here?'

I sit up in bed and rub my eyes. It's eleven o'clock on Sunday morning in mid-March and the doorbell has been ringing for about five minutes.

'Aren't you going to let her in?' I'm curious about Luke's mother. He rarely mentions her, and all I know is that she and Luke's dad live in East Sussex and she used to be a nurse.

Luke pulls on his jeans with a sigh. 'If I let her in, she'll never leave.' He grabs his jacket and his wallet and heads downstairs. 'We'll be in Mike's caff over the road. Join us if you want.'

I leave it about twenty minutes before I join them. Luke's mother is nothing like I expected. She's dressed in a dark blue raincoat and her grey bobbed hair looks like she's just come from the hairdressers. She's fiddling with the glass of orange juice on the table in front of her.

'This is Hannah,' says Luke when I approach the table. 'Hannah, my mother, Eileen.'

'I'm so pleased to meet you.' Eileen jumps up, but knocks over the orange juice and it splashes down her raincoat. I fetch some napkins.

'I was just visiting my sister in Kentish Town,' she says when she's wiped off the worst of the stain and sat down again. 'I thought I'd make a detour.' She turns to Luke. 'We don't get to see you very often these days, do we?'

I order a coffee and Eileen and I chat about Portobello Road and how much it's changed in the past ten years. There's something very sweet about her and I can't see why Luke is making such a fuss.

'We need to make a move,' says Luke after about half an hour. 'Hannah and I are going to Dungeness for the day.'

I look over at Luke. We weren't planning to leave till after lunch.

Luke picks up his phone from the table. 'But like I said, I'll call you later.'

'You always say that,' says his mother. There's nothing accusatory about her tone, just a sad resignation.

We arrive in Dungeness at two o'clock. It's a strange apocalyptic landscape that backs onto the beach, full of derelict shacks, old railway carriages and broken-down cars. Behind us the power station glows eerily beneath the pale March sun.

After egg and chips at the railway café, we visit Derek Jarman's house, a black clapperboard cottage whose shingle garden is filled with sculptures of driftwood and scrap metal. Then we head down to the beach. Luke has bought his old Super 8, so while he films the black and white striped lighthouse in the distance, I lean against the hull of an abandoned boat and read.

'I love this place.' Luke throws himself down beside me a few minutes later. 'It reminds me of the South West.' He picks up a stone from the shingle and skims it into the water. It bounces away, barely touching the surface.

'It's always been my dream to ride through Louisiana on my bike.' He says with a sigh. 'So many places, so little time.'

I glance over at him and feel the creep of dread as I often do when he talks about wanting to travel. Not for the first time does it occur to me that I've fallen in love with a younger version of my father.

'Where else do you want to go?'

'Arizona, Utah, New Mexico... I'd take off on the bike and just see where I ended up.'

I pick up a smooth round stone and aim it at the water's surface, but it does just one miserly bounce before sinking. 'Would you have room for passengers?' I ask.

Before Luke can answer, his mobile beeps with a message. He stares at it, frowns, then presses delete with a swift stab of his thumb.

'I had coffee with her this morning, what more does she want?'

'Why don't you want to see your mother?' I ask. His behaviour reminds me of my own infrequent visits to see Mum and I feel a momentary pang of guilt.

'What's the point? We have nothing in common.' Luke stares out at the water. 'Still, at least she didn't bang on about me getting a wife and two-point-four kids like she usually does...' He mimes holding a handgun to his temple. Then he leaps up and takes his small Nikon from his jacket pocket.

'Photo time.' He lines up the shot before propping the

camera on the boat's splintered bow. Then he lifts me to my feet and positions me in front of him, his arms tightly around me. Seconds after the camera has made a sharp click, the sun falls behind the power station and a long thin shadow stretches down the beach almost reaching our feet.

*

Joe and his mum are still chatting in the kitchen while Linda and I have moved next door with our coffee. She's been asking me about Nellie, saying that she's always wanted a dog. I'm about to reply and tell her that Nellie's not great with small children when I hear Rosemary's voice from the kitchen.

'I spoke to Nadia this morning. She said you two had a good talk on Thursday.'

'We did.' I hear Joe reply.

'So what happens now?'

'Would you ever have puppies from her?' says Linda.

My answer to Linda's question, that one Nellie in this world is quite enough, means that I miss both Joe's answer and Rosemary's next question, so I only hear Joe's reply.

'I hope so, Mum,' he says. 'I can't afford to blow it a second time.'

Chapter 16

'You look terrible.' Ian swings round in his chair to face me when I enter the office the following Tuesday morning. 'What's happened?' He didn't come into work yesterday because he was taking his brother to a hospital appointment.

I dump my bag on my desk and sit down hard in my chair. 'Not much – apart from the fact that Joe is getting back with his ex.'

Ian frowns. 'Are you sure?'

'Yep.' I take the final gulp of the double-shot coffee I bought on the way and repeat what I heard through the sitting room wall.

'So you didn't hear the entire conversation?'

'As good as.'

Ian sighs. 'And you didn't talk about it afterwards with Joe?'

'What's the point?' Besides, even if I'd wanted to, I didn't get the chance because Joe's early evening shift at the Paradise started as soon as we'd left his mum's.

'Don't you think you might have got the wrong idea?' asks Ian.

I shake my head.

'But you'll never know until you ask him face to face.'

I switch on my computer and stare at the blank screen. 'I already know what his answer will be, Ian. Trust me, it's happened before.'

There are a couple of five hundred word articles outstanding for the website ('Is krill the new kale?' and 'Beat the Bloat'), but I just can't face them. Instead I let my mind gnaw away at the previous afternoon like a dog on a rotten bone. The relentless looping of my thoughts only stops when I hear my phone ringing.

I know it's Joe from the number displayed but I don't pick up. Instead I sit there, staring at the flashing red light and rehearsing in my head what I'll say when I finally find the courage to speak to him.

'I need distracting,' I say to Ian when the phone is silent again. 'I can't bear being in my head any more.'

Ian pulls his paper from his rucksack and hands it to me. I flick listlessly through a few pages looking for the jobs section, but on page five there's an advert for *Guardian* Soulmates.

'I've got a better idea,' I say. 'We're going to set you up for internet dating.'

'No, we're not.' Ian doesn't bother to look away from his screen, where he's working on a new design for the website's Healthy Eats section.

'Please. It's for my mental health.'

Ian sighs loudly. 'If that's what it takes to keep you quiet. But don't think that I'm going on any dates.'

I log onto the website and we start with the physical stuff – Ian's age, height, hair colour, etc., then we move on to his character.

'So how would you describe yourself?'

'Shy?'

'We'll need more than that. How about kind, generous, funny…?' I type the words and they pop up on the screen.

Ian blushes.

168

'Come on, you're going to have to work with me here. What are your passions?'

'Cooking and photography, as you know.'

'Anything else?'

'I like watching stand-up comedy.'

'Good. What about books?'

'Mostly sci-fi.'

'Geek.'

Ian laughs. 'Oh, and the comics, of course.'

'Super-geek.'

We complete the profile, listing music and food preferences, then I press save and turn towards Ian. 'Now for the close-up.' I pull the office camera out from the drawer.

Ian gulps.

'Come on, it won't take a second. Let's have you by the window.' Ian shuffles over to the window and leans stiffly against the glass. I put the camera to my eye and line up the shot. Then I put it down again.

'The light's against us and...' I pause, 'don't take this the wrong way, Ian, but can we do something with your hair?'

'What's wrong with my hair?'

'It's just the spiky shark's tooth thing. I'm not sure it's the most flattering look for you.'

'What would you suggest?'

'Something a bit more relaxed.'

Ian puts his head upside down and musses his hair. He straightens up. 'Any better?'

'Totally.'

Ian's face splits into a grin. 'So where do you want me if the window's not good?'

'Naked on the desk next to the hole puncher? The chicks will really dig that.'

'Ha ha,' says Ian.

It's almost one o'clock by the time we finish uploading Ian's profile and picture. We eat our sandwiches in Luigi's because it's drizzling, and afterwards I head off to Charing Cross Road to buy Megan a belated birthday present. In the window of Zwemmer's, the art bookshop, I spot a book about early Renaissance artists. On the front is a painting of Tobias and the angel. The angel is twice the height of Tobias and dominates the picture – its two wings spread out behind it like a magnificent canopy made from bright red feathers.

*

April 2007

'This was my favourite picture in the exhibition.' Victor is pointing to the second page of his catalogue. 'It was painted by an artist called Andrea del Verrocchio.'

'It's glorious,' I say and bend forward across the café table to study the Archangel Raphael's fiery red wings as they fan over the smaller figure of Tobias.

'I try to see all the National Gallery exhibitions,' says Victor. Then he pauses for a second. 'Perhaps you would like to accompany me one day?' he says shyly.

It's two weeks since he told me the final part of his story with Claudette and something has shifted in our friendship. There's a new level of trust, and Victor no longer needs my prompting to open up about what he does when he's not working. He tells me about his weekend trips to museums and galleries and the French food shops in South Kensington; the books he loves to read (mostly French romantic writers –

Dumas, Rousseau and Hugo) and the concerts he likes to attend (mainly chamber music and choral). I now realise what a rich inner life he has.

Because Victor has been so honest and vulnerable with me, over the next few weeks I find myself more able to discuss those things I usually keep hidden away. I admit to him that I too had never imagined my life turning out like this, that I used to believe that with luck and perseverance I'd find a job which I actually enjoyed and a man with whom I could fall in love. But as the years passed and the prospects of finding either were shrinking around me, whatever faith and optimism I once felt was slowly being replaced by a creeping cynicism.

Just like our visits to Monsieur Henri's cinema, there's no formal agreement to what becomes our Sunday ritual. But starting the next weekend, we meet at a different location, alternately chosen by each of us, on the last Sunday of each month. In April we wander along the Serpentine, stopping at the clock tower café to admire my favourite bridge and the pleasure boats that drift on the dark green water beneath it. In May we visit Brick Lane market, sampling Malpua pancakes dripping in syrup. In June we walk through the Chelsea Physics Garden amongst rows of medicinal herbs grown for the nearby hospital. July sees us heading for Tooting Bec lido, with its brightly painted changing rooms and ninety-metre pool. In August we laze on the sun-scorched grass by Kenwood House and listen to a single piano performing Ravel's *Miroirs* at dusk. In September we take a trip to Keats' House to admire the garden's plum tree from which the famous nightingale sang each morning.

During the winter months we tend to stay inside. At the

National Maritime Museum we pore over parchment maps of the stars drafted by ancient astrologers. We study the intricate circuitry of the brain at the Wellcome Collection and we gaze at the works of the Italian Renaissance painters in the National Gallery.

I look forward to these Sunday outings more and more. Just like the Monday night films, they act like a beautiful painting slipped between the grey canvas of workday routine, or a line of poetry squeezed into the dull text of everyday life. I find myself remembering how I felt as a child when cynicism hadn't yet stained the landscape, and slowly, almost imperceptibly, I feel the wonder I once had for this strange and beautiful world returning.

*

Inside Zwemmer's I immediately find something for Megan – a book on the eighteenth-century sculptor, Messerschmidt. I pay for it and walk back to the office. Ian is sitting at his desk, eating a post-lunch Snickers bar and reading one of his Silver Surfer comics. I decide to ring Mum on her mobile while she's taking her lunch break.

'Hello, darling,' she says when she hears my voice. 'I was just thinking about you.' She tells me that she's in Chorleywood bakery, having a sandwich.

'You used to take me there when I was young,' I say. 'We'd eat Chelsea buns and drink hot chocolate. Do you remember?'

'Of course I do,' says Mum. 'I haven't gone gaga quite yet. How are you, Hannah?'

'I'm OK.'

'You sound a little down, darling.'

'It's just boyfriend stuff.' My answer takes me by surprise.

I've not mentioned a boyfriend to Mum since I was about sixteen.

'Would it help to talk about it?' The concern in her voice makes my throat tighten.

'I can't right now because I'm a bit behind at work,' I say, 'but thank you.'

'You can ring me anytime,' she says. 'I'm a good listener.'

We continue chatting for a few minutes, then Mum says she needs to get back to work, but we can talk again tomorrow if I want.

I put the phone down. The combination of Mum's kindness and a sleepless night make me feel like crying.

'Take this.' I hear Ian saying next to me. He pulls a handkerchief from his pocket.

'Thanks.' I quickly wipe my eyes then hand it back to him. 'I don't know what's wrong with me,' I say, 'I never cry.'

Ian rests his hand gently on my shoulder. 'You should. It's good for you,' he smiles. 'So when are you going to have that talk with Joe?'

I tell him that I've decided to do it when I see him tomorrow night after a book reading that his friend Caitlin is giving.

'Promise?'

'Promise.'

After work I head over to Megan's place, which is just three streets away from the Paradise. When I arrive she's in the kitchen, and Billy is stretched out on the sofa with a beer, watching television. Nellie's next to him with her eyes closed and her chin resting on his stomach. I bend down to ruffle the fur on her back and she does her one-eye-open thing while giving me a lazy half-grin.

Billy pats the small space next to him after I've kissed him hello. 'Take a pew, Hannah. *Place in the Sun.* Majorca.'

'No, she's chatting to me while I make supper,' says Megan over her shoulder as she heads towards the kitchen. 'We want to talk about tampons, so no men allowed.'

I follow Megan into the kitchen where I give her my present, which is wrapped in the spring edition of *Health and Wellbeing.* She rips it off like a small child and stares down at the book, whose front cover features one of Messerschmidt's famous head sculptures.

'For someone who knows bugger all about art, that's a brilliant choice. Thank you.' She goes to hug me then pulls back at the last moment and we both laugh. We've never been the kind of friends that hug each other.

'Did you have a good time in Wales?' I ask. She and Billy were in St David's staying at her mum's for her birthday.

'It was OK,' says Megan. 'But we couldn't afford to do much so we just hung around the house.' She spoons a final dollop of mashed potato onto the shepherd's pie and slides it into the oven. 'So how's it going with Joe?'

I pour two glasses of the Merlot that I brought with me. 'Honestly?'

'Of course.'

'Not brilliantly.' I haven't told Megan much about what's been happening with Joe, mainly because I get so tired of hearing myself repeating the same old stuff. But since she's asked, I explain about the conversation I overheard between Joe and his mother.

'I can't get it out of my head that he's going to get back with his ex.'

Megan eyes me over her glass. 'Confront him then.'

'Yeah, like it's that easy.' My voice drips with sarcasm.

174

'What's the alternative? You wait until he breaks your heart into tiny little pieces?' She takes another sip of wine. In the background I can hear Amanda Lamb enthusing about a two bedroom split-level apartment in Deia.

'I'm going to speak to him tomorrow,' I say.

'Good,' says Megan.

'Is it safe to get myself another beer?' Billy is standing in the doorway, grinning.

'Sure,' says Megan, swivelling round to face him. 'What's that – the fourth this evening?'

'Third actually,' says Billy. 'But I'm glad you're keeping tabs.' He laughs then bends down to kiss Megan on the forehead. 'Besides, I'm working this evening, so I'm allowed.'

Megan rolls her eyes, then turns to me. 'First gig in nine weeks. Wa-hay!'

Supper is ready and Megan, Billy and I squash down on the sofa, having relocated Nellie to the floor with her own bowl of shepherd's pie. We're playing one of the daft games that we sometimes play when we're together – this time we have to decide what songs we want played at our funerals when the casket disappears into the furnace.

'Disco Inferno,' I say.

'Feeling Hot, Hot, Hot,' says Billy.

'Hell Ain't No Bad Place To Be,' says Megan.

'The Heat Is On,' I say.

'Living In A Box,' Megan chips in.

'Loser!' Billy and I shout. 'That's a band, not a song.'

'It's both,' says Megan, sticking out her tongue. She jabs her fork victoriously in the air with a grin.

'You look beautiful when you gloat,' says Billy, leaning over to kiss her softly on the mouth.

I watch Megan return his kiss and smile. Despite their problems, there's more love between these two than any other couple I know.

'So when am I going to meet *your* new fella, Hannah?'

'Hmmm,' I say, 'there are a few teething problems to sort out first.'

'Like what?'

'He's got an ex and they have a child together.'

'He has a past. Who hasn't?' Billy shakes his head. 'Don't go creating problems where there aren't any, Hannah. That's what'll mess it up.'

After supper, Billy heads off to his deejaying slot at the Mason's Arms on Harrow Road, while Megan and I polish off a second bottle of red wine. Nellie is curled up in the corner on one of Billy's jumpers.

'Jesus,' says Megan. 'That dog snores like a lorry driver.'

I smile and twist around to watch Nellie. Her frilly pink gums are quivering and she's making little snuffly sounds.

'Buying her for me was one of the best things Victor did.' I say. 'Even when things got so bad afterwards, I wouldn't have done anything because I always had Nellie to think about.'

Megan glances sideways at me. 'You wouldn't let yourself get into that situation again, would you?'

'No,' I say. 'Never.'

'In which case,' says Megan, setting her glass firmly down on the table. 'Let's go and see what your man has to say for himself. Where is he?'

'What now?'

'Now.'

'He's at the Paradise. Probably not the best time to have a heart-to-heart. Besides, I said I'd do it tomorrow.'

Megan pushes herself up from the sofa. 'No excuses. We're doing it now.'

Twenty minutes later, Megan and I are standing by the main bar of the Paradise, after dropping off Nellie on the way. I was feeling three-glasses-of-Merlot brave before we left the house, but now I'm suddenly very unsure about pitching up here. The pub is jammed – there's a band on tonight in the upstairs room, where I've just been told that Joe is working.

'See?' I say to Megan. 'It's really not a good time.'

Megan says nothing but I can feel her hand in the small of my back pushing me towards the stairs.

There's a long queue of people at the top, waiting to get tickets. Megan marches straight to the front, while I hang back.

'My mate has to talk to the barman, so she doesn't need a ticket,' she says to the woman on the door. Then she grabs my hand and drags me forward so that I stumble into the music room.

I see Joe immediately, unloading glasses from the dishwasher behind the bar. He looks up.

'What are you doing here?' He leans over the bar and kisses me briefly on the lips.

'I wanted to see you.' Any residual red wine bravado has gone, but now I'm here, I can't just stand in silence. 'And I needed to say something.'

Joe nods to the queue of people outside. 'Better make it quick. The rabble's about to be unleashed.'

'It's about Sunday.' I stop and take a deep breath. 'When I was sitting with your sister, and you and your mum were—' There's a screech of feedback as the singer tests the microphone. I wait till he's finished, then start again. 'You and your mum were next door and I overheard you saying that—'

'Two glasses of house white, please.' The first customer, a woman in a fake leopard-skin jacket, has been let in and is standing at the other end of the bar.

'Be with you in a minute,' says Joe, before turning back to face me.

I force the words from my mouth. 'What did you mean when you said to your mother that you didn't want to blow it?'

'I thought this was a bar,' says the woman in leopard-skin, 'where people can buy drinks.'

'I'm coming,' says Joe. He mouths a sorry to me and walks down to serve the woman. I watch the lead singer tuning up his guitar as four more people from the outside queue rush through the doors.

'Two pints of Guinness,' shouts the bloke at the front.

I head down to the far end of the bar just as Joe is taking the change for the white wine.

'It's really not a good time, Hannah,' he says over his shoulder.

'Can you come round later?' I ask.

Joe, who's now pouring a pint of Guinness, shakes his head. 'I'm going to be knackered. Double shift and all.'

'What about before Caitlin's tomorrow night then?' More people have been let in and are jostling me from behind in their eagerness to get a drink.

Joe winces. 'I'm at Nadia's till six thirty.'

'What are you doing there?' The question shoots from my mouth before I can think.

'Err, looking after Maya.'

'Will Nadia be there?'

Joe cocks his head to one side. 'Why are you acting so weird?'

I take a deep breath. 'I just need to know if you still—' The band chooses that moment to launch into the first song, a raucous rendition of The Clash's 'Revolution Rock'. I can't possibly compete against three guitars and a full set of drums.

'Forget it,' I say, and burst into tears. 'Just forget it.'

Chapter 17

Caitlin's reading is in a small bookshop on Charing Cross Road, a couple of doors down from Zwemmer's. Joe and I have arranged to meet outside just before seven but he's not here yet so I go straight inside.

There are just two other people browsing the shelves – in the poetry section a woman wearing a large green necklace and in the classics a girl with a savagely cut black fringe reading Dorothy Parker. The air is musty and the dark wooden floorboards tilt markedly to one side which, when added to the tall oak bookcases and the low timber ceiling, give the feeling of being below deck on an old sinking ship.

I wander to the back of the shop, where the foreign books are kept, and my eyes skim the shelf marked with the letter H: Hafiz's *Odes of Hafiz*, Hesse's *Siddhartha*, Homer's *Odyssey*, and right at the end of the shelf a collection of Victor Hugo's poetry, *Les Contemplations*.

'If you're here for the reading, it's about to start,' says a woman from behind the till, so I make my way up the steep wooden staircase to the small room at the top. A man in a dusty green corduroy jacket points me to the few remaining free chairs in the first row, directly in front of the three authors.

Caitlin, who's first in line, is flicking through the pages of her book when I take my seat.

'OK, then,' she says, addressing the audience with a smile. 'You know how everyone always writes about how the Oirish love a drink and how boring that is? Well, I'm going to read a bit about...' she chuckles, '...a night on the piss in Dublin.'

Her reading opens with a woman standing in front of her wardrobe, trying to decide on an outfit for a date with a man she met the previous weekend. Having selected a thirties-style tea dress, tights and heels, she sets off for a pub in South William Street where they have arranged to meet. The first part of the evening goes well and the guy seems to be really into her. But then his ex turns up. Two hours and four large glasses of Sauvignon blanc later, after a misunderstanding with the ex-girlfriend, things aren't looking quite so rosy. The evening ends with a long walk home, a lavish vomit in a bush and a drunken telephone call to her date, in which he tells her she needs help, but unfortunately he's not the one to give it to her.

'Bet you can't guess who that story is about,' Caitlin finishes. She's answered by a round of boisterous clapping and catcalls from the audience, most of whom seem to be her friends.

I glance at the door behind me but it remains firmly closed so I resign myself to the fact that Joe isn't coming.

The second author, a man with pointy black suede boots and a Dalí-esque moustache, rises from his seat. He bows deeply before reading a piece about a guy who's turned into a giant penis, but who then discovers he isn't able to masturbate any more because he doesn't have any hands. Even if I'd wanted to, I wouldn't be able to concentrate because I'm too busy imagining what Joe and Nadia are doing at that moment... I can see each scene as clearly as if it was happening in front of me... the two of them sitting just a little too closely on the sofa together, the invitation to stay for supper, the bottle of wine, the kiss…

The man with the pointy boots has finished and sat down, grinning despite the reserved applause. I consider leaving but I'm stuck in the front row and the third author, a bald guy in a leather jacket, is already standing.

'Any of you ever been cheated on?' he asks, opening his book. Without waiting for an answer, he launches into a passage about a man standing in a Brighton phone box. On the wall in front of him are numerous cards for call girls offering full body massages and unlikely vital statistics, and at his feet is an empty packet of condoms. He's lost his mobile phone and is trying to call his girlfriend to say that he will be back a little later. He dials the landline of their flat because that's the only number he can remember. While the phone rings, he thinks about the first time they met, bumping against each other in a crowded Brighton pub. He smiles to himself, remembering his clumsy attempt to chat her up and how, just when he was about to admit defeat, she'd invited him to a party.

The phone continues to ring as the man recalls that first disastrous beef stroganoff supper he'd cooked for her, having failed to check if she was a vegetarian; those rocky few months when he lost his job; and now, after almost three years, the flat they had moved into the previous week. He grins, picturing the wrought iron bed from the Brighton flea market that was being delivered that afternoon. He's looking forward to christening it when he gets home.

His thoughts are punctuated with the silence between each telephone ring. Eventually he hangs up, trying to fathom where his girlfriend might be. A variety of possibilities flit through his mind, but there's one scenario that he doesn't contemplate – the one where she is fucking his best friend in the new wrought iron bed.

'Isn't it funny,' the author breaks off to gaze out at the audience, 'how we can know so little about the people we love so much…' He pauses then closes the book with a soft thud while my mind spirals back in time to another city and another bed.

*

'This mattress is buggered, Luke,' I say, shifting position to avoid yet another spring that's gouging into my lower back. 'When are you going to get a decent one?'

Luke and I are sprawled on his bed, eating pizza and watching Hitchcock's *North by Northwest*. It's a Sunday night in early April and rain is pattering against the windows.

Luke takes a swig from his bottle of Corona. 'It's not really worth it. I won't be here for much longer.'

My stomach lurches. 'What do you mean?'

Luke's eyes are fixed on Cary Grant, who's running through a dusty cornfield. 'The landlord's coming back in the autumn. He wants to move back in.'

'Oh, right.' I let out a breath. 'Do you know where you're going to live?'

Luke shrugs. 'Not yet.'

I take a swig of my beer – for courage. 'What about getting a place together?' I say. I watch his expression closely before adding, 'That way what we save on rent by sharing, we could put towards a few trips?'

Luke bites into his slice of pizza and chews slowly. 'Hmmm, maybe that's not such a bad idea.'

After a week of gentle persuasion and subtle reminders of what we could do with the extra money, Luke agrees. By that time I've already rung the local estate agent, so we start our search the following weekend, looking at places mainly round the corner from me in Kensal Green. Every Saturday afternoon we view three or four 'compact one-bedroom flats within easy reach of Portobello' (ahem!) and each time we're left feeling pretty dispirited. The places are either located above a Chicken Village or barely bigger than a biscuit tin, but they still cost around three hundred pounds a week, minimum. After six weeks of searching, I make another suggestion. Surely it would be better to buy somewhere, instead of throwing away a grand each month? Then, if we wanted to travel, renting it out would be a cinch. As for the deposit, I still had most of the money left by my dad, and since it was earning almost zero interest it made much more sense to put it into property.

Again Luke doesn't give me an answer straight away. He says he needs to think about it. He's still thinking about it two weeks later when we go to a party given by his boss. It's in a smart white four-storey house on Elgin Crescent, with waiters handing round plates of tempura prawns and cocktails made from sake and pomegranate juice.

We've been there for about an hour, chatting to some of Luke's work colleagues, when a man with curly black hair and a Sundance Film Festival T-shirt rushes up to Luke.

'Justin!' shouts Luke. 'What the fuck are you doing here?' The two men hug, slapping each other on the back and laughing.

'I haven't seen Justin since I was in LA,' says Luke, after he's introduced us, 'we did a couple of jobs together. The best AD in town.'

Justin smiles at me and shakes my hand before turning

back to Luke. 'Actually I'm back there again next week for another job.' He hesitates, then adds, 'I think Catherine's working on it as well.'

No one else would have noticed the momentary flicker in Luke's expression. It's only there for a second before he's grinning again.

'Great,' he says, slapping Justin on the shoulder. 'Say hi to her from me.'

'So who's Catherine?' I say when we're alone again. We're standing in the kitchen next to a vast chrome fridge where Luke has just found a stash of Asahi beers.

'Just a woman I went out with in LA.'

'How come you've never mentioned her before?'

'Probably because she's not a part of my life any more,' says Luke. He twists around to scan for a bottle opener.

'So how long were you together for?'

'Four years, on and off.'

'Wow, that's quite some time! When did you split up?'

'Last July,' says Luke, slotting the bottle opener onto the metal top of his Asahi.

'Two months before we met?'

'Something like that.'

'Oh,' I say, not sure how to react. It seems ridiculous that I don't know about such a recent ex-girlfriend of someone I want to spend the rest of my life with.

'So why did it end?'

'She's a nutcase and I got tired of being messed around.' Luke flips the bottle's top off with a jerk of his wrist and takes a long slug. 'You know what?' he says, slamming the bottle back down onto the table. 'Let's do it. Let's buy a place together.'

*

The Q & A with the authors has finished and the bookshop owner is giving a closing speech, thanking the writers for taking the time to do a reading in such a small venue and urging the audience to keep buying real books from real bookshops. We're just filing down the stairs into the shop below, when outside I see a figure sprinting down the street.

'I'm sorry,' Joe pants and leans against the window of the bookshop to catch his breath. 'Nadia didn't get back till past eight.'

'Shame,' I say. 'You missed a good reading. Caitlin was funny.' I try to keep my voice as casual as possible. I don't want a repeat of last night, so whatever I'm going to say will have to wait until we're on our own.

'You two lovebirds coming with us?' says Caitlin from the door of the bookshop. 'We're going to Bradley's bar for a drink.'

Joe and I follow Caitlin and her friends up towards Tottenham Court Road. The July night air is clammy, clinging to my legs and arms like damp muslin. We turn into Hanway Street and a snatch of flamenco music pulses towards us from one of the bars.

'Things were OK with Nadia?' I say.

'Yeah, fine.' Joe nods.

I wait for more, but nothing comes. He hasn't even mentioned the fact that I turned up half-cut at the Paradise yesterday, and burst into tears before running out.

'You're very quiet.'

'Just in another head space,' says Joe. He kisses me on the side of my temple as we enter the bar. 'Sorry, I'll snap out of it.'

Somehow we've all managed to squeeze into the small downstairs room. Joe is on my right beside a girl with blonde corkscrew curls and Caitlin is opposite us. The table is littered with bottles of San Miguel and David Bowie's 'Sweet Thing' floats down from the jukebox on the floor above. A waitress brings over a plate of Manchego cheese and someone stands up to take it, knocking over a bottle, just as a snatch of conversation catches my ear.

'Why weren't you at Nadia's on Saturday?' says the girl with the corkscrew curls to the guy next to her.

'I was out of town,' he says. 'Any good?'

'Great.' The girl helps herself to a piece of Manchego.

'Did you meet Daniel?'

The girl nods and finishes her mouthful before replying. 'I like him. I think he's good for Nadia and he adores Maya.'

I see Caitlin flash her a warning look.

'Who's Daniel?' says Joe, setting his beer down on the table.

A hush falls over the crowd.

'Who's Daniel?' Joe repeats, this time louder.

'Nadia's new boyfriend,' says Caitlin.

'Since when?'

'I'm not sure. You'll have to ask Nadia that,' says Caitlin gently.

'But you must know, you two talk all the time.' Joe's hand is gripping his beer bottle so tightly that the white bones of his knuckles gleam through his skin.

'Like I said, you should ask Nadia.' Caitlin's voice is calm but there's a visible flush to her cheeks.

Joe rises abruptly, letting the chair topple backwards behind him as he elbows his way through the crowd and storms towards the stairs.

Up on the street, Joe is standing by the open door of the flamenco bar opposite. One hand clutches his mobile to his ear and the other is balled into a fist. Having followed him up here, I wait in the doorway of Bradley's, unsure of what I should be doing at this moment.

'When I asked you earlier this evening, you said you were just friends.' Joe slams his fist against the wall. 'What the fuck do you mean, it's none of my business?'

I feel a hand on my shoulder and turn to see a man in a crumpled fedora, struggling to do up his flies. 'Where's the party?'

'I don't know,' I say, one eye still on Joe.

'Come on, pretty girls like you always know where the party is.' The guy thrusts a red, puffy face into mine.

'Please go away,' I say.

'You're not much fun, are you?' He shuffles off, just as Joe snaps his mobile shut and leans heavily against the wall.

'Joe?'

For a second, it seems like he doesn't recognise me.

'I'm sorry, Hannah. I've just had a bit of a shock.' He shoves his mobile back into his pocket.

'Do you want to talk about it?'

Joe levers himself off the wall. 'Not right now.'

'Are you coming back inside?'

Joe shakes his head. 'It's probably best that I go home. I don't want to ruin yours and everyone else's evening.' He puts both his hands on my shoulders. 'Honestly, I'm going to be crap company tonight.' His fingers squeeze my shoulders through my shirt. 'You go back in though, and I'll call you later this evening. OK?'

I nod. What else am I going to do – Beg him to stay? Follow him home? Plead with him to tell me the truth and admit that he's still in love with Nadia? I want to do all of these things, but I don't – I just stand there nodding, like the coward that I am.

Chapter 18

I stare at my reflection in the bathroom mirror. My eyes are swollen and red from lack of sleep and my head throbs so hard it feels like my skull is about to explode. I hold the cold flannel against my face and listen to the telephone ringing from the sitting room. Joe has called four times on both my mobile and landline since yesterday evening but I haven't picked up. I just can't face what I know he's going to say.

I've already rung Ian to tell him that I won't make it into work, at least not until this headache has gone. I open the bathroom cabinet, pull out some paracetamol and shake a couple into my hand. Behind me, I hear the door being pushed ajar and the soft pad of paws on lino. A nose nudges against my leg and I look down at Nellie's crumpled furry face.

'It's alright, Nell,' I say as much to myself as to her, 'I'll survive.'

I swallow two paracetamol and am just replacing the packet in the cabinet when something soft brushes against my fingertips. I peer inside but it's too cluttered to make out anything, so it isn't until I've removed a large wad of cotton wool that I see what it is – a bright red feather.

I stare at it for a good few minutes, trying to figure out how it could have found its way into my bathroom cabinet. When I finally pick the feather up, I place it in my palm, where it rests, light as a dream.

Looking at it, I suddenly feel an overwhelming urge to see Victor. My former reservations evaporate and I remember only his heartfelt invitation for me to visit him again, when I bumped into him outside Monsieur Henri's old cinema. Besides, although I'm not a great believer in signs (unlike Roz), even I can't put the feather down to pure coincidence.

Outside in the street, summer seems to have departed without warning, leaving a dull, faded Thursday afternoon. A jaundice-yellow sun hangs listlessly in the grey sky and the few trees in my cul-de-sac, which only two weeks ago were bursting with birdsong, now droop with exhaustion.

Nellie, however, seems far from exhausted as she trots perkily several paces in front of me.

In the distance I can hear the rumbling engine of a bus and I watch the No. 52 curve around the corner and pull into the bus stop.

Once on board we take the two front row seats on the top deck and the bus sets off up Chamberlayne Road. We pass the school with the car boot sale, and further down I see the entrance to Meanwhile Gardens, and I think of the afternoon that Joe, Nellie and I spent there just two weeks ago.

Nellie and I had never been to Meanwhile Gardens before. In fact I didn't even know it existed, so it was Joe who led the way past the walled rose garden and along the maze of little bridges to the large pond at the end. We sat on the wooden jetty, eating Hassan's pastries flavoured with rose water while Nellie chewed determinedly on a thick slice of Ramón's Jabugo ham. All around, wild flowers bloomed: bright red poppies swaying in the warm breeze; blue-tongued irises lolling over the water; purple foxgloves fizzing with bumble bees. Behind us, music spilled from the open windows of the flats in Trellick Tower: the sad lilting voice of Billie Holiday; the slow steady beat of Steel Pulse and Dizzee Rascal's 'Dirtee Disco'.

'I love the fact that they mate for life,' said Joe, pointing to two swans necking beneath the small willow tree.

'Isn't that just a myth?' I replied.

There was a short silence, filled by the sound of a moorhen calling up from the water.

Joe set down his half-eaten pastry. 'Were you always this cynical, Hannah?'

'No. It's taken years of practice.'

'It's just that sometimes…' he paused.

'What?' It was unlike Joe not to finish a sentence.

'It doesn't matter.' He shrugged and turned back to watch the swans, one of whom had broken away from its mate and was swimming towards the far end of the pond.

I watched Joe study the remaining swan and I wanted to tell him. Tell him that I hated being like this and that I'd do anything to believe it was possible for two people to love each other for a lifetime. But that part of me was broken and I didn't know how to mend it.

Just as well, I didn't say anything, I think as I stare out of the bus window. It wouldn't have made any difference.

'Last stop,' the conductor calls from below, and Nellie and I clamber down the stairs and step off the bus with the three other remaining passengers.

In daylight everything looks much livelier than last time. There's a lorry in the salvage yard unloading some Victorian fireplaces and the Brazilian café is full. A group of teenagers are chatting on their mobiles outside the hairdressers, while in the distance I can hear the Met line tube rattling past.

The urge to see Victor is still as strong by the time Nellie and I set off down the street. Above us, the sun has broken through the grey clouds, bringing a hazy light to the gardens on either side. Honeysuckle and jasmine froth over the walls and when we reach the video shop I notice a tree outside, which I didn't spot the previous time. From its branches hang creamy trumpet-shaped flowers that smell faintly of vanilla.

The door to the video shop is open, and inside I can hear Victor whistling one of the old Maurice Chevalier songs that Bernard used to play on his gramophone.

'Victor?' I call tentatively. 'I've brought an old friend to see you.'

Victor obviously hasn't heard so I call out again a little louder and step inside. He emerges from the foreign section around the corner, wearing a pair of jeans and a blue and white checked shirt, both of which have seen better days.

At the sight of him, Nellie hurtles towards his legs with a loud yelp.

'Hello, stranger,' says Victor and bends down to scratch her back. His hair is still uncombed and it's now tangled enough to house a small family of field mice.

I stand there watching the two of them, Nellie wagging her stump-tail from side to side in delight and Victor stroking her. Eventually he straightens up.

'I had hoped you might return a little sooner.'

'Sorry,' I say lamely.

'Never mind. You are here now.' He motions towards the back of the room, and seconds later, I find myself following him down the corridor and through the door on which is painted 'Cinema Lumière' in gold letters.

The tiny auditorium with the single red velvet seat is bathed in a gold glow from the little torch lights and the reflection of the wallpaper. There's music playing and I recognise Ravel's *Miroirs* from our evening together at Kenwood House.

The projectionist's booth is just as I remember – the shelves stacked with silver film reels, the brightly coloured bottles on the drinks cabinet and the shiny walnut wood of the cinematograph. The only difference is that there are two open cardboard boxes in the middle of the room.

'What made you come today?' Victor is standing beside the cinematograph, removing the film reel from its slot on the hub inside.

I open my mouth. 'I just wanted to…' Suddenly I can't hold it in any longer and I burst into tears.

Victor points to the two chairs and waits for me to sit down before taking the second one. Nellie flops down at his feet, watching us with her black button eyes.

'Start at the beginning,' he says gently.

So I do. I tell him everything: how when I met Joe, I was determined not to get involved; how that determination slowly dissolved the more time we spent together; and how I really wanted to believe that I had found a good, kind man. I end with the previous evening at Caitlin's book reading and Joe's outburst when he heard that his ex-girlfriend was seeing someone else.

'So that's the story,' I say. 'It's happened all over again.'

'And you are sure that he still has feelings for this woman?' says Victor.

'It's obvious.'

Victor shakes his head. 'Until you talk to him it is just a story based on your previous experience.'

'I may not be the smartest woman when it comes to relationships but even I...'

Victor holds up a hand. 'I know it is hard, Hannah, but you must stop dragging the past around with you.'

I shake my head. 'That's easy for you to say.' There's a spike of anger in my voice which I immediately regret.

'I'm sorry, Victor,' I say. 'I have no right to be telling you all this.'

Victor says nothing but hands me his handkerchief so I can blow my nose.

'Would you care for a drink?' He gestures towards the drinks cabinet. The words sound so old-fashioned, as though he's hosting a 1920s cocktail party, that I can't help smiling.

'I assume that is a yes,' says Victor, also smiling. He stands up and walks over to the cabinet, selecting the second bottle in the row.

'This one is for the heart,' he says and removes the cork. Then he pours the green liquid into two glasses, handing me one of them.

I take a tentative sip of what tastes like crème de menthe and feel the cool liqueur slide down my throat. Next to me, Victor swills the contents of his own glass around his mouth, before swallowing. Then he wipes the sticky green residue from his lips with his cuff and heads over to the shelves of film reels.

'Last time we met, I mentioned a film I had recently made. I would very much like you to see it.'

I hesitate. 'Is it anything like the first film?'

Victor shakes his head but holds my gaze. 'I think you will find it easier to watch.'

'OK then,' I say. Admittedly, watching a film isn't top of

my wish list – crawling under the duvet for several months is much more what I had in mind – but I don't have the energy to argue. Besides, at least it might give my head a rest. I'm so tired of thinking about Joe that anything is preferable at the moment.

'But first I have to do a little paperwork.' Victor points to the box nearest him, which contains about a dozen film cans. 'I need to register these films before they get mixed up.' He bends down to pick up one of the cans and examines the name printed in neat red letters on the side. Then he lays it carefully on the floor and pulls from his pocket a sheet of paper on which more names are written. After checking off the first name against the list with a small tick, he selects a second, then a third can from the box and repeats the process.

It's clear that he needs to concentrate, so I watch him quietly logging each film. On the side of each silver can are printed the words 'Lumière Productions', a fitting title given Victor's admiration for the brothers. Seeing it, I am reminded of his story about Louis and Auguste Lumière's very first film, which showed a train pulling into a station. When they premiered it at Grand Café in Paris in 1895, the audience had shrieked and ducked behind their chairs for cover, thinking that the train was about to plough into the theatre. Yet despite the crowd's obvious enthusiasm, Louis said afterwards that people would soon tire of watching images on the screen and that cinema was 'an invention without a future'.

At the time I was intrigued by these two men, whose fascination with the moving image had furnished the world with the means with which to film itself. I also wondered at the strange coincidence that they were named after the very thing without which films could not exist: light.

Victor is nearing the end of the first box and the stack of logged film reels is growing. He catches me watching him and sits back on his heels, placing the list of names by his side.

'Looks like you've been busy,' I say, taking it as a sign that he can talk. 'Are you still getting funding from the same backers?'

Victor nods.

'Who are they exactly?'

Victor reaches behind him for his second glass of the crème de menthe drink. He takes a sip and swallows before he answers. 'They are silent partners who have an interest in what I do. I was introduced to them shortly after I retired.'

'Presumably they get to see the finished product?' I don't say it, but I'm obviously wondering if they are happy with funding such experimental films, which clearly aren't about to break any box office records.

Victor smiles. 'This is not a commercial enterprise,' he says. 'It is an act of love.' He points to the second box. 'Give me five minutes to register these last few, then I am finished.'

I sit back in my chair and wait while he logs the final reels. I still have so many questions about his late-blooming career, such as who else is making the films with him, because I can't believe he's doing it all on his own. What made him decide to return to film-making in the first place? And did the cine camera that I gave him have anything to do with that decision?

*

I spot the cine camera at Portobello Market one Sunday morning, well over a year after Victor and I initiated our monthly weekend outings. It's an old 16 mm Kodak model from the seventies but the stall owner assures me it still works. After giving me a short demonstration, he throws in a box containing several spools of empty film reels for the same price.

Both are stashed in my bag when Victor and I enter the café the following Monday night. Mahler's Symphony No. 5 is playing, but despite the melancholy music, Bernard, who's been visiting his sister in Besançon, is in a particularly good mood. He recommends that we both try the plum tart, but Victor declines.

'Not hungry?' I say to him once we've sat down.

Victor shakes his head. I sense that his mood might have something to do with the Louis Malle film we've just seen about an old man trying to find a reason to live.

'That's the third depressing one in a row,' I say. 'Maybe we should switch to Richard Curtis romcoms.'

Victor attempts a smile. 'You know, Hannah, I am no different from Alain, that man in the film. I have done nothing in my life which has made a difference to anyone.'

'Yes, you have,' I say. 'For a start, you have been my friend. In fact...' I reach into my bag and pull out the package which is wrapped in an old copy of *Sight and Sound* magazine. 'I even bought you a present at the weekend to prove it.' I set the package down on the table in front of him.

Victor stares at it for several seconds, then very slowly he pulls off the paper and lifts out the cine camera.

'I know it's not exactly state of the art, but...'

'How did you know?' he whispers.

'Know what?' I push the second present – the roll of film in its book-shaped box – towards him.

'That it is my birthday today.' He picks up the cine camera and inspects it from every angle. Then he sets it carefully back onto the table and looks over at me. 'Thank you, Hannah,' he says in a voice cracked with emotion.

I feel embarrassed that, despite knowing Victor for almost three years, I haven't bothered to ask when his birthday is, and I don't have the heart to tell him that I only bought it on a whim. Instead, I tap the camera. 'I'm giving you this on one condition: that you promise me you will use it.'

Looking back, it seems a sinister coincidence that I should give Victor the camera on the very same weekend that I met Luke; that the seeds of the end were already sewn into the beginning.

*

'All finished!' Victor has just placed the final reel from the second box onto the middle shelf. He smiles at me encouragingly and walks over to the cinematograph.

Nellie is still sparko on the floor in front of me. It's almost eight o'clock and normally she'd be starting on her supper campaign by now, but the journey here must have whacked her out.

'I should not really be showing you this.' Victor flips open the side panel of the cinematograph and adjusts the film reel inside. 'It will be our secret.'

I leave Nellie with Victor and walk down the aisle towards the solitary seat. Behind me I can hear the familiar whirring from the booth, and seconds after I've sat down, the lights fade and the crimson curtains inch apart. In front of me the gold-scripted words 'Lumière Productions' appear on the screen. Once again the little red feather that forms the *accent grave* of Lumière floats down across the otherwise white expanse.

The film opens with a man sitting alone at a kitchen table. His shoulders are hunched and there's an empty bottle of whisky in front of him. He's staring at a window through which a woman with long strawberry blonde hair can be seen hurrying away down the street. He watches her until she rounds the corner and disappears from view. Then he takes the whisky bottle and hurls it against the opposite wall.

There follows a sequence of fast-moving black and white images showing a little boy and his mother. First they are on a beach building a sandcastle, then they're at the zoo watching penguins playing in the water, and finally, they're curled up together in an armchair. Just as in the first film, it seems as if I can feel what the boy is feeling, so when he puts the final seashell decoration onto his sandcastle, I too experience a burst of satisfaction. The sight of the penguins triggers in me a sensation of excitable delight, and as I watch the boy snuggle into his mother's lap, I feel the warm rush of love.

From then on, only the boy's father features in the snapshot images. I see the two of them cheering from the sidelines at a rugby match, then at a school awards ceremony in which the boy, now a teenager, is given first prize for a wood sculpture he has made, and finally saying goodbye to each other before the young man drives away to start his new university. Although I can feel the boy's surging adrenalin at the rugby match, his glowing pride when he wins the school prize and his nervous anticipation before his first day at university, alongside these emotions lies something else – a deep and paralysing sense of abandonment. It's a feeling as familiar to me as my own face.

Moments later the film turns to colour again, and I watch the man from the first scene sitting once more at the kitchen table. He's still staring at the window, although the street outside is empty. A tear slides down his cheek, and seconds later he lowers his head into his hands, sobbing like a little boy.

The film ends abruptly as if the reel has simply been spliced in two, and the curtains glide across the screen once more. I sit there, trying to make sense of what I've just seen and more importantly what I am now feeling.

I'm still sitting there when the lights come up and the cinema's rich interior reassembles itself around me: the gold flocked wallpaper, the worn red carpet and the torch lights which I assume are an exact replica of the ones in Studio 28 that Cocteau designed. There's even a small piano in the far right-hand corner by the screen like the one Victor described, which was used when Charlie Chaplin showed his films there.

Up in the projectionist's room Victor has just removed the film reel from the cinematograph when I walk in. Nellie is fast asleep with her head propped on her paws and her back legs splayed out behind her.

'What did you think?' asks Victor.

I sit down and try to gather my thoughts. My chest still feels tight and that painfully familiar ache of abandonment hasn't gone away. I rub my hands along Nellie's back to bring some warmth to my fingers. She squirms appreciatively in her sleep.

'It wasn't exactly a laugh a minute,' I say eventually.

'No,' says Victor. 'But that is only the first part.' He fixes me with those pale blue eyes. 'Every story has a second part, where we can put right what did not work before.' He slots the film into its silver can and sets it back onto the shelf.

'And you, Hannah,' he says, 'how will the next half of your story unfold?'

I shrug. 'Hopefully very differently from the first half.'

'In which case you must do things differently.' Victor pauses. 'What is that Einstein quote again? "Insanity is doing the same thing over and over again but expecting different results".' He moves over to the drinks cabinet and pours two more glasses of the green liquor. He hands me one and sits down in the other chair.

I take a couple of sips. Whether or not it's the alcohol from that first drink, I have to admit that I feel a little better. At our feet Nellie is stirring, presumably her stomach is telling her it's suppertime. She stretches her front paws rigidly in front of her and yawns loudly. Victor reaches down to scratch her under her chin.

'Would you like a biscuit, Nellie?' He points to a large tin on the lowest shelf beneath the film reels.

Nellie lets out an excited little bark.

The tin is filled with every type of biscuit imaginable from Garibaldis, Gypsy Creams and Wagon Wheels to Jaffa cakes, Penguins and Rich Tea. I take a chocolate-free digestive for Nellie and a Jaffa cake for myself, while Victor selects a Wagon Wheel.

'Biscuits! Such a marvellous invention! Why did I never try them before?' he says, chewing contentedly.

Nellie gulps her digestive down in one go then stares pointedly at the biscuit tin again. Victor and I watch her and smile.

'I never thanked you properly,' I say. 'I can't imagine life without her now.'

Victor eyes me from his chair. 'I wanted to make sure that you would be alright, when I had gone.'

I take another sip of the crème de menthe. 'What made you come round that night?' I say slowly.

'I had a feeling something was wrong, Hannah,' he says.

'You realise that I wouldn't be here now, if you hadn't come.'

'I know,' he says quietly.

Victor, Nellie and I are still in the projectionist's booth. Nellie is prostrate on the carpet in a huff because I wouldn't give her another biscuit. Victor is standing next to the cinematograph where he's been telling me about the film he is about to start work on.

'It is going to be a feature film,' he says proudly. 'It will be a co-production but I will be directing it.'

'That's amazing.'

Victor beams.

'What's it about?' I say. 'Give me the elevator pitch.'

Victor chuckles at my choice of words. 'It is about a life well lived.'

'That's it? You're not really selling it to me.'

'I do not have to,' Victor laughs. Then he checks his watch and frowns slightly. 'I have a screening at six. I would ask you to stay and watch, but once again it is a private viewing.'

'Don't worry. We should be going anyway,' I say. I don't know if it's a direct effect of the film I've just seen or Victor's words, but it's suddenly very important that I talk to Joe.

'Come on, Nell,' I say.

Nellie gives the biscuit tin one last lingering look and heaves herself off the floor.

'Will you visit me again?' says Victor.

I nod. I feel different having seen him again. Something – although I can't say exactly what – has lifted.

'Do not leave it so long this time,' he says.

I pick up my bag and smile. 'I won't.'

The three of us walk down to the cinema door and out into the corridor. Just before we reach the curtain at the far end, I hear the shop door slam. Through the small gap I glimpse a man of about my age marching towards the counter.

'Anyone serving here?' he calls angrily.

'Yes,' says Victor stepping out into the video shop with a little bow. 'There certainly is.'

Chapter 19

Joe is waiting outside the flat when Nellie and I return. He hasn't shaved and dark purple rings are etched beneath his eyes. His clothes look rumpled and he's leaning against his bicycle. When he sees us he immediately props it by the railings and runs towards me.

'Where have you been?' he says. 'I've been trying to ring you.'

'I figured you needed some space to sort things out,' I say in the calmest voice I can manage. Inside, my heart is pounding.

'But why didn't you return my calls?'

I take the keys from my bag. 'I wanted time to think after what happened last night.'

'What do you mean?' Joe places both hands on my shoulders, twisting me towards him. 'What's going on, Hannah?'

'I don't know,' I say. 'I was hoping you could tell me that.'

Joe and I are on the sofa in the sitting room. I've made us both a cup of tea, mainly to give me time to prepare for what I want to say. Nellie is in her kennel, facing outwards and watching us.

I take a breath and count to three. I know that if I look at Joe then it will be even more difficult, so I stare at the opposite wall, where a large crack jags its way from floor to ceiling. At the top, the wallpaper that once covered it has come away, exposing clumps of pink plaster below, like a raw wound.

'I know that these things can happen...' I try but fail to keep my voice steady.

'What things?' says Joe.

The words catch in my throat but I manage to force them out. 'That something you thought was finished... well, it's not finished.'

'Hannah, what are you talking about?'

'You and Nadia.'

'What about me and Nadia?'

'It's alright.' I twist my head further to the wall so he won't see that I'm crying. 'I'll deal with it.'

Joe prizes my mug from my fingers and places it on the table next to his. Then he turns my shoulders towards him so that I am forced to look him in the eye. 'I don't understand.'

I stare up into his eyes, willing myself to hold it together at least for a few more minutes. 'It's obvious that you're still in love with Nadia, and...'

'*What?*'

'Please,' I say, 'I need you to be honest with me.'

'But why on earth would you think that?' Joe's eyes are wide with surprise.

'Because of how you reacted when...' again the words catch in my throat, 'when you heard about her new boyfriend.'

'You thought that was because I was in love with Nadia?'

'Why else?'

Joe shakes his head. 'It was because of Maya. I panicked.

I don't want strange men in the house with her. He could be anyone.'

'But when we were at your mother's, I heard you say that that you didn't want to blow it a second time round…'

'I didn't mean that I wanted to *be* with Nadia, just that I needed her to trust me again, to show her that I could be a good father to Maya.'

I take at least a minute to absorb this. 'But why do you keep pushing me out? Whenever I try to talk to you about Nadia, you change the subject.'

'It's because I don't want to involve you in Nadia's and my baggage,' says Joe. 'It's not fair on you, and besides, I wanted us to start cleanly.' He folds his hands around mine. 'Is this what you were trying to tell me the other night?'

I nod.

'Why couldn't you say it before?' He shakes his head. 'Hannah, you're going to have to start talking to me, telling me what you're thinking, because otherwise I don't see much of a future for us.' He picks up his mug but doesn't drink from it.

'I mean, do you see this as a serious relationship? Because most of the time you act as if it's just something casual. Only once in a while I'll catch you looking at me and then I think maybe you do want this to be something more.' He sets the mug down again. 'What is it that you actually want, Hannah?'

'I want to be with you,' I say quietly. More than you will ever know.

'Why don't you show it then?'

'Because I'm scared,' I say. 'I'm really scared.'

Chapter 20

The August heatwave is sizzling across London and office workwear for Ian and I has taken on a distinctly holiday feel. I've been turning up in T-shirts and a light blue cotton skirt while Ian prefers a jungle green top and a pair of khaki trousers. We've taken to buying flowers on alternate weeks to liven up the office, and Phil from the guitar shop found us another poster of Elvis, from *Blue Hawaii,* which is now tacked on the wall in the 'kitchen'.

I've visited Mum a couple of times in the last month and I'm still ringing her at least twice a week. Today when I call her at work she tells me that she's in the sorting room sifting through some recently delivered bags of donations.

'I've just found a Hermès scarf,' she says excitedly.

'Pocket it,' I say.

Mum laughs. 'I know when you're taking the mickey now, Hannah.' Then she asks me what I've been up to and I tell her that I've just been writing about myrrh oral hygiene spray.

'I'll bring you some next time I visit,' I say. Mum's always had a thing about bad breath and can get through half a bottle of Listerine in under a week.

'How's Nellie?'

'Fat and fine,' I say and go on to describe the previous day's trip to Sainsbury's, where Nellie had snuck up on a chubby little boy holding a Boost bar in the car park. Before I could stop her, she'd snatched it from his fingers and wolfed it in one. I apologised to the mother and bought the child another Boost while Nellie smirked from the sidelines. *What's the big deal? It's not like the fat kid needs it.*

'You did that once,' says Mum. 'You were about three. We were in the Chorleywood bakery and you took an iced bun from Mrs Weston's little girl and ate it. Like daughter, like dog.'

'That's just cruel.'

We both laugh.

'And how's it going with that man of yours?' Mum asks.

'Good,' I say and tell her about the previous weekend when Joe, Nellie and I took the train to Whitstable and ate oysters and crab sandwiches on the beach. Afterwards, Joe and I went swimming while Nellie sulked on the shoreline.

'Will I…' she hesitates, 'will I get to meet him sometime?'

'I don't see why not.' I smile into the end of the phone and I can sense Mum smiling back.

'What are you doing the Friday after next?' I ask. 'I was thinking of taking the day off work and coming down.'

'In which case, I am completely free,' says Mum.

'But I want to do the cooking,' I say.

'Is that wise?'

'Coming from you, Mum…' I chuckle.

We're both still chuckling a few moments later when we say goodbye and hang up.

'How does this sound?' says Ian from his desk. He reads out his recipe for this week's Healthy Eats – gluten-free goat's cheese tart with a side salad of beetroot and chopped chives.

'Nice,' I say. 'Pudding?'

'Strawberry fool with spelt cinnamon biscuits.'

'You know,' I say, 'any yeast-intolerant woman would be happy to be your bird.'

Ian laughs. 'Thanks, Hannah.'

We knock up another couple of recipes for the next print edition of *Health and Wellbeing*, by which time we're both so hungry that we go for an early lunch. Having fetched sandwiches from Luigi's, we take them to the garden in the middle of Soho Square. We sit by one of the flowerbeds, which is filled with yellow roses whose delicate lemony perfume scents the air. All around us office workers sprawl on the grass, shoes off and collars loosened while they eat their lunch.

Ian tells me that his aunt's been staying for the week to give his mother a rest during the daytime. He's paid for them both to have a massage and facial that evening at a local beauty spa. They're also planning a trip to Scotland with Matthew in August.

'Brilliant.' I take a bite of my baguette and pause to savour the velvety texture of the mozzarella. 'I love Scotland.' I tell him about one of my first holidays with my parents when we went to Edinburgh on the night train.

'Are you going anywhere this summer?' Ian asks.

I nod. Joe and I are visiting a friend of his who has a cottage in Galway at the end of August – with Nellie, of course.

Ian chews thoughtfully on his sandwich. 'I'd love to go away somewhere with a girlfriend. I've never done that.'

'You will,' I say, 'but you may need to go on a date first. Don't think I haven't noticed that you've not been on one single date from that website.'

Ian sighs. 'I'm working up to it.'

'But you've been on it for three months now. What's stopping you?'

Ian looks at me. 'Confidence?'

'Right,' I say, 'in that case we're going to have a dress rehearsal this afternoon. You and me – after the relaxation CD reviews.'

We finish our sandwiches and Ian takes out his paper to do the crossword. I prop myself up on one elbow and look around at the other lunch-timers. Lounging beneath the beech tree a few metres away is a young woman with two men. One of the men is playfully tugging at her hair while the other one is sketching her.

'Keep still,' says the latter, frowning, 'you're making it impossible to capture you.'

The other man laughs. 'Forget it, mate. You'll never capture her.'

I watch the three of them – the woman with her two obvious love rivals – and I can't help remembering one particular Monday evening with Victor, shortly before everything started to unravel.

*

March 2009

'That was a beautiful film,' I say. 'It was almost like a painting.' Victor and I have just left the cinema, having watched Eric Rohmer's *L'amour l'après-midi*. Rather aptly we are standing in front of the artists' supplies shop.

'That is one of the reasons I admire Rohmer so much,' says

211

Victor. 'The other is his ability to portray human relationships.' He pauses to inspect the mannequin which is propped against the side of an easel, wooden arms reaching rigidly towards the glass. 'He shows us how we can never really know the truth about anyone.'

'I don't agree,' I say. 'I think if two people spend enough time together and genuinely love each other...'

'That is so naïve, Hannah.' Victor's tone is unusually harsh. 'Humans will always hide their true desires from one another. It is in their nature.'

I shrug. 'That may be your experience,' I say, 'but mine is different.' I glance surreptitiously at my watch, trying to work out if I can get to Luke's by eight so I can make supper.

I still haven't told Victor about Luke despite the fact that we've been together for five months. There are two main reasons for this – the first is that I know how much Victor cares for me, so it would feel tactless and cruel to start blathering on about my love life in view of his own romantic history, or rather the lack of it. The second is that I tend to keep the time I spend with Victor separate from the rest of my life. I'm not quite sure why, perhaps because I believe other people will think it strange or even a bit suspicious that a seventy-year-old man is hanging around a thirty-something woman, and I don't want their comments to tarnish our friendship.

Victor and I turn away from the wooden dummy and head towards Cambridge Circus. 'I'm going to have to leave you here, Victor,' I say. 'I need to be on the other side of town by eight thirty.'

'Oh?' says Victor. It's the first time that I have cut short our post-cinema talks and he looks hurt.

'I am meeting an old school friend,' I say. The moment it

212

leaves my mouth I'm aware of the irony that it's the first lie I have ever told him.

I arrive at Luke's just after eight, having shopped for ingredients on the way. I'm attempting to make a tortilla with chargrilled peppers, a recipe I spotted in one of the Sunday supplements. If it works, it will expand my culinary repertoire by about twenty-five per cent.

While I whisk the eggs, Luke opens the bottle of rioja that I've brought.

'You're becoming a proper little housewife,' he says as he pours two glasses.

I laugh and nod at the sticky mess of eggshells which has somehow spread across the sideboard. 'I've got some way to go yet.' I take a glass from his hand and chink it against his.

'So how was the movie?' says Luke.

'It was beautiful.'

'What's the name of the guy you go with again?'

'Victor.'

'Aaah, yes, Victor,' Luke laughs. 'My rival.'

I smile. 'He's hardly your rival. For starters, he's almost seventy.' I reach over for the pan of water, which has been boiling for the potatoes. 'I'm just a friend to him.'

Luke arches both eyebrows. 'You really sure about that?'

''Course I am.' I lift the pan, but as I do so a few drops splash onto the naked flame of the gas ring, causing it to hiss and flare an angry, vibrant orange.

*

Back in the office after lunch, I do a quick two hundred words on the importance of magnesium for a healthy heart, bones and brain function. After that I dash off a review of *Pure Calm*, the relaxation CD that came in this morning's delivery. Then it's time for Ian's dress rehearsal.

'What here?' says Ian.

'Unless you'd prefer to do it in the toilet?' I drag open the shop drawer and study the contents. 'First I need to set the scene.' I pick up the azure Eco eye shadow and dab it over both my eyes, then I spritz my mouth with some of the myrrh oral hygiene spray.

I spin round to face Ian at his desk. 'Right, I'm a chick, you've met me online and now you're meeting me in person. I'm twenty-six, blonde and I'm a trained nurse. Oh, and I'm called Suzy.'

Ian bursts into giggles. 'Sorry, I can't do this in front of you. I feel too silly.'

'You have to role play, Ian,' I say in my strictest voice, then I rummage around in the shop's miscellaneous department and pull out the Trayner pinhole glasses. 'Put these on.'

Ian perches the glasses on the tip of his nose and squints through the miniature holes.

'You look all weird and fragmented,' he says.

'That's good, it'll make it easier for you to pretend I'm Suzy.' I position my flower arrangement for that week, a spray of blue cornflowers, between us.

'So we're in a bar, nice and casual, you've just bought the drinks,' I nod to my cup of tea, 'and now we're getting to know each other a little.'

There's a lengthy pause and Ian giggles again.

'No giggling, Ian. This is serious stuff.'

Ian pulls the sides of his mouth down with his index fingers.

'So, Suzy,' he says, his face contorting with the effort to stop smiling, 'did you always want to be a nurse?'

'Oh yes,' I say, 'ever since I was a little girl. In fact I used to walk around the playground and put plasters on the other children's knees even though they didn't need them.'

'Right,' says Ian.

There's a pause and I hear a gentle humming start up.

'Ian, you're humming.'

'Oh, sorry.' Ian takes a swig of his coffee and chokes.

'I'll take over,' I say when he has finished spluttering. I clear my throat. 'I read on your profile that you like photography. What kind of camera do you have, Ian?'

'A Leica,' says Ian, 'and an old Canon.'

'And you're doing an online photography degree?'

'I am,' Ian smiles. 'It's really interesting. I've been taking pictures of landscapes and developing them on dyed printing paper so they look quite surreal.'

'I'd love to see them sometime,' I smile.

'What? You, Hannah would like to see them, or you Suzy?'

'Ian,' I tut, 'we're role playing here. I'm Suzy, the twenty-six-year-old nurse.'

'Yes, sorry,' says Ian. 'Another drink?' He taps my tea mug.

'Why not? Let's get trolleyed.'

We continue for the next few minutes covering music tastes, favourite foods and the high and lows of being a nurse in the NHS. Then we move onto hobbies.

'I go swimming a lot,' says Ian. 'Oh, and I also like comics.'

I wrinkle my nose.

'Not good?'

'Let's focus more on the cookery. What's your signature dish?'

'Well, Suzy,' Ian adjusts the pinhole glasses so that he can peer over them, 'last night I made marinated swordfish steaks with a parsley, coriander and garlic tapenade.'

'I think I'm falling in love with you.'

'Really?' Ian's cheeks flush a bright pink.

'As Suzy,' I say gently.

Ian nods then grabs his coffee and takes a gulp. 'Of course,' he says. 'I knew that.'

Chapter 21

'What's this for?' Joe watches me place two plates of sloppy scrambled eggs on the bed, along with the papers. It's Saturday morning, mid-August, and we are having a lie-in at mine.

'I'll give you two guesses.'

Joe hoists himself up to a sitting position. 'It's my birthday?'

'No.' I hand him the plate of toast. 'That's in March. Remember?'

'I've been awarded the Not So Young Playwright of the Year?'

'No, but you will be.' I kiss him and give him a fork. 'It's because I love you and you make me very happy.' Ever since seeing Victor's second film I've been making a big effort to tell Joe how I feel, despite the fact that it makes me feel incredibly vulnerable. It hasn't been easy to change what I now see is a pattern of a lifetime, but I'm determined to keep it up.

The curtains are open and the sun pours in, spilling pools of light like liquid honey onto the newly varnished floorboards. The flat has seen a bit of a makeover in the past few weeks – gone are the nicotine yellow walls, the faded brown carpets and limp curtains. Now my bedroom is pistachio green, the sitting room a bright turquoise and the kitchen a warm sunflower yellow. Joe even managed to unstick all the windows so that whenever it's hot – like today – a gentle breeze blows through the flat.

From next door I can hear Nellie snoring. It's taken a while to convince her that sleeping in the same room as Joe and me isn't really an option any more. But I think she was ready to move on anyway, mainly because she clearly couldn't get her head round the idea of sex and would begin to growl whenever Joe and I got frisky. At first I worried that if she was sleeping on her own the nightmares might return, but there's been no trace of them.

'Carnival's next weekend,' says Joe. 'I asked Nadia if we could take Maya for the kids' day on Sunday.'

Although Joe now sees Maya twice a week, I still haven't met her. Up until now he's thought she needs more time to get used to him being around again before he introduces me, and I agree with him. There's also Nellie to consider – somehow neither of us can picture a cosy Lassie-type relationship developing between dog and child.

'Did Nadia say yes?' I ask.

Joe shakes his head. 'She and whatever-his-name are taking her away for the weekend.'

'You mean Daniel?'

Joe doesn't reply.

'I know it's difficult,' I say, 'but you're going to have to get used to the idea that he's sticking around.'

Joe turns to me. 'Have you any idea *how* difficult it is?'

'No,' I say, 'but I'm trying.'

Joe pulls me into a one-armed hug. 'I know you are. And so am I.' He nods down at the two plates of scrambled egg. 'Eat up, Miss Bailey. Don't forget we're meeting Megan and Billy at two o'clock.'

After we've showered and dressed and convinced Nellie that going outside is a good idea, Joe unlocks his bike from the railings outside. Recently it's become our favourite way to travel – Nellie wedged in the front basket, Joe peddling and me perched behind.

We whizz down Ladbroke Grove towards the market with Nellie's ears flattening against her head and her gums flapping in the wind. Once we hit Portobello Road, we offload outside Falafel King (which causes two separate strops – one that Nellie is being forced to walk, and two, that we don't buy her a falafel) and wander down to the Westway. We pass Cashmere Paul and his stash of second-hand cashmere jumpers, and Mirko's orange VW van selling the best al fresco coffee in Portobello. But Nellie isn't interested in cashmere or Italian coffee vendors. Nellie's got just one goal – the food stalls. As we near them, her nose begins to twitch.

First in line is Arnaud, sporting his crowd-pleasing beret and exaggerated French accent as he drizzles melted chocolate over dinner-plate sized pancakes. Then comes the Italian bread man with his piles of warm focaccia stuffed with feta and rosemary. By the time we reach the Jamaican jerk chicken stall, Nellie is dribbling violently. Finally, in front of a row of thick sausages spitting on the open grill of the German bratwurst stall, she has a massive meltdown and lies on the floor like an obese child, refusing to move.

Waiting in the queue for our Bavarian bockwurst, the sounds of the market filter past us: the swelling voices of the gospel choir outside the Salvation Army building; the old West Indian man on the corner of Talbot Road pling-plinging on his steel drum and the shouts from market traders offering everything from bananas, J-cloths and lilies, to cheese, papaya and plungers.

Half a bockwurst later (Joe had the other half) and Nellie is on her feet again, so we stroll down to Laura's stall, where Joe always buys his fruit and veg. Everyone on the market knows Laura and her boxer dog, Alf, who today is sheltering from the sun under the stall, peering out from behind a length of acid green Astroturf.

'How's the play going?' Laura asks while she loads handfuls of shiny red vine tomatoes onto the scales.

'It's finished,' says Joe. 'I just need someone to take it now.' He tells her that he's had more than twenty rejections from various directors and theatres.

'You should put it on yourself,' she says. 'There's that empty post office near Paddington station. You could use that.'

The two of them continue chatting but I'm not listening any more. Instead I'm watching Nellie, who's crawling on her stomach towards Alf. I've never seen this particular expression on her face before – a cross between a leer and a certain wide-eyed coyness. Closer and closer she edges until she finally reaches Alf, whereupon she sinks down next to him with a contented grunt, Astroturf draped over her head like a bridal veil.

Joe and I turn to each other at the same time. 'Nellie's scored.'

Such a momentous event needs to be celebrated, so after we've said goodbye to Laura and Alf, the three of us make our way down to Finches to meet Megan and Billy. Joe goes into the pub to get the drinks and, I suspect, to keep an eye on the finals of the men's basketball. He's been glued to the Olympics for the last two weeks, while I only bothered with the gymnastics.

Outside, Nellie flops down by my side to bask in the sun and I gaze over at Ted's stall and the profusion of flowers that spill out onto the pavement. There's about five bunches of my favourite tea roses, whose cream petals are stained red at the edges, just like the ones Bernard used to buy for the café.

*

April 2009

'Bernard's been to Covent Garden market again,' I say to Victor as I study the single cream rose with the petals that look like they've been dipped in blood.

Across the table, Victor smiles then picks up the china teapot to pour my Earl Grey. We've just been to see a Chabrol film, but I have a feeling we won't be discussing it. Instead I've picked today to tell him about Luke. I wait until he has set down the pot and is lifting his own cup to take a sip of coffee.

'I've fallen in love,' I say simply.

Victor's hand and the cup freeze in mid-air – just for a split-second but long enough for me to notice.

'Who is he?' he asks quietly.

And so I tell Victor. I try to select details which I think he'll be interested in, like Luke's obsession with American films from the seventies, his passion for his *Easy Rider* documentary, the old-school Super 8 camera he takes almost everywhere he goes... I don't say anything about the daft things he does, such as leaving peonies on my doorstep in the middle of the night so they are there in the morning when I go to work, or slipping love notes into my coat

221

pockets. Nor do I tell Victor that I am so in love I can barely breathe.

'I am very happy for you,' says Victor when I've finished. He looks briefly towards the window, which is smudged with raindrops. Then he checks his watch. 'I should be leaving now.'

'We've only just arrived!'

Victor is already picking up his coat. 'Really, I have to go.'

Without looking at me, he pushes himself up from the table, and walking quickly – almost running – he hurries for the door. But just before he reaches it, he stumbles and knocks into one of the tables. The white vase with its tea rose teeters for a few seconds, before toppling sideways and falling to the floor, where it smashes, leaving the rose with its red-tipped petals stranded in a tiny pool of water like an exotic fish. For a moment Victor hesitates, then he picks up his stride once more, unwittingly crushing the delicate petals beneath his right foot. After wrestling with the handle of the café door, he disappears into the rain outside.

By the time I catch up with him, he's already reached Cambridge Circus. His hair is slicked to his head and large droplets of water are sliding off the end of his nose.

'You left your hat.' The crowds are jostling around us to get into the theatre. 'And your umbrella.'

He takes them silently.

'Victor, what's wrong?'

He still won't return my gaze. 'I think it is best if we do not go to the cinema any more,' he mumbles into the collar of his coat. 'You do not want an old man taking up your time.'

I suddenly feel guilty for my distracted behaviour the last few occasions I've seen him, and I wonder if he noticed me clock-watching.

'Victor,' I say. 'I love spending time with you, and even if I am with someone now, nothing will change between us.'

Victor's eyes finally meet mine. 'Honestly?'

'Honestly.'

'It is not just because you feel sorry for me?'

I place both my hands on his shoulders. 'No, Victor,' I say. 'It's not.'

Victor allows himself a hesitant smile and I suggest we return to the café before Bernard clears our tea away. I link my arm through his and we start walking back. Moments later, I hear sniggering close behind us. It's a group of teenage boys and one of them taps Victor on the arm.

'Bit old for her, aren't you, granddad?' The boy makes a round shape with his left thumb and index finger, jabbing the other index finger in and out of it.

Victor's mouth sets in a hard line and his face turns a livid red. He starts shouting – I'm not sure what because it's in French, but it only makes the boy and his friends laugh even more.

'Leave it, Victor,' I tug at his arm. 'It doesn't matter.'

'But it does,' he shouts in English. 'Of course, it does.'

The boys move on and Victor calms down a little, although his cheeks are still bright red.

'Who cares what anyone else thinks?' I thread my arm through his again. 'Besides we do make a pretty odd couple, don't we?'

By the time we get back to the café, Bernard has taken away our tea things. Another cream-coloured rose has been placed in the vase on our table, but it's not as fresh as the previous one and the petals are already turning a dull brown.

*

'Hannah?' I hear Megan's voice from across the street. She's wearing her old AC/DC T-shirt over a brown suede skirt and she's carrying her portfolio.

'Sorry I'm late,' she pants, 'I've been hanging paintings for that group exhibition in the Tabernacle.' She takes my Guinness off me and has a swig. 'Billy not here yet?'

I shake my head.

'He must be still in Rough Trade.' Megan rolls her eyes and sits down next to me on the pavement. 'Hi, Nell,' she says, scratching Nellie's back. Nellie grunts and wags her stump of a tail.

'A lager for the artist,' says Joe, who's just emerged through the pub doors. 'I heard your dulcet tones from inside.' He hands Megan a pint of Red Stripe and sits down beside us. They've now met quite a few times and I love the fact that they get on so well.

'That's what I like to see,' says Megan. 'A man who gets the beers in.' She kisses Joe on both cheeks. Behind us, a cheer goes up in the pub. Someone must have just scored a goal – or whatever the terminology is – in the basketball match.

The three of us sip our drinks in the sunshine and chat about Megan's exhibition, along with the possibility of Joe staging his play in the empty Paddington post office. The Saturday crowd shuffles past us along Portobello Road – almost everybody is eating something: plates of garlicky paella; freshly blended fruit smoothies; chocolate-drenched churros and cones of thick Italian ice cream. Billy turns up about fifteen minutes later, carrying a Rough Trade bag.

'Anything good in there?' asks Joe. He and Billy have also met several times and are even planning to do an evening deejaying together at the Paradise.

Billy pulls out a Parliament record and a compilation of seventies funk.

'How did you pay for those?' asks Megan.

'With money,' says Billy. 'You know, the gold and silver stuff.'

'And where did that come from?'

Billy frowns slightly. 'From that gig I did last week.'

'Oh yes, the first paid gig in what… six weeks?'

'Not here,' says Billy.

Megan sets her half-drunk pint down on the pavement. 'Why not here? Hannah knows it all anyway, and Joe, well, I'm sure he'll work things out for himself.' She stares at Billy for a couple of seconds.

Billy turns to Joe and me. 'Sorry about this.' Then he swivels back to Megan. 'I think I'll head off somewhere else, where I can have a pint in peace.' He kisses me briefly on the cheek and shakes Joe's hand. 'Let's meet up another time, when someone's in a better mood.'

We watch him stride down Elgin Crescent and turn into Ladbroke Grove.

'I'm sorry,' says Megan. 'He drives me nuts. He still hasn't got a job, yet he can buy records every weekend. How does that work?'

We carry on chatting, this time about the two actors that Joe's just cast for his play, before Megan says she needs to go back to the Tabernacle and finish hanging her paintings. We say goodbye, then Joe, Nellie and I walk back to my place, where Joe decides that he wants to make savoury pancakes. He and Nellie disappear into the kitchen while I tidy up next door in the sitting room. I grumble loudly to myself as I pick up dirty coffee mugs, socks, jumpers and a pair of Joe's jeans.

'Joe,' I shout into the kitchen. 'How tricky is it to walk the few extra feet to put your filthy clothes in the wash basket?'

'Very,' Joe shouts back.

I march into the kitchen where he's whisking milk and eggs. Nellie is stationed at his feet, awaiting overspill.

'Besides, I'm busy creating.' He tips some of the mixture into the bubbling frying pan.

'Busy creating a big old mess.' I stomp over to the sink to put the mugs down, but on the way I slip in some pancake mixture which Nellie must have missed.

Joe catches me just in time. 'You want to watch yourself – one pint of Guinness and you're all over the shop.' He turns to toss the pancake into the air, but on its descent it misses its mark completely and slaps down onto the kitchen floor. Nellie is on it in seconds.

I glare at the piles of dishes in the sink, the food-encrusted pans littering the sideboard and the trails of what looks like pancake batter down the cupboards near where Joe's been whisking.

'I'll clear it up,' he says.

'I've heard that one before,' I say. Joe's not exactly strict about when he does the washing up. Last week, when I went on strike, the dirty plates sat on the sideboard for three days before he finally got around to it.

I sigh. 'It's not fair, Joe. I spend half my life clearing up after you and I'm sick of it. I have enough trouble keeping myself clean.'

Joe points to his second attempt at a pancake, which is now ready. 'I'll finish making these, then I'll do it.' He laughs. 'I may need a clean plate to put them on, though.'

I point to the overflowing sink. 'There aren't any. We'll have to eat off the floor.'

Joe winks. 'You might want to wash it first.'

'Oh, you…' In my frustration I grab one of the plates and hurl it at the wall. It shatters into dozens of pieces, smearing last night's leftover curry across the skirting board.

I stand there, not quite knowing what to do next. Then Joe starts clapping. 'The plate throwing needs some work, but otherwise quite impressive.'

We've eaten the pancakes, Joe has washed up, and I've calmed down. Now we're lying on the sofa, watching one of Joe's favourite films from the sixties, *The L-shaped Room*, with Leslie Caron. Nellie's asleep in her kennel.

'Tantrums suit you,' says Joe. 'I'm loving this new expressive you.'

'Despite the nagging?'

'Despite the nagging.' Joe grins. 'You really hate the domestic stuff, don't you?'

I nod. 'It ruins everything.'

'It doesn't have to.' He leans up on one elbow. 'What you and I have doesn't happen often – at least not to me, and I'm not going to let anything ruin it.' He turns down the volume with the remote control and looks at me. 'So when we do decide to move in together, I'll do *all* of the cooking and *all* of the washing up.'

I nod and attempt a smile.

'Did I say something wrong?'

I pluck at the sleeve of my shirt, stalling for time. 'It's just that I hadn't really thought about…'

'I'm not talking tomorrow,' says Joe, 'but maybe sometime in the New Year.'

'Why can't we just carry on as we are?'

Joe stares at me. 'You don't ever see us living together?'

'If it isn't broken and all that.'

'Oh,' says Joe simply. 'I'd always imagined that one day...' he trails off. 'Well, if that's how you want it, then I guess I have no choice.' He turns up the volume with the remote and the sound of Leslie Caron sobbing alone in her bedsit fills the sitting room.

Chapter 22

'What else did you have in mind, Hannah?' Mum and I are standing in her kitchen early on Friday evening, trying to decide what I'm going to cook for supper. I had thought I'd tackle a lasagne, but now I've looked up the recipe it seems a bit complicated.

'Something simple,' I say.

'There's some chicken in the freezer,' says Mum.

'Now that's a surprise,' I grin.

Mum hands me her ageing copy of Constance Spry. 'I happen to like chicken.' She nods down at Nellie. 'She does too, so you're outvoted.'

I smile and shrug my defeat before opening up Constance under the C section to read the first recipe.

'"Chicken Koulibiaca is a Russian speciality, generally served hot at the beginning of a meal, or it may be included in the 'zakouska' or hors-d'oeuvres..."' I look over at Mum, who is trying to suppress a giggle.

'Maybe not.' I trace my finger further down. '"Chicken Millefeuilles is an alternative to bouchees of chicken and is a pleasant and attractive dish for a luncheon or buffet..."'

'Shall we just do a stir fry?' says Mum.

While Mum defrosts the chicken, I chop the vegetables. Nellie is in the sitting room in a grump because I made her walk from the tube station to Mum's. I've given the pram back to Joe for Maya.

The radio murmurs quietly in the background while Mum tells me about the week's holiday to Cornwall that she's planning for early September.

'Maybe I could come down for a few days.'

'You don't need to,' says Mum. 'Pam says she might visit for a couple of days if her sister is mobile enough after her hip operation. Besides I'm quite alright on my own.' She takes the knife from me to finish slicing a red pepper.

'But I want to.'

'In that case, I'd love you to come.' Mum's face breaks into a smile.

'And maybe Joe could come down for a few days in the middle of the week?' We've been trying to find time for him to meet Mum but his weekend shifts at the Paradise make it quite difficult.

At that moment Nellie ambles back into the kitchen. Chin tilted upwards, she scans all visible surfaces for any signs of food.

'You'll have to wait, Madam. It's not ready yet,' says Mum.

Nellie sinks to the floor with a dramatic sigh.

Mum chuckles. 'I suppose she'll be coming to Cornwall too.'

Mum continues chopping the rest of the vegetables while I sit up on the sideboard and shred the chicken. Just before six, the shipping forecast comes on the radio and together we listen to that resonant voice reeling off the list of faraway places, which as a child I'd imagined to be teetering on the edge of the earth. 'Viking, North Utsire, South Utsire, Forties, Cromarty, Forth, Tyne, Fisher, Dogger...' I remember sitting in the exact same spot as a little girl while Mum cooked supper and how we used to try and recite the names along with that voice. We only ever made it to German Bight before our tongues became tangled around the strange-sounding words and we'd dissolve into laughter.

I catch Mum looking at me as the familiar voice fills the kitchen and I feel a warmth spread through me.

A programme on Maria Callas follows the news, with extracts from an old recording of *Madame Butterfly*. Mum stops chopping and closes her eyes to listen to the soaring notes of Callas singing 'One Fine Day'.

'I could listen to that forever,' she says when the song ends. Picking up the knife again, she starts to dice a courgette.

'Ouch,' she says a few seconds later. She sucks her finger, while dark red drops of blood drip onto the chopping board. 'You wouldn't get me a plaster, would you?'

I run upstairs to the bathroom cabinet and eventually find a box of Elastoplast behind Mum's generous supply of Listerine and a bottle of beta-blockers.

I head back down to the kitchen with the plasters. 'Since when have you had high blood pressure, Mum?'

'Since about five years.'

'It's not dangerous, is it?'

Mum shakes her head then nods down at her finger. 'Come on, Ms Nightingale, let's get that plaster on.'

I smooth on the Elastoplast then point to several little scars on the back of Mum's hand. 'What are those?'

'Gilmore,' Mum laughs.

Gilmore, my guinea pig, had been rescued from the window of the Chorleywood pet shop, but after the initial honeymoon period, he'd undergone a bit of a character change, which manifested itself mainly in scratching and biting anything that came near him. Consequently the novelty of owning a guinea pig wore off even faster than it would usually have done for a seven-year-old. Dad said we should return him, but Mum refused, saying that she couldn't bear to see Gilmore's little face staring out at her every time she passed the pet shop. So she spent the next four years caring for him until one winter morning she found him stiff as a scouring brush on the floor of his hutch.

'Did I ever thank you for looking after Gilmore?' I say.

'No, I don't think you did. But it's OK – that's what mums are for.' Mum glances over at Nellie, who's scowling at us both, presumably because supper's still not ready. 'But if you think I'm looking after that one, you'd better think again.'

We eat the stir fry and chat about St Mawes and the nearby beaches we would like to revisit together. Afterwards we watch a DVD of *The End of the Affair*, which Mum brought back from the hospice shop ('paid for, not pocketed, Hannah'). She goes to bed around ten but Nellie and I stay in the sitting room. The late-night film about a detective with pocked skin and a drinking habit fails to enthral us, so while Nellie dozes, I pull out one of the old photo albums from the cupboard beneath the telly.

I pause at a picture of my school's prize-giving day, in which my father and I are sitting on a tartan rug, squinting into the sunshine. I am twelve and it is the final term before I go to Watford Grammar.

We've just endured an hour of prize-giving, where it appears that everyone apart from me has won something. Claire Easton bagged the English prize, Sally Ford – Maths, Tessa Shaw – Biology. Even Fiona Wharton got a new leotard for her 'outstanding gymnastics display' that was basically just a couple of somersaults and a hand-stand crab.

I am still sulking when Mum spreads out the tartan rug for lunch.

'I enjoyed that,' she says brightly, opening a Tupperware box. 'Egg and cress or chicken and tomato?'

'Egg and cress, please,' Dad and I say together.

Just then, Miss Simms walks by. Miss Simms is our biology teacher and has hair like Brian May and still wears T-bar shoes at the age of fifty. She and Mum start chatting about how clever Tessa Shaw is for growing a broad bean from a seed. I pretend not to listen and concentrate on picking out the pieces of peppery cress from my sandwich.

'But Hannah did a lovely picture of a spirogyra this term, didn't you, Hannah?' said Miss Simms.

'Can't remember.'

'Yes, you can,' she insists before turning to Dad, who has an amused expression on his face.

'A spirogyra is a single cell organism like an amoeba, only it has flagella,' she explains.

'Is that a fact?' says Dad with a little smile.

Two red circles stain Miss Simms's cheeks, and a hand makes an unsuccessful attempt to smooth down the Brian May hair.

'You are a clever girl,' says Mum.

'No, I'm not.'

'What's the matter with you, Hannah?' asks Dad when Miss Simms has finally gone.

'Nothing.'

'Let me take a picture of you two,' says Mum, and she rifles in her bag for her Instamatic. 'Smile!'

But just as she's about to take the photo, Dad leans down

233

and whispers in my ear, 'You don't need prizes to make me proud of you.'

On the way back home in the car, I sit snugly behind the driver's seat. Dad asks me if I am considering a career as a biologist, given my talent for drawing single cell organisms.

I laugh and tell him that I want to travel to as many different countries as possible and then live in the one that I love the most. I don't really want to do that, but I know he'll approve.

'What about me?' says Mum. 'Are you going to leave me all alone?'

'I'm not going to stay in Chorleywood all my life, am I?' I say, waving my hand over my mouth as if to suppress a yawn, 'I'd die of boredom.'

Sitting in Mum's armchair, I feel the sharp ache of remorse at yet another hurt that I must have caused her, for all those times I sided with my father, trying to secure his love and in doing so deliberately excluding my mother. Suddenly it seems very important that I tell her how sorry I am.

I make my way upstairs leaving Nellie to sleep in the sitting room. Mum's door is slightly ajar and I can see her propped up in bed with a book resting on the top of her pink and green flowered eiderdown. I knock and go in.

'You OK, Mum?'

Mum nods and closes the book, setting it on the bedside table next to a box of tissues and a small framed photograph of Dad and her standing outside Edinburgh Castle. We both stare at the picture.

'You still miss him, don't you?' I say.

Mum does a stiff little shoulder shrug. 'It's been so long since he died. It's pathetic, isn't it?'

I sit down on the edge of the bed. 'It's not pathetic, Mum.' I twist around to look at the photograph again. 'I'm sorry that I wasn't more supportive after he left.'

She shakes her head. 'You did your best, Hannah.'

'No, I didn't,' I say, 'and I want to apologise. For a long time I blamed you, and that wasn't fair.'

'You were only a child, Hannah. You needed someone to blame.'

'But even before that I wasn't very nice to you.' I pick at a loose thread on the eiderdown. 'I was so busy trying to please Dad that I never really thought about you.'

'That's alright,' says Mum softly. 'I understand.'

There's a short pause while details from that Sunday lunch reel through my mind: Dad slowly threading his napkin through the wooden ring, his stilted voice, his silhouette in the doorway, with that overnight case.

'You remember the letter he wrote me?' I say a few moments later. 'In it he said that he hadn't been happy for some time. Is that true?'

It's the first time I've ever discussed the letter's contents with Mum.

Mum nods slowly. 'I always knew that he wanted a very different life from the one he would have with me. He made it clear from the beginning that raising a family wasn't part of his plan.' She takes a deep breath and returns my gaze. 'I thought that if I had a child he would change his mind. If I hadn't stopped taking contraception and become pregnant he would never have married me.' She reaches over to take a tissue from the box. 'In those last years before he left, he was miserable, but I refused to see it.' She wipes her eyes with the tissue. 'Even when he took an overdose...'

I take her hand. 'Dad always said that you were the kindest woman he had ever known.'

'Is it kind to trick someone like that?'

'You did what you felt you had to, and Dad did the same.' I glance back at the photo and my throat tightens. 'I still miss him too. I just find it hard to talk about.'

'I know you do, darling.' Mum folds her hand over mine and together we sit there, quietly contemplating the picture of the man we both loved and still love, whose absence after twenty-five years is as palpable as his presence once was.

Chapter 23

By three o'clock on Bank Holiday Monday even the pavement outside the Pelican has a pulse, throbbing underfoot to the bass lines belted out by the stacks of speakers on All Saints Road, where thousands of bodies dance beneath the red, green and yellow banners proclaiming 'Carnival – Europe's Biggest Street Party'.

The air is thick with the smell of beer, sweat and spliff, and trapped in the haze of heat, the music from the sound systems fuses into a frenetic mixture of reggae, soca, calypso, hip-hop and ragga. Another cheer erupts from the crowd, accompanied by a volley of head-splitting whistles as Ganja Cru's classic 'Super Sharp Shooter' slowly winds from the CMC speakers, in front of which Joe and I are attempting to dance.

'You're doing pretty well for a broom,' laughs Joe, one hand round a can of Red Stripe, the other waving manically in the air.

'And you're not bad for a spirogyra.' I try to imitate him but succeed only in elbowing the forehead of the small blonde woman dancing next to me.

After I've apologised and the song has ended, Joe and I join the slow-moving herd to shuffle our way past the Mangrove Community Centre. I spot a walnut-faced Benjamin from the Pelican contorting his wiry body to the deep bass line blasting from the eight-foot-high speaker stack. Sally is next to him, puffing on a massive joint.

We reach the end of Powis Terrace, where nestled in the raspberry pink doorway of My Beautiful Launderette, is Mama C's Kitchen – a home-made BBQ swirling in smoke. Mama C stands behind it, dressed in a red frilly apron and a home-made chef's hat and prodding at jerk chicken, corn on the cob and fried plantain. By her side two little boys with an ice box on wheels wave slices of watermelon and plastic bags filled with a lurid orange liquid at the passing crowds.

'What's next?' I say, licking my fingers clean of the jerk chicken we've just shared.

Joe leans down to kiss me, leaving the faint sting of sweet chili sauce on my lips. Then he points to the float outside the Globe bar, which is covered in palm trees and where a man in a big panama hat stands behind the decks, swigging from a bottle of rum.

'More dancing,' Joe chuckles, pulling me towards Gaz's sound system. 'Come on, Broom, let's really see what you're made of,' he shouts above Screamin' Jay Hawkins's 'I Put a Spell on You'. And with that, he's off again, head jerking from side to side, feet kicking out in all directions like an epileptic pony. Not one part of his body, except his heart, is in time to the music.

After more pit stops for Red Stripe, saltfish fritters and a half-hour wait for a soggy cubicle in an overflowing Portaloo, Joe and I jostle our way up Ladbroke Grove. The float in front of us is loaded with twenty or so steel drums, on which dozens of pairs of hands are beating out a frenzied rhythm. Grass-skirted hula girls undulate in the road behind

238

it, along with a mass of schoolchildren dressed as warriors, red Indians and butterflies.

Finally we reach the Good Times bus, where Norman Jay is playing Kool and the Gang's 'Celebration'. Joe throws his arm protectively around me and we merge with the heaving mass of bodies.

'What are you looking at?' I ask Joe. He's stopped dancing for a moment and is staring at me with his head cocked to one side.

'You,' he says, flinging his other arm around me. 'Have you any idea how much I love you?'

I look up at him, feeling the weight of his arm around my shoulders, and once again, it strikes me how incredibly relaxed and secure I feel with him.

*

July 2009

'What are you staring at?' I say to Luke, who is standing by his window, looking out at the street below. It's seven o'clock on Wednesday evening and I've just arrived back from work.

Luke doesn't answer me, but continues to stare out of the window.

'What's happened?'

'The funding fell through,' he says dully, without turning to look at me. 'The producer just called from the States.'

I walk over to him. 'I'm sorry,' I say. 'I know how much the documentary means to you.' I wrap my arms around him. 'So what happens now?'

Luke sighs. 'Nothing. It's the end of the line. Three years down the drain.'

'Surely you'll be able to find other funders?'

Luke twists his head towards me. 'Do you have any clue what state the film industry is in?'

'No,' I say, 'but it's such a good idea and...'

Luke shrugs and turns to stare out of the window again. A plane passes overhead and his eyes follow it as it curves westwards.

'Come on, I'll take you out for supper,' I say.

We're sitting in one of the green leather-clad booths in Jimmy's, the diner around the corner, which is Luke's favourite place to eat. The restaurant is full of locals and a few bankers who've obviously heard that this is a hip place to go. The flame grill at the far end is working overtime and the waitress has just bought Luke's Californian cheeseburger along with my Maryland crab burger and chips.

'I interviewed a raw food advocate today,' I say. 'She hasn't eaten anything hot for over two years.' I dunk a chip into the bowl of ketchup. 'She looked so peaky, I just wanted to take her to Luigi's and give her a steaming plate of spaghetti.'

'Sure,' says Luke, but I can tell he's not listening. After six months I'm used to his moods and I can usually cajole him out of them by making him laugh, but obviously not tonight.

I place my hand over his. 'It's going to be OK,' I say, 'something will come through.'

Luke shrugs. 'It better had because I'm not going to stick around here making pissy pop promos for the rest of my life.' He leans out into the aisle and calls to the waitress. 'I'm still waiting for that chili sauce I ordered.' He sighs loudly. 'You'd think it was a simple enough request.'

The manager, a guy in a green baseball cap, is passing our table. 'Is something the matter?'

'Your waitress is deliberately ignoring me.' Luke takes his knife and stabs his burger with it. 'I ordered chili sauce to have *with* this, not *after*.'

'I'm sure she's doing her best,' says the manager. 'We're pretty crowded tonight.'

Luke stares at him for what feels like minutes. 'You know what, forget it,' he says dropping his knife back onto his plate with a loud clatter.

'Is it really that important, Luke?' I say when the manager has walked back up the aisle to talk to the waitress.

There's a brief silence while Luke glares over at me. 'Sorry, I'm being an arse, aren't I?' he says eventually.

'Just a bit.' I tap his plate with my own knife. 'Maybe we should stick to raw food from now on then this sort of scene would be avoided.'

Luke smiles briefly then picks up his Californian burger and bites into it. I do the same with my crab burger but it's been sitting there for so long that its contents have congealed and are already going cold.

*

Kool and the Gang's 'Celebration' has finished but the crowd is still moving. I'm being kettled from either side and it's difficult to keep my balance. I'm not sure if it's the spliff, the beer or the heat, but a wave of nausea swirls up from my stomach. I stumble and slip on a discarded chicken wing.

'Joe,' I say, 'can we move—' But I don't finish my sentence because Joe is staring in the opposite direction at a little girl on a man's shoulders. Her T-shirt is red and says 'Pop Kid' on the front.

'Dad!' shouts the little girl across the heads of the dancers.

Joe fights his way towards her. I follow a few paces behind.

'You must be Joe,' shouts the man on whose shoulders Maya is sitting. 'I'm Daniel.' He holds out a hand.

Joe ignores him and tilts his head towards his daughter. 'Where's Mummy?'

'She's over there.' Maya points to the other side of the road.

'Getting something to drink,' adds Daniel.

Joe stares at him. 'Will you put my daughter down please?'

'It's safer for her on my shoulders,' says Daniel.

Just then a woman with short bleached hair, a denim miniskirt and trainers pushes through the crowd. She hands Maya an open can of Ting.

'Sorry that took ages,' she says. 'Hello, Joe.'

'I thought you said you were going to your parents,' says Joe.

'We were,' says Nadia. 'Until Dad decided to take Mum to Madrid for the weekend.'

'Is there a problem?' says Daniel.

'Yes, there *is* a problem,' says Joe loudly, still addressing Nadia. 'You drag Maya out into the crowds on a Monday – not even the kids' day, then you leave her with some random man…'

He's shouting now and Maya has begun to cry. Daniel lifts her off his shoulders and hands her to Nadia.

'Calm down, mate,' he says, swivelling to face Joe, whose fists are now clenched in his pockets. 'Besides, Nadia and I've been going out for over five months, so Maya knows me pretty well by now, in fact she probably—'

The blow catches Daniel just above his jawline, causing him to stumble back against the wall of people dancing behind him. His expression shows more a look of surprise than pain.

'Oi!' A voice shouts from behind Joe and within seconds two policemen have jumped on him, slamming him down onto the pavement. One of them whips out a pair of handcuffs and snaps them sharply around his wrists.

It is almost eleven o'clock at night by the time they let Joe leave the police station. It turned out that they had mistaken him for a dealer and we had to wait for his sister, Linda, to bring some ID for him. Most of the Carnival goers have dispersed, leaving the streets to ferment beneath the vinegar stench of stale alcohol, vomit, urine, chicken bones and broken flip-flops. A few solitary whistles try in vain to keep the party going as stragglers weave and stagger their way home, stumbling into overturned crash barriers and stopping to piss in basements.

Joe and I head up Portobello Road towards the flyover. The right side of his face is bruised from where he hit the pavement and his wrists are ringed with red weals from the handcuffs.

'I'm sorry, Hannah,' he says, just before we reach the Mexican takeaway. 'I ruined everyone's day.'

'Is that how you usually settle things – by hitting people?' I say.

Joe shakes his head. 'I haven't hit anyone since I was fifteen.' He stops abruptly. 'You believe me, don't you?'

I study his face and feel a flood of relief when I see the expression in his eyes.

'Joe, you're going to have to accept that Daniel is part of Maya's life now,' I say. 'You can't change that.'

'I know,' Joe mumbles.

I take his hand. 'He's not going to replace you.'

'How do you know?' Joe's voice is so quiet I can hardly hear him.

'Because you'll always be her Dad.'

The look on Joe's face makes me want to cry.

'Will I?' he says.

The small red button on the answering machine is flashing when we get back to my flat, and there are three messages on my mobile which I had left at home to avoid losing it in the crowds. Joe feeds Nellie while I listen to them. I am still shaking when I run into the kitchen to tell him what's happened.

Chapter 24

The heavy steel lift inches its way up to the fourth floor of the hospital, stopping with a shudder every few seconds, as if fighting for breath, before lurching upwards again. Only two other people are in the lift with me – a woman of about my age, whose neck is covered with eczema, and her little boy, dressed in a Spiderman outfit.

When I finally spoke to Pam, Mum's neighbour, the previous evening after we got in from Carnival, she was already at her sister's in Somerset. She told me that she'd asked Mum for lunch on the Bank Holiday Monday, and when she didn't turn up, she'd gone round and spotted her through the window, face down on the kitchen floor. She wished she could stay so she could visit Mum in hospital, but her sister needed her help after her operation.

A sound like a submarine's sonar and one final shudder announce that we've reached the fourth floor, and the lift doors open onto a wide corridor whose walls and ceiling are painted a watery green. Dusty double-glazed windows on one side filter the sunlight to a sickly yellow haze which, when mixed with the blue vinyl floor and muted sounds from the street below, only add to the impression of being in an oversized aquarium. Two white-uniformed nurses pass me, their soft-soled shoes squeak-squeaking as though conversing in some curious underwater language.

The geriatric ward, which also acts as the hospital's stroke unit, lies at the end of this aquatic tunnel, and through the round porthole windows of the swing doors I can see the strange world on the other side. An elderly woman in a pink dressing gown is shuffling past reception, towing her drip stand. A nurse is removing the sheets from an empty bed as she chats to a doctor carrying a clipboard. A man in a green cardigan arranges a mug of sweet peas next to his wife's bed, while she stares on, expressionless.

Iona, whose hennaed hair is lanced with a chewed pencil, leads the way in her white uniform through the ward. We pass a woman who is being helped from her bed by a male nurse, her puffed ankles bulging from sheepskin slippers like two Yorkshire puddings. Further down, a man in a mustard-coloured pullover is watching a morning chat show on a small television. In the bed next to him a very old woman stares slack-jawed at the ceiling. The covers have partially slipped from her body and her nightdress has ridden up to expose thin, mottled legs and a pair of baby blue pants several sizes too large. The radio on her bedside table is tuned to Radio 4, where a chef is discussing how to make the perfect seafood salad.

'The stroke has left your mother paralysed down one side of her body,' says Iona in a soft Scottish accent. 'We still have to do an MRI to see the extent of the damage, but she's as comfortable as can be expected.' She pulls back the plastic curtain around the bed next to the far window.

'Look who's come to see you, Mrs Bailey.'

I stare at the sleeping figure in the bed, a little wax doll that someone has dressed in an oversized nightie. Her grey hair sticks up in all directions like a newly hatched chick and her left eye and left side of her mouth droop as if they're being pulled down by an invisible thread. Drips burrow into her wrists and lower arms, which are mapped with green and purple bruises.

Iona checks the bottle that's attached to a metal stand, then adjusts the thick tube which is filled with beige liquid. I sit down in the chair next to the bed and take Mum's limp right hand in mine.

A voice calls over from reception for Iona to help with a patient who has wandered out into the corridor and needs escorting back to bed.

'Will you be OK on your own?' asks Iona with a hurried smile.

I nod hesitantly. The curtain gives a plasticky rustle when she leaves, then it swings back into place, sealing Mum and me in our own little world.

'Hello, Mum,' I whisper. 'It's me, Hannah.'

Mum's right eye flutters open for a moment then closes again before opening a fraction once more. She looks at me and tries to smile, but only the right side of her mouth is working, so it's more of a grimace.

'How are you feeling?'

Mum coughs dryly several times. 'Been better,' she says hoarsely.

Beneath my fingers her skin feels like tissue paper, so thin it might tear at any moment, exposing hollow bird bones beneath. I shift position and my knee brushes against something warm and clammy hanging over the side of the bed. I look down and see a clear plastic bag filled with an amber-coloured liquid, the same colour as the liquid which fills the tube snaking under the sheets: Mum's catheter.

Mum is opening and shutting her mouth, making a

rasping sound. It takes a while before I can make out what she's saying.

'Why wouldn't I come, Mum?'

'Kind… busy…' The words are spoken from the right-hand corner of her lips, like someone talking with a cigarette in their mouth.

'Of course, I'm not too busy, Mum,' I say, with a flush of shame as I remember all those times I've cut short conversations with her.

Mum is saying something else. I lean forward so I can hear, but the smell of her breath makes me jerk back involuntarily.

Mum points with a shaky hand to her mouth, croaking a couple of words.

'No, Mum. Your breath doesn't smell. It's fine.'

Her tongue lifts to the roof of her mouth and clicks down again. 'Liar.'

'Well, maybe a bit.'

'Spun.'

'Sorry, Mum. Can you say that again?'

Her right eye slides over to the bedside table, where there's a small Petri dish of water and a sugar-lump-sized sponge on a stick.

'Oh, I see. Sponge.' I dip the stick in the liquid, then place it gently inside her mouth so that she can suck the moisture.

'Thank you, darling,' she whispers.

She sleeps for the next hour or so and I hold her hand, studying the scars left by Gilmore, the pale brown freckles dotted along her fingers and, just at the base of her thumb, a small dark red birthmark that I've never noticed before. It is in almost exactly the same place that I have one.

On the other side of the curtain I can hear the sounds of hospital life: chairs being scraped forward and back as visitors come and go; a clatter of plates as lunch is served; the rattling bronchial cough from a nearby bed. The chat show on the television has turned into a home makeover programme in which an excitable presenter is discussing new ways to stencil dining room chairs. Through a gap in the curtains I watch the man opposite, who had been arranging pink and white sweet peas in a tooth mug. His cardigan is inside out and he looks like he hasn't slept for days. The woman in the bed, presumably his wife, lies completely still, not even registering when he bends over to whisper in her ear.

Mum's curtain opens and another nurse appears, carrying a bowl of water, flannels, soap and a towel. Her starched white uniform is slightly too small and contrasts sharply with her blue-black skin. She's here to give Mum a bed bath.

I wake Mum gently. 'There's someone here to wash you, Mum.'

'It's only me, Mrs B,' says the nurse, resting a hand on Mum's shoulder. 'I came by this morning to introduce myself. My name's Fahima. Remember?'

It feels intrusive to watch Mum being washed, so while Fahima soaps her back I stare out of the window at the park. Joe will be walking Nellie and the other dogs by now. He had planned to go to Holland Park and I'd meant to warn him to keep Nellie away from the flowers in the walled garden, where she once wrecked a bed of freshly laid primroses by rolling in it.

Through the slit in the curtains I can see Iona tucking a woman – presumably the same woman who wandered out into the corridor – back under the covers, but each time she smoothes down the blankets, they are kicked off again. By the side of the neighbouring bed is the lady from the lift, brushing what remains of the hair of an old woman as carefully as if she were brushing cobwebs. Her son, still wearing the Spiderman mask, is playing with a toy fire engine, running it over the hills and furrows of the blanket that covers his grandmother's inert body.

Fahima looks up from washing Mum's arms. 'Your mum's a lovely woman,' she says to me. Then she leans down so she is eye to eye with Mum. 'Your daughter is very lucky, isn't she, Mrs B?'

Mum gives her a crooked smile.

'All done now.' Fahima folds the towel over her arm. 'I'll be back the day after tomorrow,' she adds, before she slips out through the plastic curtain.

Mum's right eye opens as soon as the nurse has left and I realise that she was awake all the time. 'Hannah,' she rasps. 'I don't want this.'

'What do you mean, Mum?'

She casts her eye around the small space inside the curtain, taking in the grey metal hospital bed, the feeding tube and the catheter coiling from under the sheets. 'This,' she whispers.

Iona comes in twice during the afternoon, once to check Mum's blood pressure, then again to change the feeding bottle. I stay by the bedside and watch her sleep, while memories float through my mind: Mum cleaning out Gilmore's cage on a cold December morning; Mum hopping jerkily in a hessian sack on school sports day; and Mum sitting by my bedside in hospital after I'd had my tonsils out, telling me that I had to come home soon because she and Gilmore missed me too much.

There's a clanking of wheels from the supper trolley and the smell of cauliflower cheese wafts through the curtain. I look down at my watch. The hands say that it's five forty-five and for a moment I can't work out whether it's morning or evening. Time has taken on a dreamlike quality, contracting and expanding to make three hours feel like five minutes and half an hour feel like a day. Inside the plastic curtain, normal life has been suspended so that it seems Mum and I and the hospital bed are hovering outside the laws of time and space with nothing to anchor us to the everyday world.

I hear the muffled sound of the shipping forecast from the old man's radio. I look down at Mum as the sonorous voice runs through the list of mysterious places: 'Viking, North Utsire, South Utsire, Forties, Cromarty...' The names register briefly before dissolving into the ether again, but Mum doesn't respond.

Through the slit onto the outside world, I watch the man in the green cardigan lean over and kiss his wife's forehead, before he lifts himself stiffly out of the chair. Some time later I feel a hand on my shoulder and hear Iona telling me that it's eight o'clock and I should go home for some rest.

Mum's breakfast things are still on the kitchen table. The contents of the half-finished bowl of muesli have solidified into a gluey mass and two slices of toast stand rigidly in the rack. Next to them is a catalogue for garden furniture, open on the 'Special Offer' page saying that if you bought one wood-effect bird bath, you were entitled to two free hand-painted chaffinches. I wonder which part of the kitchen floor Mum fell on and how long she had lain there.

I ring Pam in Somerset and tell her what Iona said about

Mum. Then I call Joe, who's already on his way down with Nellie, to give him directions from the tube.

They arrive shortly after nine o'clock, with Nellie panting theatrically from the walk up the hill.

'Are you OK?' Joe wraps his arms tightly around me.

'Not really,' I say. I stand there with my head against his chest, buried in the folds of his jumper. Nellie is at my feet, looking up at me with her button eyes.

Joe unpacks the takeaway that he picked up from The Mandarin Palace in Chorleywood, while I have a shower. I've just stepped out when Megan rings.

'I'm so sorry, Hannah,' she says. 'Is she going to be OK?'

'I hope so,' I say shakily.

She asks if I want her to come down but I say that Joe and Nellie are here with me.

'Call if you need me.' It's the catch in her voice that sets me off because Megan is even less of a crier than I am. I brush the tears away with my sleeve and I tell her I will ring tomorrow when I know a little more.

Behind me, Joe is spooning some noodles and stir-fried vegetables onto two plates. At his feet, Nellie lets out a cross bark.

'I know, Nell, we're all hungry.' He pulls a bowl from the cupboard and tips the rest of the noodles into it. Then he places the bowl down in front of her.

Nellie looks down at the bowl then back up at Joe.

'It's rice noodles. If you don't like them, I'll eat them,' says Joe. He extends a foot as if he's about to nudge the bowl back towards him.

Nellie growls and plunges her face into the food.

After Joe has added the sweet and sour prawns to our plates, we sit down at the kitchen table. But neither of us picks up our chopsticks.

'Do you want to talk about your mum?' says Joe with his hand on mine.

I shake my head. 'Later,' I say. 'Right now I need some light relief.'

'In which case you might want to hear about our walk?'

'Yes, please.' I smile gratefully. 'You didn't go near the flowerbeds, did you?'

'We went to the Kyoto Gardens, the one with the ornamental pond with those huge carp.' Joe hands me a pair of chopsticks. 'Poor Nellie was so busy drooling over the fish she nearly fell in.'

'She wasn't too cruel to the other dogs?'

Joe lets out a little laugh. 'Depends on what you mean by cruel.' He glances down at Nellie. 'She tried to mount Stan, if that counts.'

Nellie, who has just demolished her dinner in about four seconds flat, raises her head, shakes it a couple of times and lets out a massive sneeze, spraying Joe's jeans with snot.

See who's laughing now, matey.

After dinner, Joe and I go upstairs while Nellie settles in on the sofa. I clean my teeth, but before I join Joe in my old bedroom, I go into Mum's room. The bed is unmade and the eiderdown has slipped to the floor, where it lies in a crumpled floral heap. The pillow still has a faint indentation from her head.

I am awake for most of the night, thinking about Mum. At around 4 a.m. I get up and go down to the kitchen for a cup of tea. It's here, as the light begins to filter through the curtains that I remember Victor telling me what happened to his own mother.

*

July 2009

After I tell Victor about Luke and assure him that nothing will change between us, our friendship soon resumes its former rhythm. Over the following weeks I make a big effort not to miss our Monday cinema visits.

One muggy summer's evening, we watch Marcel Carné's *Les Enfants du Paradis*. It's not our standard *Nouvelle Vague* film, but a sumptuous tribute to French theatre set in the 1830s.

'That was one of my mother's favourite films,' says Victor in the café afterwards. 'She must have seen it at least ten times.'

Victor rarely mentions his mother. I only know that she brought him up singlehandedly, she was a seamstress, she adored the comedies of René Clair and her favourite church was the Saint-Eustache.

'You must have missed her when you came to London,' I say. 'How often did you go back?'

Victor stirs his coffee. 'Every other year, although I would write or telephone as often as I could.'

I take a forkful of my strawberry tart. 'Why didn't you go back more often?'

He shakes his head. 'I was too proud and too ashamed. I had told my mother so many lies: how well I was doing in London; the films I was working on; the new friends I had made… I just could not face her because I knew she would see through me.'

He stares down at his hands. 'I never even knew that she was ill. But one night, about eight years after I left Paris, I had one of those vivid dreams that are somehow different from the usual ones. In it, my mother and I were both back in the sitting room of the apartment in Montmartre and I was showing her a film.

"'I did not make this,' I said to her, shortly after it had begun. "I have never filmed inside the Saint-Eustache Church."

'My mother looked back at me with the most beautiful smile, and at that moment I noticed that we were no longer in the sitting room but standing inside Saint-Eustache itself. Light streamed through the stained-glass windows, making the air sparkle with hundreds of colours. The magnificent organ was playing, accompanying a full choir, and I recognised the hymn immediately because it was my mother's favourite – "Ave Maria". Soon the whole church resounded with a harmony of voices so rich and so unlike any others I had heard before that if I had believed in them I would have said that angels were singing.

'When I awoke the following morning I tried to telephone my mother but there was no reply. When I finally reached Madame Valjean, she said that she had found her that morning, sitting upright on the sofa with her supper tray still on her lap. When they did the post-mortem, they discovered a tumour the size of a grapefruit in her stomach.'

Victor pulls his handkerchief from his pocket. He wipes his eyes then says in barely more than a whisper. 'I will never forgive myself that I let my mother die on her own like that.'

*

The following morning, Joe and Nellie take the train back to London and I return to the hospital. Mum is asleep, but during the night she has been hooked up to a respirator because her lungs are too weak to pump out the excess fluid. The oxygen mask is made from see-through plastic, held in place by a piece of grey elastic around the back of her head. With each gurgling exhalation, steam puffs out of the two round holes at the side like a cartoon dragon.

'Hello, Mum,' I whisper.

Her right eye flickers open. Beneath the mask her lips move slightly, but it takes a while before I can decipher what she is mouthing.

'You came again?'

'Of course I did,' I say. I point to the bottle of Listerine on her side table that I brought with me. 'You feel like a mouth freshener?'

Mum nods and I take the sponge from the Petri dish and dip it into the mouthwash, before raising the mask and putting it gently into her mouth. She sucks at it for a few seconds then lets her head fall back onto the pillow.

Outside I can hear Iona and another nurse discussing Mrs Coombes, who escaped yet again from the ward during the night and was found at 6 a.m. by the print works roundabout in her short hospital nightdress waving cheerily to passing cars. Through the gap I see that the bed opposite, where the man with the inside-out cardigan had been, is empty and stripped down to the mattress. The blankets, along with a lilac dressing gown and a small green hairbrush, lie in a neat pile on the chair next to it. Collapsed over the edge of the tooth mug, the sweet peas on the side table are wilted and brown.

Two beds away, the man with the mustard pullover is watching the same morning chat show. This time a guest is talking about how she has just had her teeth whitened and how it changed her life because she can now smile without being ashamed.

'What about it, Mum?' I say. 'Let's treat ourselves to some LA teeth.'

Beneath the misted mask Mum tries to smile, but it's such a lopsided, wonky attempt that my eyes fill with tears. I quickly wipe them away before she can see, then I take her hand in mine again as her eye flutters shut.

Moments later Iona appears around the curtain. 'Dr Perkins would like to see you now.'

The man behind the desk gives me a quick professional smile when I enter the box-shaped room to the right of reception. With his babyish pink face and a small trimmed goatee, he looks much too young to be a qualified doctor. A framed picture of a young blonde woman holding a small baby sits next to his computer.

Dr Perkins starts talking and I watch his mouth opening and closing, accompanied by slight nods of his head. I find it difficult to look at him without crying, so I scan the office for something else to focus on. The walls are bare except for a calendar with pictures of Sardinia on it. The last week in September is marked with the words 'My Holiday!!!' Just above the calendar is a round white clock, whose hands quiver and jerk when they move forward as though they're fighting against time.

I feel like I'm trapped in an elaborate stage set, which might collapse at any moment, revealing the real world behind it once more. The world in which Mum is on her way to the hospice charity shop and I am sitting on the tube into work and all this – Mum's stroke, the doctor with the baby face, the man with the inside-out cardigan – is nothing more than a momentary lapse in reality, a temporary glitch in the system.

I find that if I focus on the calendar I can take in what Doctor Perkins is saying. He's talking more slowly now, emphasising certain words and phrases: CAT scan, quality of life, no mobility, ventilator, palliative care…

When he finishes, I nod, swallow, and tell him that he should do whatever he believes best, as long as Mum doesn't suffer. Saying the words, I feel like a character in that stage play, going through my lines without any rehearsal, a character pretending to be a grown-up but underneath still a child.

Back at Mum's bedside she is still asleep and doesn't wake for the rest of the afternoon. I sit with her hand in mine in that strange floating world, with just one thought, the same thought that was circuiting my mind throughout the night. Have I ever told her that I love her?

That evening Joe and Nellie arrive at Mum's house just a few minutes after me. Joe makes omelettes, which we eat in the sitting room. I don't feel like talking, so instead we watch a David Attenborough programme on the imminent extinction of a cave-dwelling salamander.

That night as I lie in bed, I pray. It's not a long prayer because I don't expect anyone to be listening and I only have one request – that wherever Mum is going, assuming she is going somewhere, there will be people there to love her.

They have already fitted the drip by the time I arrive the next morning. The machine next to Mum's left arm is the size of a cigar box, and printed on the side in red letters is the word 'Diamorphine'. Every so often it makes a whirring noise, the sound of the next dose of oblivion being released into Mum's veins. Iona tells me that Mum has been unconscious since early that morning.

I put my fingers to Mum's cheek. Are you scared, Mum? What do you think will happen? Is it going to end here in this hospital bed with these thin faded sheets? Or will it carry on elsewhere?

For some reason I remember a conversation I once had with my father. Prompted by a biology lesson, I was asking him about the brain when he said that scientists had never found the exact part where memories were kept. They could locate the bit that told your left eye to blink, or the part that could work out the square root of three hundred and eight, but precisely where memories lay was still a mystery. Afterwards, I spent quite a lot of time thinking about this and wondered where else, if not in the brain, they could be safely stored. I ran through a list of possible places ranging from the inner ear to the eyes. Eventually I came to the conclusion that the safest place for memories to be housed was in the most vital organ of the human body – in the heart.

Several years later, I came across an article in the newspaper about a woman who had undergone a heart transplant and who appeared to have inherited specific memories from the heart's former owner. Although the article gave no scientific explanation as to how this was possible, the story struck a chord and seemed to confirm my theory as an eleven-year-old that the heart was indeed the safest place to store my most precious memories.

I don't know why I should recall this in the last few hours that I spend with my mother, but listening to her breath becoming weaker and weaker, I imagine those memories of her, the ones I had pushed away for so long, slowly weaving themselves through the chambers of my heart like insoluble gold threads.

Through the window I see a silver plane slicing across the sky with a trail of cloud in its wake. Moments later, the trail dissolves into little puffs of mercury.

'Mum,' I say. 'I need to tell you something.' Even though she's still asleep, somehow I know that she can hear me.

I stroke her face, tracing each detail and hoping to imprint it indelibly onto my mind long enough to last a lifetime. Then I thank her for being my mother and for all the childhood memories she has given me, filled with so much love that they will last forever. I say that if I had my time again, I would be a very different daughter, and that one day I hope to be able to love as unconditionally as she did. Finally I hold her and tell her that I love her.

By the time I have finished the sun is setting. Streaks of orange, pink and gold, brighter than any technicolour film, are splashed across the sky. Yet behind the colour is something else, something luminous and alive, which glows with such intensity that, despite everything, I feel a wave of joy wash through me.

'Look, Mum, isn't it beautiful?' I say, clasping her hand tighter inside mine.

I hear a tiny wisp of breath, barely audible but there, as though she is letting me know that she too can see the sky. I look back down at her, thinking for one moment that she has heard me and that her eyes will be open once more – but she has gone.

Chapter 25

I am sitting on the brown slatted bench outside the main entrance to the hospital, waiting for Joe and Nellie to arrive in the cab from Watford station. The last drift of cloud has dissolved into the purple night sky and above me a thin waxy light drizzles from the street lamp. Nurses are hurrying off duty, chatting as they walk together to the bus stop. One of them has a date that night and is trying to decide whether to wear her new Topshop dress.

The ground in front of me is spotted with cigarette ends, sucked so hard that their spongy filters are crushed and soggy. I'm not sure why but I start to count them. I have just reached fifteen when the taxi pulls up and Joe gets out.

Joe and I sit in the back of the taxi heading towards Mum's. His arm is around me and my head is on his shoulder. Nellie is at my feet, her chin balanced on my knee. I can't talk – there's nothing more to say – so we sit together quietly. The evening news comes on the radio – President Assad's army has pushed rebel forces out of Aleppo; Ellie Simmonds has won another gold in the 400-metre Paralympics; and a celebrity is suing a Harley Street surgeon after her breast implants imploded.

Back at the house, the clock in the sitting room has stopped, the hands frozen at five to nine, so Joe spends a few minutes winding it up again. After a cup of tea, he and I start to draw up a list of all the things to be done: talk to Mum's few remaining relatives, register her death, ring the funeral home, the vicar… hymns… flowers, solicitors…

The next day, the three of us head back to the hospital in Mum's Golf to pick up her belongings. Iona hands me a see-through bag that contains the last things Mum wore in her life. Amongst them are her pale blue cardigan, a plain cotton skirt and her favourite pearl earrings, one of which still has a grey hair twisted around it.

After we have left the hospital we drive to a large redbrick building on Bushey Road to register Mum's death. Inside the front door are three different signs – Births, Marriages and Deaths – pointing to the three rooms in which to register life's most important milestones. According to their function, each room seems to diminish in size and state of repair. The first, for registering births, has recently been painted a cheery daffodil yellow, and inside I see a young woman filling in a form, while her husband cradles a tiny baby, whose bald head is covered in milk spots. The second room is mint green, and over the mantelpiece hangs a framed picture of a bride and groom standing under a rose bower. Aside from a Hoover propped up against the wall, it's empty. The room where deaths are registered comes last in the corridor and is painted a murky beige colour, which looks like a mixture of the leftover paint from the first two rooms. Presumably the people who use this room are too consumed with grief to notice.

Joe and I sit on the hard plastic seats waiting for the registrar. On the table in front of us are a glass vase of fake white tulips, a box of Kleenex tissues, a neat stack of death registration forms and three black biros. The only sounds are the hum of traffic on Bushey Road and the drone of the Hoover, which has just started up in the marriage room.

'What's your mum's date of birth?' says Joe, spreading out one of the forms on the table.

I scrabble in my bag for Mum's passport. Although I know her birthday, I can't remember if she's sixty-three or sixty-four.

'Do you know which hospital she was born in?'

I shake my head.

We work our way through the other questions on the form: the name and address of the deceased's GP, blood group, religion… there are so many basic things I don't know about my mother.

We are early for our one thirty appointment at Todd and Sons Funeral Directors, and as the bell echoes into the hollows of the building, I wonder what sort of person would choose to deal with death on a daily basis. After a short delay, my question is answered by the appearance of Patricia, who's wearing a white shirt, frilled around the neck, and a dark blue jacket with a matching skirt. On her upper lip is a little piece of what looks like egg, which quivers when she speaks.

After Joe and I have shaken hands with her, she glances at Nellie. 'We don't usually allow pets inside the building.'

Joe shoots Nellie a warning look. 'She's very well behaved.'

Patricia's flesh-coloured tights make a chafing sound in the otherwise silent corridor which leads to the consultation room. The green walls are covered in pictures of sunny country scenes featuring either lambs or children, or both. The air smells of dusty carpets and feels heavy against my legs, as though each person passing through has left a tangible trail of grief behind them.

Inside the consultation room, everything – the chairs, the curtains, the sofa coverings, the carpet, even the lampshade – is maroon, making me feel as though we've walked into a giant liver. The double-glazed windows that look out onto a busy road are sealed shut and it's incredibly hot. Joe and I sit on the sofa while Nellie flops down on the thick pile carpet. Patricia is opposite behind a polished dark wooden desk. There's a half-eaten sandwich inside a Boots 'Shapers' wrapper on top, and I watch her open one of the drawers and quickly push it inside, making the wrapper's stiff plastic crackle. By the lamp is a Twix, which she's either overlooked or doesn't mind being on display.

'I think we covered most of the details on the phone,' she says, 'so we just need to decide which casket you would like for your mother's internment.' The piece of egg is quivering and I wonder if I should tell her about it.

I feel Joe take my hand.

'We operate a monthly instalment plan, if that helps,' Patricia adds kindly. The shade on the lamp is giving her cheeks a weird maroon glow.

'You said on the phone that you wanted something simple, so here are some options…' Patricia opens the drawer and tries to pull something out but she's obviously forgotten about the egg sandwich, so that has to be removed first. She carefully places it next to the telephone before taking out a large blue hard-backed book.

Nellie's chin jerks up off the carpet. She lumbers to her

feet and marches over to the side of the desk to sit down almost on top of Patricia's navy blue shoes.

'Nellie, can you come back over here, please,' I say.

Nellie doesn't move. *Busy.*

'At the front of the catalogue you'll find the more elaborate casks,' says Patricia, who's obviously determined to ignore Nellie.

Nellie, whose eyes are drilling into the sandwich, lets out a plaintive whine.

Joe stands up and walks over to Nellie. 'Sorry about this,' he says to Patricia, before bending down to circle Nellie's stomach with his hands.

Nellie flattens herself on the floor like a fat slug, but he manages to get one hand under her belly. Having hoisted her to her feet, he lugs her back over to the sofa, where she sits in a sulky heap, staring at the liver-coloured carpet.

'So…' Patricia stuffs the Boots egg sandwich back into the drawer for the second time. 'Perhaps we can move on.' Catalogue in hand, she walks over to Joe and me.

'Take your time,' she says, handing it to me. The egg has gone from her top lip. It must have fallen off en route.

I feel Joe take my hand again as I turn to the first page which features the 'Deluxe Casket Range'. I stare down at 'The President' – 'This heavy oak coffin with high-gloss stained lacquer finish and a choice of elaborately designed side panels depicting scenes from Christ, Our Lord's life is one of our most…'

From the corner of my eye I notice Patricia extend a frosted nail to nudge the Twix behind the telephone.

I look down at the catalogue again. 'The Tea Rose is a walnut casket with full couch lid, featuring a rose motif and sculpted viewing panels. The interior drapery consists of luxury white ruched velvet with a matching satin headrest...'

Up until now, I've tried not to think about the fact that I will have to choose a box in which to put Mum's body before burying it beneath the ground. But with the pictures in front of me and the thought of Mum sealed inside, my eyes blur with tears.

I stare out of the window, where a woman with a small child is standing outside a newsagent's. The little girl is holding an ice lolly which has left an orange stain around her mouth, and the mother is kneeling down to wipe it off, first licking her tissue then rubbing the little girl's cheeks.

'Have you given any thought to the deceased's outfit? We have a small range at the back of the catalogue,' says Patricia, rising from her seat again. 'It's one less thing to think about.'

On autopilot, I turn to the final page where, displayed against a backdrop of white velvet, are the 'Burial Outfits'. For the men, there's a suit in dark blue or black viscose and a white Viyella shirt, and for the women, a viscose shirt with 'leg of mutton sleeves and matching elasticated-waist skirt, available in midnight blue or discreet salmon pink.'

I'm not sure if it's the maroon room, the egg sandwich, or the discreet salmon pink skirt, but suddenly I begin to laugh, an hysterical high-pitched laugh, which seems to ricochet like gunfire around the room. But then the laugh turns into a long thin wail, followed by a sort of guttural choking sound.

I can barely breathe because it feels like someone is squeezing their hands around my throat and my heart is beating so fast it's going to explode. I launch myself up from the sofa and run towards the door.

Back in the car park of Todd and Sons, I'm sitting in the passenger seat of the Golf. Joe is next to me and Nellie is on my lap. Huge sobs rattle through my ribs, making me shake violently and leaving me gulping for breath.

Joe is holding me tight and his hand is stroking my hair. 'Just cry, Hannah. Cry as much as you can.'

I can feel Nellie nuzzling my jumper and a damp patch of drool spreading across my skirt. When the sobbing eventually subsides, Joe gives me a handkerchief. I blow my nose, then look across at him and down at Nellie.

'Thank God, you're both here,' I say.

Chapter 26

'Hello, stranger.' Ian rises from his chair and folds me into a lanky hug. 'I missed you.'

I rest my head briefly against his cotton shirt and tell him that I missed him too. It's been three weeks since I was last in the office.

'Are you alright?' he asks gently.

'I'm getting there.' I pull back to survey the room which looks even smaller than before. It feels really weird to be back, like I'm just pretending to be me, going through the motions of my old life.

Ian reaches into the top drawer of his desk. 'This is for you.' He hands me an envelope. 'I wanted to say how sorry I am about your mum.'

I pull out the card and read the message. Immediately my eyes fill with tears. 'Thank you,' I say.

Ian puts an arm around me again, while I wipe my eyes with the cuff of my jumper.

'Sorry,' I say, 'I seem to be crying almost every day at the moment.'

'That's a good thing,' says Ian. 'Keep it coming.'

For the first part of the morning, Ian fills me in on what's been happening over the past few weeks – he's been on holiday to Edinburgh with his mum and Matthew – one of his landscape photographs won a competition in a national newspaper – and apparently the freelance writer who stood in for me wasn't nearly as much fun as I am.

As expected, there's a mountain of work, but I start small, with a piece on the benefits of a daily dose of flaxseed oil (reduced risk of cancer and heart disease, quicker burning of body fat, healthier-looking skin). Every so often I glance up at the picture of Mum on my desk. It's one of the very few recent photographs that I have of her. Pam took it in the spring and she's standing in her garden beneath her favourite tree, the purple lilac, which is in full flower. The sun is lighting up her face and her eyes are shining with happiness.

It's almost two weeks since her funeral – according to the calendar in the doctor's office, he'll be away in Sardinia now. But it doesn't feel like that, sometimes it feels like six months and sometimes just a few days. And it isn't only time that seems out of sync. I also feel detached and out of step from everything that's happening around me. I wonder how other people manage it. How do they bridge the before and after?

Joe's been brilliant, dragging me out to films and plays and taking me away for a weekend in Hastings, because we obviously had to cancel our trip to Ireland. We also spend a lot of time taking Nellie for walks, not to the cemetery any more, for obvious reasons, but round the corner to Meanwhile Gardens.

Joe's also come with me to visit Mum's grave. She's buried in the grounds of the Norman church, where she and Dad married. A simple wooden cross marks the spot, to be replaced by a headstone after the earth has settled. When the man in the memorial shop asked me what I wanted written on the stone, apart from her name and the dates of her life, I didn't know what to say. 'What about something like "Sadly missed by her loving daughter", he suggested, but I shook my head. I didn't tell him why, though – that I felt like a fraud using the words 'loving daughter'. It's hardly as if I earned them. I thought about it for over a week, and in the end, I asked him to engrave the words 'One Fine Day'. Somehow, they just seemed to fit.

I've been back to the house a couple of times to sort through Mum's things, but I haven't made much progress. I can't bear the thought of boxing up the remnants of her life and sending them away. I know it's ridiculous. I've spent the last twenty-odd years shutting her out, and now I am unable to even part with the old muddy brown lace-ups that she wore to do the gardening.

As for her other things, not her jewellery, which I'll keep even though I probably won't wear, but her hairbrush, her faded pink Carmen Rollers, her powder compact – I can't bring myself to even pick them up. Years of her using them means that each one carries a trace of her, like an echo, and if I touch them the echo will fade.

One Saturday afternoon when I was tidying her bedside table, I found an old black and white photograph at the back of the drawer. The picture showed Mum holding me as a newborn baby, no more than a few hours old. She's smiling at me and tracing a finger down my cheek, with a look of such pure love that my eyes immediately fill with tears. It was only then, sitting on Mum's bed with the photo in my hand, that I realised I wasn't just grieving for myself. I was grieving for Mum and for the sort of relationship that she must have imagined she'd have with her only child, the relationship that we actually had, and the distance between the two.

'Hannah?' I feel a hand on my shoulder and I look up to see Ian place a sandwich next to my computer. 'Cheese and tomato. You don't have to eat it if you don't want to.'

'Thanks,' I smile up at him and start to remove the wrapper even though I'm not really hungry.

'Want to talk?' says Ian.

'Maybe later.' I take a bite of the sandwich because I don't want to look ungrateful.

'Want a distraction?'

I nod.

Ian taps something into my computer and brings up the home page of a website devoted to British bulldogs. 'I stumbled across this the other day. It's a competition to find the best-looking bulldog in Britain. If you win you get a whole year's supply of Beef-Stick dog treats. Shall we enter Nellie?'

'Why not?'

Ian presses the download key and the screen fills with the questionnaire, which rather bizarrely asks the same type of questions that a potential Miss World might have to answer. Ian reads from the top section, fingers poised over his keyboard.

'Vital statistics?'

I think for a moment. Mr Tierly has weighed and measured Nellie a few times over the years, but I can't remember what the figures were.

'Fat as fuck.'

'Be serious, Hannah. We want those dog treats.'

I agree to measure her again that evening.

'Weight?'

'Sixty pounds, give or take.'

'That's impressive,' says Ian. 'Favourite pastimes?'

I think for a while. 'Fine dining.'

'Dream job?'

'You could put "working with small children" for a laugh.'

Ian chuckles. 'I made that one up, but let's put it in anyway.'
He clicks the save button. 'They also want a picture of her.'

'It's just like Readers' Wives – only with less tacky
underwear and more fur,' I say. 'Either that or a racy dating
website.' I watch Ian upload Nellie's profile. 'Which reminds
me, have *you* been on any dates yet?'

'A couple,' says Ian.

'And?'

'The first girl never turned up and the second one got so
drunk that I had to put her in a taxi home at nine o'clock.'

'But did it go OK until she got drunk?'

'Not really.'

'Why not?'

'Nerves,' says Ian. He picks up his coffee cup and mimes a
bout of bad shaking.

'Did you hum?'

'There may have been some humming.'

We agree that we should try another date dress rehearsal
later in the week, after I've waded through some of the work
backlog.

The rest of the afternoon slips by with several articles and
some CD reviews. I leave the office just before six and head
to Foyles to buy Joe a book of Alfred Fagon plays to thank
him for being so wonderful over the last few weeks.

Walking down Charing Cross Road I see a figure coming
towards me. Although the face looks craggier now and the back
is bent with age, I'd recognise that walrus moustache anywhere.

'Monsieur Henri,' I say when I reach him. 'It's me,
Hannah.'

'Mademoiselle Bailey!' He grabs my hand and shakes it hard. 'What a pleasure!'

We talk for a while and he tells me about his part-time job at the French cinema in South Kensington. It's his day off and he's just been to a screening at the Curzon round the corner so he thought he'd pass by his old cinema.

'Do you ever see Victor?' I ask.

He looks surprised at my question. 'I have not seen Monsieur Lever in over three years. The last time he came to the cinema, he was very ill.'

'Oh, he's completely fine now.' I say. 'I saw him not so long ago. In fact I'm due another visit. Did you hear that he has his own cinema?'

'No!' says Monsieur Henri, incredulous.

'He shows films that he has made himself.'

'A miracle,' Monsieur Henri shakes his head in disbelief. Then he claps his hands together and laughs like a little boy. 'See! It worked out for him after all.'

On the way home I think about what Monsieur Henri said. Although I clearly remember Victor being ill a few months before he retired, I had assumed that it was just a particularly nasty bout of summer flu.

*

August 2009

In all the time that I have worked with Victor, I have never known him to be unwell. But around two months after he told me about his mother, he fails to turn up for work on a Monday morning. When he still hasn't appeared by

273

Thursday, I begin to worry. It's never been necessary to call him before because we always make our arrangements at the office so I don't have his home number, and he refuses to get a mobile. When I ring the HR department for the management company that own the building, they say that he is sick and won't be returning to work for at least another week. I try to get his address from them but they won't give it out for privacy reasons. However, I know from Victor's and my conversations that he lives in Stafford Road in West Kilburn, and from his description of his next-door neighbour's banana plants, I reckon I can work out which flat belongs to him.

'What are you doing here?' Victor stares at me from the doorway of his ground-floor flat. He's wearing a dark blue towelling dressing gown and slippers. His cheeks are a pallid yellow and his forehead is damp with sweat.

'I've come to play nurse.' I nod to the bag of Covent Garden soups, grapes, lemons, fresh ginger and a pot of honey that I've brought with me. 'Where's the kitchen?'

Victor's flat is small but surprisingly cosy. The galley kitchen, which looks onto a neat back garden, has rows of jars filled with pulses and beans, and pots of basil, thyme and rosemary line the windowsill. In the adjoining sitting room the walls are covered with prints by Gauguin and Cézanne, along with a picture of *Tobias and the Angel* by Andrea del Verrocchio. Above the mantelpiece is a framed picture of the Saint-Eustache Church, and to the right of that is a bookcase, filled mostly with the French romantic writers I know he loves. On the top shelf is a small picture of Victor standing beside Truffaut, and next to it is the cine camera that I gave him.

While I unpack the shopping, Victor lies on the sofa beneath a thick blanket. I try to make small talk, telling him how the lift jammed between floors that morning, and how Luigi's nineteen-year-old niece has come to work with him and is already causing chaos amongst the male customers.

'Sorry,' I say, 'work's probably the last thing you want to hear about.' To change the subject I point up to the cine camera. 'You've never used it, have you?' I walk over and take it down from the shelf, blowing off the fine layer of dust.

'What would I film?' asks Victor.

'The same sort of things you filmed when you were younger. People in the neighbourhood, the woman next door tending her banana plants, the guy from the local greengrocer – whatever catches your eye that you can film without getting into trouble.' I note Victor's non-committal shrug. 'Come on, if not for you, then do it for me.'

'How is Luke?' says Victor a little later when I've handed him a bowl of chicken soup.

'He's well,' I say. 'Although the American funding for his documentary has been cut so he's trying to raise the money over here.' I don't elaborate because I don't want to bother Victor with my problems, but I am getting quite worried about Luke. He's become obsessive about the documentary and talks of little else. The flat hunting, which at first he was so enthusiastic about, has clearly been put on the back burner so now it's mostly just me who goes to the viewings.

'I'd still like you two to meet,' I say. 'You'd have a lot to talk about, film-wise.' I hand him a spoon. 'When you're better, we'll make a date.'

While Victor eats, I look through his books. He has all of

Hugo's works including his entire poetry collection, which is bound in red leather with pages edged in gold.

Victor watches me from the sofa. 'I started to write a book once,' he says.

'Really? What was it about?'

Victor wipes a dribble of soup from his chin. 'An awkward young boy growing up in Paris who dreams of making films. I never completed it. I could not think of an ending.'

After Victor has finished the soup, he lies back on the sofa with his eyes closed, dozing. I pick out a volume of Hugo's *Les Contemplations* and let the book fall open in my hands. The poem, whose English translation appears on the right-hand side of the page, is dedicated to the writer and poet Théophile Gautier. When I turn over to read the final few lines, a red feather flutters to the floor. I bend down and pick it up.

'I found that in the street the same morning that I started to write my book,' says Victor from the sofa, his eyes now open. 'In French, the word for feather, "*plume*", is also the word for pen, so I believed it to be a sign.' He adjusts the cushions behind him so he can sit up a little straighter. 'Which poem have you just read?'

'The one dedicated to his friend Théophile Gautier. It's beautiful.'

Victor nods. 'I would like you to have that book, Hannah.'

'But it's part of your collection.'

'I do not need one with an English translation in it,' says Victor. 'Please. It will be something to remember me by.'

'Why? You're not planning on going anywhere, are you?'

Victor laughs gently. 'I have been considering a trip to Honolulu but perhaps not today.' He shakes his head. 'No, Hannah, I am not planning to go anywhere.'

'Good.' I tuck the feather back into the folds of the pages. 'Tell you what,' I say, slotting the book back onto the shelf, 'why don't you come over for tea next Sunday if you're feeling better?' I pull a biro and piece of paper from my bag to jot down my address. 'Then you can finally meet Luke.'

Victor is still unwell the following Sunday and Luke and I are busy over the next couple of weekends. In fact, it's another six weeks before I am able to introduce the two of them, and when I do it sets in motion a series of events, whose outcome I could never have predicted.

Chapter 27

We spread out Joe's red blanket beside the tennis courts in Holland Park and unpack the picnic. It's still warm for the end of September, and the early evening light fingers its way in long shadows across the grass. A blackbird calls to its mate from the nearby eucalyptus tree, and the sweet scent of roses hangs in the air.

Monitored closely by a drooling Nellie, I unwrap Ramón's freshly made chorizo from its greaseproof paper and cut her a small slice. Meanwhile, Joe opens various tubs and pots to lay out green olives stuffed with slithers of red chili, roasted artichokes and a block of Manchego cheese, all from Ramón's.

'Do you want the good news or the bad?' Joe takes a bottle of cava from the bag.

'Start with the bad.'

'My landlord has sold the flat so I have to move out,' he pauses and looks at me for a second or so, 'but if nothing else comes up, my mate Saul says I can move in with him. On the plus side, I heard today that I got that grant from the Portobello Business Trust.' Smiling, he loosens the cork of the bottle. 'That means I can start rehearsals by the end of the month.'

I fling my arms around his neck. 'That's so brilliant, Joe.'

'And there's more,' he grins. 'Nadia has agreed to let me

have Maya for a whole weekend in November.' He pours the cava into two glasses. 'Finally you'll get to meet her properly.' Although I've obviously been introduced to Maya, I still haven't spent much time with her and I have to admit the prospect makes me a bit nervous.

'To your play and to the weekend with Maya,' I say, touching my glass against Joe's. We both take a sip, then Joe passes me the pot of olives. I pick one out and pop it into my mouth. Immediately my tongue begins to buzz and my eyes start to water.

'That's hotter than Hades.' I swallow another slug of cava, which only seems to make it worse. 'My mouth's about to blow off.'

'I thought you had taste buds of steel,' Joe laughs.

We've polished off most of the picnic and now we're chatting about where we might take Maya when she visits. Next to us, Nellie is digesting the chorizo she's just guzzled. Her chin is resting on her paws and every so often she lets out a little belch.

'I'd love you to meet Nadia as well,' says Joe. 'Now that she and I are getting on again.' He tilts his head towards mine. 'You'd be OK with that, wouldn't you?'

'Of course, she sounds like a good woman.'

'She is.' Joe squeezes my hand. Then he nods to the two peaches next to the empty cava bottle on the rug. 'I bought those especially for you. They're the French ones you love so much.'

I kiss him then take one and bite into it, wiping the trickle of sweet juice from my chin. As I lie back on the grass to watch the clouds above me, it strikes me that I'm actually looking forward to meeting Joe's ex.

*

September 2009

'Sure I can't tempt you?' I say to Luke as I hold out the bag of peaches I've just bought from Ted's fruit stall. 'They're those delicious French ones I always buy here.'

Luke shakes his head and continues walking in the direction of the Coffee Pot. Although it's a sunny Saturday afternoon, it's been an effort to drag him from his flat. Ever since the funding fell through, he barely goes out except to work.

We've just reached the café and are scanning for an outside table when I hear a voice behind me calling Luke's name.

'Well, what are the chances?' A woman with long dark hair, wearing a bright orange silk scarf around her neck, stops in front of Luke and kisses him on the cheek.

'Hello, Catherine,' says Luke. 'I thought you were in LA.'

Catherine flicks the orange scarf behind her shoulder. 'Not any more,' she replies in her West Coast accent. Then she turns to look me up and down. 'Hi,' she says, proffering a limp, cool hand.

'Hi,' I say, shaking the hand, 'I'm Hannah.'

She gives me a cursory nod before swivelling back to Luke. 'So how's tricks?'

'Tricks are fine,' says Luke, just as a guy with curly black hair who I recognise from Luke's boss's party in Elgin Crescent walks up to stand beside Catherine.

'Hi, Luke,' he says.

'Justin,' says Luke evenly.

There's an uncomfortable pause.

'We'd better get going,' says Justin. 'We're having lunch with my folks so we can't be late.'

Catherine looks over at Luke. 'Small world, huh?' she says with a smile, before linking her arm through Justin's and heading off into the crowds.

'So that was the famous Catherine,' I say when Luke and I are sitting by the window inside the Coffee Pot a little later. The place is packed with tourists because it's a Saturday and the thudding techno music is so loud that we have to shout to make ourselves heard.

'Yip.' Luke rips open a sachet of sugar and tips it into his double espresso.

'She's very beautiful,' I say. 'I wonder how long she and Justin have been together.'

Luke stares over at the Electric Cinema opposite, whose notice board shows a list of forthcoming attractions. 'How should I know?'

'But I thought you two were mates.'

Luke shrugs. 'We only worked together on a couple of jobs.'

I take a sip of my cappuccino. The froth's gone flat and it's lukewarm. 'By the way, they finally sent the details on that place near Kensal Green tube.' I rummage in my bag and pull out the envelope I'd stuffed inside that morning.

Luke stares at me. He clearly has no idea what I'm talking about, although we've discussed the flat several times. I tap his sleeve with the corner of the envelope.

'The flat,' I say. 'The one that actually looks half decent.'

Luke glances down at his sleeve. 'Jesus, Hannah, is that all you can think about?' He picks up his espresso and drains it in one. 'Come on, let's get out of here. This music is doing my head in.'

'Are you going to finish that peach?' I hear Joe say from beside me, 'because if you're not, I'll have it.'

I smile and reach over to let Joe take a mouthful. Out of the corner of my eye I spot a small blue butterfly that's landed on the grass by his elbow. Its blue wings are quivering in the breeze and I can even make out its minuscule antennae.

'Look at that,' I point to it and Joe follows my gaze.

'Did you know that the ancient Greeks believed when someone dies, the soul leaves the body in the form of a butterfly?' he says.

'I bet you read that in one of your "special" books?' Joe's special books, as I call them, range from *The Tibetan Book of the Dead* to Eckhart Tolle's *A New Earth*. Since Mum's funeral I've even found myself dipping into a few of them, although I'd never admit it to Joe.

'I did, as it happens,' Joe laughs. 'It's a beautiful thought, isn't it?'

I agree that it is.

Nellie is also watching the butterfly, inching towards it on her belly and extending her nose to sniff its wings.

'Be nice to it, Nell,' I say.

Nellie glances at me for a split-second then, before I can react, she lifts a paw and slams it down on top of the butterfly.

'Nellie!' Joe and I shout.

Nellie gurns back at us, then raises the offending paw to reveal the butterfly's crushed body on the ground. It lies there for a few seconds, before a small tremor flickers through its wings and, closely studied by a quizzical Nellie, it struggles up, shakes itself briefly, then flies off.

Above us, sunset is spreading across the sky and shafts of light pierce the pink and orange clouds, reaching down to the grass like dozens of luminous ladders.

'Did I ever tell you about the sky on the night that Mum died?' I say to Joe.

Joe shakes his head.

'The colours were extraordinary, so much sharper and brighter than usual. It looked like a layer had been peeled away.'

Joe props himself up on one elbow. 'I noticed that too when my grandmother passed away. Bizarre, isn't it?'

I nod and it's then that I tell him about those final minutes with Mum, how I held her long after her last breath, because I couldn't bear to let her go. Yet even though her body was growing colder with each moment, I had the very definite feeling that she was still there in the room with me.

'This morning I found myself asking Mum to send me a sign that she's OK,' I say. 'How daft is that?'

Joe takes my hand. 'I don't think it's daft at all.'

In the brief silence that follows we hear the sound of a woman singing from Holland Park opera house. She's obviously practising for tonight's performance, and her falsetto voice has a plaintive, melancholy quality that makes goosebumps prickle my skin.

'That's strange,' says Joe. 'I knew they did concerts here in the summer but I thought they ended by September.' He pauses to listen to the soaring melody. 'It's amazing. Do you know what it is?'

I nod, hardly able to believe what I am hearing.

'It's from Madame Butterfly. It's called "One Fine Day".'

Chapter 28

Although it's already the beginning of October, the evening is warm when I walk down the street towards Victor's video shop. Dusk is just descending, softening the edges of the houses, but I can still make out the flowers of the gardens in front of them: fuchsias like tiny crimson ballerinas, pale pink tuberoses and clouds of white winter jasmine. The tree at the bottom of the video shop steps is also still in bloom and the creamy trumpet-shaped flowers are breathing their vanilla scent into the hazy air.

The door is open and I can see Victor tacking up a poster in the foreign section. It's a picture taken from Michael Haneke's *Amour*, featuring the still-beautiful face of eighty-four-year-old Emmanuelle Riva.

'Not interrupting, am I?' I say from the doorway.

Victor turns round and smiles broadly. He's wearing a pair of wine red corduroys and the frayed blue shirt. 'Of course not.' He hurries towards me and gives me a hug. 'How wonderful it is to see you again.'

'You too,' I say, returning his hug. I pull back and look into his eyes. 'I should have come sooner.' Seeing him here in front of me, I suddenly feel the weight of the past two months. Tears gather, so before I start crying again I cough and point to his trousers.

'Check out those toff strides.'

'It's my new look. To go with my promotion.'

'What do you mean, "promotion"?'

Victor nods to the back of the room. 'Give me a minute and I will show you.'

After he has locked the video shop door, we walk to the back of the room, through the curtain and down the corridor. I notice that the photographs of the *Nouvelle Vague* directors have gone. In their place are pictures of more contemporary French filmmakers – amongst them Jacques Audiard, Claire Denis and Jean-Pierre Jeunet.

Inside the projectionist's booth there have also been a few changes. The cinematograph is still here, as is the drinks cabinet, but this time there are no boxes on the floor and only a few film reels remain on the top shelves. The bottom shelf is now home to a random selection of groceries. A poster hangs from the wall, advertising a film that I've not heard of – *Une vie passionée.*

'So how have you been?' asks Victor, taking the chair next to mine.

I look over at his face, which is full of concern and again, I feel my eyes welling up.

'Mum died,' I say. 'She had a stroke.'

Victor shifts his chair closer to mine. 'Would you like to talk about it?'

I nod and start to describe the last few days I spent with my mother. I tell Victor how those hours by her bedside will always be amongst the most precious of my life. It's the final hour that I find myself focusing on – that extraordinary sky, her peaceful last breath and how I was still able to feel her presence around me long after she had died.

'I'm so grateful that I was able to tell her I loved her,' I say. 'I would never forgive myself if I hadn't.' As I say this, I hear an echo of Victor's words after he'd told me about his own mother's death. I glance over at him and see that his eyes are also filled with tears.

'Thank you for showing me that first film,' I say. 'Without it, things would have been very different.'

Victor takes my hand in his. 'I am so proud of you, Hannah.'

'I still miss her, though,' I say. 'Every day.'

'I know,' he says softly.

Victor is standing by the glass cabinet because we've both decided we need a drink. He's just selected the third bottle in the row, whose contents are the colour of blackcurrants.

'This is my favourite.' He pours a glass and hands it to me.

I take a sip. The drink does have a hint of crème de cassis, but there's something else behind that, which I've not tasted before. I take another mouthful, then point over to the bottom shelf which is stacked with the groceries, including two tins of ambrosia rice pudding and some Mr Kipling's Bakewell Tarts.

'What's with that lot?'

Victor smiles. 'Like the biscuits, there is so much that I never tried. I am making up for lost time.'

'Which reminds me,' I say, 'I brought you these to taste… now that you're getting so adventurous.' I pull the packet of pork scratchings from my pocket and hand it to Victor. He immediately opens it, takes one out and studies the bristle of hairs on the surface. Then he pops it in his mouth. He crunches thoughtfully, grimaces then gives me back the packet. 'Save the rest for Nellie,' he winks, then quickly downs the last of his drink.

'So tell me about this promotion,' I say.

Victor glances over at the film poster which features an old man standing in an art studio, surrounded by an array of richly colourful paintings. He's smiling and light seems to be emanating from his body. The title is written as if with a fine paintbrush.

'I have finished my very first full-length film,' says Victor. 'Would you like to see it?'

This time I am genuinely interested to watch Victor's film. I'm still amazed that he's managed to make a full-length feature, even if it is a co-production. The title of it – *Une vie passionée* – also intrigues me because I'm always curious about people who have found their passion in life. As I take my seat in the auditorium, I can't help thinking back to the time when I too believed that I had finally found my own.

*

October 2009

It's difficult to say exactly when the idea for the book first formed, but I know for certain that it happened in Monsieur Henri's cinema. For there, cocooned within the burgundy walls, I fell in love with and was inspired by Victor's favourite directors: Godard and his empathy for the outsider; Resnais with his themes of time, memory and regret; Chabrol, whose tales of friendship and failed ambition never failed to move me; and Truffaut, whose characters found it so difficult to express their emotions.

The idea crystallises in my mind the day Victor and I watch Resnais's, *La Vie est un Roman*. As soon as the title appears on the screen – which I translate literally to mean

Life is a Novel, although I know this isn't correct – something sparks inside me. Suddenly I know that there's a story I want to tell, Victor's story.

Instead of concentrating on the film, I spend the next two hours sifting through the conversations between Victor and me in the café each Monday and on our Sunday outings. There's so much material I can use, from his childhood fascination with his neighbours' lives, his friendship with the projectionist at Studio 28, his meeting with Truffaut...

I know instinctively that the first half of the book will be rooted in reality – Victor's life in Paris and his early days in London. But after that I will have to fictionalise the story, to find an ending in which he is somehow able to return to film-making. I certainly don't want to portray him as a broken old man who settled for the life of a lift operator.

I'm realistic enough to know that my day job of knocking out copy about echinacea and Healthy Eats probably won't equip me for the long haul of penning a novel. And I'm pretty sure that my earlier attempts to write fiction won't be much help. But as I sit there with Resnais's film flickering across the screen in front of me, I'm determined to at least give it a go.

I start the first draft a few days later, and almost immediately experience that same feeling I used to get as a teenager and in my twenties when I wrote. I'd forgotten how much I loved it – that sense of complete absorption and quiet contentment. With it comes a feeling of connection – to what exactly, I don't know. But it's so delicious and I'm so immersed in the act of writing that the hours glide by unnoticed. When I finally leave the desk I find that the fictional Victor is still with me, prompting me with words and images which I can use to tell his story.

I decide to keep quiet about the project because first I want to make sure that I can complete it. Then I'll probably get Megan to take a look. After that – and only if I think it's good enough – I'll show it to Victor. As for Luke, I'll wait until he's in a better frame of mind before I tell him anything about it.

I'm still preoccupied with the story when Victor and I take the guided tour around Kensal Green Cemetery. It's our first Sunday outing since Victor's illness and he still looks frail but he says he needs the fresh air, and although he was a little surprised at my choice of destination, he is as fascinated as I am by the tales of the cemetery's famous inhabitants. His favourite is the story of Graham Ducrow, the circus performer, renowned not only for his feats of horsemanship but also for his vanity and filthy language.

After the tour, Victor says he is tired so we sit down on the bench near The Dissenters' chapel. It's a crisp autumn afternoon and the leaves on the nearby chestnut tree are turning to a burnt orange. A shiny black crow hops from gravestone to gravestone, cawing crossly at the sky.

'The tour has made me homesick for Paris,' says Victor, turning his face towards the sun's last rays. 'Père Lachaise is my favourite cemetery in the world.'

'Aaah, but does it have as many exciting inmates as we have here?'

Victor smiles. 'Well, apart from Oscar Wilde and Jim Morrison, there is Balzac and Bizet, Marcel Marceau and Modigliani, Edith Piaf and Proust…'

'Alright,' I laugh. 'No need to brag.'

We sit in silence and watch the sun sink behind the gasworks. In the distance a train rattles past, beginning its journey to Bath or Bristol or some western tip of the British Isles, but here in the cemetery everything is still.

'Where would you like to be buried?' I ask Victor.

He turns with a look of surprise. 'Why do you ask?'

'Just interested. You know I have a morbid streak.'

Victor gestures towards a spot beneath the chestnut tree, near where the crow is now perched on a stone urn. 'If it cannot be in Père Lachaise, then that looks like a good place.'

'Smart choice,' I say. 'And I'll be just around the corner, next to that foulmouthed circus performer. He should keep us entertained for a few centuries.'

Beneath the chestnut tree the crow lets out a loud caw, flaps its wings, then flies off towards the cemetery gates.

*

The lights in the cinema have dimmed and the curtains are already open. The familiar 'Lumière Productions' appears on the screen and the red feather untethers itself from its mooring and floats down. When it reaches the bottom, a burst of choir music fills the auditorium. Hundreds of heartbreakingly beautiful voices swirl around me, so rich in harmony and so perfectly pitched that I feel a lump in my throat. Seconds later the film begins.

Immediately I can see that this is a very different production. Although there are still traces of Victor's former *Nouvelle Vague* style, there's a much smoother flow to the images and the stark realism has been replaced by carefully lit camera angles.

The opening scene shows a young man trudging through the drizzle to catch the bus to work. His hands are buried deep in his pockets and his face has an expression of barely suppressed desperation. Once at work, he sits in front of a stack of papers, occasionally answering his fifties-style telephone before chewing listlessly on a dry sandwich for lunch.

Again, it's as if I can feel what he is feeling – that slow, leaden walk to work, the same numbed resignation and the weighted sense of wasted time.

Eight hours later the man takes the same grey route home. It is only when he climbs the stairs to the attic and pushes open the door that a burst of colour explodes onto the screen. Green, blue and red canvases line the walls, shiny tubes of oil paints litter the floor and light floods the room from an overhead window. The man walks over to the old-fashioned turntable, sets on a record and the sound of a Rossini opera swells around him. Then he begins to paint.

The following day the man repeats the same resigned walk to work, but on the bus home in the evening, he sits behind a woman who is telling her friend how the art course that she runs will be cancelled unless she finds more students. The young man listens intently and when she has finished, he taps her on the shoulder.

The next scene shows him standing in front of an easel in a massive studio, daubing bright yellow oil paint onto a canvas. The same woman from the bus, and now his tutor, stands behind him, offering advice. By now I'm experiencing completely different emotions – gone is the leaden weight from my shoulders and in its place is a feeling of lightness and that same sense of connection that I get when I write.

From then on, the screen becomes a blur of fast-moving images showing the man's wedding to his art tutor, the birth of their first child and the opening night of his first exhibition. Each one of these snapshot pictures radiates a tangible, almost visceral feeling of joy.

More light-flooded images flash by with the births of his other two children, holidays with his family beneath a dazzling cerulean sky and several more art exhibitions. The final scene shows the man, now in his late eighties, standing in his studio, listening to Rossini and gazing with rapturous delight at the dozens of paintings around him.

I stay in the seat after the final credits, savouring that sensation of lightness. And it's here that I make a silent promise – that whatever happens, I will not let myself continue to drift in a job which gives me no joy. Somehow I will track down whatever it is that will make me happy.

'Did you enjoy the film?' Victor has come down from the projectionist's booth and is standing beside me, one hand resting on the back of my seat.

'It was beautiful,' I say. 'What an amazing life.'

Victor smiles.

'And that's a wonderful idea,' I say, referring to a particular discussion between the man and his new wife. 'That we choose what we will do in this lifetime before we are born.'

'Go on.' Victor gives me a nod of encouragement.

'But when we come into the world we forget, so we have to follow our intuition. If we go too far off the rails, something or someone will nudge us back on track.'

'Do you believe it could happen in real life?'

'I want to. I really do…' I trail off. 'But anyway, it's a truly lovely film. Congratulations.' I glance around me at the cinema's plush red interior. 'And you've created a brilliant place here.' I nod over to the right-hand corner by the screen. 'You even found a piano like the one used for the Charlie Chaplin films.'

Victor grins and does a little bow. 'It is all in the detail, my dear.'

'Do you play?'

'A little.'

'Give us a tune then.'

'Now?'

'Of course.'

I stay where I am while Victor walks down to the piano, sits on the blue velvet-covered stool and opens the lid. He places his fingers on the yellowing keys and begins to play. The melody is immediately familiar – it's the third movement from Ravel's *Miroirs*, which I first heard that lazy August evening at Kenwood House. Now, as then, I find the simple sweeping arpeggios incredibly poignant.

While Victor plays, I lean my head back against the chair and let the memories of those happy Sundays we spent together wash through me. Each one trails scents and sounds unfaded by time: the yearning calls of seagulls circling above the Serpentine Bridge, the syrup-sweet taste of Malpua pancakes in Brick Lane, the eucalyptus fragrance of sage leaves in the Physic Garden.

When the movement comes to its bittersweet end, Victor stops, leaves his hands to rest for a second or two on the keys, then twists around on the stool.

'You're good,' I say. 'Did you learn as a child?'

Victor shakes his head. 'I always wanted to but I never made the time.' He smiles. 'So when I realised that I would not be going back to Paris, that was one of my gifts to myself – to buy a piano and learn to play Ravel.'

'You've learnt to play like that in just two years?'

Victor grins. 'I have an extraordinary teacher. He's also French, from the Basque country.' Then he closes the lid with a joyful laugh and walks back up the slope towards me.

'So what happens with the film now?' I ask, back in the projectionist's room where Victor is standing by the cinematograph and I'm sipping another glass of the blackcurrant liqueur.

'It is almost time for its official screening,' Victor removes the reel from inside the panel and places it carefully in one of the metal film cans. Then he pulls a small blue cloth from his back pocket and begins to polish the glass of the cinematograph's lens.

'What made you decide to go back to film-making?' I ask, still curious if the cine camera had anything to do with it.

Victor continues with the polishing. 'When I left my job, I was extremely ill,' he says. 'During that time – actually a little afterwards – I was shown a film. It was an incredibly sad film and it made me realise how much of my life I had wasted.' He gives the lens a final swipe. 'I resolved to return to my passion and try to prevent others from making the same mistakes as I did. And I was lucky enough to meet people who could help me.' He turns to me. 'See, Hannah? We all find our way in the end. It just takes some of us a little longer than others.'

I watch him tuck the cloth back in his pocket then run his fingers lovingly over the walnut wood of the cinematograph.

'Victor,' I start. 'I need to say something.'

Victor eyes me intently.

'I know I've already told you, but I need to say again how much I loved watching films with you in Monsieur Henri's cinema.' I take a quick sip of my drink. 'Sharing *tartes aux pommes* in the café, gazing at those paintings in the National

Gallery, wandering around Keats's garden… all of those memories are incredibly precious to me.'

Victor smiles over at me from the cinematograph. 'To me too, Hannah,' he says. 'I shall take them with me wherever I go.'

Victor and I stay talking and drinking in the elevated booth for almost two hours. We've got through at least a third of the bottle, but surprisingly I don't feel drunk.

'And how is young Nellie?' Victor asks.

'She's getting grumpier and greedier by the day – and I love her all the more for it.' I gaze over at him. 'It was a big risk, making me get her, but it worked.'

Victor raises his glass in a little toast and I do the same.

'And you are happy with Joe?' he asks.

'I am,' I say, grinning.

'Do you think you will live together?'

I shake my head and tell him about Joe's and my conversation a couple of nights ago. Joe had asked me again if I would consider sharing a place, but I said that endless bickering about who'd do the washing up would drive us insane, not to mention his habit of littering the floor with dirty clothes. This wasn't the first time we'd talked about the subject, but this time Joe stormed off. He came back a couple of hours later and we called a truce over a bottle of Merlot.

'Is that the real reason you do not want to live with him?' asks Victor.

I nod quickly and there's a short pause. 'I just wish he and Mum could have met,' I say, edging the conversation to something else I've been meaning to tell Victor. 'She would have loved him.'

Victor smiles.

'You know what's weird? Even though she's gone I can still feel her,' I say. 'When I'm thinking about her, I'll suddenly smell the scent of lilacs, which used to be her favourite flowers, or I'll hear her laugh.' I take another mouthful of liqueur and swallow. 'It's probably just my imagination.'

Victor cocks his head. 'How can you be so sure?' Then he takes another sip from his own glass. 'Do you remember when I told you about the dream I had the night my own mother died?'

I nod. The image of the sunlight streaming through the Saint-Eustache stained-glass windows and his description of the choir has never left me.

'At the time I did not believe in angels,' he says with a little smile. 'But now I do.'

Victor comes outside to say goodbye and stands with me at the bottom of the stairs. The light from the video shop shimmers on the pavement beneath our feet, washing it with gold. The moon is full, round-bellied and glowing amidst the thousands of silver stars scattered across the night sky.

'Take care of yourself, Hannah,' says Victor, hugging me closely.

'You too.' I watch him turn to slowly climb the stairs. 'Next time I'll bring you some Newcastle Brown Ale. Maybe even some B&H fags. See what you make of those,' I say, but I don't think he hears me because he's already reached the top step.

Chapter 29

Ian and I are in Phoenix Gardens, the hidden pocket of green that we've recently discovered behind the Curzon Cinema. The early November sun slants through the trees and the air smells faintly of the pink viburnum flowers that smother the wall near where we're sitting. In front of us the gardener is already planting bulbs for next spring, and two girls with prams are chatting on the bench beneath the old walnut tree.

Ian has been telling me about a date that he recently went on. 'I really liked her,' he says, 'but she never returned my phone call.' He shakes his head. 'I'm done with website dating.'

'But you only went on three dates.'

'Trust me, I've had enough,' he says. He removes the greaseproof paper from his baguette and takes a bite. I do the same with my sandwich, closing my eyes to savour the contrast of the sweet roasted peppers with the salty tang of goat's cheese.

'Don't move.' Ian reaches down to his rucksack and pulls out his Leica camera. 'I need more pictures for my course.'

I grimace, my mouth is still half full of peppers and cheese, but Ian is already lining up the shot.

'Perfect!' I hear a click.

'I was still chewing!'

'Yes, but your expression was priceless.' He tucks his camera back inside his rucksack. 'So what are you up to this weekend?'

'I'll be hanging out with Joe and his daughter,' I say. 'It's the first time and I have to admit, I'm pretty nervous.'

'She'll love you,' says Ian. 'How could she not?'

'Maybe because I'm not very good with children?' I take a swig of Luigi's Lavazza coffee. 'And you?'

'I'll probably take Matthew to our local farmers' market on Saturday. Other than that, not much.'

'Any hot chicks at the farmers' market?'

'Even if there were, I wouldn't have the confidence to talk to them.'

I sigh. 'Well, how else are you going to meet someone?' On the other bench I see the two girls with the prams preparing to leave. 'What about them?'

Ian laughs. 'I'm not sure gymslip mums are my style.'

'Italian au pairs,' I correct. 'I heard them talking the other day. Come on, which one's your type?'

Ian nods towards the smaller girl with brown hair, who's wearing a bright green bobble hat and a short red jacket.

'I dare you to go up and say hello.'

'Are you nuts?'

'You want me to do it for you?' I put down my coffee and rise from the bench.

Ian grabs my arm and pulls me back down again.

'OK, then. Not today, but next time you're going to talk to her, aren't you?'

'I doubt it,' says Ian.

After lunch, Ian goes off to the camera shop to buy a new lens, while I walk around Soho making the most of the winter sunshine. On my way back to the office, I pass what was once Bernard's café. It's been gone for over a year now, bought by a coffee chain a couple of months after Bernard moved back to Besançon to open a restaurant with his sister.

I glance through the window at the solitary customers drinking oversized coffees and staring listlessly at their iPhones. In my mind I try to recreate the interior of the old café: the wobbly tables with the worn green paint, the mismatched china and Bernard's cherrywood gramophone – and I think back to the last time Victor and I were there.

*

November 2009

'Please, Victor,' I say. 'I'm getting desperate. He's hasn't picked up his Super 8 camera for weeks, he won't take his bike for a ride, in fact all he wants to do is sit in front of the television and drink bourbon.'

'How do you think I can help him?' Victor stirs his coffee and eyes me from across the table.

'I'm not sure,' I say. 'Maybe you could talk to him, give him the same sort of advice you always give me.' Of course, I don't mention the other reason that I want Victor and Luke to meet – that he might act as a warning, showing Luke that if he gives up now, he may well end up like Victor, just watching other people's films instead of making them himself.

I pick up the chipped teapot and pour myself a second cup of Earl Grey. 'So you'll meet him?'

Victor nods. 'If you really believe it will change things, then I will.'

Persuading Luke isn't so easy. But eventually after several days of coaxing on my part, he agrees to meet Victor the following Monday – I suspect more to shut me up than because he wants to get to know him.

Truffaut's *Jules et Jim* is showing the night we get together. There's still fifteen minutes before the film starts, so while I chat with Monsieur Henri by the ticket office, I leave Luke and Victor to talk on their own. Luke takes a while to warm up, but soon I hear them both animatedly discussing the fact that it was Truffaut who was originally chosen to direct *Bonnie and Clyde*.

I sit in the middle of them during *Jules et Jim* and once again – for I have already seen the film three times – am immediately drawn into the story of two friends and their love for the same woman. But next to me Luke constantly coughs and fidgets in his seat.

'Are you alright?' I whisper to him in the dark.

'Yes,' Luke snaps, 'why wouldn't I be?'

Afterwards we stand in the foyer, while Monsieur Henri sits behind the ticket booth, counting the evening's takings. I can never understand how this gem of a cinema survives – there were only six other people in the audience with us tonight.

'Did you enjoy the film, Luke?' says Victor.

Luke shrugs. 'It was pretty unrealistic. Two men infatuated with the same woman and still remaining friends. I don't think so.'

'I don't agree.' I button up my coat. 'But let's talk about it in the café, it's warmer there.'

Luke glances over at the exit. 'Actually, I've got to go.'

'Go where?' I say.

'I'm meeting an American producer for a drink.'

I am conscious of Victor studying Luke and me so I shift slightly around so that I am facing Luke directly.

'You never mentioned it before,' I say quietly.

Luke zips up his flying jacket and winds his scarf around his neck. 'Sorry, I forgot I had to run everything by you first.'

'Fine,' I say, suddenly too tired to argue, 'go and see your producer then.'

In the café Victor and I take the window seat after Bernard has scribbled down our order.

'Is Luke often like that?' says Victor.

'More and more so recently,' I say. 'I just don't know what to do.' I don't mention the mood swings, which are getting even worse, nor the late-night drinking binges.

'And you are still looking for a flat to share with him?' There's a hint of doubt in Victor's tone.

'Of course,' I say a little too defensively. I've been back three times to view the flat by Kensal Green tube and I'm hoping to put an offer in next week. Somehow I've convinced myself that things will improve once Luke and I are living together. I'm also hoping that the flat will help to anchor Luke in London and stop him moving back to the States.

Victor takes a small mouthful of his Dijon slice and chews thoughtfully. 'Have you considered that there might be something else troubling him?'

From the way he asks it, I immediately assume he's talking about another woman.

'What do you mean?' My tone is much more abrupt than I'd intended, probably because the question has been at the back of my mind for weeks.

Before he can reply, Bernard stops at our table to tell us

about his forthcoming trip to Besançon and promises to bring Victor back a block of Comté cheese.

'I have some news for you, Hannah,' says Victor after he's gone, obviously sensing my discomfort at his previous question. 'I have started filming again.'

'That's brilliant.' I say, glad to be talking about something other than Luke. 'What sort of things?'

'Just the people in my neighbourhood – the old man who sits outside the betting shop, the woman who walks to the pub in her bedroom slippers… This weekend I plan to take the camera to the Serpentine and film from the bridge that you love so much.' Victor smiles. 'You know, Hannah, when you gave me that camera, you gave me back a piece of myself.'

'I'm so glad,' I smile back at him. 'Who knows, this might even be the start of your second film career.'

Victor raises his coffee cup and smiles. 'Who knows?' he echoes.

*

When I get back to the office, Ian is still out. I have just two new e-mails – the first tells me that unfortunately Nellie was not selected as Best-Looking Bulldog in Great Britain. The second, which is from the publishing house, informs me that due to the recent drop in advertising revenue, the company will be closing the magazine in five weeks, at the end of the year. All copy for the website will now be supplied by freelance writers and therefore my position is now redundant. I will be paid the standard redundancy fee: one month's salary for each year I have worked.

I sit there and stare at the e-mail. My head's already gone into meltdown mode, imagining escalating rent arrears, bailiffs and brutal eviction, filthy shop doorways, and then the inevitable decanting to West Riding.

No, Hannah, I think, let's be rational here. I take several deep breaths and try to visualise an alternative future, in which I am thrifty enough to survive on the redundancy money until I can find another job, which might actually prove more fulfilling than my present one.

I'm just garnishing the final details of this rosy new existence (Abundance Judy would be proud of me) when my phone rings. It's Joe.

'Something will definitely turn up,' he says after I've told him what's happened, 'and if it doesn't, we could always take to the road,' he laughs. 'Run our own little Victorian sideshow with Nellie as the star.'

'Be serious,' I say. 'I could be eating offal burgers in West Riding by the end of the year.' It's all very well spouting Judy's abundance principles, but it'll obviously take a while to really believe in them.

'Listen, Hannah,' says Joe. 'I'm not going to let you starve, and besides there are other options...' he pauses. 'Let's discuss this later. I should be home from rehearsals by nine. I'll cook dinner and if you're really lucky I might even wash up.'

Ian arrives a few minutes later with his new lens and a slice of Luigi's date and walnut cake, which he sets down on my desk.

'What's up?'

'My job,' I say. I open up the e-mail again and read it out to him.

'Oh, shit!' Ian sits down hard in his chair. 'What the hell do we do now?'

'We?'

'Well, if you're going, then I'm not sure I'd want to stay on.'

'Don't be daft.'

'Really,' says Ian. 'It's not as if this is my ideal job.' He pulls out his newspaper from his rucksack. 'Let's be proactive about this.'

We spend the rest of the afternoon scanning the newspaper and every possible job website. I'm sure Ian is only saying he'll leave to make me feel better, but he still takes the time to doctor his CV. Then he does this week's Healthy Eats menu while I ring a couple of employment agencies. We keep our spirits up by playing Judy's *Abundance Mentality* CD and doing bad impressions of her Californian accent.

Just after five o'clock Ian heads home and I make my way to Wormwood Scrubs to pick up Nellie. When I arrive at Megan's studio, she's standing by the far window, staring out at the prison. Nellie is curled up asleep in her favourite brown cardigan next to the gas heater.

'What's wrong, Meg?' I say.

'Billy,' she replies. 'We've broken up.'

'What?'

Megan turns from the windowsill. 'It's finished.'

'But you can't finish it. I mean, I know you two have your stuff, but you always work it out in the end.'

Megan walks over to Nellie and squats down to rub her back. 'We can't work this one out.' She looks up at me. 'Hannah, I want a baby. You know that. But I can't have one because I'm already looking after a child – Billy.'

I stare at her, trying to take in the fact that she and Billy might split up.

'What did Billy say when you told him?'

'Oh, the usual,' Megan waves a hand. 'That he'll get a job, that he'll stop drinking, that everything's going to be fine. But it's not fucking fine, is it?' She pushes herself up off the floor. 'I'm going to my mum's for a few days while he finds somewhere else to live.'

'Are you really sure about this?'

'If I don't do it now, I never will.' Megan straightens up and looks closely at my face. 'What's up with you then?'

I tell her about the redundancy.

'You and I need a drink,' she says, and burrows in the paint cupboard to bring out a half-bottle of Bell's whisky. She pours two measures into a chipped red mug and an old jam jar.

'Here's to our shit lives,' she says, 'may they continue to prosper and thrive.'

'Well, actually,' I say, 'I know I've just lost my job, but apart from that my life isn't so shit right now.'

Megan takes a slug from her jam jar of whisky then laughs. 'Oh, fuck off!'

Chapter 30

'Who are you?' The little girl standing in the doorway of my sitting room is staring at me with big serious eyes. She's wearing a glittery silver tiara on her head and carrying a tiny red overnight case.

'You know, Hannah,' says Joe. 'You met her a few weeks ago when she and I picked you up from Mum's. We're staying at hers for the weekend.'

'Why?'

'Because I'm moving out of my flat, and everything is already packed up, to go to my friend's. We'd have to sleep in one of the cardboard boxes and I didn't think you'd want that.'

Maya continues to stare at me.

'I like your tiara.' I say, hoping that old-fashioned flattery might ease things a bit.

Maya shrugs then glances around at the sitting room.

'Oh, and that's Nellie,' I say, determined to persevere. I point to the glowering mound of fur just inside the kennel door.

'She's silly,' says Maya.

Joe and I have been preparing for Maya's first visit for some time. We've bought a little blue blanket which looks like the one on her bed at her mum's, we've got the ingredients for her two favourite meals and there's a video of *Finding Nemo* to watch, with the accompanying colouring book.

She and Joe are working on it right now on the sitting room floor while I'm in the kitchen creating what I hope will be a satisfying first supper for Maya – spaghetti Bolognese. Nellie's here with me, stationed hopefully at my feet.

I hear Joe's mobile ring from next door and moments later he calls through to me, saying that the side door to the post office where they are doing rehearsals for his play has been left open and he needs to bike over and lock up.

'You'll be OK to look after her for half an hour, won't you?' he says from the sitting room door.

I peer round the door and see Maya is still happily colouring. 'But don't be any longer or supper will be cindered,' I say.

Maya is perched up on the sideboard in the kitchen, watching me stir the tomato sauce. The colouring session seems to have thawed her a little and we're listening to a CD of *Wind in the Willows*. Nellie has flopped next to the fridge on a stake-out.

'What's that?' Maya points to the pot on the windowsill above the sink.

'It's a chili plant. Your dad gave it to me.' I take it down so she can have a closer look.

'Did you grow it from a seed?' Maya asks. Last week she gave Joe some blotting paper in a jam jar on which she'd grown some cress.

'No,' I say. 'I'm not very good at growing things.'

Maya pulls off one of the bright orange chilies. 'Why is it that colour?'

I gently take it from her fingers before she pops it in her mouth. 'It just is.'

'When it's a seed, does it know that it will be orange when it grows up?'

'I suppose so.'

'How?'

'It's in its DNA, I think.' The tomato sauce is beginning to turn brown and claggy. I really need to focus.

'Do I have DMA?'

'DNA,' I correct. 'Yes, you do.'

'And did I grow from a seed?'

'Sort of,' I say, wondering if five isn't a bit young for the facts of life. I remember Miss Simms's lesson on reproduction: 'And then the man puts his erect penis inside the woman's vagina…' Best not, I think.

'Who's that lady?' Maya points to the picture of Mum smiling in her garden that I've hung above the kitchen sideboard.

'That's my Mum.'

'She looks nice,' says Maya.

'She is,' I say. I don't correct myself to the past tense.

'Daddy says that she's gone to heaven.'

'That's right.' Even though I don't buy into the idea of heaven, it would be churlish to tell Maya that.

'What's heaven like?'

'I don't know exactly, Maya. But I bet it's fun.'

'Why?'

'Well, I'm sure they'd lay on some entertainment.'

'Like what?'

I try to imagine something that might satisfy a five-year-old. Egg and spoon races? Trampolining? Gymkhanas? Or are those too old-school?

'Discos,' I say. 'I'm sure they'd put on the odd disco.'

Maya nods as if this would be acceptable. 'What else do you do in heaven?'

I think for a moment. 'I read in one of your dad's books that you get to watch a film of your life.' I've obviously oversimplified this – giving Maya a detailed breakdown of the Buddhist *bardo* state as described in the *Tibetan Book of the Dead* might be a bit daunting for her.

But Maya has lost interest anyway and is eyeing up the grocery cupboard.

'I'm hungry. Can I have a snack?'

'Of course.' I flip open the cupboard above me. 'We've got crackers and Ryvita, and some weird brown rolls.' I rustle around some more. 'Or what about a rusk?'

Over by the fridge I see Nellie's head jerk up expectantly.

'Rusks are for babies,' says Maya, adjusting her tiara, which keeps slipping down onto her forehead.

'I know but they're pretty tasty. Nellie loves them,' I say. 'In fact, why don't we give her one now?'

It's just gone seven and Joe's still not back. I've rung him twice, but presumably he's on his bike so he can't answer. Having swallowed a rusk in one gulp, Nellie is snoozing in her kennel. Maya and I are on the sofa, having our own little rusk moment while we watch Nemo trying to find his way home.

I hear my mobile ring from next door and I head into the kitchen to answer it. But it's not Joe – it's Ian. I glance into the sitting room to make sure Maya is OK, then I answer it.

'Sorry to ring you at home,' he says, 'but I'm just buying tickets online for a comedy club as a pre-Christmas treat for Matthew. I thought you might like to come with us.'

'I'd love to, Ian,' I say, after I've asked when and where it is. I am about to ask him for some advice on how to de-congeal Bolognese sauce when I hear a menacing growl from next door. I hang up and run into the sitting room. Maya is kneeling in front of the kennel and attempting to balance her tiara on top of Nellie's head. Nellie is looking uncannily like an enraged Bette Davis in *What Ever Happened to Baby Jane*?

If you don't get this thing away from me, I'm going to rip its fucking head off.

'Princess Nellie!' says Maya, giggling while she nudges the tiara to a more central position.

A bone-chilling snarl erupts from Nellie's mouth and her jaws snap open exposing two rows of needle-sharp yellowing teeth, millimetres from Maya's nose.

'NELLIE!' I shout at the top of my lungs.

'It's nothing to do with you, sweetheart,' I say a few minutes later. I am drying Maya's tears in the kitchen and Nellie has retreated to the back of her kennel. 'Nellie hates anybody touching her head.'

My long-distance lunge across the sitting room floor to wedge myself between Maya and Nellie was successful and Maya and her nose are still intact. In fact the only injury is a sprained left wrist on my part.

'Nellie doesn't like me,' sniffs Maya.

'Yes, she does,' I say.

'Really?' Maya's face brightens.

''Course she does,' says a voice from the kitchen door.

'Dadddeee!' shouts Maya when she sees Joe. She hops off the sideboard and runs over to him.

'Hello, poppet,' Joe hugs his daughter tightly to his chest.

I stare at the blood smeared across his forehead. 'What happened?'

Joe tentatively touches the skin just below his right temple. 'The bike and I had a run-in with a taxi. The taxi won.'

After I've washed away the worst of the blood from Joe's face, the three of us tackle the gluey spaghetti, while Maya chats cheerily away about her own run-in with Nellie. After that, she describes in gleeful detail another girl at school whose nose was partially bitten off (and swallowed) by an Alsatian. The story ends with the dog getting 'shotted'.

'So what else did you two get up to while I was gone?' says Joe.

'We listened to *Wind in the Willows* together while I sweated over this delicious dinner.'

'And I had a rusk,' says Maya. 'It was really stale.'

'You said you liked it,' I say.

Maya shakes her head. 'No, I didn't.'

'Yes, you did.'

'No, I didn't.'

Joe's head is imitating a Wimbledon spectator.

'How come you ate it all then?' I say, playing my master shot.

Joe chuckles. 'Hannah, you can't argue with a child like that.'

I catch sight of Maya's cross expression. 'You're right, maybe it was a bit stale.'

Maya grins smugly, looking for a moment just like Joe. 'I already told you that.'

'You'll learn, Hannah.' Joe laughs.

It's ten o'clock and Joe and I are on the pull-out sofa, propped up with a glass of wine each and a packet of salted dark chocolate. Nellie is snoring on a cushion next to us and Maya is in my bed, having finally gone to sleep after Joe read her three stories.

'Why do you think she snapped?' Joe leans down to stroke Nellie's back.

'Maya touched her head,' I say. 'You know how she hates that.'

'You never told me why, though.'

I point to the little pink scar on top of Nellie's head which is usually hidden by her fur. 'That probably has something to do with it.'

Joe leans closer to inspect it. 'How did she get it?'

'A brick,' I say. I explain how a month after I'd brought Nellie back from Battersea Dogs Home, she was still whimpering in her sleep, so I called the kennel worker to ask more about her history. Apparently she'd been found dumped in the corner of the men's toilets at Kennington Road garage with a bleeding head and a broken foot. The vet who stitched her up reckoned it was a brick.

'You poor old girl,' says Joe, rubbing Nellie's neck.

'Maya will be alright, won't she?' I ask.

Joe nods. 'We'll just have to keep a close eye on the two of them.' He smiles. 'She really likes it here. Just before she fell asleep she told me she wants to come again – as long as you don't make spaghetti next time.'

'What?' I twist around, indignant. 'I put a lot of effort into making that.'

Joe kisses the side of my neck. 'Only joking – about the spaghetti anyway. The rest is true.' He takes a sip of his wine. 'You realise how big a deal for me it is, her staying here?'

'I know.'

'And I'd like to think that one day, things could be a bit more permanent.'

I fiddle with the stem of my glass. 'What do you mean?'

'I think you know what I mean.' Joe sets his own glass on the side table next to him.

I nod. It's not as if I haven't thought about this.

'I want more than this, Hannah, you know I do.' He shifts position on the sofa so he can look me directly in the eye. 'I'd like a place with you, where Maya can also feel at home.'

My heart is thumping in my ears. I take a sip of wine to stall for extra time. 'If that's what you really want, then...'

Joe shakes his head. '*You* have to want it too.' He takes my free hand in his. 'What is it that you're so scared of?'

It's the same question that I've been asking myself for the past few months. All I know is that whenever I think about moving in with Joe, I feel that familiar cold clutch of fear.

'I can see that Maya's already getting attached to you,' says Joe, 'and if you're not willing to make a proper go of it...' The rest of his sentence hangs in mid-air.

'What are you saying?' My throat is so dry I can barely speak.

Joe stares at me for what feels like minutes. 'I'm not sure if this is enough any more, Hannah.'

It's one o'clock and I'm lying alone on the pull-out sofa. After we had finished talking, Joe said that he wanted to check on Maya and he never returned. When I went in an hour ago, he was lying on top of the bed, awake. I asked him if he wanted to come back next door, but he said he would prefer to keep an eye on Maya.

Nellie is in her basket in the corner of the room. I've been staring up at the ceiling for half an hour, wondering why after all these months with Joe, I still believe that every man I love will leave me.

*

November 2009

Luke and I don't see each other in the week following the cinema visit with Victor. We speak a couple of times on the phone, but it's always brief because Luke's in a hurry to get somewhere. Apparently the American producer has extended his stay in London and he and Luke have been putting together a rescue plan for the documentary. Given how he's been behaving over the last few weeks, I figure it's better to let him have some space so I say that I'll make supper for us both on Monday, when I hope that we can finally have a proper talk. There's also the small matter of the Kensal Green flat that I've just put down a whacking deposit on.

When I arrive at work that morning, Victor is waiting for me in the foyer. His voice is low and urgent. 'Hannah, I need to show you something. Can you come to my house tonight?'

'I'm busy tonight. Why can't I see whatever it is here?'

Victor shakes his head. 'You remember I was planning to take the cine camera to the Serpentine this weekend?' he says. 'I have to show you what I filmed.'

'But I'm making dinner for Luke this evening.'

'Please, Hannah, this is very important.'

For some reason his insistence annoys me.

'And so is my relationship,' I say. But seeing Victor's expression, I add. 'We'll do it another time. OK?'

I sneak off early that evening so that I can do some shopping for dinner. Victor is on a tea break so I don't see him before I leave.

'What are you doing here?' When Luke opens his front door, he's wearing his dressing gown. He's obviously just stepped out of the shower because his hair is wet.

'I told you I'd make supper tonight.' I hold up the bag containing the home-made tortilla and the bottle of Médoc. 'Don't you remember?'

Luke mumbles something and holds open the door.

'You don't need to sound quite so excited,' I say, heading for the kitchen counter while Luke flops down on the sofa, remote in hand.

I unpack the tortilla which weighs roughly the same as a six-month-old baby. I'm determined to keep to myself what I need to say until we've eaten but watching Luke splayed out on the sofa, barely acknowledging my existence, something snaps.

'For fuck's sake, Luke! I've made you dinner and lugged it all the way over here. You could at least pretend you're pleased to see me.' I pull the bottle of Médoc from the bag and slam it down onto the counter. 'I wish I'd taken Victor up on his invitation.'

'What? For a candlelit dinner à deux?' Luke presses the remote and the TV switches to the Channel 4 news.

'No, actually. He's made a short film, which he wants me to see.'

Luke raises an eyebrow. 'A short film?'

'Don't make it sound lewd.'

Luke shrugs. 'You know he's infatuated with you.'

'Don't be ridiculous.' I jam the corkscrew into the bottle. 'It's only some footage he shot by the Serpentine this weekend. He wants me to see it because he used the cine camera I gave him.'

There's a pause, broken by the voice of a TV reporter saying that parts of Cumbria have been devastated by torrential floods.

'Which day was Victor filming on?' says Luke slowly.

'I don't know. Why?' I pull out the cork with a loud pop.

It's a couple of beats before Luke replies. 'Just curious.'

I chip off the burnt edges of the tortilla to the sound of the forecast for the whole of the UK. Rain and sleet are predicted for the Christmas period with snow in the Highlands. Luke is still slouched on the sofa with an open can of Budweiser.

'You know that one-bedroom flat by the railway in Kensal Green?' I say tentatively.

'Aha.'

I take a deep breath before I continue. 'I've put down a deposit on it.'

'You bought it?'

I nod.

'Why did you do that?'

'Well,' I say, 'it was such a good deal, and as you know the money my Dad left me is barely earning interest any more, so it just made sense.' What doesn't make sense is why the bank agreed to give me a mortgage that I can't possibly afford on my own.

'Are you going to say something?' My heart is pounding in my chest.

'You bought a flat. Great,' says Luke. 'I'm happy for you.'

I try to suppress the creep of panic. I've used all the money that my dad left me for the deposit and if I pull out now, I'm not even sure I can get it back.

'You realise that this is a huge deal for me,' I say.

'I said I'm happy for you.'

'For us, Luke. It's for us.' The words ring out in the flat, sounding ridiculous. Of course I know how stupid I've been – trying to tether Luke to London with the lure of a flat.

I return to chipping the charred bits off the tortilla. When

I finish, I sweep the burnt debris into my hand, along with a scrap of paper that I assume is the receipt for the wine. But when I tip the small load into the bin, I see it's a receipt for something else.

'So who did you have coffee with at the Serpentine café last Sunday?'

'What?' says Luke.

I repeat the question slowly although I know he heard the first time.

'Why are you always interrogating me these days?'

'It's just a simple question.' I untwist the corkscrew from the cork, which makes a sound like a creaking door being pulled shut.

'Jesus, Hannah. Do I ask you about your cosy little Monday evenings with Victor?' Luke leaps up from the sofa and marches towards the bathroom.

'Why are you so angry?' I say to his disappearing back.

'I'm not angry,' he shouts over his shoulder. 'I'm just sick of you being on my case.' He slams the bathroom door so hard that one of the photographs, an aerial shot of LA, falls to the floor and smashes.

There's a sharp pain in my palm where I've been clenching the corkscrew. I open it and see a tiny blood blister forming beneath the skin.

*

It's 4.45 a.m. and I still can't sleep. I throw off the covers and go into the kitchen. I don't bother turning on the light but I switch on the kettle to make myself some camomile tea. My foot brushes against something soft on the floor. In the half-darkness I make out Joe's favourite T-shirt, the dark blue one.

I bend down to pick it up, running my fingers over the soft fabric. I can remember the last time that he wore it, propped up in bed two days ago when we were watching Wim Wenders's *Wings of Desire*.

Outside the kitchen window the bare branches of the sycamore tree shudder in the night breeze. A freight train rumbles past on the Great Western. A fox barks from over in the cemetery.

I sit down at the table, trying to warm my fingers on the mug. That final scene from Victor's second film is looping through my mind and it feels like I have exchanged places with the man sitting at the table. That feeling of frozen fear has seeped into every cell of my body.

Behind me I hear the kitchen door opening. Joe comes in and walks over to the sink. He takes a glass from the shelf above and holds it under the tap.

'You can't sleep either?' I say.

Joe shakes his head and stares out of the window for a moment. Then he puts down the glass and turns to look at me. I can't see his expression because it's too dark.

'What's going to happen?' My voice sounds like a twelve-year-old child's.

It's at least a minute before Joe answers.

'I don't know, Hannah,' he says quietly. 'I really don't know.'

Chapter 31

Chortles Comedy Club is not what you might call one of London's premiere comedy venues, despite what it says on the website. In fact it's misleading to use the word 'club' at all to describe a room about six metres by seven, with a minuscule bar, a makeshift stage and a curtain fashioned from what appears to be a dirty duvet cover draped with some limp tinsel.

Matthew and Ian aren't here yet, so I take up position at the bar. To be honest, a night in a comedy club is the last thing I'm in the mood for. It's now three days since Joe got up on Sunday morning and left with Maya, and I've been able to think of little else since. Before he went, he asked me to give him a week to sort out his head and make some decisions.

I feel a hand on my shoulder.

'Sorry we're late,' says Ian, 'there wasn't a wheelchair ramp so we had to go round the back.' He gestures towards Matthew, who's wearing a bright orange jumper and looks just like his brother, with the same reddish hair and brown eyes.

'Matthew, meet Hannah,' says Ian.

'Hello,' I smile and hold out my hand towards him.

Matthew grins at me then nods at his right arm, which hangs loosely by his side. 'I can't shake your hand because my arms don't work.'

'Oh sorry, I didn't realise…' I stammer.

'It's OK,' says Matthew. 'I'll forgive you if you buy me a Coca-Cola.'

'Done,' I say.

It's a busy night for the 'club' with a large group of thirty-something women wearing T-shirts printed with the words 'Kath's Hen Night', downing tequila shots at the bar. Kath herself is sporting a big 'Learner' sign on her chest along with a red feather boa and the requisite blue garter on an exposed thigh. There's also a group of guys at the bar, dressed identically in Le Coq Sportif shirts and sparkly silver wigs. The rest of the audience, including a rowdy office party, have already taken their seats.

I'm still waiting to be served. I feel my mobile vibrate and I snatch it from my pocket. But it's only Megan, asking me how I am. I've told her what's happened with Joe and she's been ringing me every day from her mum's place in Wales.

'You're very pretty,' says Matthew, who's wheeled his chair next to me at the bar. 'Are you Ian's girlfriend?'

'No, Matt,' says Ian quickly. 'I've already told you that Hannah has a boyfriend.'

'That's a shame,' says Matt, 'because you said that…'

'Ssssh, Matt,' says Ian with a smile in my direction. 'You mustn't give away trade secrets.'

Matthew opens his mouth to say something else, but is drowned out by a deafening drum roll. Seconds later, a skinny man in a red tank top and tight checked trousers runs onto the stage and grabs the microphone. I pay for the drinks and we hurry down to the few remaining seats in the back row.

'Good evening, Wembley.' The compère pauses expectantly

and receives an enthusiastic round of whooping from the hen and stag parties.

'I'm Dave and tonight I'm warming up for...'

'Get your cock out, Dave!' shouts Kath.

'Tonight, we've got a fantastic...'

'Go on, get your cock out!' shouts Kath again.

'Line-up, kicking off with...'

'GET YOUR COCK OUT, DAVE!' The rest of Kath's crowd join her in the chant.

Whether or not Dave has a more extensive introduction, we'll never know because he clearly knows defeat when he sees it.

'So without further hesitation, I'd like to welcome...'

Silence.

'I'd like to welcome...' Dave's face is very red and his hands are shaking as he tries to slot the microphone back onto its stand.

'If you can't remember, make it up,' one of the stag party shouts from the audience, just as a second man appears around the duvet, dressed in baggy tracksuit bottoms and a T-shirt advertising a veterinary college in Tring.

'It's alright, Dave,' says Ross, the first comedian on the night's bill. He shakes his thatch of peroxide yellow hair. 'I'll take over from here. You go and put your feet up.'

Relieved, Dave does a rather uncoordinated attempt at a bow, waves frantically as if he has just completed half an hour of gut-twisting comedy, and then legs it backstage.

Ross takes the microphone. 'Right, what did the barman say when twenty miniature owls flew through his pub?'

And with that he's off, delivering a string of surreal nonsense about miniature owls, DFS double divan sofas and by-elections in Leamington Spa. He's so carried away that he barely takes time to breathe, and even the hen night women in front of us are captivated. In fact, Kath is so captivated that she hasn't noticed her boa has slipped from her shoulders and now lies at her feet in a pile of red feathers.

*

December 2009

I've been trying to weave the theme of red feathers into Victor's book, partly because of his love for Verrocchio's painting of Tobias and the red-winged angel and partly because of the linguistic link between feathers and pens in French. Given that Victor always longed to be an *auteur* – an 'author' of films – it seems fitting.

Writing has proved to be a welcome respite from constantly worrying about Luke's and my relationship. I've now reached 40,000 words and am midway through Victor's life after he arrived in London. He's working as a lift operator in Soho, and every Monday evening he visits Monsieur Henri's cinema, where for two hours he loses himself in French films.

It's at this point, however, that something starts to shift in the book. A sinister note has crept into the text, and the fictional Victor no longer resembles the Victor that I first described. Neither is his friendship with a young woman at his workplace quite so innocent as it once appeared.

I know the reason for this, of course. It began with Luke's comment that Victor was infatuated with me. Somehow the idea has taken root and festered in my mind. As a result, I begin to search for evidence and find exactly what I'm looking for. All the things that Victor has said over the years, I begin to reinterpret: how I am the only person he can really talk to; how sharing his love of film and spending time with me means more to him than I can ever know; how he and I are so alike. Then there is his reaction when I first told him about Luke, the expression in his eyes and his hand frozen in mid-air. There's also his behaviour when the teenage boys accused him of being a dirty old man. For why else would he be so angry and defensive if there wasn't a kernel of truth to it? And finally, there is the story of Claudette and how he couldn't tell her about his feelings, so instead he made her a film, just as he has made one for me.

In my warped mind it all begins to make sense, to slot together like scenes in a film, in which the character's underlying motives are hidden at first, but as time passes and more clues come to light, they are revealed. In a twisted rerun of Truffaut's *La peau douce,* Victor is playing out the film's narrative in real life, re-enacting the story of a tragic old man and his obsession with a younger woman.

The more I write, the more distorted my portrayal of Victor becomes. His quiet, gentle nature has turned into something much creepier and his passion for films and his eagerness to share his knowledge of cinema are simply a means of seducing a naïve young woman.

And the longer I spend rewriting this fictional figure, the more my perception of the real Victor changes. Over the following weeks, the pity, disdain and dislike I feel for the main character of my story is mirrored by the disdain and pity I have begun to feel for Victor himself. I now view his comments and questioning of Luke's and my relationship as a subtle tactic to plant suspicion in my mind and widen the rift between us.

By the time I start the second draft, the initial quiet joy and contentment I experienced while writing has gone. Instead, I've come to hate the book, perhaps because deep down I know that it says more about me than about Victor. So I abandon it, dumping it in the bottom drawer of my wardrobe beneath a pile of old moth-eaten jumpers.

By now it's the beginning of December and the situation between Luke and I has become intolerable. After that night when I told him I had bought the flat and I ended up running from his place in tears, I begged him to tell me what's wrong. But all he ever says is that I'm paranoid and that I'm pressurising him too much. Can't I see that he has to focus on his career?

Of course, I'm too much of a coward to ask him the most important question – does he want to be with me? – because I'm petrified of what the answer might be. Pathetic as it sounds, I'd rather have a relationship like this with Luke than none at all.

Worries about Luke and the flat that I can't afford mean that I am barely sleeping at night. Bleary with exhaustion, I stumble through the days at work, hoping that things will get better but knowing they won't.

I recognise the signs of depression from the bouts that I suffered in my early twenties – the insomnia, the lethargy, the bleak dark landscape – but unlike those depressions which usually passed within a few weeks, this one seems permanent. For the first time I really understand what my father was talking about in the letter he wrote to me.

Victor, the man I once turned to for advice, is now the last person I want to see. In the mornings I hang around outside until others are waiting for the lift so that I don't have to go up with him alone. In the evenings I wait until I know he has gone home before I leave the office. Whenever I do run into him, I make excuses as to why I don't have time to talk or go to Monsieur Henri's cinema any more, but we both know that I am lying.

One Thursday morning when I am hurrying to the lift, I hear Victor's voice behind me.

'Did I do something wrong, Hannah?'

When I turn around, Victor is standing inside his booth.

'No,' I say, 'but like I told you, things are a pretty busy right now so I don't have much time to talk.'

Victor is staring at my face. 'Have you hurt yourself, Hannah?'

My hand automatically reaches to the cut on my left cheek, which I snagged on the metal catch of Luke's front door when I ran crying from his flat.

'Did Luke do that?' he asks.

'No,' I say coldly. 'He didn't.' However else Luke has behaved over the past weeks, he has never hit me. The fact that Victor would even think it is further proof of his motives.

Victor nods. 'And the cinema?' he says. 'Are you too busy for the cinema?'

'At the moment, yes.'

'But I thought that you enjoyed it.' Victor raises his hands in defeat.

I look at him and see only the sinister character from my story and the obsessive old man from Truffaut's film. And at that moment all the suppressed emotion of the past few weeks, the fear that I am losing Luke and the panic about the flat I can't afford, comes to a climax.

I stare at Victor, wanting only that he will leave me alone.

And that's why I utter the cruellest words I could possibly say to him. 'I only went because I felt sorry for you.'

*

Ross has finally wrapped up his act and Ian, Matthew and I are back at the bar. To our right, Kath is being chatted up by one of the stag party, mascara streaking splendidly down her cheeks and her blue garter sagging by her ankle.

'That was really funny,' says Matthew. 'I like Ross.'

'Me too,' I say. 'Good choice, Ian.'

Ian does a little bow then leans over the bar to order the drinks. I sneak a look at my mobile but there are no messages from Joe. Out of the corner of my eye I notice one of the stag guys weaving towards us with a pint in his hand.

'This is for you,' he slurs and thrusts the glass towards Matthew.

Matthew looks at the pint, then back up at the man. 'Thanks, but my brother is buying me a Coca-Cola.'

'That's not very grateful,' says the guy. 'I'm offering you a drink.'

'And that's not very polite,' Matthew nods towards the glass which is a few inches from his face.

'What are you drinking Coke for anyway?' asks the man.

'Why are you wearing a lady's wig?' asks Matthew.

It's difficult to know how the man would have responded if Ian hadn't walked over from the bar to stand next to his brother.

'Leave us alone.' His voice is trembling with rage.

'And who are you?' says the man.

'I'm his brother.'

'Lucky you.'

It happens so quickly that there's no time to react and the sound of Ian's fist smacking into hard bone reverberates around the room. The man howls and clutches his cheek and a stream of blood splatters down his sports shirt. Next to us, a collective and excitable 'Oooh' erupts from Kath's crowd.

Chapter 32

'How's that fist of yours?' Ian and his bandaged hand are already at his desk when I arrive half an hour late the following morning.

'Not good,' Ian winces. He swivels round in his chair. 'But I'm glad I punched that prick. I'm just sorry that we got thrown out.'

'Hell,' I say, 'all good nights out end in a ruck, don't they?' I sling my coat over the back of my chair and sit down. 'What did Matthew say about it?'

'The same as he always does,' says Ian, 'that I shouldn't get so angry.'

'He's got a point.'

'I know.'

'What about if you—'

Ian interrupts before I finish. 'Hannah, I really appreciate that you care but let me deal with it my way.' He studies my face. 'Looks like you didn't get much sleep either.'

I shake my head, then I tell him what's happened between Joe and me. 'I can't even call or text him,' I say, placing my mobile next to my computer, where I can see it. 'It feels horrible.'

'Why on earth didn't you say anything last night?'

'Because I didn't want to spoil it.'

Ian grabs me by both shoulders and shakes me. 'Hannah, you're my mate. Next time, tell me.'

I'm trying my best to distract my mind so I start on the day's freebies. There are two relaxation CDs – *Tranquil Shores* and *A Guide to Breath Work* – some lavender skin moisturiser and a tube of Silicea Gastrointestinal gel to prevent wind, bloating and constipation.

'They're all yours,' I say and shunt them over to Ian's desk. 'Go easy on the Gastrointestinal gel, though – I know what you're like.'

'You're so funny,' says Ian drily. 'Ever considered a career in stand-up?'

Next I check my e-mails. There's one from Roz, who says that the deputy editor at *Learn to Knit* is leaving in January and the position is mine if I want it. I e-mail back, telling her I will decide by the end of the week, if that's OK. There has to be something better for me out there than writing about wool.

My phone beeps and I grab it, knocking over my mug. But it's only Orange telling me that my phone bill is available online.

Next to me, Ian is checking the job classifieds. 'Come on, it'll take your mind off things,' he says, so I drag my chair over to his and we scan the adverts together.

Halfway down the page I spot something. I tap the screen. 'What about that?'

Ian reads aloud. 'Website manager for Scope charity.' He pauses then reads on. 'Option to work from home for two days a week.' He shakes his head in disbelief, reads the advert again, then sits back in his chair.

'There's just one major problem.'

'The interview? You'll breeze it,' I say. 'You're a genius with computers, you've got plenty of experience of disability AND you're a pretty good person to share an office with. What more could they want?'

'Confidence?' says Ian.

'In which case,' I say, 'they'll get it. We just need to put in a bit more practice.' I reach over to the shop and select the Trayner pinhole glasses, which I jam onto my nose before taking out an imaginary notebook and pen.

'Right, take three deep breaths and imagine how it would feel to be calm, collected and full of confidence.'

Ian swallows loudly.

'Now, tell me what you think you can bring to Scope.'

Ian swallows again and I hear the sound of light humming.

'Humming won't get you the job, Ian.'

'That wasn't a hum,' Ian frowns. 'I was thinking.'

'How about "I'm passionate about building and managing websites, and given my experience of disability..." '

Ian shakes his head. 'I don't want to use Matthew as my meal ticket.'

'You're not. You're explaining why you're the best person for the job.' I smile over at him. 'You can do this, Ian. I know you can. Now repeat what I've just said, but in your own words.'

We do a couple more run-throughs, until Ian says that he can now at least contemplate an interview without throwing up. I'm about to make us both a cup of coffee when my mobile rings. I race over to my desk and snatch up the phone.

'Please, Hannah. You have to get her to talk to me.' It's Billy and his voice is choked with emotion. I've been expecting him to ring.

'I know I shouldn't involve you but I don't see any other way,' he says.

'I'd love to help,' I say with a sigh. 'But you know Megan. She won't listen to anyone once her mind is made up.'

'What can I do?' Billy sounds close to tears. I know that this isn't an easy call for him to make.

I hesitate. It's not really my place to tell Billy what Megan has told me, but at the same time I'm not going to lie to him. 'The booze doesn't help,' I say gently.

'I haven't touched a drink in two weeks. And yes, I know I've quit before, but if it's a choice between drinking and Megan… and…' his voice lifts a little, 'I've got a job. It's only painting and decorating, but it's a start.'

'Megan knows that?'

'No, because she won't speak to me.'

I pause again, torn between my loyalty to Megan and helping Billy. 'OK then, I'll see if I can get her to call you. But I can't promise anything.'

When we've said goodbye, I set the mobile back down on my desk, aware of the irony of advising Billy on his relationship when my own is in tatters. Then I pick it up again. I know Joe asked me not to contact him but it's unbearable. The text I write is simple – just three short words – and I press send before I can change my mind.

Ian wants to go to the comic shop before lunch so we arrange to meet in Phoenix Gardens. After I've picked up both our sandwiches I walk down Charing Cross Road, passing the bookshop where Caitlin did her reading. I remember the last time I was there, waiting for Joe to turn up.

I head inside the shop and find myself standing once again in the foreign section in front of the shelf marked with an

H. There's still the copy of Hugo's *Les Contemplations* that I'd spotted before Caitlin's reading. I pick it up and flick through the pages until I find the poem that had caught my eye on the evening I visited Victor's flat.

*

December 2009

The last time I see Victor at work is two weeks before Christmas. I am just leaving the office, assuming, since it is well after six o'clock, that he's already gone. But when I emerge from the lift he's standing by the booth. He walks stiffly towards me and I notice that he still hasn't put on the weight that he lost when he was ill.

'Hi,' I say hurriedly.

Victor holds my gaze for what seems like minutes. 'I am leaving my job, Hannah,' he says. 'I am retiring.'

I stand there and mutter something inane about being sorry to see him go. Naturally, I wonder if my recent behaviour has anything to do with his decision.

'I hope to return to Paris at the end of the month, but before I go, I would like to give you this.' He hands me a wrapped package.

I take it and mumble a thank you. Glancing down I see that it's the same size as the box that the extra cine camera film stock came in and I assume that it contains the footage he shot by the Serpentine. I shiver – he really has made me a film like he made Claudette.

'Goodbye, Hannah,' says Victor quietly. 'I wish you well.' Then he turns and walks towards the lift.

When I get home I lie on my bed, staring up at the ceiling.

Shame, guilt and sadness are mixed with a relief that I won't have to face Victor any more. I won't be constantly reminded of how cruel I have been.

I don't open the parcel until the next day. And when I do, I see that it's not the cine film after all. It's the copy of *Les Contemplations* that Victor had wanted to give me when he was ill. Feeling utterly ashamed, I open it nevertheless and turn to that beautiful poem dedicated to Hugo's fellow writer, Théophile Gautier. The red feather is no longer there, although I can see a very faint indentation where its spine has pressed into the yellowing page, like a slowly fading memory.

*

Ian is sitting on our usual bench when I arrive at Phoenix Gardens. In front of him the gardener is loading handfuls of leaves onto a big pile of dead branches, presumably to burn later. Otherwise, the place is empty – not even the Italian au pairs are braving the cold.

'Festive turkey and cranberry,' I say, handing Ian his sandwich. I sit down with my own baguette and the Victor Hugo book I've just bought. Then I take my phone from my pocket to put it on the bench beside me.

'He said a week, Hannah,' says Ian, 'and we're only on day four.' He holds out his hand and reluctantly, I give him the phone.

'Just for lunch,' says Ian, 'otherwise you'll drive yourself insane.'

We unwrap our sandwiches and take a bite each.

'Let's talk about the job that Roz offered you,' says Ian, when he's finished his mouthful. 'Think you'll take it?'

'If I don't see anything else by the end of the week, I'll have to.' I admit to him that the idea of writing about wool and soft toys again makes me want to stick knitting needles in my eyes. 'But it'll only be temporary,' I add. Since seeing Victor's last film, my determination to find something I love, and which I am good at, hasn't dwindled, however unrealistic it might seem, given the current recession. If anything it's even stronger.

'You realise that we only have two weeks left of working together?' Ian sets his sandwich down on his lap. 'I'm really going to miss you, Hannah.'

'Me too,' I say, 'but it's not like we won't see each other again. We could even make the comedy club punch-up a weekly thing.'

'Not funny,' says Ian with a smile.

Together we eat our sandwiches and watch the gardener tip the last load of leaves onto the pile of branches before retiring to the shed for a roll-up. I've just swallowed my final mouthful, when I spot the Italian au pair with the green bobble hat pushing her pram through the gate.

I nudge Ian with my elbow, and before he can say anything, I rise from the bench and walk over to her.

'Hello,' I say. 'You're an au pair, aren't you? I overheard you talking to your friend a while back.'

The girl nods and smiles at me warmly. She has a kind, freckly face and wide brown eyes.

I bend down and peek into the pram at the fat, pink, thumb-sucking face that's peering from the nest of blankets.

'I do love babies. What's it called?' I need to spin out the conversation until I can think of a way of bringing Ian over.

'Emma,' says the girl.

'And your name is?'

334

'Isabella.'

I hold out my hand. 'I'm Hannah.' I gesture over to the figure sitting rigidly on the bench, staring at his right knee. 'And that's my friend, Ian.'

'Ian, this is Isabella,' I say a few moments later. We're standing in front of the bench on which Ian's still sitting, rod-straight. 'She's only been in London for a few months so she doesn't know many people yet.'

Ian blushes a deep beetroot and stammers a hello.

'I thought it would be a nice idea if we took her to Luigi's café sometime.'

Ian stutters something and I can hear the beginnings of a hum. But before it can gain momentum I turn to Isabella. 'Luigi serves proper coffee and he makes great cakes. In fact,' I say, glancing at Ian, 'why don't you two go there this afternoon? There's so little going on at work, you could take an extra hour off.'

I leave Ian and Isabella talking in the park (at least I *hope* they're talking) while I walk back to the office. I have an interview with a nutritionist in Edgware Road at 4.30 p.m. and I need to finish a couple of articles beforehand.

Two hours later, I am sitting on the No. 7 bus, heading for the Columbia Hotel. Outside, hoards of Christmas shoppers stagger along Oxford Street, faces tight with festive tension. Above them, the giant silver sleigh decorations – which have been there since early November – look limp and faded.

*

23 December 2009

The silver stars strung along Portobello Road blur in the early evening sleet. It's seven o'clock on Tuesday night and Ted from the market is trying to offload the last of his Christmas trees, while his wife doles out free glasses of glühwein. On the corner by Finches a rogue bunch of drunk carol singers are shouting 'Silent Night'.

I'm standing outside Luke's flat, ringing the bell. I've been trying to call him for days but he won't pick up.

'Who is it?' When Luke finally answers his voice sounds stilted and unfamiliar.

'It's me, Hannah.'

'It's not a good time, Hannah.'

'I need to talk to you. Please, Luke.'

After a long pause, Luke presses the buzzer and I push open the door, edging past his motorbike, which is still in the hallway.

Luke is standing outside his flat when I reach the top of the stairs. He's wearing a grey cashmere jumper that I've not seen before.

'Can we go inside?' I shiver.

Luke reluctantly opens the door, and once inside he walks over to the far window in the kitchen. There's a half-empty bottle of Wild Turkey and the remains of a Mexican takeaway. Cardboard boxes are strewn around the floor, filled with clothes and shoes.

'What's going on, Luke?'

Luke mutters something about having to tidy the flat before Christmas. It's only when he mentions the word 'Christmas' that I realise we have made no plans whatsoever for the day.

'The thing is, Hannah…' Luke picks up a paper cup, pours a measure of Wild Turkey and knocks it back. 'I don't want this any more.'

'Don't want what?' I feel dizzy and sick. Of course I've known this was coming but that doesn't lessen the shock.

'This. Us. You.' The words are delivered in three short syllables, sharp as a blade.

'Why? What have I done wrong?' My voice is high and shaky.

Luke at least has the grace to look at me. 'You've changed, Hannah. This used to be fun and exciting, and now all you want to do is make nice little dinners and talk about the flat you've bought. I feel trapped and I can't stand it any more.'

'But I thought that was what you wanted.' Given his behaviour over the past few weeks, this sounds utterly ludicrous and we both know it.

Luke glances down at his watch. 'I have to go out now, Hannah. You need to leave.'

I stare back at him. Suddenly I am twelve again, frozen with fear as I watch my father walk away.

Luke's hand is on my arm, pushing me towards the door. I grab onto his other sleeve. He tries to shake me off.

'Don't you get it?' Luke's face is flushed. The look in his eyes is cold and full of seething anger at the same time.

I'm crying now and snot is bubbling from my nose. 'Please, let me stay.' I despise the pleading tone in my voice. It reminds me of my mother.

'You can't.' Luke pushes me again, this time harder. I stumble backwards, knocking my head against the window. It's only now, from this angle that I spot the orange scarf tangled amongst the bed sheets, like the recently shed skin of a snake.

The bus has reached Marble Arch and this is where I should get out. It's twenty past four and I'm already cutting it fine for the interview. But I watch the people at the stop get on, shifting towards the window when a large man with a Selfridges bag takes the seat next to me.

I send a text to the nutritionist's PR, saying that I'll have to postpone due to a stomach bug. The bus pulls away and heads up Edgware Road towards Paddington station. Next to me, the man takes out a Lion bar and eats it in two bites.

I get out at Praed Street bus stop and walk up past the Frontline Club towards St Mary's Hospital. I know from Joe that the post office is to the left of the paediatric department, a few doors down from the Hilton hotel. I also know that the actors usually start rehearsals at five o'clock.

The post office is a dark squat building, with a large contractor's board outside. Metal grates block out the windows and graffiti is spray painted across the front wall. A large padlock and chain secures the main door, beside which is a stack of soggy telephone directories. But down the side alley I can see another smaller door with a bicycle chained to the railings outside.

I make my way down the alley, pushing past a filthy mattress and an abandoned fridge. Having wrenched open the door, I enter a dark corridor. There's no light switch so I feel my way along the damp right-hand wall. Silence roars in my ears.

A minute or so later, I am standing in what was once the post office's main room. It's freezing and there's still no light, although I can make out the glass counters along the back wall and several weighing machines stacked in one corner.

Most of the floor tiles have been ripped up and thrown onto a dusty pile next to a red metal pushcart.

The sorting room is directly behind the main post office area and is lit by a solitary bulb suspended from the ceiling. Wooden cubicles for letters and parcels line the walls and there's a long table down the middle. Joe is kneeling in front of it, tearing off a strip from a roll of white tape.

I watch him stick the piece of tape to the floor, then get to his feet. He walks over to the sorting table and picks up the script that's lying on top. He flips it open and takes a pencil from his pocket.

My heart is hammering so hard I can barely speak.

'Joe?'

He jumps at the sound of my voice and it's a few seconds before his eyes locate me standing by the doorway in the semi-darkness. My feet feel frozen to the floor but I force myself to walk over to the table, where I stand awkwardly in front of him.

'I know that you asked for a week,' I say, 'but I can't wait that long.'

Joe puts down the script on the table and looks at me. I move a step closer, but there's still a good two metres between us.

'I want it as much as you do,' I say, shakily.

'What do you want, Hannah?' Joe's voice gives nothing away.

'For us to live together,' I say. 'With Maya, whenever she's able to visit.' I reach out a hand to steady myself against the table. 'I'll do whatever I need to, to make it happen.'

In the background I hear a train pulling out of Paddington station. The rumbling shakes the concrete floor of the post office. It seems like minutes before Joe replies.

'I'm not sure that you wanting it is enough any more, Hannah.' His voice sounds flat and detached.

'I'll make it enough.'

Joe shakes his head. 'I don't see how you can, when you keep so much hidden from me.'

'That's going to change,' I say. My heart feels like it's going to burst from my chest as I wait for his reply.

'You said that before,' says Joe eventually.

I clear my throat. 'I know, but this time I'm going to get help.'

An ambulance siren pierces the silence that follows. The solitary light hanging from the ceiling flickers, sending tiny shadows skittering across the table.

'If you're just doing this for me, it's not going to work,' says Joe.

'It's for me,' I say. 'I went to the GP this morning and she referred me to a counsellor.' I take another step towards Joe. My right foot is on one of the spots he'd marked with tape for the actors.

'Whatever it is that happened, why can't you tell me?' says Joe.

I stare down at the white tape by my foot. 'Because I'm so ashamed.'

'Don't you see that it's always going to come between us?'

I nod and make the final step. I'm standing next to him now and our arms are touching. My throat is so dry I can hardly swallow, but I look Joe straight in the eye, take a deep breath, and then I tell him.

*

23 December 2009

Luke's hand is still on my arm when the sound of the downstairs doorbell knifes through the air.

'Just go,' he says, and gives me another push towards the door.

But I can't move. My limbs feel rigid, as if they're encased in blocks of ice.

Luke gives me a second push, much harder. I stumble across the sitting room, my legs propelling me forward as if on autopilot. Suddenly I want nothing more than to get as far away as possible, as quickly as possible. I run for the door and out onto the landing, down the stairs two at a time and into the corridor below. But the bike is blocking my way so I have to squeeze around it before I can wrench open the front door. My head is down as I wipe away the tears so I can see where I'm going. But I forget about the metal catch, and I feel a searing pain in my forehead where it slices into the skin above my left eye.

I know exactly who's standing on the other side of the door, but it's still a shock when I see Catherine's face. She also looks shocked – maybe it's the blood that's dripping down from the gash on my forehead. I push past her into the street.

After that, I can remember only snapshots: the crowd spilling from the Electric Cinema; a woman with tinsel wrapped around her head; a man with a Christmas tree slung over his shoulder. I have a vague recollection of standing at the till of the local off-licence and paying for a bottle of vodka. The next minute I am back at the flat downing as much of it as I can stomach.

Some time later I am standing in front of the bathroom

341

cabinet. The whole left side of my face is smeared with blood. I need something to take away the pain – and not just the physical pain.

I reach inside and grab a full packet of paracetamol, popping them as fast as I can out of their little plastic cases and shoving them into my mouth…

'Hannah, wake up!' I hear a voice shouting at me. A face is inches from mine and fingers are digging into my collarbones, shaking me hard. For a moment I think it's Luke.

'Hannah, can you hear me?' It's not Luke. It's Victor.

I try to work out how he could have got into the flat and why his arms are covered in blood. But my thoughts feel random and disconnected.

'Leave me alone,' I say. My voice is slurred and distant as though I am speaking from beneath the floorboards.

'I need to know what has happened, Hannah.' Victor is so close now that I can feel his breath on my eyelids. But his voice is dissolving into the background and his face is fuzzing in and out of focus.

'Wake up. Please wake up.' When I come round for the second time, Victor is still shaking me and repeating the same phrase over and over again. A cold breeze shivers through the shattered glass of the sitting room window, where he must have forced his way in.

I try to fling my arms across my face to block him out, but my limbs feel leaden and I succeed only in knocking over the half-empty vodka bottle by my side.

I summon all the strength I have. 'Let me go, Victor.'

Victor bends his head even closer to mine and his palms cradle the sides of my face.

'No,' he says. His fingers brush the edges of the gash on my forehead and his tone hardens. 'Where is Luke?'

I let my head fall to one side, so that another section of the sitting room swims into view. For an instant the photo on the mantelpiece catches my eye – the one of Luke and me laughing on the beach at Dungeness.

'He's gone,' I say.

My breath is shallower now and I can feel myself slipping once again into the warm blanket of oblivion. But Victor is begging me to stay awake and keep talking. Then, suddenly, I feel his body stiffen and see his head twist towards something on the side table. He leans over and grabs it.

'Hannah,' he shouts, shoving the empty packet of pills into my face. 'How many did you swallow?'

*

I tell Joe everything. How Victor forced me to drink three glasses of salt water until I vomited thirty-two paracetamol and half a bottle of vodka into the loo. How he wanted to take me to hospital but I refused, so he insisted that he stay until he knew that I was going to be alright. And how, two hours later, having dressed the wound on my head and made me ring Megan, he quietly left.

I never saw Luke again. I only found out what had happened to him when I bumped into Catherine's ex-boyfriend on Portobello Road, six weeks later. Justin told me that Luke and Catherine had left for LA the day after New Year. Apparently they had been planning it for months.

I don't know what I expected to feel after I finish talking, but there's no big drum roll, no fanfare announcing the end of the pain. Instead, as I stand there in that derelict post office with Joe beside me, I feel something loosen then shift very slightly, and with that shift comes the realisation that whatever happens from now on, things will be OK.

Chapter 33

'Have you tried meditation before?' asks Sue from the blue chenille armchair opposite me.

'Yes,' I say from the green sofa, 'but it doesn't work.' I tap the side of my head. 'It's like a madhouse in there.'

Sue smiles. 'Isn't everyone's?'

It's 8.30 a.m. and Sue and I are sitting in her Shepherd's Bush flat. As well as referring me to a counsellor, Dr Ling advised me to book three sessions with Sue, who specialises in meditation. I have to admit that I had pictured a very different woman from the one in front of me. Sue reminds me of Ma Larkin from *The Darling Buds of May*, all floral and blowsy, as if she's just gusted in from 1950s Kent.

'Close your eyes and focus on the sensations in your body,' says Sue.

I suppress a sigh. I'm hard-pushed to see how she'll be any different from the dozens of other meditation experts that I've met for work over the years.

'Breathing deeply, work downwards from your head, relaxing each part of your body,' says Sue. 'Your forehead, your cheekbones, your jaw...'

I try to concentrate but my mind is busy with images of Sue, aka Ma Larkin, bustling into her 1950s kitchen and bringing out a massive pork pie with a side serving of piccalilli.

'Your neck, your shoulders, your chest… let all the tension drain away,' says Sue.

What was the name of the actress who played Ma Larkin? Pam somebody. I fish around in the backwaters of my mind but the only Pams I can dredge up are Pam Ayres, who was on Radio 4 recently, and Pam Anderson.

'Your knees, your calves, your ankles…' says Sue.

Whatever happened to Pam Anderson? Must Google her when I get home.

'Now take several more deep breaths,' says Sue, 'consciously noticing the space between each one.'

I abandon the search for more Pams and do as Sue says, breathing deeply and trying to linger in the gap between each breath. In. Pause. Out. Pause. In. Pause. Out. Pause. It's actually quite relaxing.

'Whenever you notice your mind wandering, come back to that space,' says Sue.

I take a few more breaths and feel a slight slowing in the incessant, inane mind chatter.

In. Pause. Out. Pause. In. Pause. Out. Pause. This is really quite nice.

In. Pause. Out. Pause.

It's about now that I feel a sort of click, a shifting down of gears followed by a profound stillness.

'You can open your eyes now.' I can hear Sue's voice. I have no idea how much time has passed, but I don't want to open my eyes yet. I want to stay here with this delicious feeling.

'It stopped,' I say, when I've finally dragged myself back to Sue's sitting room. 'My mind just stopped.' I shake my head,

346

amazed. There simply aren't any words to describe what I've just experienced. Peace, joy, love… nothing comes close.

'Thank you,' I say to Sue a little later, as we stand on her porch together.

'Just ten minutes each day,' says Sue. 'Try it and see if it makes a difference.'

'I will,' I say. You'd have to be crackers to get a taste of that feeling and not want to try it again.

I give Sue a hug, which she returns with just the type of hug Ma Larkin would give – a big, warm, Kentish embrace – which feels like haystacks, apple orchards and home-made sponge pudding all rolled into one. As we pull apart it comes to me. Pam Ferris.

I head off, smiling, into the December sunshine. I turn the corner and pass beneath a cherry tree. Above it, the sky stretches out like a freshly painted canvas, big and blue and beautiful.

I arrive at work just after ten. Ian is already sorting through the shop, making little piles of spelt crackers, boxes of herbal teas, hemp bars, tubes of fennel toothpaste and relaxation CDs. Today is our last day and we need to clear the office by 4 p.m.

'How was the meditation session?'

'Extraordinary.' I hold my fingers to my lips. I don't want to say too much about it, because I don't want to dissipate the feeling.

Ian points to the pile of samples on my desk, which includes the two exfoliation gloves, the Eco eye shadow, the Menop-Ease mug and the Trayner pinhole glasses. I pick up the glasses and throw them over to him.

'Think of me whenever you wear them.'

'Cheers,' says Ian. 'I'll wear them on my first date with Isabella.'

'You've got a date with Isabella?'

Ian grins. 'I rang her last night and asked her out.'

'That's brilliant. Where are you going to take her?'

'I'm not sure yet but we're meeting at Luigi's after work.' Ian tosses me the RSI squeezeball that he's just pulled from the shop drawer.

'Well, Joe's deejaying at the Paradise Christmas party tonight,' I chuck him a fistful of detox foot patches, 'so you could always bring her to that.'

We spend the rest of the morning lobbing freebies back and forth. By one o'clock we've given up trying to palm each other off with Nutri pots and Hopi Indian candles. Instead, we load the surplus stock into a cardboard box to put out in the street. I scribble a note. 'Healthy Stuff. Get It Here'.

We're just having a recuperative cup of real coffee when Roz rings, wanting to know what I've decided. I thank her for considering me but say that I won't take the job.

'So what are you going to do?' says Ian when I've put the phone down.

'Well, as of yesterday I have two new careers. The first is helping out Hassan in his café for three days a week, providing I leave Nellie at home. And…' I pause to heighten the suspense, 'it looks like I may be proofreading manuscripts.' I smile. I still can't quite get over Caitlin's and my conversation last night when she told me her publishing company were looking for freelance proofreaders, and if I gave her my CV she would happily recommend me.

'And if that doesn't work out,' I say, 'something even better will turn up.' I surprise myself by the conviction in my voice. Somehow it doesn't feel at all like wishful thinking any more.

'What about you? Any news from Scope?'

Ian shakes his head. 'But you know what? I feel quite…'

'Confident?'

He grins, then opens his rucksack to whip out a package which he hands to me. 'For Christmas and for being such a brilliant friend.'

I take the present and pull off the paper. Inside is a mug featuring a photograph of Nellie splayed out on the sofa at home and looking like Caligula. It's the same one we sent in to the best-looking bulldog competition. Below the picture it says 'Nellie for President'.

There's also a cardboard envelope, and inside is a framed photo – the one that Ian took of me in Phoenix Gardens. My mouth is bulging with baguette, my coat is covered in crumbs and I'm grinning like a loon. On the back Ian has written 'With love and thanks'.

I feel a lump swelling in my throat.

'I have something for you,' I say quickly and dig into the shop's bottom drawer. I pass Ian the package I wrapped yesterday in the final edition of *Health and Wellbeing*.

Ian opens it carefully. 'You bought me a ukulele!' he laughs.

It's the sight of his face that finally sets me off. He's beaming so much that I can barely see his eyes.

'Where's your hankie?' I say. 'The weeping has commenced.'

It's obviously impossible to do any work on our final day, so after a lengthy lunch at Luigi's, Ian and I spend the rest of the afternoon chatting while we clear our desks. At 4 p.m. we pull down the blinds, split a hemp bar for the road and leave the office for the last time.

Chapter 34

After we've deposited the 'Healthy Stuff. Get it Here' box outside the main door, Ian and I go for a pint at the Coach and Horses. One pint turns into three and by the time I get home it's almost seven. Nellie is waiting for me by the back door so I give her some supper, then I shower and change into the green silk dress I recently bought at Portobello Market. Nellie wanders into the bedroom as I'm zipping it up. She plumps down next to my feet and tilts her head expectantly up at me.

'Sorry, Nell, it's a party. It'll be too crowded.'

Nellie lets out a plaintive whine. *Pleeease.*

'No, Nellie,' I say, 'you'll be bored.' I look down at her face. Her wonky teeth poke out at cross angles from that equally wonky smile. *Oh, go on.*

'All right,' I sigh, 'half an hour – max.'

By the time we arrive at the Paradise, the party is going full pelt with well over a hundred guests, including Megan, Hassan, Ramón, Mrs O'Connor and Duke and Benjamin from the Pelican. There's a long trestle table loaded with plates of warm flatbreads, bowls of baba ganoush, grilled halloumi, Esme's patties and a selection of Hassan's sugar-dusted pastries. In the centre is a whole suckling pig, studded with cloves and glazed in honey.

Joe is behind the decks, attempting to dance to Beyoncé's 'Crazy in Love', so Nellie and I fight our way over.

'Hello, you,' I say, kissing him on the lips. It's now two days since I went over to the post office, and last night we stayed up making plans till 3 a.m.

Joe kisses me back, then bends to ruffle the fur on Nellie's neck. 'Will she be alright?'

I point to the suckling pig. 'What do you reckon?'

After I've installed Nellie safely under the trestle table, I hurry over to Megan, who's by the bar. She's wearing a pair of red velvet hot pants and a Mott the Hoople T-shirt.

'Nice pants.'

'Ta,' says Megan. 'Nice frock. Guinness?'

While Megan orders, I scan the room for Billy. I know that he and Megan have talked a couple of times after I told her to call him, and somehow I'd expected him to be here.

'He's coming later,' says Megan, obviously clocking my search. 'He's still at work.'

'So he's sticking with the job?'

'Seems to be.' Megan passes me my Guinness and picks up her own glass of red wine.

'And you're back together?'

Megan chinks her glass against mine. 'Let's see,' she says, smiling.

Megan has headed off to request AC/DC's 'Back in Black' from Joe, and I've spotted Ian and Isabella sitting in the small side room next to the log fire. I walk over with my Guinness.

'Hello, you two.' I kiss Ian and then Isabella on both cheeks. When I pull away from Isabella, she whispers 'Thank you' in my ear.

'You look pretty,' says Ian.

I pluck at the emerald silk material of my dress. 'This old thing.'

Ian points to the dance floor, where Benjamin is doing his Cuban sideways shuffle. 'When can I see you dancing?' he asks. 'I hear you're quite a mover.'

I laugh and turn to Isabella. 'He's getting a bit cheeky these days. You want to watch him.'

From where I'm standing I can see Nellie beneath the trestle table. Above her, Ramón is stationed next to his glazed pig, chatting to Hassan. He's waving a piece of ham around, either about to eat it himself or perhaps trying to get Hassan to bend the rules a bit. Nellie's eyes are following the ham's every movement. When Ramón tosses it into his mouth, she lets out a frustrated bark. *You greedy shit!*

Ramón looks down, laughs, then picks up a second piece of ham, which he dangles a few inches from Nellie's mouth.

I leave Ian and Isabella and hurry over to the trestle table.

'I'm not sure that's a good idea,' I say.

Ramón chuckles. 'But I wanna see if Nellie can jump.'

Nellie's eyes have narrowed ominously and her ears are flattened against the side of her head.

'Trust me, that's really not a good idea.'

'If Nellie want ham, Nellie jump.' Ramón raises his hand a little further out of reach. 'Jump, Nellie, jump.'

By now Nellie's face is twisted with fury. *Just give me the fucking ham!*

I grab Ramón's arm but at the same moment, I see a quivering in all four of Nellie's legs as though an earth tremor is passing beneath the pub. Seconds later, she springs straight up into the air and snatches the ham from Ramón's fingers, swallowing it in a single gulp.

'See!' says Ramón, quickly wiping his fingers on his trousers. '*Un perro muy intelligente.* You want some too?' He hacks off another slice of the suckling pig and flaps it in front of my face. I'm just wondering if I'm also meant to jump for it when the music suddenly stops.

I look over to see Joe behind the mixing desk, frantically twisting various knobs.

'Sorry about this, folks,' he says into the mike. 'Whatever it is, won't take long.' He waves me over.

'In the meantime, Hannah's going to keep you all entertained.' He thrusts the microphone into my hands. 'Tell them a joke,' he smiles.

'But I'm crap at jokes.'

'Do your special broom dance then,' he chuckles. 'They'll love that.' He squats down beneath the desk and starts fiddling with the tangle of wires.

I stand there, looking over at the dozens of expectant faces in front of me. And that's when I have a thought. Here I am, in a packed room with a mike in my hand. It's the perfect opportunity to say something really, really filthy or do something totally weird...

I am still trying to think what exactly I could say or do when I have another thought: This is my first twinge of the Mentals in months and I can't even come up with anything decent. Brilliant! I've cracked it. It's my final liberation. I can meet people's mothers without shrieking hysterically about the size of their breasts. I can sit down to Sunday lunch with my boyfriend's parents without imagining myself hurling lumps of lamb at their dining room walls.

I clutch the microphone. I'm normal, I repeat to myself. Hallelujah! But at that precise moment I have an extremely vivid image of me can-canning butt naked in front of the crowd. I lift the mike to my mouth.

'Happy Christmas, you cun—' The screech of feedback cuts me off mid-sentence, but not before I glimpse Mrs O'Connor staring at me with a look of astonishment. Joe straightens up from beneath the mixing desk.

'Are you alright?' he says, peering at my face.

'Yeah, great,' I say with a big fat grin. 'Just great.'

At eleven o'clock Billy takes over the DJ decks and Joe and I hit the floor, where we dance in our own special way to a random mix of alt-J, Lady Gaga and The Jackson Five. Next to us, Mrs O'Connor is really getting down, wig in one hand and bottle of cherry brandy in the other. Megan is chatting with Ian and Isabella by the fire in the side room, and Nellie is spark out under the trestle table, snout smeared in grease.

By two o'clock only a handful of people are left. Amongst them are Benjamin and Mrs O'Connor, who've both collapsed on the sofa, Sally and Duke, and Hassan. Ramón, who's clearly overdone it on the pig, is now slumped in the corner room, sticky-fingered and sated. Nellie is still under the trestle table, grunting in her sleep.

'Come on, Nell,' I say, bending down to ruffle her fur.

Nellie opens one eye and lets out a little belch.

'It's bedtime.' Joe kneels next to me and hoists her into his arms, where she flops against his chest, lets out another much bigger belch and promptly falls asleep again.

Chapter 35

'Why are you up so early?' Joe reaches a hand from under the duvet.

It's 8.30 a.m. the following morning and although I'm knackered from the night before, I'm already half-dressed.

'I had a dream,' I say, 'and I can't get back to sleep.'

Joe mumbles something, then rolls back beneath the duvet while I pull on my jeans.

The dream, which is still looping through my mind, was like a trailer for a film. In it, all my most treasured memories of Victor were compressed into one glorious technicolour sweep of celluloid: the two of us sitting side by side in Monsieur Henri's cinema watching that first Truffaut film; sharing an apple tart in Bernard's café; wandering along the banks of the Serpentine... Playing in the background throughout, like a subtle soundtrack, was the delicate, poignant melody of Ravel's *Miroirs*.

It's only when I've finished dressing that it dawns on me how I can use the dream. Since watching that third film at Victor's cinema, I've been trying to work out how to rewrite the story of his life. And now I know how I can do it. I'll write it like a film, scene by scene, and this time I will describe Victor exactly as he is – a kind, gentle man who showed me the way out of a very dark place.

So now I need to ask for his permission before I start. It'll also be a good opportunity to drop off his Christmas present – the collection of Hugo's poems that I bought at the Charing Cross bookshop to replace the copy that he gave me.

Surprisingly, Nellie is already awake and lumbers into the hallway after me. I'm not about to argue, and besides, an early-morning bike ride is just what we both need after last night's indulgence.

With Nellie and the book in the bike's basket, we hurtle up Chamberlayne Road, following the No. 52 bus route. There's almost no traffic – it's Christmas Eve, after all – so it's a clear run over the railway bridge, past the old school, then through the streets of Willesden until I reach the salvage yard.

I see the For Sale sign outside the video shop from the top of the street. Then as I draw nearer, I spot the metal grate bolted across the shop door. Leaning the bike against the tree with Nellie still in the basket, I search for a note pinned to the grate, a forwarding address or a final goodbye – but there's nothing.

Three doors down a man is putting out his rubbish.

'Excuse me,' I call over, 'how long has the video shop been closed?'

The man straightens up and squints into the early-morning light. 'A couple of weeks now.'

'Do you know what happened to the French man who worked here?'

He shrugs apologetically. 'Sorry, never used the place myself. More of a Sky Sports man these days.'

The only other place I can think to try is Victor's old flat. So I peddle back the way I came then make for West Kilburn to the house next to the garden full of banana plants. I prop the bicycle by the sidewall and lift Nellie down for a leg stretch, then I walk up to the front door. The curtains of the downstairs flat are closed and when I press the bell there's no answer.

'Can I help you?' I look up to see the head of a black woman emerging from the second-floor window next door. I recognise her marked West Indian accent although I don't know why.

'I'm a friend of Victor's,' I say. 'I'm pretty sure he doesn't live here any more but do you know where he moved to?'

'Mr Lever?' she says slowly.

'That's right.'

The woman stares at me. 'Didn't no one tell you?' It's now that I remember where I've seen her before – in the bus all those months ago, when the feather from her hat landed at my feet.

'Tell me what?' I ask. My heart is thumping, and somehow – though I can't think how – I know what she's going to say.

'That Mr Lever pass away from cancer almost three year ago.'

The sun is just rising above the trees as Nellie and I speed back down Chamberlayne Road, past Esme's and Ramón's, past the launderette and the Paradise pub and then onto Kensal Green Cemetery.

Once we're inside, we leave the bike by the gates and make our way through the graves. I know exactly where to head for – to the spot beneath the chestnut tree not far from the bench where Victor and I sat on that autumn afternoon. Around us, the morning mist has cleared and the cemetery is suffused with a light so intense and so vibrant that everything in sight, from crumbling Corinthian column to simple wooden cross shimmers and glows with a strange luminous quality.

I see Victor's statue long before we reach it – the angel with the outstretched wings and arms raised towards heaven. Up close, it's about level with my shoulders, and carved into the white marble beneath the angel's feet are two lines of poetry that I recognise from *Les Contemplations*.

And all of this Light is yours
Spread out your wings and soar.
Victor Lever, 1937–2010

Above me I hear the sound of wings brushing the air and I look up to see a large white bird, a seagull perhaps or maybe a dove, flying towards the sun. As it rises, the rays catch the tips of its feathers, turning them to a crimson red. Moments later, it dissolves into the bright light.

But from out of that light something is floating down towards Nellie and I. Swirling and looping against the dazzling blue sky, each moment of its journey is captured in perfect detail like a slow-motion clip from a film until the final shot when the red feather comes to rest on the tip of the angel's wing.

And that's when I hear it, or rather sense it – a voice inside me, telling me that death is not the end but just the beginning, and that one day when the world has woken, we will all remember this. As I listen, those words feel oddly familiar, like the echo of a distant melody that I once heard but somewhere along the way, I forgot.

I smile, nod down at Nellie, and we start our journey home.

Acknowledgements

There's a long old list of people to whom I'm very, very grateful:

My family – Mum, Anna, Charlie, Jamie, Gabriella, Max, Tom and Hugo. For so much support and love and for unflagging encouragement, despite the ridiculous amount of rejection letters.

My friends, who like my family, waded through endless drafts of the book - Jacqueline, Lee, Sue, Tanja, Sadie, Sarah A, Tim, Fi, Victoria and Joe C, along with Lucille, Kim, Jo and Mark, Gigi, Johannes, Frosty and Angelika.

To Fausto Maria Dorelli, Mrs Kanji and Teresa Leong.

To Clare Christian who came along in the nick of time.

And finally, to all those filmmakers, whose glorious films have inspired the world to dream, to find beauty and truth, and of course, to feel.

Thank you.

About the Author

Hattie Holden Edmonds has attempted lots of careers, including junior assistant on Separates in Clements (of Watford) department store and chief plugger-in of cables in a Berlin recording studio. For ten years she was the London correspondent for a German pop magazine, interviewing many, many boy bands. After that, she spent three joyous years as the in-house copywriter at Comic Relief. Now she writes full-time (including a weekly blog on the Huffington Post) and teaches meditation to people whose minds are as manic as hers.